Dedicated to Paul Meloy
and *i.m.* Sheila Furnell and Jeanne Neagus,
John Balance and Peter Christopherson.

Montag Press
ISBN: 978-1-940233-10-9
Cover art © 2014 Daniel Serra
Jacket design, layout, & e-book © 2014 Rick Febré
Author photo © 2014 Jonathan Jewell

Montag Press Team:
Project Editor – Charlie Franco
Managing Director – Charlie Franco

A Montag Press Book
www.montagpress.com
Montag Press
536 E. 8th Street
Davis CA, 95616 USA

Montag Press, the burning book with the hatchet cover, the skewed word mark and the portrayal of the long-suffering fireman mascot are trademarks of Montag Press.

Printed & Digitally Originated in the United States of America
10 9 8 7 6 5 4 3 2 1

VENTRILOQUISTS

BY DAVID MATHEW

MONTAG

'It's just a story, though,' Rosie said.
'You can die of stories,' Spofford said.

John Crowley, *Dæmonomania*

You have to think yourself worth saving before
you get angry at someone who wishes to kill you.

Tom Wolfe, *I Am Charlotte Simmons*

VENTRILOQUISTS

BY DAVID MATHEW

contents

Grey Voices

Finders Keepers

The Moron and the Nurse's Dog

Housewarming

Salty *Entr'acte*

Show and Tell

Party Animals

Lesser Characters

Toenail Island

Hospital Patience

Relationship Problems

Whipping Boy

Night Pursuit

Unpatrolled Borders

Wish Fulfilment Vignettes

Wild Nature

Thought for Food

Confessions and Accusations

Delivery

Goodbye to the Carnivores

Property Viewings

The Edlesborough House

Reunion

Number 77 (and the Camp)

Cabin in the Woods

The Shredding of Sleep

Troubled Trances

Homes of Wherefore

Faithful Following

The Canines of Strangers

Descent

An Absence of Light

Guided Tour of the Atrocities

The Village Idiots

Beneath a Storm of Voices

Aftermath

Benny Hill

Stand-Offs

The Intra-Rationalist

Children of the Overlap

Group Activity

Scenes from the Vivaria

Skull Rendezvous

The Can-Do Spirit

GREY VOICES

WHEN THE LARGE MAN HUFFED and waddled his way up the slope to the station platform, Nero kept his eye on the cross-footed gait and hoped that the man wouldn't take the next bench along. But the man did. And when the large man took the next bench along, he deposited at his feet a laptop case, the contents of which clinked together to join the sounds of the man's sighing heavy breathing.

Wine bottles, Nero decided. *Couple of drinks on his way home. Must've been at the conference centre. Late one.*

Nero's girl, Jess, was not bothered about the man's arrival: she continued to kiss her man's neck as though nothing had changed – as though they were still the only two people in the sickly beige illumination on this rural platform. Nero, on the other hand, was sorely disappointed: he had intended to spider his fingers up Jess's short purple skirt; now *that* was out of the question, wasn't it? Although his erection still drummed in his boxers, the pulse was not so insistent – the tune was difficult to hear. And to think, this might have really *gone* somewhere.

Still might, Nero told himself. 'Last train's not for another half hour, mate,' he called over to the large man. But where else could the man wait? Nettle (spiky by name and by nature: old joke) was in the middle – dumped deep in the heart – of nowhere. A village-worth of overpriced houses; The Rook public house; the newsagent and general convenience shop; the confer-

ence centre... Like it or lump it, thought Nero, the man had a
right to travel.

'Thanks. Bit quiet out here.'

Indeed, the loudest sounds were Jess's kisses, planted peck-
peck-peck on Nero's face. Deciding not to let the moment dwindle (in a spirit of waste not want not), Nero returned his full attention to his girl. Their faces caught and held, tongues tapping.
Nero anchored one heavily jewelled hand in the sea of flesh at
Jess's hip.

There we are. Nero felt some of the force return to his groin.
Might be a limit to how far they could go, but this was still nice.
*Yeah, this'll do. Maybe under the jumper a bit, not as far up as the bra, but
feel the skin on her side...*

A crack and a click from the other bench.

*Guy's opening a bottle. Twist top, not a cork. Prepared. Quite thirsty
myself.*

Nero turned his face away from Jess, as much for a breather
as out of any genuine desire to confirm his deductions. What he
saw surprised him. The fat man was staring straight at them!
Audacious innit! Swimming up from his erection, via his belly, to
his well-moistened face: a solid clot of embarrassment. It was
Nero who turned away, but not for long. The large man was still
staring when Nero tuned back in: staring and raising his bottle
of wine to his lips.

White wine: girl's drink, was Nero's gobbet of constructive
criticism. He didn't like the man's gaze; he was feeling fidgety –
ferrety. *Do you need a picture for your mobile, knobcheese?* This Nero was
on the cusp of posing, when the voyeur, prompted it seemed by
the lovers' inactivity (maybe drunk, too), threw in:

'Don't stop on my account, whatever you do.'

Nero's mouth set, gripped in a temporary oblong of inac-
tive rage; his lips hardened as Troy jellied, Troy fell (a favoured

expression of Nero's). When words came back to speak, seconds later, they scratched with obnoxious loathing.

'You some kind of perv, summing, mate?'

The fat man tipped the neck of the bottle in the direction of Nero and Jess. 'Indeed I am! Fire away!'

'Let him look, I don't care,' Jess giggled.

'I don't do public,' Nero stated with priggish conclusivity – a plosive click, not altogether unlike that of the wine bottle being opened, on the final disdainful consonant.

'Oh but you do,' said the fat man. 'That's *precisely* what you do. What's more, I'll pay you for the show.'

It was the word *pay* that did it: planted an itch on Nero's disgust. 'Do what, mate?'

'You heard. Pay you.' Eyes pinched, eyes squinty: *rat's eyes,* thought Nero. 'Twenty quid if you kneel down and suck his cock. More if you do more, so to speak.'

'You filthy bell-end,' said Nero.

'Cash?' asked Jess.

'Yes, cash. I can spend up to a hundred and forty.'

'What, on expenses?' Nero replied, bitter.

'No, in cashflow. In my wallet of calfskin. Right now. I only watch. You do what comes naturally, no holds barred.'

'I could smack you for the very suggestion.'

'You could. Something tells me you won't.' The fat man took a pull on the bottle. 'What's in it for you to hit an old man with a diabetes problem?'

'What's in it for you to watch teenagers at it?'

'Gratification, of course, by proxy. Do we have a deal?'

It was Jess who answered. She said, 'Fifty.'

'Thirty. And that's my final offer, I'm afraid.'

Jess turned into Nero's uncomprehending glare. 'I'd blow you for thirty,' she offered.

'I think you're missing the point, girl.'

'Maybe. But we can get lashed on thirty. And sides,' she added slyly, lowering her voice, 'I was gonna to do it anyway.'

'Here?'

'Yeah, why not? No one around, warm evening…'

'Someone around now.'

'But not *then*. Show us the cash, mate,' she said. 'Not thy'm suspicious or nuffing.'

'Of course. Would you like another drink, by the way? I have ample.'

'What do you mean, another?'

'You've had a few if I'm not mistaken, at The Rook no doubt. A short or two in the legally acceptable pint of Diet Coke. Something of that water anyway. Honest offer.' Again, the fat man tipped the bottle in their general direction. With his other hand he plucked the calfskin wallet from his inside jacket pocket. Expertly, with nimble dexterity, he fished two bills free of the concertinaed leather. 'Thirty for a dirty,' he announced.

After salmon-leaping free of Nero's halfhearted embrace, Jess plucked the money from the fat man's pudgy hand. Without a word she bloused it: deep in the brassiere.

'Show must go on,' she announced. 'You up for this, Rambo?'

'…Not sure.'

'Well *get* sure. We won't be fifteen forever. Seize the day all that.'

'*You're* in a funny mood,' Nero observed.

'Fifteen!' the fat man noted.

Gymnastically Jess dropped to her bare knees. She did not check for other people on the platform – she knew there was no one else present. No cameras either. *Tricky work, cameras*, Nero reflected. To hell with it. *Show on the road*, fiddling the fiddle free. Jess absorbed what he revealed – seemed to *absorb* him into her nasal passages, into her sinuses, into her *brain*.

Done this before. Fair enough, probably Jonno. She likes a challenge. Lumpy Goth… what's in it for this twat? Concentrate – train lines. Tongue on me glans – she can't reach the balls. Best bit.

A sound of shuffling. The voyeur was standing up. *If he takes out his wand, I'll what? Voice my protest? Behave yourself. Don't be an infant. Paid for a wank innit. Bound to. Just don't look. Up to him dirty cunt. Get what you pay for…*

As the man approached – a matter of gentle strides – Nero focussed on the tracks, twisting them in his mind into sigmoidal shapes, into knots. *Tying up the line. Worse if another bloke sees the fall of Troy. Silly, really, given the circos.*

The fat man used what remained of his bottle as weight, as heft, for the club that he bounced off Jess's skull. Wine splashed; Jess yelped. Nero's thigh muscles twanged with his velocity off the seat. But he hadn't been paying attention; he hadn't seen that the fat man carried something other than wine. A canister.

The contents were sprayed into Nero's face.

Getting darker. Too fast. Does what it says on the tin…

What had he inhaled?

'Train's coming,' said Nero as he fell over, chuckling. 'Lucky train.'

His voice to his own ears grew grey.

FINDERS KEEPERS

1.

The directions were blunt but accurate, and he made excellent time through the towns, arriving at the camp before six on a damp, cold morning – a good half-hour before he'd expected to. The wipers smeared greasy rain as thick as curd across his windscreen as the engine panted softly and he tried to talk himself out of driving in. All it would take was a three-point turn in the narrow trash-strewn road between two unkempt fields, and he would be heading back the way he'd come. But he was more nervous than predicted, and he took this internal disquiet as a good sign. If he drove home now, he would never come out here again, he was sure of it. The opportunity would be lost forever. Indignant rage, in the visitor's opinion, flared briefly.

Having engaged first gear he crept onto the driveway. It was smoother underwheel than he'd imagined it would be, and the slickness sickened him: it was wrong that scum could accumulate enough money to maintain frictionless driving conditions. By the time he had reached the end of the drive, where the first of the trailers gleamed dully in the smudgy rain, his anger was stoked and puckered. As he passed between two grey trailers, a dog italicized itself noisily at the end of a three-metre length of rope, its snarls intermittent with soprano-pitched barks that the driver feared would wake up the camp.

The trailer he wanted, he'd been told, had a fresco painted

on its side of the moon and stars, in royal blue. (Shyleen had made an earlier trip to the camp and had made enquiries.) Crawling slowly in first gear, it was not hard to find. He disabled the engine; he watched the fuel gauge ease down from a quarter tank to empty. (He had come here deliberately short of petrol: the possibility that he'd have his car set alight had been uppermost.) Then he exited the vehicle, experiencing the full sub-coastal slap of sozzled wind across his bows.

Next door to the moon-fresco trailer sat a smaller caravan. A short, stocky man in his mid-forties was already outside, in his checked shirtsleeves and a pair of water-resistant green plastic jekylls. He'd been fastening a tarp to the back of his red miniloader, and he only stopped doing so now to watch the visitor unfold out of his own vehicle. There was no expression of cordial greeting on his grey bearded features.

'Are you lost, son?' he asked.

'No. Good morning to you,' the visitor replied.

'Yeah, good morning. Now what is it you'd be needing here so early?'

'A word with your neighbour.'

'She's asleep.'

'Oh? How can you be so sure? *You're* awake.'

The caravan's owner smiled briefly. 'Man's gotta work,' he answered. 'Them draincovers and hubcaps won't be stealing themselves now, will they?'

'Pardon?'

'Cuz that's all we do all day, right?'

'I never said that. I don't *believe* that either. But now you mention it, I *am* particularly fond of my hubcaps, so if you wouldn't mind –'

The stocky man had taken a few steps to close the gap between them. 'Now don't be chatten the bollocks,' he said. 'Are you the law?'

'No.'

'Then I'd advise you to make a swift exit. You're on private property.'

'I beg to differ.'

'Oh you do. Listen, son. You've woken up Excalibur −' He had to be referring to the dog on the rope, near the entrance, still yapping in an earnest but frustrated manner. ' −which means you've woken up the camp.' Indeed, the visitor had noticed a few lights winking on in the caravans and trailers nearby. 'So it's not looking handsome, is it?' As if to suggest some further point of protocol he took another step closer: his plastic trousers swished and the visitor heard his boots squelch in mud underfoot.

The visitor had come prepared for confrontation. Stood his ground. 'I'll need a name.'

'What name?'

'*Your* name. Sir.'

Again, the caravanman smiled − it was even briefer this time, little more than a twitch. 'They call me the Brazilian, son. Do you know why?'

'You were born in Buenos Aires?'

'Cuzza me tendency to tear strips off a poor cunt. So be going, why don't you, before I have cause to give you a free demo. We protect our own here.'

The visitor shook his head. 'I'm no threat to you,' he elaborated.

'I should say you're not!'

'Unless my car's damaged, of course. Took me a lot of cold Saturdays to earn that car, and I repeat what I said about my hubcaps.'

'...Cheeky bastard,' the other man muttered, closing the gap again to a distance of two metres. Then they both heard:

'Leave it, Tommy.'

The voice emerged from the frescoed trailer. When the visitor turned at the waist, the voice's owner was standing in her narrow doorway. Dressed in a little pink housegown, she had pale hair piled in a haystack on top of her head. She was somewhere in her early twenties, but with a rinsed longsuffering air that made her appear a decade older.

'Are you for me?' she asked the visitor calmly.

'For Eloise.'

She paused. 'You'd better come in then,' she said.' You'll catch your death.' She turned her back. 'Don't you boys believe in coats?' she added. 'Or did the Prophet prohibit the bloody things?'

2.

'She's sleeping. She wouldn't go down until about five, I'm *exhausted*... Would you like a cup of tea?'

'Thank you, yes.'

'Take the weight of your indignation, sir. The sofa won't bite.'

Unnerved more by the hostess's civility than he had been by the Brazilian's aggression, the man sat down. It was like an interview: one of the dozens he'd attended, seeking a job that would facilitate his escape out of his world of frozen fingertips and charmless punters.

'Do you take sugar?' he was asked.

'No, thank you. Are you alone?'

Three metres away, in the narrow kitchen, the woman sniggered. 'Are you scared now?' she asked teasingly.

'No. Are you alone, I asked.'

'Me Da's on nights. Be home soon.'

'And what does *he* make of the Eloise business?'

'It was his idea.' She sniggered again and crossed towards him. 'It's a bit strong,' she warned, handing him a mug of brackish soup-like tea, for which he thanked her regardless.

She sat close by (there was no choice as to the distance), in the compact dining area. On the table before her, her Man U mug sprinkled steam into the air. 'What's your name?' she asked him.

'Yasser.'

'As in Arafat? That's a funny kind of name, Yasser.'

'I'm a funny kind of guy.'

'You're surprised I've heard of Yasser Arafat, aren't you now?'

Despite himself, Yasser smiled. 'I am a bit. What's yours, if we're getting acquainted?'

'Maggie. Maggie Earl.'

'Well, Maggie Earl, how about we go straight from the *h'ors doeuvres* to the cheese board? You know what I want: I want the child. I want Eloise. More specifically, her *parents* want Eloise. Me, I'm just a go-between.'

Maggie blinked at him and asked, 'How's your tea?'

'My tea's fine. The other matter, on the other hand, remains *not* fine...'

'Why, you haven't so much as sipped at it, Yasser. I've been watching.'

Yasser shook his head. 'My tea's not in doubt... Maggie. The issue at stake is the child that belongs to someone else, sleeping where?'

Maggie jerked her makeshift bouffant in the direction of a closed door beyond the kitchen area. With a smile on her face she said, 'Did you think I might've put her up in the South Wing, you dafter? Where else? I'm sorry if she's more accustomed to a *room with a view.*'

Yasser sat back against the sofa; his back was tense – the muscles more clustered than he'd imagined. The thought trampled through his head that Tommy the so-called Brazilian might be waiting outside for him – and the longer he spent in this long box the better chance the bastard had of rounding up troops.

He took a sip of the tea: strong as cyanide. Again he said, 'Thank you.'

'You're welcome, Yasser. So what happens next, if you've got a script?'

'I return Eloise to her parents, that's what happens next.'

Maggie nodded. 'Out of interest,' she said, 'how did you find us without a name?'

'Pardon me?'

'You didn't know my name. So how did you find us, Yasser?'

'I employed the services of a professional.'

'You cheated, in other words.'

'If it pleases you to think so...'

'You're a college boy, aren't you?'

Yasser frowned. 'That's not relevant.'

'But aren't you though? Central Beds or Barnfield?'

'Barnfield College. A.V. course, level 2. Mature student.'

'What's an A.V. course?'

'Audiovisual.'

Maggie brightened. 'So you'll be making a *film* about me? I wasn't far off with what I said about a script after all!'

Feeling mildly ashamed, Yasser looked away and did his best to let her down gently. 'I'm not exactly making a *film*...'

'Your face, Yasser! I'm only teasing. Why would you waste time and celluloid on *us* scum, eh? Shall I put the kettle on for another cup of tea?'

From outside came the rumble of a vehicle drawing closer.

'I don't think we've time for tea, Maggie. I'm taking her. You know that, don't you?'

Maggie nodded.

'Irrespective of who that is. Even if it's your dad.'

Maggie nodded; she brushed back a stray frond of hair that cornered down over her left eye.

'Because it's the right thing to do,' said Yasser, as softly as he dared. He stood up. Light on his feet, he moved towards the door at the end and opened it. He peered in, leaning slightly. He was able to see pencilly outlines, not much more, but he believed he could make out a cot beside the bed. The cot surprised him a little bit: he had expected the child to be wrapped in a towel or a blanket or something, asleep on the bed itself. But they'd bought a cot. And the sight of it made Yasser's temples throb with heavy-weight disgust. What better indication of their arrogance – of their belief that they'd get away with the abduction – was there, than the fact that they'd gone out and *bought a cot*! Or at least obtained one from somewhere… maybe the transaction of filthy lucre had had nothing to do with it…

The important thing was that the girl was inside it. Yasser bent at the waist… Part of his preparation for today had been to ask his cousin for a hold of her baby, and now he knew how to do it, reasonably well. He picked up Eloise – and he took it as an added slice of good fortune, the contented near-silence that she maintained as he transported her, gifted in a wrapping of blue blanket, towards the door. Her breathing was soft and still sleep-dunked, near Yasser's left earlobe.

When he carried Eloise past Maggie, he tried to catch the woman's eye. A transmitted note of apology (but from whom to whom?) he might have expected; but Maggie was having none of it. Her eyes stared at the surface of her drink, and Yasser shook his head. That Maggie had moved not a muscle to defend her newfound property might have come as little surprise to Yasser – not since he'd met her, although his doubts in the car over would have begged to differ – but her shameful reluctance to look up from her cup of tea was what he found disconcerting. Not even to say *goodbye*? he wondered.

Well, some people found farewells terrifying – brittle and hollow. If that was the way she wanted it… maybe it was for the best. Keep the break clean.

Yasser unfastened the door; the wind outside did the rest. A brassmonkey sou'wester stole the door from Yasser's grip and flung it back against the side of the trailer, where it collided with a fearsome *clump*.

If the noise of the door was not enough to rouse Eloise, the wind and the rain combined certainly were. It took the girl a second to get her emotions straight, as if to make sure, then she started crying with a vengeance, her lungs sucking in moist, chilly air.

Yasser heard the noise – he had no choice but to hear the noise – but it was something distant, something dreamy. What occupied his attention at this moment was his welcoming committee, all three of whom were armed in one way or another. The man that Yasser had met originally – the Brazilian – was tapping a crowbar into the palm of his left hand. A second man (a stranger to Yasser) was older, but by no means necessarily wiser; he was carrying a petrol can. A third man (the oldest still) had parked a blue van next to Yasser's car, angled slightly in front of the headlights of the latter in a way that might impede but not prevent an escape. Yasser guessed that this third man was Maggie's father. Not that Yasser was any good with estimating ages, but he figured the man would be about right. Early fifties? Mid-fifties? Shoulder-length grey and white hair, not a bald spot or receding enclave to be seen; a thick but tidy grey beard. Surely this man – a father himself no less – would see reason. Surely Maggie had been fibbing about the kidnapping having been this man's idea…

On the other hand, this oldest man of the three held a simple but effective weapon. Simple and effective, at any rate, if it was used in conjunction with the second man's petrol can.

A box of matches.

They wouldn't, Yasser told himself as he descended the three steps down from the trailer. But if he was so sure, what accounted for the sudden doughy texture about his legs? What accounted for the fact that despite the wind and rain, his body had broken out in a rash of perspiration?

A waft of ugly perfume − the smell of petrol − reached Yasser's nostrils. It might well have reached Eloise's too, for she emitted a fresh scream, as piercing as a needle through skin.

'You'll be leaving the child, son,' said the man in the middle − Maggie's dad's workmate, perhaps. They might have arrived back in the van together.

'She's not yours,' Yasser replied.

'She's not yours either.'

'And she's not Maggie's,' Yasser continued. 'I'm taking her back to her parents in Luton.'

Eloise squealed.

The oldest man spoke next.

'You've got two choices, my boy,' he said, his eyes following Yasser as he executed the short crossing from the steps to the car.

Trying to ignore the implied threat, Yasser pointed his fob at the door; the locks clunked open. 'My choices are stay here or do what I came here to do,' he called across his car roof.

'Your window was open a crack,' said Tommy the Brazilian.

'…What?'

'The passenger side,' Tommy explained. 'This came in handy.' He brandished the crowbar. ' −widen the gap a bit, you know what I mean?'

Yasser shook his head − and the man who had spoken first

shook the petrol can at the car.

'No!' Yasser shouted.

The three men burst into laughter. The man with the can tipped the vessel upside-down; no more than a few drips fell out. They were bluffing. They'd been bluffing the whole time. So why…

'You soft bollocks,' said the oldest man.

…so why could Yasser still smell petrol?

'Leaving your *window* open? Around *here*?' the man continued. 'You never know what might fall in, son…'

Yasser opened the driver's side door. Sure enough, a weak puff of fuel vapour exited.

'You're talking about murder,' he told the men.

'Not necessarily,' said Tommy. 'Depends how many people *get in* the fucker, don't you see?'

Yasser shook his head; Eloise squealed again, her breath having deteriorated into desperate little sobs.

Petrolcan Man explained.

'If you get in that car on your lonesome, then I dare say not one of us'll fancy a fag and let our sparks fly willy-nilly. At the other extreme, though, it's two oyiz getting into a car that's been soaked in a gallon of petrol. And nature'll take its course.' He shrugged.

Yasser experienced a chill that had nothing to do with the weather.

'People know where I am.'

'Accidents will happen,' the old man told him, also shrugging.

'And they know where this little girl is too,' Yasser continued. 'You think you're hated *now*? Just *imagine* the persecution when the locals find out you incinerated a baby!'

For the first time the older gentleman smiled. 'You've got spirit, son. Go on about getting in your wheels, why don't you. Before I change me mind.'

'Da?' protested Tommy.

'I wanted to be sure you meant it,' said the elder. 'A test of your convictions, if you care to call it. Go on now. Don't make me beg.'

As swiftly as he had with his cousin's offspring in the back seat of her four-by-four, Yasser strapped the wailing Eloise into the child's seat he had attached to his passenger side chair. Seconds passed; Yasser felt hot with panic, but his preparations at least had been thorough. When he sat down (he didn't bother with the belt) an ice-cold shower of sweat passed from his skin to his shirt and back again.

The engine started reliably. Were they really going to let him go so easily? To test the question Yasser engaged reverse and squelched away from the trailer, trying not to make eye contact with any of the committee.

He swung the car on to the smooth driveway and headed for freedom.

3.

Standing on the landing, Bahrati wagged a finger and said, 'You'll eat some breakfast before you leave ho.'

Yasser was sitting on the edge of his bed, pulling on a white sock. So far he had dressed only in his boxers.

'Get out, Mum! I'm getting my kit on !'

Bahrati chuckled as she stepped into the bathroom. 'Aho! You think I haven't seen my own boy in the nip? Eh? *Eh?*'

'I'm twenty-three!' Yasser protested. *For fuck's sake,* he added under his breath. Leaning forward, he tapped the door closed and resumed his preparations for work.

Before his mother locked the bathroom door she called out a parting shot – a reminder.

'And eat some breakfast ho! Your father and I don't want you wasting your earnings on a bloody Mickey D innit!'

Yasser clipped downstairs when he was ready, trailing a wash of aftershave and hair gel. His mother had left him a bowl of Coco Pops on the breakfast bar; but how long ago? Yasser's stomach squinted at the sight of the cereal congealed in a puddle of filthy brown milk. *No thanks, Mum.*

In sweats and found hundred-quid trainers, Yasser jogged to his Saturday job: to the market in Luton's High Town, two-and-a-half miles away.

By eight o'clock, an hour after his arrival, the market was in full swing. Not even a sandalwood sky threatening a cloud-burst could keep the local Saturday shoppers away this morning... The plot where Yasser sold gardening equipment, under the wing of his Uncle Wafiq, stood next to a stall brightly-coloured with herbs, fruit and vegetables, and the aroma of berries was sweet in Yasser's nose. If he had to work anywhere at all, this was as good a patch as any to fritter away the lion's share of his weekends. Before he'd ordered his first bacon sandwich of the morning he had personally swapped two shovels, a set of green waste sacks and a pair of sturdy gloves for hard cash. His mood was buoyant.

The snacks van that he frequented was one of three clog-ging up High Town Road. Its competitors sold Polish and Carib-bean food, but it was too early in the day for cabbage or curried goat for Yasser. He queued patiently for Snow White's attention. Behind the counter, Snow White, a hyperactive, septuagenarian Rasta who claimed to have studied under Steve Biko back in the old country, finished preparing a sausage-and-egg baguette for the guy who sold paperbacks of dubious provenance, and Yas-ser tapped his toes to the disco beat slamming out from Snow White's iPod. Snow White dished out the man's change and clocked his next customer. So wide was his welcoming grin that

Yasser was able to see past his tan-coloured large front teeth, right to the back of his mouth, where the gold was buried.

'Yo, Yass! Usual innit?'

'Safe, man. You okay?'

'When it don't rain it shine, blood. You's onions?'

'Nah. Too early for onions.'

Yasser took a step back from the counter when Snow White turned his concentration to his grill plate. Without looking up while he flipped bacon, Snow White asked Yasser if he wanted a coffee. Yasser lit a smoke and declined politely. Then Snow White added: 'Woah, boy!'

'What?'

'Them creps, man! They the shit!' And he pointed his dripping tongs at Yasser's new footware. 'You win the Lotto or sumpin?'

'Been saving for a rainy day.' Yasser smiled, delighted that his investment had been noticed.

'They cost you what?'

'Four ton.'

Snow White whistled, then revealed his teeth once more. 'Someone *paying* you too much, Yass!' he declared.

'Well it ain't Wafiq!' Yasser replied.

'Then who is it?' said a voice behind Yasser's left shoulder. Yasser turned. Immediately he felt prickly with anxiety. The face was familiar – more familiar than that of any regular Saturday morning market-haunter.

'You don't tell me that's your babysitting money paid for that,' the man went on.

'...What do you want, Tommy?' asked Yasser.

It was the Brazilian, from the camp. Close up, closer than he'd been three mornings earlier, the man held about him the odour of swamp and sweat. He was dressed in the same clothes as he'd worn then.

'I owe you a freebie, son,' Tommy replied. 'Never let it be said I don't honour me word.'

'You owe me nothing,' Yasser told him. 'The business is concluded.'

'Can I help you?' Snow White called from behind a crackling hedge of silver fat fumes.

Tommy asked Yasser: 'What is it we drink? You got any petrol, mate?' he asked Snow White.

'Any *what?*'

'I asked you what you wanted, Tommy,' said Yasser, his voice level but his heart ranting.

'And I told you, boy: I tear strips off poor cunts, and you qualify.'

'The baby's well, by the way. Eloise.'

Tommy shrugged. 'I don't give a fuck. That was none of my business. You think I ask their permission to scratch me bollocks?'

'No. And there was no petrol on my passenger seat either,' said Yasser. 'The smell receded as I drove away. It was the can I could smell.'

'Oh it *receded*. You college boy...'

Yasser turned his head by twisting his neck. To Snow White he said: 'Have you got your camera with you?' When Snow White nodded, his dreadlocks whipped like horses' tails. 'Get a picture of this prick, would you then?'

Malice leaked through Tommy's features. 'You'll not be taking my photo,' he stated flatly.

'Then get away from me.'

'Why? I'm here to buy a wheelbarrow,' Tommy answered. 'I hear you're doing em cheaper than Homebase.'

Yasser shook his head. 'We reserve the right not to sell to

psychopaths. How d'you find me?'

'No, son. How did *you* find *me*? Is the question. See, it had to be here. No other connection.'

'Well, well done, Inspector Morse.'

'You bacon is ready,' said Snow White.

'Do you sell trowels?' Tommy asked, grinning.

'Yes. But not to you.'

'We'll see what your Paki boss thinks about that opinion, so we will.' Tommy laughed as Yasser took possession of his bacon sandwich. It was wrapped in kitchen roll. 'That looks good,' he added. 'Can I have a bite?'

'Buy your own.'

'Maggie sent me.'

'What? I have work to do, *Tommy*.'

'Maggie sent me. To retain your skills for finding things. Mainly children.'

'What are you on about?'

Tommy nodded towards Snow White. 'Are you sure you want Bob Marley to hear this?'

'Yes. I'd like a witness,' Yasser answered.

'The only reason she took the white girl is she had her own girl stolen from her. And she would like to pay you to find her. You *impressed* her, boy.'

Yasser's heart was calming and steadying. A cauldron of questions bubbled in his mind, but one in particular made a much louder pop and flashed an image of a pair of Gucci loafers.

'How much is she offering?' Yasser asked.

4.

Maggie was early. Yasser knew she was early without needing his wristwatch: he was early himself and she arrived only a few minutes after him. Without so much as a word of invitation from Yasser, Maggie entered on his passenger side.

'Not a bare hint of petrol,' she said by way of a greeting.

'They were bullshitting me.'

'They were *testing* you. There's a big difference.'

'How did you get here?' Yasser asked.

'How do I get anywhere? The 61 bus... Thanks for meeting me.' Maggie had yet to meet Yasser's eyes; her focus was straight ahead. 'I'd've understood if you told me no.'

Yasser started the engine. 'Where to?'

'Do you know Hockliffe?'

Yasser moved the car towards the car park's exit ramp. 'It's a name on a sign,' he told her. He reached out the window to feed his ticket to the machine. The barrier rattled erect to let them out.

'I'll direct you... A prepaid ticket, eh? Man of means.'

Yasser indicated left. 'I paid for thirty minutes. That's all I was gonna wait,' he said.

Maggie laughed. 'Treat em mean and keep em keen, eh Yasser? What happened to a woman's prerogative to be late for everything?'

'What happened to a child's – to live like a child?'

'Amen to that,' Maggie whispered, and turned Yasser's way for the first time. She only saw him in profile – he was watching for a space in the Dunstable traffic on West Street – but perhaps he had sensed her. 'We need to turn right, by the way,' she said, blinking back tears. 'Then left at the crossroads, up the A5...'

After nearly a minute a works van and a motorcycle allowed them to cross the thoroughfare and ease into traffic. Having negotiated the manoeuvre, Yasser experienced a failure of patience with Maggie. 'Tell me about your little girl,' he said. 'Where did you lose her?'

'I didn't *lose* her. She was *stolen*.'

'Where was she stolen?'

'In Hockliffe.'

'...Are you serious? You're taking me to the scene of the crime?'

A red light at the crossroads held them still. For the first time in this vehicle their eyes met. Something nervous but mischievous tinkered with the left side of Maggie's mouth.

'Where else did you have in mind to start the search?' Maggie wanted to know.

'I haven't *agreed* to anything yet!' Yasser protested.

'Yes you have, Yasser. You turned up.'

'To *discuss* it!'

'Baloney... The light's green. And besides, I've got something in my handbag for you. It'll soothe your doubts, to be sure.'

5.

Hockliffe is a pleasant Bedfordshire village, smeared a brown-chrome combination this morning, about eight miles from the camp where Maggie lived. She knew the way adroitly: as though she were directing Yasser to her own refrigerator.

For Yasser's part, he had believed he was being led to a house or a pub – either of which would have fit. But *this*?

'A *dog-grooming* shop?'

The sign outside said LEIGHTON PAMPERED POOCH.

'Bridget lives here. Follow me. Though don't speak too much,' said Maggie, opening the passenger side door.

'And who's Bridget when she's at home?' Yasser demanded, stifling the murmurs of the expensive engine.

'She *is* at home. She's my cousin. She used to look after Paloma.'

It was the first time that Yasser realised that he didn't even know the name of the allegedly abducted daughter. Well, now he did. And furthermore, he knew a bit more than the black and white of fib versus truth. The existence of a child carer lent Maggie's story a puff of wisdom and verisimilitude.

If this is a set-up, Yasser considered, it's a good one.

He had deliberately not brought cash with him this Monday morning. Only now – with a bell tinkling above the door as they entered, and Yasser's sphincter muscle ceasing its endlessly curious gulping – did he start to wonder if he'd overplanned.

'Bid!'

'Mags! Hang on a mo,' said the young woman standing at a table on which a West Highland Terrier stood proud but snuffling under the influence of some sort of canine chill. 'I've just got his gonads to go around.' With which she flicked a switch, and the electric razor that she carried fired back into life.

The dog did not so much as blink as Bridget reapplied the tool of her trade to the tools of his. The dog was no fool.

'This is Yasser,' said Maggie.

'Well, I didn't think it was Stevie Wonder,' Bridget responded. 'Put the kettle on, Mags, and for fuck's sake let the teabags drown. Enough of your cat piss. I can afford a couple of teabags.'

Yasser waited near the door for further instruction. One question in his mind among many was this: *What the hell have I got myself into?*

6.

'Paloma was taken from us about three months ago,' said Bridget.

'Two months and twenty-three days,' Maggie interrupted.

' –and it's all my fault.'

'No it's not, Bid.'

'Yes it is.' To Yasser she said: 'I hold myself utterly responsible. It was a shopping centre – the one in Aylesbury.'

Yasser was frowning. 'And the police couldn't trace the CCTV?' he wondered.

'There *were* no police.' This was uttered as a Maggie and Bridget duet.

Yasser continued to frown. 'You didn't *report* it?' he asked, incredulous.

'Report what?' Bridget sounded angry. 'Another Pikey kidnapping?'

'No we didn't,' Maggie said simply.

Bridget sipped her tea (it had been deepened appropriately dense as a brew) and said: 'I had a stomach upset. At any one time I was one fart away from disaster, Yasser. I had a bowel like a *depth-charge*.'

'I get the picture.'

Bridget shook her head. 'I went into the Ladies. I left her outside in her pushchair. And it was the last time I saw Paloma.'

Maggie copied Yasser's frown. 'I won't have you giving up on her, Bid, I'll give you that for a starter right now.'

Bridget sighed. 'I'm not giving up, Mags,' she said, straight but quiet.

Seconds drifted past. It was Yasser who broke the silence.

'I thought you said she disappeared in Hockliffe,' he said to Maggie.

'I did,' Maggie started to say.

'She was seen here afterwards,' Bridget explained. 'I was frantic. *Frantic.* I didn't *know* what to do. I went from shop to shop, searching. I remember screaming. *God knows* how I drove back here – I couldn't get anyone on the phone, so I get it into my head – this is stupid, I know it – but I got it into my head she'd got home here. On her own. Somehow. She'd either been picked up and collected, or... or I don't have a clue what. She didn't bloody *fly*.'

Yasser nodded. 'Who saw her here?' he asked.

'Lulu. Louise,' said Bridget. 'She works for me. She swears blind she saw Pamona walking through the door.'

'Walking?'

'I *know*! She's barely at a crawl, but Lulu's adamant. What do you call it? A visitation?'

'I suppose. A haunting.'

'She was here, Yasser,' Maggie said quickly. 'I don't doubt it for a second. Not that I can explain it but I believe it.'

'Okay.' Yasser breathed deeply. 'Okay...'

Maggie repeated, 'She was here...'

THE MORON AND THE NURSE'S DOG

1.

Connors stared at Dorman in disbelief.

'You're having me on.'

'Nope.' Dorman was eating chicken from a bucket: one drumstick, one slurp, one chew, and down it went; on to the next, the bone discarded into a small paper dish. There were already a lot of wet bones; and on the table, only the coleslaw remained untouched: Dorman believed coleslaw was the Devil's work.

Connors persisted. 'There'll be law *all over* the place,' he said. '*Swarming.*'

'Don't care. I'm going back.' Dorman slurped. 'Gonna do what I shoulda done before.'

'But it's just a *dog*, mate!'

'Yeah. A dog that *bit me.*'

'A dog that bit you while protecting his property!'

Dorman chewed – the muscles in his temples bulged – and replied: 'Dog ain't *got* no property. It's just a dog. As you say.'

'*His* property. The owner's.'

Dorman sniffed. Although he disapproved of such logic, he was a man for the easy life, or so he said. Besides, the job had exhausted him, and he couldn't be fussed to fight. So he changed the subject. 'Are you sure you don't want no chicken?' he asked.

'No I don't. Thanks.'

'It's delicious. I wish I had a place like this near me.'

They were eating (or Dorman was eating, Connors had taken no more than a few fries) at a table half a mile from the house they'd entered. Dorman had been firm on this point: to buy dinner afterwards. *Some* professionals, he explained, spent the following twenty minutes, thirty minutes, trying to race out of the immediate neighbourhood, usually in light traffic. They bought attention. The car got noticed; or your mug was caught on the station camera. Whatever. But if you kept a clear head (no alcohol: another of Dorman's rules) and did something normal, like order a family bucket, somewhere close to where you'd explored, no one asked. You were invisible. At the very worst, it was their word against yours; and yet…

He was determined: he would return to the house, to butcher the family canine. The one that had taken out – forcibly removed – what felt like a pound of flesh from his left glute. The wound stung. It was only fair that Dorman should have his own pound of flesh, was it not?

'Finished?' Connors asked. Barely a few minutes had passed, but Dorman was one of the fastest eaters he'd ever seen. Defeated by Dorman's stubbornness, Connors had sloped outside for a cigarette and when he'd got back there was only one piece left for the other man to suck clean. It was hardly worth sitting down again.

As the two men exited, they made a point of saying goodbye to the guy behind the till. If it ever came down to it, they'd want to be remembered.

2.

Massimo helped them with the bags. 'Anything to report?' he asked.

'Pretty routine,' Connors replied.

'Apart from the German Shepherd you failed to mention,'
Dorman added sourly.

'Really? I didn't know nothing about a dog.' Massimo
sounded genuinely surprised. 'Sorry about that, lads.'

The bags were laid on a table and Massimo said, 'Right.
Let's be having you then. What have we got?' He opened the first
one. 'Laptop…nice… A *games* console. Blimey! Bit old to be playing computers, I woulda thought. Grandkids, maybe.'

'Maybe,' Connors agreed. 'Do you mind if I get a drink,
Mass?'

'Bar's in the games room, three doors down on your right.
I'll have a brandy. No ice.'

'Dorman?'

'Diet Coke… Use your privy, mate?'

'Second on the left,' said Massimo, now opening the second
of the seven rubble-strength black bags. 'And clean up if you
splash, eh? Gail's a demon for toilet hygiene.'

In the corridor Connors whispered to Dorman: 'But he
must be something else as well. Place is even bigger than it looked
outside! You don't' get a gaff like *this* being a fence.'

Dorman sniffed. 'Don't let him hear you call him that: he
hates it,' he whispered back.

'What's he prefer?'

'A transferral executive, believe it or not.'

'…You're pulling me leg.'

'Straight up! Here's me,' Dorman added, referring to the
door he'd been directed to.

Connors wondered what might be behind the other doors
he passed. There were even a few further on from the one *he'd*
been directed to. Parenthetically he considered how cool it would
be to tap *this* place.

The games room was larger than the library, where they'd

left Massimo to rifle through the haul. The baize on the pool table – a vibrantly bloody red – matched that of the eight-foot-high curtains. A pinball machine winked different colours in random arrangements. An exercise bike stood in the right-hand corner, facing a vast plasma screen that was currently switched off.

Most importantly, the bar was to the left. Connors trekked over and fixed the drinks. After a moment's hesitation he had a swift shot for his troubles – down in a swallow – and then filled his glass up again.

Dorman was exiting the bathroom. 'See the *mess* that canine's caused!'

'No thanks!'

'I tell you…if not tonight, then soon.'

'Keep on with the not-tonight idea,' Connors suggested.

Massimo had concluded (or cancelled) his inventory. As Dorman and Connors re-entered the library, the Italian was browsing the spines along one shelf of the floor-to-ceiling bookcases that hemmed in the room. He didn't turn.

Connors placed the glasses on the table, near one of the bags. Dorman claimed his Diet Coke and said, 'Mass? Everything okay?'

Massimo didn't turn. He spoke to his book collection.

'You'll have to go back, boys,' he said. 'You were in the wrong house.'

3.

Bernadette had calmed down considerably by the time she'd returned home. She was definitely still irked – she knew her tempers well enough to understand she'd have to sleep it away – but she was nowhere near as enraged as she had been when that drunken wit had spewed up half of the Last Supper on her regulation shoes. He'd been bugging her before this – demanding to be next to see a doctor, complaining about civil liberties and the importance of his own individual National Insurance contributions – but the tepid vomit footbath had been the end of the line.

She'd told him to leave. She'd warned him that Security would want a word…and then – *then* – of all the damned things, that bossy cow Margaret had admonished *her* to keep her voice down!

Bernadette's night was thirty seconds away from becoming worse.

Scented bath, glass of wine, slice of toast, she predicted; then *bed*. Decisively and defiantly – bed. Tomorrow being another day, and all that.

She turned the key and opened the front door. A few seconds later, in the pokey front room, she breathed, 'Oh my God…'

No TV where a TV should be – where she'd left it this afternoon. No player, no console… Just Chelsea, the four year-old German Shepherd, nudging up to her, happy to see her, the long tongue extended – wanting to play, whatever the hour.

'I've been burgled, haven't I, hon?'

Not moving from the spot, she called Chris.

'Is it important? Only I'm holding a straight flush and the boys are shitting a rucksack *apiece*.'

Bernadette heard a chorus of taunt-filled laughter.

'They think I'm *bluffing*. Well it'll cost you, Tommy, to find out!'

More laughter.

'We've been robbed,' Bernadette said through the noise. 'Can you come home?'

'Aw, you said it was okay I played tonight, babe. I won't be long.'

'Did you hear the first part of what I said?'

'No.'

Bernadette repeated herself.

'Arsecakes… Give me fifteen minutes.'

4.

Dorman said, 'But it *can't've* been. They had a sign on the side of the door!'

'Saying what?'

'Seventy-seven! Seventy-seven Wilberforce Drive.' Dorman turned to Connors for moral support, and the other man nodded enthusiastically.

Finally, Massimo span on his heels and faced them across the table.

'If I'd wanted you to go to seventy-fucking-seven,' he said slowly, 'I would've *sent* you to seventy-fucking-seven.'

'But you did, Mass!'

'*Eleven*. The job was *eleven* Wilberforce Drive.'

'It fucking weren't!' Connors protested.

'You got the paper?' said Dorman.

The sheet had been torn from a ledger. On it, in black ink, handwritten, was the address. Gratefully vindicated, Dorman snatched the paper from between his partner's fingertips and skirted around the table.

Massimo read the address. 'Eleven Wilberforce Drive,' he said.

'You blind?' Dorman retorted, indignantly. 'It clearly says–'

'They're *ones*, you idiot!'

'…Well they look like sevens! Why've they got them silly *hats* on? A one's a stick, Mass. It don't have…'

Massimo was not to be out-decibelled or out-logicked. 'A seven has a *line* through it.' He prodded the sheet of paper. 'And *they* don't. That's a one. And *that's* a one as well. You put em together and what've you got? Bibbadee bobbadee boo. *Eleven…*' He shook his head sadly. 'You pair of jokers. And to think you came *recommended*…Get back in your van.'

Dorman hung his head.

Connors, on the other hand, stood his ground. 'With due respect, I think we're entitled to at least a percentage of our fee. For the work so far.'

Massimo drew closer. 'Oh you do, do you? For a table full of shit I'll be hard pushed to punt at a car boot sale.'

'That's not what you said five minutes ago.'

Massimo smirked. 'So what sort of percentage did you have in mind, eh? I'll tell you what, son. Here's me best offer: take it or leave it. Nought per cent and a kick up the arse on your way. Or you can go back to the *right* house and *do the fucking job I told you to do.* Now get out of my home.'

'It was an honest mistake,' Connors persisted. 'The Continental style of those ones – we both thought they were sevens.'

'Well you were both *wrong*, weren't you?' Massimo told them.

5.

'Nothing we can't replace,' Chris concluded, drawing Bernadette in for a squeeze. 'It's nothing, babe. Don't let it worry you. It's random. We were *out*, they came *in*,' he sing-songed. 'They don't *know* anything.'

Bernadette sighed. 'I think Billie bit him. She had a tiny bit of blood on her tooth.'

'Good. I hope it was on his dangle.'

'…I'm sorry I spoiled your game. I don't suppose you really had a flush, did you?'

'No. I made a hundred, though.'

'Excellent. We can put a down payment on a new laptop,' Bernadette said sourly.

6.

'Now we face an uncertain but interesting premise,' said Dorman, indicating left.

'We need a different vehicle,' Connors interpreted.

'Exactly.'

'So what's the interesting part?'

'Concept of two birds with one stone,' Dorman answered. 'Have to go back there anyway…'

'No. I'm not standing there while you do in a dog! Forget about it! We're going to the right house and we'll see how the land lies.'

'It's just up the road!'

'I don't care, Dorman. You didn't think I'd *accompany* you, did you? This is you and the dog's problem, not mine. The bugger didn't bite *me*.'

'No. He wouldna been able to *catch* you.'

'…What's *that* supposed to mean?'

'You're light on your feet, that's all. The benefit of youth.'

'Oh…'

'Why, what did you think I was implying?'

'Nothing. So what do you say? We park this – and what?'

'Well let me think now. If we park, we add on the inconvenience of having to lift the stuff, maybe two or three streets away. Or more.'

'As I say: we need a different vehicle.'

'Right.'

'And we ain't got one.'

'*Right.*'

'…So your suggestion is?'

They had drawn up to a red light. There were two cars ahead of them. Dorman drummed on the wheel; he revved the engine as if he was going somewhere in a hurry.

'What do you think he was expecting?' he asked, ignoring Connors's question.

'I've been curious about that for the last twenty minutes,' Connors admitted.

'He got a laptop, some electrical shit,' Dorman continued in a ruminative manner. '*I* thought it was pretty decent.'

'We both did.'

'No jewellery, I suppose…'

'No; but there *weren't* any!'

'No. It'd be helpful if we knew what we were actually *looking* for.'

'I don't think *he* knows,' said Connors.

For the moment Connors declined to comment further. He engaged first gear and pulled away, but he didn't keep his counsel for long.

'Should've trusted my instincts,' he said. 'This had a funny feeling from the start.'

'How do you mean?'

'Well, for openers – why did it need two strangers? No disrespect intended, but you get to my age you get a good idea who you want to work with. Then Benny's telling me, "You're working with a new kid." I'm like, "Why? Everyone on holiday or summing?" He's gone, "It's a job for Massimo. Bloke don't need to supply reasons." So I went along with it – obviously – but I had a taste in my mouth. No offence.'

'None taken. I thought it was odd too,' said Connors. 'And the *urgency* of the thing. Has to be Monday night. Homeowners at a funeral up north. Well okay. I don't doubt *that* exactly…'

'*I'm* starting to.'

'…but if they're away, what does it matter what *time* we hustle? Don't make sense.'

Dorman agreed. 'None of it does. If I thought I could get out of this with my reputation intact I'd be out of here, mate. I don't like the flavour.'

Somewhat uncertainly Connors asked, 'What's the worst that could happen?'

'We get killed.'

'No, I mean – what's the worst that could happen if we refuse to do the job?'

'That's what I was talking about.'

'...Jesus.'

'Oh, not *directly*, maybe,' Dorman conceded. 'But I seen it happen. Bad jobs leading to a... to a devaluation of a reputation. The next thing you know the guy's frozen out and half blind with hunger. No work to be had, see. Moves on. End of story. Good as dead...But this *one* guy – Feathers his name was – he thought he'd tough it out. Started taking risks. *Silly* risks. The last time I see him, guy's punting for change outside the bookies, slowly starving to death. They say they saw him strangling a pigeon. For a meal, presumably. Only, by then the poor cunt was so doo-lally with fatigue and the munchies and desperation, he tried to eat the fucker *there* – raw – on the street.'

'Yuck.'

'Exactly. Yuck. Thereafter he was busting into places just to get a cell for the night. For the toast and coffee...We'll park here.'

Connors waited until Dorman had killed the engine.

'What happened to him? To Feathers.'

'He disappeared. Poof! In a puff of smoke, like.' Dorman sighed reflectively. 'I wish *I* had someone I could look up to in a situation like this,' he said softly.

Connors was already bristling: the altercation with Massimo had had a chance to get back under his skin. And now *this*: the obligation to play the part of the grateful new boy.

'Situations like what?' he all-but demanded.

'Like this! This *amateur* stuff, mate!'

'It don't *feel* amateur,' Connors replied.

'Well, that's because *you're* an amateur.'

'Oh fuck off! We both got it wrong, Dorman, it weren't just me... Oh very funny.'

Dorman had burst out laughing. 'Don't get me wrong, mate, but you're gonna be a fucking *cinch* to wind up! Temper flaring up like a pack of haemorrhoids!'

'Yeah yeah...'

Dorman parked a couple of streets shy of their destination. 'I got it,' he said, clicking his fingers. 'Staring us right in the face. It's like going for food.'

Connors twisted in his chair. 'What do you mean?'

'We bought food, right? Why did we do that?'

'Because you were hungry? Because that's what they do on this planet?'

'Oh I see. You're being *humorous*. You're being a *wag*. Well listen up. We went for food *and acted normal* for people to remember us, Connors. And by remembering us – what happened?'

'They forget us,' Connors answered. 'We're just two blokes who bought chicken.'

'Exactly. So what could be more natural, after a dog's bit a bloke, than that bloke going back to the house? It's acting normal...'

'Except for two things,' Connors told him.

'What two things?'

Connors counted them out into the palm of his left hand. 'One: it's the middle of the night – not exactly a traditional time for making a complaint.'

'But they're night owls, mate! We just seen the bloke come home!'

'Unless he's burgling the place.'

'Good luck to the cunt if he is. We already *got* it all.'

'And two: we happened to be inside the place removing their goods when the dog bit you, as I do believe I've mentioned before.'

'Ah!' Dorman raised a finger: point of order, my lord. 'Except we weren't.'

Connors shook his head slowly. 'Weren't what?' he asked.

'*In*side. We were *out*side. And what's more, we saw the cunts coming out with a load of fucking computers and whatnot in their arms! It was *them* cunts burgling the place. *We* just happened to interrupt the proceedings.'

Connors smiled. 'I see where you're going –'

'Exactly.'

' –but why were we there in the first place? Why were we *passing?*'

'We know someone in the next village… What do you think they're gonna do, cross-examine us? We just stopped a burglary at their house!'

'Or tried to,' said Connors.

'Or tried to, exactly.'

'…How many of'm were there?'

'Three. Nice unround number, three. And big cunts. But *white*. White as us. This don't look like the sort of place as gets too worried by racial tension, you know what I mean?' Dorman laughed.

'But we just robbed a black geezer's house,' Connors argued.

'*Who* did?'

'Well, *they* did.'

'*They* did. Right. But they didn't *know* it was a black geezer's house, did they?'

'I don't know if they did or not,' Connors admitted.

'Exactly. You don't. And do you know *why* you don't know?' Dorman asked him.

'No. Because I'm an amateur?'

'No. Because you're not a bloody sociologist, are you? Let's go for it, mate.' Dorman did what his name suggested his ancestors once did for a living, or at least for tips: he opened the door. And he was about to slide out into the chilly air.

'Just so I'm clear,' Connors stopped him. 'We were in the neighbourhood, maybe asking for directions...'

'Yeah okay: we were lost.'

'...and we see em coming out of the house, carrying stuff.'

Dorman was growing impatient. 'That's about the size of it,' he told his pupil. 'Except – one look at us and they think they're onto a loser, even if *we* think they happen to be moving house.'

'At midnight.'

'It don't *matter* at what time. We scared em off and got a bite on our arse from the dog for our troubles.'

'Well *I* didn't.'

'Well *I did.* And they'll be sorry about that. They might even reward us, mate! Won't occur to em someone'd be dumb enough to return to the scene of the crime so soon afterwards.'

'I can follow *that*,' Connors added. 'This is suicidal.'

'No it ain't. Even got a poetry about it,' Dorman countered. 'We're completely in the clear – think about it. We sow the right seeds while they're still awake inside the house.'

'But why did we come back?'

'We or they?'

'*We*! Us! Why are we here after we went away for a bit?'

'It's obvious.'

'Not to me.'

'We were *chasing* the cunts, but they got away – they slipped us on the B road. *Adios.* Goodnight, Vienna. They's too fast for us. Too *skilful*.'

For a second or two Connors said nothing. The information was processed in several compartments of his brain. 'And then what?' he finally asked.

'Then we do the *real* place,' Dorman answered.

'...Why ain't they called the filth, I wonder. Place should be *oozing* blue light.'

Dorman chuckled. 'For a *burglary*? Grow up, son. What's it like here? Not exactly the Bronx.'

'That's what I mean. Burglary round here'll make the papers, I woulda thought.'

'That's your problem, son, in a nutshell. *You think too much*. Are we coming or we going? This ain't getting a bonnet for baby, sitting here getting piles. We don't want him going to sleep.'

'No, I suppose not. But what about the dog?'

'Jesus. What *about* the dog?' Dorman demanded.

'And your plans for it.'

'They can wait.' Dorman sniffed. 'I'll take the fucker out for his last walk in the near future. First, we introduce ourselves. Then we do the right house. Then in the morning, P.C. fucking Piddlestick's hot on the trail of three white skinheads in a... in a *plumber's* van. Yeah. Double burglary, dirty wankers. Don't know what this country's coming to. Now *come on*.'

Beyond the door to Number 77 the dog barked. Dorman twitched. He felt his cheeks fill with surface-level blood: embarrassment and rage. He felt ill-prepared, despite the lesson he'd given Connors. Of all the unfamiliar emotions that he might experience, he felt *insecure*. And there was no point being rational about this, he had decided. There was no point saying to himself: *Craig, my son? You're* bound *to feel a bit on edge. You just been bitten by a dog, son! The same one as wants to have another mouthful!* No point. Because if he couldn't deal with a *dog*, for Christ's sake, then his name would be rubbish before the week was out anyway: with or without Massimo's account of tonight's failures doing the rounds. *Then you notice your stock fall,* he continued. *Like it did for old George Feathers.*

He had something to prove, no doubt of that: no less than a defence of his honour... He could feel Connors slightly behind him; feel the younger man's attention. It was getting on his nerves, this assumed responsibility. Maybe better men than he could hack it... The dog barked some more. How many seconds had passed? His buttock throbbed; the alcohol in his system – the quick one he'd had at Massimo's – had been drained of any curative effect it had once possessed and was now sour and sharp in his bladder. He felt sick.

'Dorman?' Connors repeated.

Come on, Craig, he ordered himself. *Grow a pair or fuck right off like the old man did.*

Beautiful. *Poetic* timing, son! Bringing the old man in at this hardly-appropriate moment. You got enough *room* on your chest for another medal? You *sulker.* Perhaps we could pin it to your fucking *spine.*

'Dorman?'

'Yes yes,' the older man hissed irritably. He extended his reach towards the doorbell.

7.

Unable to sleep, Bernadette lay in bedclothes that she felt guilty owning. It didn't matter that honest gambling had bought them: it's the way she was. *All gamblers are guilty.* This was fifty per cent of something she thought of from time to time: it came back to her at the oddest moments. Inopportune was not the word. *All gamblers are guilty of something,* was what he'd said – what Chris had said, returning home one daybreak after an all-nighter – and the words had chilled Bernadette. She'd thought he'd lost. She'd thought he'd lost at a time in their shared life when they couldn't afford to lose.

Disgustedly she kicked off the expensive bedware; the smoothness was an itch to her skin. She stood by the window and touched the bronze-coloured curtain; the hem was as heavy as a ham.

Down on the street, two men walked towards her house. For less than five seconds they were framed in light drizzling from a lamp, which turned their faces the colour of beechwood.

The man a stride or two in the lead was of medium height and lean build; he was in his late forties. He wore either dark blue or black; it was impossible to tell which. His iron-filing hair bordered a rigid monk's tonsure at his fontanelle; he appeared angry. A mood had tugged his eyebrows together into an admonishing frown.

The second man was younger. Mid-twenties, was Bernadette's instant guess. He had a fuller figure; not fat, but broad in the beam. The look of a man who was serious when he arrived at the gym. A ratty face: something *rodent* about the small nose. He was wearing a navy tracksuit and a pair of formerly white trainers, now stained beige by mud or puddles.

Bernadette had no way of knowing it, but these two men were about to change her life for the worse.

Behind her, Chris snuffled in his sleep. Bernadette turned to watch him, to calm him; she believed that a loving unbroken gaze could soothe him when he suffered the nightfears, and on this occasion it worked too. If Chris had been worming his way up out of cover, Bernadette's patient attention – her bedside manner no less – coaxed him back down again. Simultaneously his mouth and his rectum emitted proximate noises. Then he settled, and Bernadette returned to the scene on the road below.

Then Chelsea started barking downstairs.

Then the doorbell rang.

Chris lifted his head from the pillow. 'What's going on?'

'I'll get it.' Bernadette wanted this first hand, not reported back to her. She'd be safe enough: Chelsea had always been a good guard dog. Hadn't tonight's events, and Chelsea's performance therein, proved as much?

All the same, Bernadette took the phone from the charger cradle on the bedside table. She thumbed 999. All it would take was a thumb on the green button to send the alarm. With the phone in her hand she pulled on her dressing gown as Chris sat up in bed.

'Hell's *that* at this time of night?' Chris demanded, his voice slurred with half-dissolved sleep.

'It's nothing. Probably someone lost.' Bernadette stepped onto the landing (the floorboards creaked reliably) and skipped down the flight, to where she saw Chelsea fronting up to the door. 'It's all right, girl.'

The dog turned. This was better, the eyes seemed to say as they watched Mistress descend. The bark altered: something friendlier now; something less territorial.

Aware that Chris was behind her – at the top of the stairs, in his dressing gown – Bernadette took a breath and opened the door.

8.

A matter of minutes later, and Dorman and Connors were on their way down the road to Number 11. 'That weren't too tricky,' Connors conceded.

'Told you. Now comes the hard part. They might be back from the funeral by now.'

'In which case...'

'In which case we might need to rethink. But let's look on

the bright side, eh?'

'There's a bright side?' Connors asked.

Aside from some differences in external decorative styles, Number 11 appeared much the same as Number 77. There were no lights on inside.

'Did you notice,' the younger man continued, 'she didn't even seem flustered. She's had her home broken into and you're showing her a bite on your bum – and she's not lifted an eyebrow.'

'Your point being?' Dorman enquired.

'They're hiding something.'

'Well I know *that*. Stands to reason, mate! But what they do in the privacy of their own house is none of our business tonight. Are you focused?'

'Course I'm focused.'

'Good.' Dorman opened his jacket: the tools of his trade were neatly contained in a strap that he wore aslant his chest. He removed a set of picks on a ring. 'Round the back again,' he decided, and he set off across the front lawn to address the gate that would lead to the garden at the rear. The gate was made of wrought iron, the pieces in floral shapes. A padlock held the gate in place, and wordlessly Dorman set to the padlock with one of the picks. Just as Connors was about to tell him that it would be simplicity itself to climb over the gate, the lock sprung and Dorman pushed the gate wide. The two of them followed the path; it was bordered with brown pots of various flowers that meant nothing to either man. The back garden was tidy and trimmed. The homeowners had left the lawnmower out (Connors wondered parenthetically if *this* could be what Massimo was so desperate to receive, and what might be the best way to move it quietly back down the street to the van without its rattling waking up all of the neighbours) but Dorman paid it no mind. 'Conservatory,' he muttered; 'nice job.' With which he started work with a different sized pick.

Connors leaned towards the conservatory's glass. Not *too* close, of course – he had heard of burglars being convicted on the basis of a nose-print on glass, and although he didn't *know* this to be true he was not willing to take any chances – but close enough to see what was inside. The conservatory was obviously a chill-out area. An upright piano; some up-market loungers; a small bookcase filled with volumes whose titles Connors could not read in the darkness and which would have meant little to him, even if he had been able to see them clearly.

Dorman swore under his breath. 'New locks,' he explained elliptically. The more modern the door, it seemed, the more difficult life was for honest professionals in the burgling game. Why, Dorman thought from time to time, it was almost as if no one *wanted* to be burgled anymore! What was the bloody world coming to?

'...Hell's that noise?' Connors asked quietly.

'Ssshhh.' Dorman removed his glass-cutter from the same belt, taking care to replace the picks in their original place.

'Seriously, Dorman. Can't you hear it? It's inside...'

Either prompted by the questions or because the information had filtered through his determination and work ethic anyway, Dorman said, his voice similarly low, 'Sounds like water.'

Indeed it did: like water, not merely running (it was no babbling brook somewhere close, the acoustics distorted by the pristine silence of the early hours) but *surging*. Water *pounding*. But against what? And from where?

Connors said, 'I don't like this...'

Dorman didn't like it either, but he didn't like the notion of failing Massimo even more. By applying the glass-cutter to the area around the conservatory door lock he hoped to blot out what the two of them could hear. Then something unignorable caught his eye. He looked up.

The two of them watched spellbound and speechless as the wave approached them. The conservatory was a vast TV screen, but this show would only be a few seconds long.

The wave had smashed through the house and was now going to tear its way through the conservatory. Dorman stared into the glass as if it had just asked him to dance.

Connors started to back away, stumbling deeper into the garden. 'Dorman, *move*!' he shouted as the tsunami inside the house – *inside the house*! – made contact with the front of the glass shell, pushing out with tons of force. Dorman was hypnotised; he was skewered to his spot on the patio paving, a glass-cutter in his hand and something imbecilic on his face.

The noise was astounding. As the wave smashed through the glass, the sound was close to deafening; on currents of sound shards and sheets of the broken glass exploded outwards.

Moving in a mixed choreography of backward stomping and crab-walk, Connors had made it to a spot nearly ten metres away before he dared to look again past the forearm he was using to shield his face instinctively. Although his brain registered the presence of flying glass in the air, his full attention was claimed by his work partner. Dorman hadn't shifted his position one iota: but he did now. No choice in the matter: the ceiling-high wall of water had caught him full frontal; he was lifted off his feet in time for his face to meet the hypotenuse of a perfectly right-angled slice of glass, approximately the size of a trumpet. Through the water Connors was able to see the glass slice into Dorman's face. The top of the man's head was sheared off as neatly as the top of a boiled egg, and his scalp, forehead, eyes and the bridge of his nose landed in a wet red parcel in a raised bed of courgettes that were being grown. Dorman's body sailed the sea for a few more metres, then crashed down in a lump.

Connors kept moving towards the rear of the property. Then something hit him powerfully from behind.

9.

'I'm still not sure about this,' Bernadette said softly, in one of those voices that she would use more normally to ask *Are you awake, Chris?* A voice soft but not *too* close to silent; at which point he would either say nothing at all (if he was asleep), or he would mumble something about *wanting* to be asleep; or, as he did right now, he would surprise her ever so slightly with a fully conscious response.

As clear as a bell Chris now said, 'No, I'm not sure about this either, babe.'

Bernadette sat up and flicked on the table lamp. She took a second to think things through, but either as a result of fatigue or touched nerves, she found it all-but impossible to stick to the facts. Her unconscious insisted on feeding her lines that seemed not only from other occasions, but from other *lives*.

The fact that Chris had been unable to sleep on it either did not help calm Bernadette down. Even though the two visitors had only left a few minutes earlier, Chris could sleep on the edge of a cliff and dream the sweet dreams of the righteous and the safe. If the conversation was bothering *him*...

A glutton for punishment, Bernadette returned to the window. 'I don't like any of this,' she admitted. 'What if they've found us?'

Chris sighed heavily. Twisting his upper body, he opened the drawer on his nightstand and retrieved a box of cigarettes.

'Not in here, Chris,' said Bernadette, irritably.

'I wasn't going to.' While Bernie kept her watch on the road a storey down, Chris pulled on the dressing gown that always lived on top of the bed and under which he slept by way of it being an extra blanket. 'I'll go out the back with Chelsea. Poor girl'll be wondering what the fuck.'

'She's not the only one. I'll come with you.'

Dressed for bed, then, the two of them stepped downstairs, the cords of their dressing gown flapping like tails. When they entered the kitchen, Chelsea watched them from where she lay but decided not to move to greet them. It had been a busy night already; Chelsea's jaws remained still on her forepaws, only her eyes shifting.

'She's probably confused with the dark as well,' said Bernadette. 'Thinks it's getting-up time. But it's dark, she's thinking, so how *can* it be, eh girl?'

Chris unlocked the door to the garden. 'We often walk her when it's dark,' he said.

'Yeah, after she's been *asleep*.'

'I won't be a second,' he continued, abandoning any attempt at debate. It was too deep into the small hours for them all, not only Chelsea... Wielding but a lighter and a smoke, he took the step down into the small back garden, leaving Bernie behind to fuss the dog for a few minutes – or to make a brew, or to do whatever it was that she thought it best to do in these insomniac hours.

Chris was only halfway through his cigarette, but he tasted that he'd had enough. Taking care to extinguish it in the dish of water that stayed on the windowsill for just such a purpose, Chris was about to step back into the relative warmth of the kitchen when he heard a noise that held him to the spot, with one slippered foot on the doorstep and one on the ground.

The roar of water. The din of glass smashing.

HOUSEWARMING

1.

The driveway was a quarter of a mile long. It felt longer. As though in awe of the spectacle, the bewhiskered chauffeur had maintained a purring crawl since giving his passenger's name into the voicebox at the gate and being granted entry onto the estate. Or perhaps (the passenger considered) the slow speed of progress was for the passenger's benefit − a chance for him to savour the full autumnal spread of all that he now owned. It didn't matter. The passenger was in no hurry to reach the house, and so new to him was the notion that this was *his* that he didn't wish to miss a thing anyway. Furthermore, he had yet to decide on the level of superiority to assume when addressing his chauffeur. He didn't know if it was proper to instruct the man to speed up: never before had he employed staff.

'Here we are, sir.'

'Thank you, Curtis.'

They had pulled up near the front door, gravel crackling like crossed wires beneath them. The passenger felt it might be dangerous to tear his eyesight away from the tall, wide front doors − as though attempting to take in the full picture would be too much for his mind − although he'd seen the place twice before purchase.

'Allow me to get your door, sir,' said Curtis, opening his own.

'No need.' No need, *mate*, was what he'd almost said. He

had already admonished himself for blokey language: it was names all the way from hereon in.

He angled himself free of the Jag.

The house doors opened, and Dorota threw wide her arms at the top of the shallow flight of bleached stone steps. She descended nimbly; her face was a picture of happy magic. Like the man she was shortly to embrace, she could not really believe her luck either.

Wordlessly Curtis had removed a small piece of travel-battered luggage from the Jag's boot. Now he stood, grey-suited, sombre, stoic, a respectful two metres from the embrace, which now broke with a short duet of laughter.

'Eastlight's here already,' Dorota said. 'He's in the snooker room. The *snooker room!*'

They laughed again.

'I'll take that, Curtis,' the new squire of the manor said. He held his arm out to take charge of the suitcase.

'It's no trouble, sir.'

'Not for me either.'

'As you wish, sir.' The suitcase changed hands, and the one in receipt added, to either or both of his interlocutors (or perhaps to himself):

'It's a moment. It's *me* taking *my* belongings into *my* new house… That sounds absurd.'

'No it doesn't, Vig,' Dorota told him. 'There'll be plenty of other chances for people to carry your bags. Now you're *rich.*'

Followed by Curtis they moved to the foot of the steps, Dorota saying, 'Or are you going to give me the one about not forgetting your roots again?'

'No.'

'Good. They're not slaves, Vig: you're paying them to do a job.'

'I can carry a *bag*, darling…'

'If you want to – yes.' Dorota stepped into the hallway. 'But not because you have no other choice.' She turned and grinned. 'Come on, step over the threshold – like a vampire. I invite thee.'

When he did so Vig felt small and not big; humbled, not proud. 'It's going to take me longer to get used to this than it is for you, Dol,' he said to the back of Dorota's shoulders, which shrugged. Without turning her head as she led the way down the hallway that smelled of polish and chrysanthemums, she called:

'I already have.'

2.

Eastlight was in the snooker room, as Dorota had explained. When the party of three entered, he stepped away from his caressing of the green baize, a wistful expression on his face.

'Viggy-loo, Viggy-lay!' he bellowed by way of greeting.

'How are you, Charlie?' Vig replied in a more sedate fashion.

The two men hugged but it was an awkward exhibition: like rugby players in a scrum. They clapped one another on the back and separated – not a second too soon for anyone present.

'How am I, the man asks!' Eastlight said, beaming. 'Well it's a dark day, obviously! How do you *think* I am, Viggy? This is the single most exciting thing I've ever been party to!'

'You should get out more,' Vig told him.

'Well I will! Now that you're out in the country, with the weevils and the voles and all that nonsense. But listen, Vig –'

'Sir?' said Curtis.

Although Eastlight now treated the driver to a torrential surge of immediate contempt, Vig himself was in too good a mood to chastise the man for his interruption.

'Anywhere in particular, sir?' Curtis asked, once more holding up the suitcase.

Vig sipped the air, an action which made the decision seem to be of more import to him than it actually was. However, there was a reason for this: it was at this very instant that Vig understood that from now on he would be responsible for a good many more such decisions than had ever been the case up to now. *Put it anywhere*, he almost replied; but he divined that Curtis was the sort of man who appreciated an unambiguous command – an order.

'On the chair, please, Curtis.'

Dorota had moved towards an old-fashioned hostess trolley which had been either parked or abandoned near the vast uncurtained window. On top of the trolley were a few bottles in varying states of depletion.

'We should toast,' she announced. 'Your new home. Your new life!'

'*Our* new home,' Vig corrected her. 'What do we have?'

Dorota began twisting the bottles for a better look at the labels. 'Vodka, gin…'

Eastlight spoke up quickly. 'Guys. Would you mind if we waited till Don joined us? Be nice if we were all together, to wet the baby's head as it were… Well you know what I mean.'

'What time did you say to him?' Vig asked.

'He knows you're here. Doing something disgusting with insects that frankly I had no stomach to hear the end of.'

Dorota teased him, deliberately ironically. 'Oh you city boy you,' she said.

'From the girl from Gdansk!'

'He's got a point,' Vig said. 'We're all in this together, after all… Who's for a game of doubles?' And he indicated the snooker table.

3.

Don Bridges finished feeding the birds and then loitered longer than he needed to in the case that housed the Hyacinth Macows. His narrow ex-jockey buttocks perched on the edge of a waist-high ornamental waterfall; and as he rolled a thin cigarette he watched Larry, the plump and elderly lizard that he had raised from as early as the egg, as he scuttled from rock to rock, tasting the nicotine infringement to the natural air. Not for the first time Don anthropomorphized the reptile: he read stately wisdom in those somehow *academic* facial features. A professorial quality that often made Don clutch at his own elbows, bowed once again by the presence of one of the several billion creatures on the planet that exhibited more intelligence than he did himself. And not for the first time, Don wanted to crush it dead.

Standing up to the crackling applause of creaky knees, he managed to scatter birds from perch to perch. In this one aviary cage alone there were thirteen, and there were seven more cages, each similarly stocked with life. It was Don's jobs to take care of them all (no one else could). It wasn't only where he worked, and had worked for many years: it was where he loved to be – where he *needed* to be. It was the *only* place. However (sighing now as he locked the cage behind him) he had been summoned to the house by that ball-sack Eastlight; if no other reason than to start on the right foot, he'd better go. He was *expected*. That was the word Eastlight had used: *expected*. Well; they could have ten or fifteen minutes of his time – he supposed he owed the new owner this much – but if anyone had had a strange dream that he'd be changing his clothes for the occasion then that was that silly bugger's lookout, wasn't it now? They would take him or leave him, welly boots and poacher's pockets and all.

Don sighed again. Strange to be in the main house again, he thought. It had been a good few months: in fact, he had only been back a couple of times since his lordship had moved out six months previous (on grounds of ill-health and impending penury). There hadn't been much point. The birds were all that concerned him now. Or nearly all.

Custom and good manners obliged Don to scrape his boots at the kitchen door. Although he hoped to find the door locked, he was not lucky; it opened to its familiar whine that Don had vowed to oil right on a number of occasions but had never got around to doing. The kitchen was empty. Marion the cook had left with the rest of them; no saucepans rattled ably on the roof of the Aga; no stews belched out flavoursome perfumes; the puppies were not present to beg for bacon rind... Surprisingly (but briefly) nostalgic for those times, Don closed the door behind him and strode through the room to the hallway. The voices he could hear sounded happy: that was one thing at least. He followed the voices across the ground floor, arriving at the snooker room in a slightly better mood: one of trepidation.

Introductions ensued, with Eastlight the master of ceremonies.

'Hartvig Klossen – this is Donald Bridges. Don Bridges – this is the man with a heart so big he's allowed you to keep your job, when the done thing would've been to move the hell out with the rest of the staff force...'

'Charlie,' Vig interrupted. 'Please. Delighted to meet you, Don – finally.' He extended a hand, and the hand it met was as rough as pork rind, tanned to the hue of tobacco spit.

'Viggy-loo,' said Eastlight calmly. 'Don knows I'm dicking, don't you, Don?' He clapped his hands in a wringing motion. 'Now about that drink...'

'Delighted to meet you, sir,' said Don, averting his eyes to peruse a roadmap of shrub-scratches on the inside of his right arm.

Having skipped back over to the hostess trolley, Dorota called out for drinks orders.

For Don the offer led to no lessening of tension; on the contrary, the notion of social interaction alerted a taste of capers and vanilla ice-cream to his tongue. Not a man who drew breath knew the pleasure of a glass or two of brandy better than Don, but it was supposed to be a solitary activity.

'Thank you, not for me,' he replied. 'Very kind of you, but I'd best be getting back–'

'To the birds?' cried Eastlight. 'Don't forget what you *owe* Mr Klossen.'

Vig shook his head. 'If he wants to go, Charlie...'

Don imagined himself being pulled in the middle. Through his mind flashed an image of Larry the lizard, a wellyboot heel stomping down on the scales of its backbone. As far as Don was concerned, the creature was already posthumous.

'It's all right, sir,' he said. 'I'm just not a one for the drink. It's not that I'm ungrateful...' He dipped a shallow bow. 'I just need to do a feed, sir.'

'Another one?' called Eastlight. 'You fed em not half an hour ago, Don!' He gulped at his glass of port. Crinkled cuts of barely suppressed mirth twitched at the corners of his eyes. 'We need some music! I wanna *dance*!'

'Do you dance, Don?' Dorota asked, pouring port into two other mismatched glasses.

Don laughed. 'A long time ago, maybe, madam. Bit of a jitterbug boy I was, back then.'

'Well show us your shapes, birdkeeper!' Eastlight shouted.

'I don't think so, sir. I don't think me knees could stand the strain.'

'Oh go on, Don! Teach us to boogie!' Eastlight persisted.

'Leave it, Charlie,' said Vig. 'Don't be getting boisterous on me.'

'Oh he doesn't *mind*, Vig – do you, Don?'

'No, sir. But I have to be on my toes. I'm up early in the

morning, rain or shine.'

'It was nice to meet you, Don,' Vig told him. 'Catch up soon, yeah?'

Again, Don bowed. Leaving the room he heard Vig whisper *For God's sake, Charlie,* and he knew that the encounter had gone worse than anticipated. For reasons that he could only put down to stubbornness – his own, the fact that he'd refused to move out – he seemed to have made a rival in Charles Eastlight. An enemy, even. And if there was one thing he didn't need it was a competitor for the affections of Hartvig and Dorota. Not when so much rested on Don maintaining his position.

With the sounds of laughter receding in his ears, Don left the house by the kitchen door. Air as fresh as creek rain brushed the bristles bearding from his caramel-coloured nostrils. As he scratched his left cheek his jowls dappled and wobbled. One-handed he rolled a cigarette, pinching from a pouch of tobacco in his poacher's pocket. The one-handed ministration was an old party trick from his days in the saddle and not even the wind could put him off his stride as he crossed the yard, stones rattling underheel. From the aviary to his right, hidden by a buffer of seven-foot hedges, came the sounds of birds calling.

His cabin was a five-minute walk away, due west into the melting chocolate of the autumn afternoon sky. The front door gave onto the lounge and its welcoming kissy breath of stale Drum tobacco. The concepts of relief and being home were interchangeable. Don sighed and locked the door – he locked them both in – and with aching shoulders he removed his coat and draped it over the arm of a prodigiously overstuffed chair. He took the four steps required to transfer himself into the square kitchen. Sweat traced the W of his greyed hairline.

Bending at the waist, Don whipped back a plum-coloured rug that was frayed at the edges and corners. What the rug had hidden was a wooden door; it lay flush to the dirt floor – the floorboards themselves had long since been removed. (And burnt: Don had put the boards on the barbecue a month earlier and smoked a couple of kippers and a few pork chops.) It didn't matter to Don. No one came here; they'd never know.

He lifted the heavy door; a hinge squeaked, an octave higher than the sound of the kitchen door in the main house. The hole was five feet deep; the walls were smooth and sheer.

Peering out of the gloom, a tiny face looked up at Don. A briny parcel of bodily waste aroma was delivered to his hirsute nostrils, and he said, 'Hello, darling. Are you hungry?'

At the bottom of the well the little girl started to cry again.

4.

Eastlight made it home in time to prevent the kitchen burning down, but only just. Getting out of the car he noticed the smell of mown grass mouldering in a pyramid of black plastic sacks near the shed. Vowing once more to take them to the dump as soon as possible (and silently berating his partner for not having done the same), Eastlight was pulling down the garage door when the stronger smell of something being reduced to carbon flirted with his nostrils. He entered briskly.

The kitchen rolled in a peasouper of acrid fog. Massimo was throwing open the windows on top of the draining board and sink. Having done this he fetched a newspaper lying on the microwave and started to usher smoke out with eagle-wing gesticulations.

By the door leading in from the garage Eastlight asked him: 'So what's for dinner?'

Massimo summoned up a dry snort. 'Sorry.' He maintained his flapping while Eastlight twisted dials on the cooker until he found the one that needed to be returned to zero: the dial for the oven. As the smoke cleared slightly, Eastlight donned a baking glove as a precaution and opened the oven door. A fresh gust of filthy burnt air bellowed free, making Massimo cough. Inside the oven a shallow tray had taken on the appearance of a nuked submarine.

Using the baking glove, Eastlight took hold of the tray; warmth slipped through to his fingers. He pulled the tray out and deposited it, smoke leaping from its charred contents, onto the hob.

'It's dinner, Jim, but not as we know it,' said Massimo in his best Captain Kirk. It was enough to make him laugh. He ceased whipping the air with the tabloid. 'Bloody hell,' he said, relieved.

'Cooking and drinking,' Eastlight replied. 'Overrated as a pairing… What was it?'

'Chinese snacks. You were late – I thought you'd be hungry.'

'I am. I still will be, you silly sod. Come here.'

The men embraced and shared a quick kiss.

'Thought that counts, I suppose,' Massimo offered in a ruminative manner.

'Are you fishing for praise?' Eastlight asked him.

'Yes. Bad day I've had.'

'What happened?' Eastlight removed the glove and fanned some of the remaining smoke by thrusting open and closed the door to the garage. 'Let's adjourn,' he added quickly. 'Catch emphysema stay in here.'

Relocating next door to the lounge, Massimo said, 'First of all I didn't get back till four this morning.'

'I heard you.'

'Sorry again.' Massimo dropped into one of the chairs in the small room. 'I didn't mean to wake you.'

'You didn't. I was worried.'

'You were angry I was late.'

'That as well.'

'Do you want a drink?'

Eastlight nodded his head. He stretched on the couch until the joints in his knees clicked to his satisfaction. 'What house did you use?'

'The big place in Eggington. Beautiful by the way. Any offers today?'

'Not on that. They're asking too much but they won't be told. So what *happened?*' Massimo poured wine from the bottle on the coffee table; his own glass had already been stained a rabbit-eye pink by previous dolings-out. Eastlight's glass, beside it, was temporarily chaste. Handing Eastlight's over he said, 'Not only did they go to the wrong house...'

'Where was this? Thanks.'

'Edlesborough... They then went to the right house but there was some soft of explosion or something. The place was blown to smithereens... How's the wine?'

'Not bad for thirty quid a crate,' Eastlight answered.

'Thirty-five if you please.' Massimo grinned. 'I wouldn't want you to think you share your life with a cheapskate!' The grin faded as fast as a strong smell in a high wind.

'Don't make me plead, Mass. Something's given you the willies.'

Massimo nodded, but turned away. After a fortifying half-glass of the knocked-off Rioja he said simply: 'They didn't come back.'

Eastlight paused and considered, stopping short of collecting in the full range of possibilities represented by his partner's summation. His immediate understanding was grave enough: the men had found something shiny and had then gone elsewhere to fence it. Greedy and stupid; however, not the end of the world. But then his mind tacked on the word explosion. 'They were killed?'

Again, Massimo nodded. 'One of them,' he answered. 'Decapitated: broken glass.'

'…Jesus.'

'The other one's nowhere to be found.' Massimo leaned towards the coffee table for a refill.

'Go steady, Mass.'

'I'm in shock.'

'Then drink some sweet tea… How do you know all this?' Eastlight asked.

'The police called me.'

'Double Jesus.'

'Silly bastard only had my name in his phone, didn't he? And he was supposed to be teaching the young dog some new tricks!' Massimo's voice sounded disgusted.

'Go slow. What do you mean explosion?'

'The opposite of implosion.'

'Cute. What exploded?'

'The house! The fucking house exploded!'

'But specifically – what inside the fucking house exploded. The gas mains…?'

'No.' Massimo shook his head. 'They don't have gas pipes in the villages. That's just one of the places the copper got vague on me.'

'Like he didn't know?'

'She. No; more like she didn't comprehend.'

'What time was this?'

'Eight, eight-fifteen. I was still asleep – but as soon as I heard the phone I was sure it was one of them. So I rallied. I was ready to come out swinging, I can tell you that: making me wait three hours. But then it's the law, and I'm painted into a corner, aren't

I? I have to start making up stories about my relationship with the deceased – you know the way they talk, the officious bitch. Probably only seen three cocks in her life and two of them's her dad and her Uncle Jimbo.'

Eastlight was well aware that Massimo entertained certain reservations about the nationwide and local constabulary: in Massimo's opinion (Eastlight had used to believe the man to be joshing; for a long time now he had not been so sure) they were inbred and incestuous. They saw the world through the same pair of eyes.

'What did you tell her?' Eastlight asked.

'What could I? We sometimes bartered, I said.' Massimo shrugged. 'Do you want a top-up?' he said, lifting the bottle.

'Yeah, a little one.'

'And then I've got Benny on the phone, a few hours later...' Massimo poured them both another half-glass. '...asking if I've seen Dorman.'

'Dorman's the younger one?'

'No, the older one... Keep up for Christ's sake. Dorman is the one with the experience, who can't tell the difference between a seven and a one.'

'...What?'

'Never mind. The point is, Dorman's dead – and they called him too.'

'The police did.'

'No, the Bee Gees did. Of course the police – and now I've got him wanting answers! It's a right mess, Charlie. Catastrophe. It's only a matter of time before they find the van.'

'But it's nothing to do with you, Mass,' Eastlight said cautiously, browsing through his words (and given Massimo's mood he didn't dare ask who Benny was).

'Charlie, it was me who sent them!'

'I know: they were doing a job. Something went wrong, one of em's dead. But there's no comeback to you. Is there? Unless there's something more you're not telling.'

Massimo sniggered greedily. 'You know me, Charlie: there's *always* more I'm not telling.'

'All right.' Eastlight thought about it for a few seconds. He made a decision. 'I promise I won't ask you this ever again, Mass,' he said, 'and I'll appreciate it if you think I'm interfering or prying, or any of those things I swore I wouldn't do… but what were they going to that house to bring out?'

Massimo shook his head.

Depositing his glass on the table, Eastlight stood up and circuited the latter in order to get to the couch, where he perched on the end of the third cushion and took Massimo's free hand in both of his own. 'You can't or you won't?' he wanted to know.

Massimo shook his head. 'Both,' he confessed. 'It was supposed to be an anniversary present. Two years next month, Charlie…'

'I know.' Eastlight grinned. 'Come on now, Mass. We'll get through this. But until we know what the actual *problem* is, there's no point stewing, is there? Is there now?'

'No.'

'Or burning down our kitchen, for that matter.'

'No. I fell asleep watching a Jackie Chan. I'm sorry, Charlie.'

'It doesn't matter. Come here.'

They shared a kiss. Eastlight stroked what remained of Massimo's hair, trying to curl a lock of insufficient length.

'We need cheering up,' Eastlight decided. 'Let's go west. Do you fancy a trip to Eggington?'

Massimo's face brightened, a circle of sunlight peering out among his otherwise muddied features. Quite visibly his emotions were fumbling around between themselves, but his sudden joy (Eastlight voted) was a photograph.

'*Yeah*. Let's see how they're getting on. Can we make em fuck?' he asked, excited.

Eastlight smiled. 'Anything for you, husband of mine,' he said.

Massimo nodded. Warming swiftly to the theme, he added, 'We'll watchem fuck, won't we?'

'Of course we will. Where's your coat?'

'Watchem fuck,' Massimo repeated. 'Have you fed em today?'

'No.'

'Good. They can eat when they've fucked for us, can't they, Charlie? Yeah. Only *after*.' Massimo laughed. 'You burn off calories faster that way.'

Eastlight stood up. The bulge in Massimo's trousers was not difficult to discern; nor was the one in his own. There'd be gay times tonight or they would be Dutchmen.

'Charlie? I went online today. I ordered a strap-on, I hope you don't mind.'

From the hallway Eastlight called, 'Why should I mind? Where's your *coat*?'

'I want *her* to fuck *him*,' said Massimo. 'On our anniversary night. Before we kill em… It's upstairs, on the bed.'

Entr'acte

'Do you plan to lie there, boy, or do you plan to help?'

Boy? Did he call me *boy?*

'Grab that rope, the gods damn you!'

Rope? Connors wondered slowly. Why would I want to grab a rope?

Thought processes moved with a dazed insistence. Getting there in the end. Progress hampered by barricades of logic. This *couldn't be happening.*

Snapping out of a corner of his fugue, Connors twisted his body on the bare wooden boards on which he'd slept, in order to look over his shoulder.

Activity. Men in motion, pulling ropes and shouting, an arch of silver-blue water crashing down on their heads. The movement of the floor.

'*Get up, boy, for the last time I'll say it!*'

And Connors struggled to his feet. He was taller than his interlocutor, who was four or so decades older and whose face was scarred and lined and made Connors think of a walnut.

'*If you don't pull your weight, I will personally throw you overboard!*'

You and whose army, Connors thought about retorting; but the question did not need an answer. The man's *own* army, was the answer: or at least his crew. This man was the captain.

'I'm on a boat,' Connors whispered – and immediately he was thrown to one side: a swell had caught the vessel and punched it hard.

Only by clutching hold of a rope did he manage to stay on his feet. The deck was saturated, filthy with gunmetal spume; the sky over head (he noticed for the first time) was crimson and blue.

I'm on a boat; and the oxygen he could breathe was in short supply, drenched and salty. The air stank of ozone, sweat and manure. And he was on a boat.

How did I get here?

Connors was on a boat on the sea. Violently unpredictable was the motion, the vigour and the energy of the waves, which allowed Connors to add to his list of deductions.

He was on a large boat (or is it ship?) on the sea, in the middle of a storm that had rendered the hour of the day impossible to discern. Perhaps it was too light to be night-time… although night-time was the last time that (he believed) he could remember.

The boat (or ship) was being lobbed, port to starboard. Juggled.

Connors's brain protested: *This doesn't make sense.*

The old seadog shuffled his way back to Connors, skating the frothing wooden boards for part of the journey with the professionalism of one who has ridden many a tempest. Maybe one who had even enjoyed the rides, if the smile beneath his white beard was anything to go by.

'This is where the largan's buried, boy! Just below our boots, on the ocean floor!'

'The what?' Connors shouted back.

The seadog provided an expression that suggested that the question was among the top two or three most stupid questions ever posed.

'The *largan*,' the seadog repeated. 'The reason why we're in this skirmish!'

Connors felt abruptly and acutely more conscious of his

ignorance.

I must be dreaming. It's just a dream…

'Are you dreaming, boy?' the seadog demanded at the top of his voice (perhaps not the captain after all, Connors considered). 'Or are you gonna grab a rope and *tug* – tug like it's between you and the Devil! For who falls in the *Pit*, boy!'

Then the seadog slapped Connors across his chops.

Connors jumped. The slap, and the cold wet air that nursed it, lent a sting disproportionately sharp to any that he might have considered possible within the gluey confines of a dream. It was almost as though he could *feel* the colour red that he was sure his left cheek must have turned.

The sting was bad. But accepting reality was worse.

Just at this moment the boat lurched sideways and downwards; it had slid down the slope of a sudden colossal wave… and now everything was shifting – towards the starboard side.

Connors could not hold onto his rope. With a stomach-tugging drop, he was at the barrier within the space of a few seconds – the barrier that separated him from the water. The impact – chest on wood – was more than enough to wind him, and air left his body with the force of a bullet from a nozzle. Then the pain launched. It was like he'd been struck across the chest with a bat. It was all he could do to hold on to the balustrade – and meanwhile the boat rolled and listed itself, a giant being bullied among other giants.

His knuckles were pinched white: the cold, the fear, the chilling spray…

I'm going to drown.

This was what Connors both thought and dreaded at this moment.

As the waves climbed again, he emptied his body of piss and vomit.

SHOW AND TELL

1.

The road must be closed, Branston deduced: nothing else would explain the queue. An accident up ahead, perhaps; an un-exploded bomb...

Sod it!

The one day in the last month that he'd chosen to avoid the bypass! The *one day* he'd fancied a change of journey on his way to work!

Fade in...

Middle-aged man at the wheel of a small car. Anger on his face. Late somewhere. Shaking the wheel.

Pullback.

Car is one of a hundred pearls on a five-mile necklace of traffic out of Leighton Buzzard.

Sod it!

Branston chose this moment to shake the wheel for real; scripts in his head notwithstanding, he had a job to get to, and if the cars in front didn't start moving soon he was going to be late for his class. And apart from the work ethic and the stratospheric level of professionalism at which he pitched his lessons, one of the things he took pride in was his punctuality. Those learners needed him! One of them, after all, might make it big in the film business in the future; and Branston had long since believed that in the void left by his own failures to direct an arthouse classic, the best he might hope for was a mention in an awards ceremony acceptance speech.

Closeup.

The starlet's face basted in tears.

STARLET: But most of all I'd like to thank Tim Branston. He was the one who saw something…

No.

…saw a spark of potential in my work, filming Samurai swordfights in Morrison's car park.

Branston laughed. Then behind him a horn squawked. 'Oh wait your pissing *turn*,' he shouted, his eyes locked on his rearview mirror. With a brass pair of balls he'd be out of his car…

Longshot.

Man exits vehicle and strides back down the road he's traversed. Points a finger at each driver in turn, expression quizzical.

MAN: Was it you with the horn, prick? Was it *you?*

Four cars back, a sweaty man at the controls. Honks the horn again. MAN bunches a fist and punches the driver's side window to buggery –

Branston shook his head.

– to smithereens… to *splinters*. MAN reaches through the space and pulls the driver's fucking head off…

Another honking at the horn from a car behind, and Branston said, 'Keep your hair on, squire' – this time under his breath.

A policeman was approaching, following the white dotted line in the middle of the road.

Branston dabbed the switch and the window rolled down.

'Officer? What's going on?'

'House explosion, sir, in Edlesborough. The road's jammed. Where are you heading?'

'Luton. Barnfield College. I've got a class to deliver at nine o'clock.'

'Well, you won't get there this way. If I were you I'd do a U-turn. Go up the bypass.'

Branston nodded and shifted into first. 'It's the story of my live,' he told the constable.

2.

He arrived at seven minutes to nine by the dashboard read-out, and the possibility that this was not to be his day was swiftly validated: there was nowhere to park. Branston followed lane after lane, sharking for the unlikely chance of someone reversing out of a space. But the universe was not feeling kind this morning. In the end Branston parked half a mile away, at the very periphery of the premises, and halfway up a drainage verge – not a *bona fide* parking spot anyway, but sod it.

In a dash he crossed the lot and entered the building. Given everything that had happened so far, he was of a mind that his swipecard would not allow him access; in this respect at least the universe was with him. He slipped through the barrier, strode along the corridor past clumps of students, and ascended the rear stairs. It was nearly a quarter past when he pushed into the classroom, saying 'Hi – sorry, everyone! Are we all here? Hands up if you're not here!'

The class of seven students did not so much as groan: they had heard the hands-up joke on a number of occasions, and term was only a few weeks old.

Branston typed in his password and took the register. 'Now. Today's the day, as you all know: we all get to see each other's masterpieces.'

A few of the class tittered. Experiencing relief at the sound, Branston sensed the accumulated anger at his late arrival dissipate. Some of the kids – kids is a forbidden term, he heard his head of department wag – shifted places to accommodate this new understanding. Not seat to seat (no; no one moved to a different chair) but in themselves, a straightening of the backbone, a cleared throat, a readiness. *We're ready*.

'I can either flip a coin,' said Branston, 'or you can decide among yourselves. Screen's up.'

A student named Sammy said, 'I'll go first,' and rose from her seat. The room had been designed for a maximum of twenty, and the front was achieved in a matter of four or five steps. She said, 'I'm nervous.'

Branston told her, 'Don't forget, I said draft quality. No one's *really* expecting a completed *meisterwork*.'

'That's lucky,' Sammy told him, her throat clicking slightly with snapped-off humour. Into the laptop port she slotted her memory-wand (for backup, just in case the internet connection failed her), then she typed the address for her film.

'What's the piece called?' Branston asked, partly by way of setting the young woman's nerves; partly by way of asserting seniority and a semblance of control.

'"Chuck the Ripper." It was almost "Chuck the Impaler" but I preferred "Ripper" in the end.'

Branston said, 'Good. It's witty, Sammy.'

'I hope so.'

The homework assignment brief had been to film and dub something of the students' own concoction, the guidelines being three to ten minutes, strict. Sammy had chosen a scene close to home – indeed, one *inside* her own home – in which Chuck the cockerpoo went on his canine rampage around the front room, chewing and snuffling and swinging his head right to left with a broadsheet supplement in the glossy grip of his front teeth.

The film ended at three minutes and two seconds.

Feeling otherwise from how he was about to react, Branston said, 'A noble effort, Sammy.'

'Thanks!'

Wait for the *but*…

'But not much, I'm sure you'll agree, in the way of *narrative*.' Branston perched on the edge of his front desk. 'I mean this: *what* gives the dog his motivation – *why* chew that cushion? – and have you presented his story fairly?'

Sammy paused before responding.

'…He's a dog,' she said.

'Precisely. Could we not have cause to learn more about dogs in general from a similar film?'

'I have no idea.'

'My question is rhetorical, Sammy. Chuck the Impaler loves tearing things to shreds: fine. Motion pictures have been built on lesser material; but I wouldn't want you to go away from today's lesson believing that a *You've Been Framed* extended mix constitutes the basis of a short *film*. It didn't. And if…' Branston smiled. '…I've learned anything from you and the rest of this group over the past couple of weeks, it's the fact that I didn't believe you'd be so naïve. It needs a good deal of work, Sammy.'

Having grown increasingly defensive throughout the critique, Sammy told Branston: 'As you say: a first draft.'

'A first draft,' Branston replied. 'No doubt about that – and no *problem* with that… Who was next?'

Shabreel said, 'Me, Tim.'

'Up you come, Yasser.'

Yasser sashayed to the front of the class. He was as nervous as a mouse in Owltown. 'It's just called "Market,"' he said. 'I hope it speaks for itself.'

'It should!'

'Shall I…'

'Go!' said Tim Branston.

3.

Voiceover (in Yasser's accent):

The market has been a staple of Luton High Town for at least thirty years. Nearly everything you could want is for sale.

In an age in which everyone goes to the shopping centre, it's nice that the market does all right, though, week in and week out.

Longshot.

The market in full swing. Customers and vendors in a graceful ballet. Some of the stalls are not interesting, so people stroll on.

Cut.

Closeup on Yasser.

The Asian youth hands out change to an elderly Oriental gentleman, who walks out of the shot carrying a rake with a large plastic bag sellotaped over its tines.

Voiceover.

Some days are fun and the hours roll round like minutes. Other times it's the other way around, when it's slow or it's raining and no one wants to spend any money – and even Snow White in his snacks van's gone home.

But today is not going to be either of those typical days. Today is going to be something out of the ordinary for everyone involved. For the entire market community, indeed.

Cut.

Midshot.

A man in his early thirties and a woman in her late twenties wave at the camera. They are white, dressed casually; they are smiling. The man is wearing a black Ramones t-shirt with HEY HO! LET'S GO! on the front in big white letters.

Voiceover.

This is John and Eve. They're friends of mine and my uncle's. John works in a hardware shop that he's asked me not to name, and he sells stuff that he gets with his staff discount – and my uncle and I sell it on. Eve works at JB Sports. When I've saved up enough I like to buy my trainers and sweats from her because they have a commission system to supplement their peanut wages. And this...

Camera dips. Closeup on a pushchair. A little girl in a pink bonnet sleeps inside, swaddled in a red blanket.

Voiceover.

...this is lovely Eloise. Only eight months old, and already starring in her first film, with no idea she's about to be going on the ride of her life.

'Good, Yasser, good,' Branston muttered. 'Suspense: I like it.'

'Thank you, Tim,' Yasser replied, glancing now at his classmates for a sign of their thoughts on the matter. All eyes were on the screen mounted on the wall. This was sign enough of their involvement. Yasser felt protective and pleased. Then he said, on the film:

If you keep your eyes on the top left corner of the screen, you are about to witness a crime, ladies and gentlemen.

In the foreground of the shot, a man scoops chestnuts into a brown paper bag and is given a banknote, which he deposits in the wren-coloured bumbag he wears over his groin. His fingers dicker with coins until he has the right amount of change to hand over to the stooped Asian lady in her puce yashmak... In the midground, Snow White leans out of the side of his van to hand a parcel of food to the young Polish boy who sells paperbacks. Uncle Wafiq's head, on this day topped with a pigeon-fancier's flatcap, slides past; Wafiq does not grant the lens so much as a cheeky grin; but his failure to acknowledge his moment in the spotlight is not noted by the class. After all, they have been instructed to watch the upper left corner of the screen.

This is where John and Eve are mulling over the possibility

of a purchase, at the stall selling ladies' fashion. The pushchair containing Eloise is three or four metres away.

Voiceover.

Eloise is asleep, in the Land of Dreams, no doubt. And her parents have taken leave of their joint responsibility. You can see them going into the cave of dresses – Eve wants a new frock for a wedding they're going to in November...

The woman that Yasser now knew as Maggie strolled into the shot, no larger than a matchstick on the big screen. She was wearing black: the hem of her greatcoat descended over her trousers or jeans, possibly leggings; it was difficult to judge, given the distance.

She hesitated: a pulse, a beat. Then in one unbroken movement, she stepped across the pavement and plucked the child from the pushchair. She straightened up; she moved away quickly; she slipped out of shot.

Voiceover.

And this is all it takes: an instant of distraction, and the little girl is taken from her parents.

Yasser heard a gasp from one of the class members; he was pretty sure it was Sammy – he'd made her gasp. Not entirely in the way he'd *like* to make her gasp, but hey! Beggars couldn't be choosers. The way to a girl's heart being via her brain, all that; and the way to her whoopsadaisy being her heart.

Zoom and closeup.

The miniloader – by this point as familiar to Yasser as snow on a mountain top – was the getaway vehicle: Tommy the Brazilian's miniloader. With the girl in her arms, Maggie slipped in and could not have secured her charge. She was away and off: like shit off a shovel, as slick as grease on a doorknob (both of these similes that Yasser had edited out of the final draft). The perfect crime.

Voiceover.

The perfect crime? (Yasser concluded). The police will tell you that this beast does not exist. There is no such thing. There is no such thing as the perfect crime.

The film stopped. Centred and frozen on the screen was the miniloader's registration plate. A second; two seconds.

Because the camera never lies. All it took was a call to the police. The vehicle was registered and the child was returned to her rightful parents, leaving us with the big question. What made her do it? What compels some people to steal a human being?

The screen darkened; then white letters showed the class the film had been 'A Yasser Shabreel Production'.

After a few seconds, Branston said, 'Wow. Is that all true, Yasser?'

'Every frame.'

One of the other guys said, 'What happened?'

Yasser raised his hands. 'The film says it all. The girl's in safe hands, back with John and Eve. Unharmed. And all because I left the camera running while I served a customer! It was sitting on top of a pile of boxes or garden hoses, on the stall. Sheer good fortune.'

'Nice one, Yasser,' said Sammy.

'Yes, a good piece of work, Yasser,' Branston added. 'Who's next?'

4.

At the end of the lesson Branston asked Yasser to stay behind for a minute; the other class members filed out, chatting.

'It was just a query really; I didn't want to raise it in front of the others.'

'What is it, Tim?'

'…Your uncle is a policeman, isn't he?'

'One of em is,' Yasser replied. 'Big family.'

'Yes.'

'…You seem unsure about something, Tim.'

Branston plunged.

'What I'm about to say to you – it might mean nothing or it might mean a lot. But here it is.

'For nearly a year now I've been seeing a psychotherapist, three times a week, in the evening after I finish here. And… if only to avoid any confusion in the future, I'll spell it out properly: when I say seeing I mean paying for a service – I don't mean… dating, or anything like that.'

'I appreciate your candour,' Yasser replied (somewhat prissily).

'You don't look surprised.'

'If it was intended to be kept a secret, Tim, someone's blabbed – someone's snitched on you. That was *last month's* news.'

'Good.' Branston hid with a smile an emotion that he found hard to define. It took him a beat to realise that it was disappointment: he had wanted to confess. 'And no, I've never tried to keep it a secret – it's nothing to be ashamed of, you see: therapy. It's no different from going to a doctor when your sniffle's gone on for a bit longer than you think it should and you're starting to worry.'

'Antibiotics of the brain,' Yasser chipped in.

'In a manner of speaking. You see, I'm doing a Masters in Psychoanalytic Studies at a London university, with a view to maybe going on to a PhD and becoming a psychoanalyst. A long-term plan. But to become a psychoanalyst you have to have gone through an analysis yourself, my reason for signing up with Dr Stegmeyer in the first place. But once I was there – I can't go into all the details but trust me – I've found out some interesting things about myself, about my lingering resentment of the bullying I suffered as a child, my anger over my father's premature death, my fear of my mother, her illnesses, my loathing of self-failure… Is this too much detail?'

'Not exactly,' said Yasser; 'but I'm wondering what it's got to do with me, I must admit.'

Branston sat on the edge of the teacher's desk. 'What it's got to do with you – fair question – is this. All patients are treated to a scheme of the purest anonymity. A code of conduct. Nevertheless, a doctor – Dr Stegmeyer included – will *occasionally* throw into discussion an anecdote or two from his personal and professional store, for the purposes of illustrating a point. Mental health experts, I suppose it's fair to say, being no less susceptible to the pleasures of gossip and tattle than the rest of us. And one of the stories he used in my session on Monday – stories is not quite right but you know what I mean – was about a man that Stegmeyer called *John* – an anonymised name I thought at the time. But *John* was not the patient: his daughter was. A girl of four months who had endured a trauma. She'd been taken from her parents and kept against her will – if children of that age *have* will – on a Travellers' campsite, see. And do you know how *John* told Stegmeyer's colleague (he didn't name the colleague) that the little girl was returned to her rightful parents, Yasser?'

Yasser waited with breath trapped at the top of his chest. It took seconds before he gleaned that he was expected to give an answer. He said, 'No.'

'I think you do. Apparently a young Asian man went onto the site and *stole her back*. Quite a brave thing to do, I agree; but quite foolish too… There's no uncle in the police force, is there, Yasser?'

'But there is! I gave him the licence plate number and he told me…' Yasser trailed off, his argument, he knew, full of holes, stinking like a cheese left on lawn cuttings at the height of summer.

'Your uncle found the address, didn't he. From the registration files.'

'…Yes. You can't tell anyone, Tim.'

'I'm not an analyst, Yasser; I haven't signed a confidentiality contract. In fact, if I believe a student of mine is in danger, it's my *duty* to report it.'

Yasser turned away from Branston's gaze. He said, 'I'm not in danger. I'm twenty-three years old and I can live without your protection, Tim. With respect. It's over.'

'But are you sure?'

'I got her back. I can't *believe* John opened his mouth. I specifically told him…'

'Why didn't they want the police involved anyway?' Branston wanted to know.

'That's their business.'

'Indeed. Confidentiality code?'

'Code of friendship… I told em I could get it done faster. All my uncle needed was to tap in a licence number. He gave me the address and asked me if he needed to know what this was about. I told him no and he left it at that.'

'But why you?' Branston asked.

'I don't want to work on a market stall all my life,' Yasser told him.

'It's quite a leap from trader to vigilante.'

'Not really. They *stole a child*.'

'I know: it's on the record now. In black and white, as they used to say in old money.'

Yasser chuckled. 'Do you wanna hear the *really* funny part?'

'I could do with a laugh.'

'I did it for these trainers. Top of the range – four hundred quid. I didn't want the money: Mum and Dad'd only ask me where I got it. And Eve works…'

'In a sports shop,' Branston interjected quietly. 'Well, it all fits, I suppose.'

Seconds drifted past.

'…So what now?' Yasser asked, breaking the silence.

'…Do you have another lesson to go to?'

'No. What now in general?'

'I could ask you the same thing, couldn't I? How do you know there won't be comeback?'

'From Maggie?'

'Who's Maggie?' Branston cocked his head. 'Oh the *kidnapper*. You were formerly introduced then… My my; this might be my finest hour as a filmmaker.'

'Funnily enough, that's what *she* thinks. The material's copyrighted, Tim.'

Branston laughed.

Yasser told him: 'I didn't just go in there guns blazing. I don't *have* a gun before you ask. I reasoned with em. Used my head, Tim.'

'Well that's something.'

'I even got some more work out of it.' Yasser chuckled again.

Branston could not believe his ears. 'Some *work* out…' he started to repeat. 'For *them?*'

Shrugging his shoulders, Yasser said, 'A quid's a quid.'

'…Do you drink coffee?'

'Yes.'

'Do you want one now?'

'All right.'

'Because I think I'd better hear about this: the unedited, un-expurgated version.' Branston stood up and started to pack his things, throwing board pens into the side compartment of his laptop case.

For the first time in days Yasser felt that he could breathe again; that breathing was once more a gift *and* a right he'd earned.

It was good to remove some of the weight from his conscious thoughts; it was liberating.

'The canteen?' Yasser suggested.

'Fine. I'm buying.'

'I know you are, Tim. Trainers don't grow on trees; I have to save my pennies. You get a ghost story in return, sort of.'

'I'm intrigued. And the full truth.'

'So help me… My uncle,' Yasser added quickly. 'I *do* have an uncle in the police, I wasn't lying about that…'

Wait for the *but*.

'But?'

'But it wasn't him who got me the address. I also have loads of cousins, and one of em – Shyleen – she works selling car insurance. Database size of Pluto.'

'Then you owe *him* a pair of trainers,' said Branston, lifting his case and moving towards the door.

'Her. And no, Tim. See, I banged her once during Ramadan and she's scared her dad'll find out. She's full of guilt, is Shyleen, she'll do anything to shut me up. So she got the address and even did a practice run. Went over to Eaton Bray *on the bus*. Just moseyed on in there and asked a few questions, calm as you please; then walked out again. Fearless. Nearly fearless, that girl… well, apart from when it comes to her old man.' Yasser brightened. 'Maybe *she* needs a psychotherapist!'

'Maybe she's already got one. Come on, let's go. I need a brew.'

Party Animals

1.

For Vig, the first week in the new house had been less *odd* than pinch-me-I'm-dreaming *weird*. Indeed, it had been something of a surreal experience; but for Dorota… things had been more natural altogether. Dorota had swum into the fresh experience, swanlike and blithe. What she didn't have, she sent Curtis to drive out to fetch: a pair of scissors, a roll of kitchen tissue. Although Charles Eastlight had gone beyond the call of duty by arranging for the house to be decked out when they moved in (selling properties fully furnished and prepared was his field and speciality, but even so), there was the occasional necessity that had either not been thought of or could not be located in any number of cupboards or drawers. Very quickly Dorota had risen to the challenge of this quest, whereas Vig had experienced, for the last seven days, the unshakeable enduring sensation that he had checked into an unpopular hotel that nonetheless commanded great views.

At the end of the first week they had a housewarming party. Hothouse flower that she was, Dorota took the opportunity to interpret what they'd written on the invitations literally, and by four o'clock the whole property sweltered in Capricorn temperatures. Vig was not impressed: he thought the heat indulgence wasteful, and he said so; but Dorota merely giggled off the suggestion.

'You don't want our guests catching… what's the English?

Chilly banes?'

'Chilblains. It's *autumn*, Dol; they won't be arriving on *sleds*.'

'Pity,' said Dorota.

'You're not in Poland anymore!'

'And *you're* not in Germany. And you're not a schoolteacher either. And both of us, most importantly, we're not *poor*… It's only one evening: if our gests get too hot they can go outside…'

'Which defeats the purpose.'

'…or go in the whirlpool with their champagne!' Dorota added excitedly.

The two of them were standing in the kitchen, wrapping and cutting spicy *fajitas* into finger food. Their friends were expected from seven onwards. Vig's forthcoming job was to barbecue chicken and burgers, on a patio half the area of a basketball court; but before he was allowed near any flames he had had to promise Dorota that he would help with the buffet spread, though it wasn't food he cared for and he felt guilty making a mess of such an expansive NASA kitchen.

'Yeah, *about* that champagne,' Vig said.

'I got three cases.'

'I saw.'

'Do you think we need more? I could go –'

'No I don't think we need more – not on top of the seven boxes of Pinot Grigio and seven boxes of Chianti. It was more a question about the *quality*.'

Dorota pouted. 'I bought the best stuff,' she said quickly and defensively.

'My point being: did you need to?' Vig asked. 'How much did that lot set you back?'

Dorota stopped cutting Mexican snacks and pointed the knife at Vig. 'I will *not* have people thinking we're skinflints, Hartvig. You've just won six million pounds! What do you care about a few hundred on drinks for a party? *Decompress,* why don't you?'

Vig smiled. 'Where did you hear that?'

'Like a puncture!' said Dorota, resuming her work and sing-ing choppety-*chop!*

Despite himself, Vig couldn't help but be amused. 'Now you want me to be a *puncture?*'

'Anything but a solid tyre,' Dorota answered; 'going round and around without friction. Boring!'

'…Not *quite* the analogy I'd expected,' Vig admitted.

'It's a metaphor – not an analogy.'

'Oh well I *do* beg your hard-on, my angel.'

'Wrap em faster, Vig,' Dorota ordered. 'You're a slacker. You *slack* for a living.'

'But don't we all now?' Vig wondered aloud.

2.

At six forty-five Vig fired up the barbecue, and was stand-ing solo when a familiar face (and the first to arrive) called his name. It was Phyllie Reydman. Phyllie taught Geography at the school in Aylesbury from which Vig and Dorota had resigned at the end of the summer term. She and Vig had been close for the two years he'd worked there: Phyllie had a crisp and spiteful line in gossip that was right up Vig's alley. It was also in Vig that Phyl-lie had once confided her doubts about her upcoming marriage; Vig had always assumed that she'd been flirting with him, testing their shared atmosphere, but she appeared content enough to-night, her husband Roger in laconic tow.

They kissed each other's cheek – peck, withdraw, peck – in the Continental fashion, and when they were alone and could talk in private (with Dorota and Roger in the kitchen, fetching drinks) Vig said to Phyllie, 'I see you ate early.'

'Isn't it horrible? And that's only *five* months,' Phyllie replied, laying both hands on the bump that she carried in front of
her, to which protuberance Vig had referred.

'Congratulations. And no, it's not horrible.'

'No Camembert, no Brie… It's like I'm in prison! No *wine*.'

'What about barbecued flesh?' Vig asked.

'As long as you cremate it.'

Vig laughed. 'Speciality of the house. I don't know any
other way, to be honest… So how are you keeping? How's the
new term so far?'

Roger and Dorota had come outside to join them, each
holding a glass in either hand. Taking hold of hers, Phyllie
thanked her husband and said, 'I'll be *looking* like an orange, the
amount of juice I'm downing… It's kind of odd, all the police
around all the time.'

Vig said, 'Police' and scooped some more charcoal bri-
quettes onto the thumb-sized flames.

'You know: the missing girl.'

'No I don't,' Vig answered, turning for support from Dorota, who shook her head.

'Oh it's been in the news,' said Phyllie. 'It's eight days now:
an eleventh year girl, Jessica Olney – do you know her? – she
went missing after a night out with her friends. Only she wasn't
really with her friends.'

'Jess Olney?' said Dorota. 'I know her. A bit forthright with
her opinions…'

'Yeah that's Jess.' Phyllie smiled thinly.

'How awful.'

'I don't know her myself, but we've all been interviewed.
What could I say? She doesn't do Geography. I was about as
much use as chocolate sunglasses.'

Roger said, 'Don't put yourself down, dear,' and sipped

from a thimble's-worth of whisky in a new expensive glass. Presumably he had heard it all before about the missing girl (and didn't wish to hear it again) for he went on swiftly: 'What time's the main feast?'

'About half an hour,' Vig answered absently. 'I'm trying to remember her. I know the name.'

Phyllie tried to help. 'Big boned?' she suggested.

'…Yeah I think so. Drama queen.'

'That was Jess. That *is* Jess, I mean.' Phyllie's face rouged. 'God, that's dreadful of me. And for once I can't even blame the chardonnay.'

3.

Arriving half-cut at a quarter past eight, Eastlight was fashionably late, dressed preposterously in a dark maroon suit, cream Cubans and a weary tam-o-shanter…

Dorota was standing by the barbecue: she had taken over while Vig took a bathroom break, and on seeing Eastlight's approach, she said to Phyllie, 'Is the circus in town?'

'God, who *is* he?' Phyllie replied through a mouthful of pasta salad.

'I'll introduce you.'

However, the chance to do so was not to be immediately forthcoming. Midway across the patio, Eastlight spotted someone in the crowd and changed his course. There was no need to wonder who he'd seen: his voice was like a sonic boom.

'*Don!*'

Dorota said, 'Oh, that'll keep him happy: someone to look down on for a couple of hours. That's Charles Eastlight – he's the one who found us this place; weeded out a hundred other also-rans; dealt with most of the paperwork… He's been amazing.' She swallowed what remained of a glass of cranberry vodka, mentally shuffling through her choices. 'I can't say I like him – he's either a bully or a toady, depending on who he's talking to – but I can't take it away from him, he's earned his commission.'

'And Vig's friendship?' Phyllie asked.

Dorota shrugged. 'Something like that,' she answered quietly, then her face warmed and she smiled. '*He* certainly thinks so, anyway. He greets Vig with *Viggy-loo, Viggy-lay* – like they've been the best of mates for thirty years.'

Dropping her paper plate into one of the rubbish bins around the patio, Phyllie asked, 'What does it mean?'

'I've no idea…' Dorota regarded the hotplate in front of her. 'I couldn't tempt you to another burger, could I? I think Vig's overestimated how many people would come.'

'Thanks, but I usually stick at four burgers and a plate of pasta,' Phyllie told her. 'This is a pretty good turnout though. And the weather's stayed dry.'

'We're pleased…' Dorota cast her eye over at Eastlight and Don. 'I wish he'd leave the old boy alone. What *is* it with some people?'

Eastlight was standing close to Don – surely *too* close – and leaning into the older man's face. Evidently it was difficult for Don to find the room to sip his pint of ale comfortably: his tankard hung at the end of his arm, the elongation of a long-dead limb.

'Vig was saying that Don came with the house,' Phyllie said.

'Kind of. Basically, he refused to leave. The old boy who lived here before had to move – he ran out of money – and he took his staff with him, those who'd stood by him. But Don wouldn't go: said he'd fight till the end to save his birds… So Vig hired him. Have you seen the birds?'

'No. I'd like to.'

'I'll show you around…' Dorota laughed. 'By all accounts it was the Battle of Stalingrad, apparently. My interpretation is: let's not underestimate the strength and resilience of Mr Bridges.'

'I wouldn't dream of it,' Phyllie told her.

4.

Having been relieved of gate duty, Curtis was tasked with guiding guests to the aviary, parties of five or six at a time. Some of the guests had brought children to the party; and the birds came as a blissful cooing revelation to them.

Watching over proceedings, Don appeared happy to answer questions. He even conceded to enter one of the cages and hold Larry the lizard close to the mesh, for all to get a better look; and as far as Don was concerned, he was putting in a formidable performance. Nerve-racking though tonight might be, Don knew that it was imperative that he remained cordial. Whether or not he wished to be here (and he didn't), he had done the right thing by turning up, even if the effort had required a mug of brandy with which to calm the raging waters of his discomfort.

It had to be over soon, Don consoled himself. They would all go home and life would revert to normality. The birds were what he cared about – the birds and his friend in the well – and so far, as a relationship, it was working well with Mr Klossen and Miss Teodorescu. Don had even learned how to spell their surnames, out of respect. There had only been that one awkward scene…

Vig and Dorota had been in the house for two days at that point, and Vig had decided to take a stroll around all that he surveyed. Despite the acres and the camouflaging woodland in which Don's cabin sat alone, it was probably inevitable that the cabin would be located sooner or later. Don supposed that sooner was better: at least he had been half-expecting the visit, squaring the chances with the factor of idle curiosity alone: Vig's curiosity. Fair enough that the man would want to see all that his one-pound lottery ticket had earned him, including the scrags. So when Vig had knocked on the door, the sound had been both unexpected and according to Fate. Get through this one initial house visit, Don could remember thinking, and he's not likely to want to come again.

Well, that prediction had proved true (so far); but the accuracy of his prophecy had not diminished the awkwardness of the moment. If Vig had been hellbent on causing a disruption, he could not have chosen a more inconvenient time: it was twelve-thirty. Don had been tucking into a toasted cheese sandwich, a mug of tea steaming on the sideboard. All well and good. The devilish side of this tranquil woodsman scene was that Don, since taking ownership of the little girl in the well in his kitchen, had always played fair with food: this meant that his lunchtime was also hers. Down below the ground, she was eating what Don had prepared for her (her usual), and if there was anything to thank for the advancing of human years, it was this; the natural insurance policy of *routine*. Being a man of considerable age, Don was also a stickler for things settling in a pre-arranged order, and without this compulsion – virtually unacknowledged at the time of Vig's visit, blessed ever since – Don might have been sunk, there and then. But routine it had been, and not so much as self-preservation, that had led Don to knocking the trapdoor down into place, and to covering it with the moth-bitten rug. Lunchtimes were for *solitary* nourishment.

Throughout Vig's short stay in the cabin (barely more than twenty minutes) the girl had not made a peep in the well. Not a murmur… The problem was that Don had left incriminating evidence in the kitchen. The *second problem* was that in a dwelling so petite, the kitchen could be viewed from the lounge. And the *third* problem was that Vig had sat down on the settee: he'd had a perfect vantage point of the surfaces in the kitchen, as long as he moved his head slightly to the left (the settee faced a spanking new television)... *For want of a nail the kingdom was lost*, Don had sighed ruefully in the intervening days: it was always the *little* things that did for you; the seemingly insignificant that upset the entire cart of apples. On cop shows too: the murderer caught out by a length of twine, a missed dental appointment, the fading ridges of a circumcision scar... In Don's case it was an empty box of Cow & Gate baby milk preparation, for all to see, there on the surface beside the microwave oven.

    For want of a nail the kingdom was lost... And for want of a roll of plastic pedal-bin liners, Don had almost cooked his own goose. He had made the child her milk; he had given her the cup and a separate portion in a bowl with some nutbread submerged inside; and he had closed the trapdoor and replaced the rug. But the pedal-bin had been full, and he had had no more liners in the drawer; he had put the job off for a next-day task. Tomorrow he would empty the bin; bad knees notwithstanding, he would cycle to the village store and buy some more bin-liners.

    Had Vig seen the Cow & Gate box, or not? Don had chewed on this question ever since. A simple peek into the kitchen: this is all it would have taken. And Don could hear Vig's questions to Dorota: *What the hell's he doing with baby milk?* Then perhaps Miss Teodorescu would reply: *Something for the birds maybe? A sick bird?* And they'd all live happily ever after. God willing...

    While the incident had taught Don some harsh lessons about carelessness and responsibility (and pride coming before a fall), he had known from that day – that hour, that minute, that moment – that his work must be squeaky-clean. He couldn't afford any unwanted scrutiny of his performance. This was why, when Dorota had invited him to this evening's barbecue, although his heart had sunk faster than a stone in clear water, he had thanked her and said of course he'd be there; it had even been his idea to volunteer to give brief talks about the birds, should they be required or wished for. The latter at least (Don had reasoned) would keep him near the birds, for most of the time away from the house (or more specifically away from strangers); it might make him feel necessary and useful too.

So it was that Don was standing by the first cage, sipping on a roll-up, savouring a second of balmy solitude, when Eastlight found him, again. He had hoped to be shot of Eastlight for the remainder of the evening; alas, no.

Seeming to swerve through his words – the compounded result of more wine than he was young enough to take anymore, on top of what he'd arrived carrying in his brain – Eastlight said, '*Donald,* my man. Are you avoiding me?'

'Evidently not, sir,' Don replied.

It took Eastlight a few seconds to find this funny, but when he did it was like a Comedy Krakatoa erupting. At one point Eastlight bent over at the waist, the laughs and his flammable breaths gasping exits in tandem. 'Evidently...' he rasped, '...not, sir... *Priceless...* Cuzzaye *found* you, Donald Duck... *not, sir...*'

Throughout this kitsch gale Don maintained his decorum; he pouted on the end of his drooping cigarette, silently cursing that use of *Donald Duck*, which instinct told him that should he object, would become part of Eastlight's lexicon from that nanosecond on. With luck the fat pig was too pissed to remember, the next morning, that he'd coined it and christened Don with its dubious charms.

'What was it I could do for you, sir?' Don asked.

'Oh lighten up, Donald, it's a party!' Eastlight wheezed in reply, the tatters of his mirth clinging to his reprimand. 'Doe shtan... doe shtannon....'

'Ceremony, sir,' Don finished on Eastlight's behalf. 'Don't stand on ceremony. I can tell you I'm not.'

But Eastlight had other ideas about how to finish his own sentence. He started to sing the chorus from 'Don't Stand So Close To Me', his voice cracking into more peals of laughter by the end.

Don ground his roll-up in the multicoloured gravel in front of Cage 1. The birds within made sudden busy movements and squawks of protest as their keeper said, 'You should take your own advice, sir, about standing so close to someone.'

The comment sobered Eastlight almost immediately. 'Meaning?' he demanded. 'There's two foot between us!'

'There wasn't earlier, when you rolled in,' Don answered calmly. 'All over me like a rash, you were, sir. I was quite uncomfortable, if you'll forgive me.'

'If I'll forgive you...' Eastlight smiled. 'Because I'm one of *them*, no doubt. Your shensh. Your shenshibilities have been affun. Affronted.'

Seeing no obvious way out of this altercation – even welcoming it in a way as something that had to be faced eventually, so why not now? – Don plucked tobacco from his poacher's pocket and rolled himself another smoke, arguing that he didn't know what *one of them* meant.

'A homosexual, Donald Duck! I'm as queer as folk! Good with colours! I'm a *poof*.'

Donald shrugged and lit his cigarette. 'Easy come, easy go,' he breathed out with his first lungful of smoke.

It hadn't been intended as a joke, but it set Eastlight off again. This time the man felt obliged to cling to the cage's wire mesh for support; the sight of his podgy fingers oozing through the mesh made Don shiver, but it also gave him a brief flash of revengeful fantasy, something like a garrotting, and Don even found it in himself to smile for a second while Eastlight laughed himself into recovery.

Presently a silence fell between them. Eastlight broke it.

'I'll tell you what, Donald, how's this for a proposition? You roll me one of those cigarettes with one hand like you just did, and you *promise* to try to teach me to do the same – and *I* promise not to stand too close to you again like the smelly queer I am.'

'You're not smelly, sir. And I didn't have a clue you made hay with the farmboys –'

'Jesus.'

' – It's just, sir… I'm a solitary man. Put the work in my hand and a pound in my pocket, do you know what I mean? Makes me happy the day's long… But yes, since you asked nicely, I will roll you a smoke. With my pleasure.'

Eastlight laughed again, briefly this time. 'Make hay with the farmboys,' he repeated, 'I'll try to remember that – tell Mass in the morning,' he mumbled on, eagerly watching Don execute his party trick. 'I say it to everyone early, Donald: saves any confusion in the long run. Or embarrassment.'

'Of course, sir.'

'Charlie. Call me Charlie, Donald. The *sir* shit is *so* nineteenth century… Thank you. What tobacco?'

'Drum.' Don flicked his lighter for the cigarette now between Eastlight's lips. A few of the birds flinched at the flare.

'Thank you, Donald… Nice.' Eastlight cupped his free hand to his left ear. 'Soft! What sound from yonder mansion breaks?' He smiled. 'I think you're on call again, Donald: some more on their way to see the birds, if my ears don't deceive me.'

'My privilege,' Don replied, shrugging once more.

'I'll see you later, pal. I'm glad we had this chat*ette*.' With which he turned, and set off to walk back to the house.

'Just one more thing, sir – Charlie,' Don called.

Eastlight turned again. 'Yes?'

'Call me Donald Duck again and I'll shatter your knees. Have a good evening.'

Don faced the birds and tried not to laugh.

5.

Phyllie and Roger were getting ready for bed.

'Did you meet those delightful twins?' Roger asked, pulling off his boxer shorts. 'Blond as butter, nine or ten?'

Phyllie was strapping the dildo around her naked waist. 'They're Dorota's sister's kids; they live in Dunstable... What about them?'

'They gave themselves a proper scare, that's what,' Roger told her. 'Went walking off alone in the woods; came across a *tiny gingerbread house.*'

Phyllie sat on the edge of the bed and reached for the bottle of baby oil on the nightstand. 'Must've been Don's – the bird-keeper,' she said.

'That's what I thought.' Roger tugged at the toes of his socks. 'I wonder why his wife didn't go.'

'He's not married, Dorota told me. Well, he's widowed – twenty years or more.'

Roger assumed his position on the bed: all fours, facing the headboard, eyes screwed tightly shut. 'That makes the twins' story doubly spooky – for them at least.'

Phyllie oiled the dildo, asking 'Why?'

'Because if Don was at the party, and he lives alone, how come the twins swear to their mother they heard a child crying inside his cabin? No other sounds, just crying...'

On her knees Phyllie moved up behind her husband. 'Do

you want to know about crying?' she asked darkly, her voice grey.

'…Yes, madam.'

'It was probably a fox.'

'Yes, madam.'

'There's no such thing as a haunted house.' And Phyllie pressed the end of the dildo to Roger's puckered flesh; his body writhed.

'No, madam.'

'I hate you, Roger,' Phyllie breathed as the reinforced plastic breached the miniscule entranceway.

'I know, madam. *Thank* you, madam… *Thank* you.'

LESSER CHARACTERS

Headphones applied, his long body grinding to a beat that only he heard, Molecule clicked open a file that added a stuttering violin sample to the mix. He was happy. The work was going well. Provided the Job Centre didn't drop some bullshit on him about having to attend a jobseeker's progress meeting (or face the consequence of a payout-holdback) he would have the piece ready by Friday, as promised. And he'd be glad to have it finished: from the start it had been accompanied by some pressure bullshit from Fonehacka, but these days he was on his skin every other hour! The last time he'd called to check on Molecule's progress, Molecule had screamed down the line: *Let me work, man! I'll have the fucker square by Friday! Jesus!*

You better, Fonehacka warned him. *Or your name as a DJ's mud, motherfucker.*

Yeah, sweet. Now may I be allowed to return to the fruits of my labour? I'm painting some strings as we speak, or I would be.

Yeah yeah.

Molecule knew that he should take it as a compliment: all of Fonehacka's streetgangsta bullshit was about supply. *Molecule's* supply, to be specific. Fonehacka had sold tickets on the strength that the world would be treated to a fresh Molecule splat. The people wanted his shit! A *good* thing! The only problem was that he only had two days left to finish it. And if he couldn't get out of the proposed bullshit meeting at the JobCentre, why that was half of tomorrow afternoon fucked as well. He'd be working past midnight; working like a motherfucking *vampire*.

Then you should've done it earlier, he told himself sharply.

Yeah yeah.

But his inner voice was right, of course. If he hadn't been chasing that Charlotte all fucking week…

Too late… It was too late to squirm over maybes. Roll with it. Get on with the piece… and those violins are an octave too high as well…

Molecule frowned; he set about lowering the violins, and he sat down at his desk to work through some samples. He reckoned he was about halfway through the mix.

Then the phone rang.

Molecule sang 'Motherfucker' in a G Minor 7, riffing off the beat-up in his cans. His mobile vibrated patiently, next to the mouse. Wearied by the burdens on the shoulders of the modern mixer, Molecule ripped off the headphones and took a breath. He was ready to tell Fonehacka his fucking fortune… but the display did not show Fonehacka's name. The display read SOME BULLSHIT, which meant an unidentified number – maybe the JobCentre!

'Fuck cakes.'

If he answered and they said he had to go to the progress bullshit, he would have to go. Not even (feigned) illness was sufficient for those wankers! (He knew this because he'd tried to cough his way through a phone call to say that he wasn't well enough to travel on the bus to sign on. The jobsworth cunt on the blower had said: 'Get a cab then!') And Molecule wasn't one to tempt fate by lying about a dead relative: the last time he had done so (a month ago) his Aunt Esme had been knocked over by a bus the following morning. She'd survived, but fuck.

On the other hand, they might be calling to say the progress bullshit meeting's been knocked into the long grass. Willy Womble, his case worker (or whatever the fuck) had lost his bullshit head off his shoulders in a weird baking accident…

Yeah yeah.

Like well fucking likely I don't think.

'Fuck it.' Molecule thumbed it and said, 'What up?'

'Is that Marvin Green?'

'Yeah, blood.'

'Bill Wondle, JobCentre Plus.'

'…Hello, Mr Wondle,' Molecule added in his semi-posh voice. 'I was just about to call you. I'm afraid I'm going to find tomorrow a bit difficult, for work reasons. I have something to deliver – I need to graft.'

'Oh. Are you being paid?'

'In a manner of speaking.'

'…In *what* manner of speaking? Is cash, cheque or a transfer of funds of some description *en route* to your bank account?'

'Not exactly,' Molecule answered truthfully: 'but I made the man a promise. He's spinning it at a gig on Friday.'

'Oh your *music*.'

'Yeah. You thought I meant what you people call proper work, right?'

'Well wonders never cease, I suppose,' Wondle muttered. 'I'll need his name and details.'

'Who?'

'Your employer. If you're proposing you miss an appointment…'

Appointment bullshit, Molecule considered. 'Fonehacka.'

'Is it really now. Double-barrelled, is that?'

'What?'

'What's his real name, Marvin?'

The fuck should I tell you, Womble… Molecule spat silently.

Don't take that fucking tone… 'His name's Reggie Green,' he confessed with a sigh.

'Any relation?'

'My brother innit.'

'And what's his work address?'

'His *what*?'

'I'll need his details I said. It looks good on your jobseeker
spreadsheet.'

'No it don't. He's my brother. He's *fourteen.*'

'Oh.'

Molecule sighed. 'He needs it for his school disco, see. He's
mixing and them kids look up to me a bit. He's in his room, next
to mine.'

Wondle cleared his throat. 'All right, noted,' he said, 'but
actually I wasn't calling about tomorrow. I suppose we can re-
schedule, though I probably shouldn't… I was calling about your
other brother.'

'Nero? I mean Noel – What about him?'

'He missed an early school leaver's appointment yesterday.'

'I'm not his keeper, Bill,' Molecule stated confidently but
not rudely.

'No, I appreciate that, but I wanted to… I wanted to run
something past you, before I called the police.'

'Woah!' said Molecule (he even held a hand up to his computer screen). 'That ain't no Fed business! An *appointment*? A *sign-
ing-on*?'

'Calm down, Marvin. You don't *sign on* at fifteen…' said
Wondle. 'Not because he's in *trouble* for missing –'

'Then what?' Molecule demanded. 'This is my brother
you're…'

'Because I called him today and it wasn't him who answered.'

Molecule chuckled. 'No I bet it weren't. Listen. You'll find out anyway, so who am I protecting? Nero's banging this chick in Lanzarote for two weeks. Thinks he's a porn star, right, but I bet she's worn him out innit. What she say?'

'*She* say? It wasn't a lady who answered, Marvin. Or a girl for that matter.'

'…Who was it then?'

'I don't know – that's what I'm trying to say. A man – slightly drunk would be my guess – a man answered Noel's phone and said… said we'd better hurry up and *find him* because they've *got* him and they're going to *kill* him. I'm sorry, Marvin…'

'Those *wankers*…' Molecule chuckled again. 'It's a wind-up, Bill.'

'Well I *thought* so, but…'

'But how'd they get his phone?' Molecule finished the other man's thought.

'I don't know. Who are you talking about?'

Molecule laughed flat-out. 'Some guys he knows from school: buncha pisstakers, Bill – nothing to sweat.'

'…What's her name?' Wondle asked.

'Who?'

'Lucky lady he's got a shine for.'

'*I* dunno. Janine or some bullshit.'

'Could it be Jess?'

'Yeah man. Jessica I confessica, he says.'

'They've got her too, *they* say.'

Molecule waited; he didn't feel much like laughing now. Through his headphones came the tinny hiss of his composition on Auto: it sounded like hornets.

'Marvin? Are you there?'

'…Yeah.'

'Do you *know* this Jess?' Wondle asked.

'Nah. You're kidding…'

'I'm serious. Do you have a number or anything? Do you know her age?'

'Her *age*? Do you want her bra size?'

'Listen, Marvin. I'm going to guess one thing: I'm going to guess that most boys of fifteen don't go out with girls of eighteen or over.'

'So? Loads of girls do it young. It's none of your biz.'

'But Marvin. Loads of *airlines* don't do it young, not as far as I know. I can check.'

'The fuck?'

'What airport did he go from?'

'Luton, I suppose. I *dunno*, man.'

'I don't think airlines allow fifteen year-olds to travel without an adult,' said Wondle. 'As I say, I can check... Do something for me, would you, Marvin?'

'...Okay.'

Marvin listened, then he stood up and walked across the landing, past Fonehacka's room (he was watching *Countdown*: he had taken a day off school, pleading the sinus trouble to which he was a teenaged martyr), and entered Nero's den.

Ever since their mother had become less and less a conspicuous presence in their lives (she'd not come home from wherever she'd ended up last night), the three boys had been broadly respectful of one another's space. This was one of the reasons why Fonehacka phoned Molecule from the next room, rather than knock on the door.) To Molecule it felt strange having to do what Bill Wondle had asked of him. (Even Willy Womble had known that there'd been no point asking to speak to the boys' mother.) But he did it: because the air tasted strange, he did it. He opened the first of Nero's drawers. He stroked his fists through bundles of socks. Nothing. Pumped up, he opened the next: T-shirts and tops... A third drawer let Molecule into a glimpse of his younger brother's private world. Among the junk were some childhood reminders – a few baked conkers on strings, some dobber marbles – along with a pack of blue Rizlas. His heart was straining.

But it wasn't until he rummaged through a pile of Nero's underwear that he found the boy's passport. He hadn't flown to Lanzarote: even if he'd intended to.

TOENAIL ISLAND

1.

Times without number (or so it seemed) Connors had attempted the clichéd strategies that were supposed to lead you out of sleep and back to the waking world: all to no avail. By pinching himself on the elbow, the best he had achieved was to score some baffled looks and the ire of one of the shiphands, who had told him to stop it immediately; it was getting on their nerves. When he'd shouted for his mother, the ocean had roared back in a different language, and Connors had stopped when his throat was raw, (correctly) assuming that if he didn't mend his ways he'd be seen as a madman... and only seadogs and Neptune himself were aware of the fate in store for a lunatic, miles from a harbour.

No; it appeared that the sole mission was to wait, to bide his time. Soon enough the curtains would be flung open, in the real world, in his bedroom, and Alannah would tell him that it was time to get up. If Connors concentrated hard, he was certain he could smell her nightscent, her salt and the fadings of her perfume, her 'Ocean Mist'. Soon soon soon; and if water in dreams had taught him anything over the years (usually after a night on the lager) he would regain consciousness with his erection unenlargeable and his bladder as full as a cow's udder. He'd be standing in the toilet for a week...

And yet... and yet it was all so *rich*, right down to the faces of the bosun and the crew; to the metal bowls of rice and figs that were tasty and filling but long past any sense of novelty, Connors having been fed nothing else since finding himself shanghaied on board. And the waves themselves: the infinite varieties in the patterns of spray and spume; the bellowing toil of their exertion; their shades, colours: all of this was so much more detailed, surely, than Connors was capable of conjuring up. Were it not for piss-up vacations on the continent, or the occasional dirty weekend in Brighton or Southend, he would never have so much as *seen* the sea, let alone ridden on its violent arching back, confirmed town boy and landlubber that he proudly happened to be.

Furthermore, there was the dog. Connors had not owned a dog since the age of five. His name was Harry, and for little Christopher it was love at first sight. Interdependence too: they had needed one another, and Christopher had taken firm charge of the tin-opener and the cans of Chum that Mum stored on the flat's balcony. It was Christopher who fed Harry; Christopher who had sung lullabyes to Harry while the dog endured the weekly torment of a shower-nozzle rinse-down in the bathtub; and it was Christopher who had almost died from grief when Harry was knocked down by a van driver making a delivery to the flats.

It was an accident: it was no use blaming the driver. As was the dog's sporadic wont, Harry had run away from Christopher, tugging the end of the lead from the boy's hand while they were out for exercise and a dump near the kids' swings, back in the days when no one cleaned up after their pets. Harry ran into the car park and the driver didn't see him in time. It was an accident. An *accident*: but Christopher had been left with no one to blame, in the absence of any accusation of speeding or drunk-driving. It was Harry's fault, not the driver's, and not little Christopher's own.

The boy had sworn never to own another pet. Grief could kill. Grief was a murderer of an uncertain face.

Was Connors reliving the experience, here on the boat in his dreams, after all these years? The dog was certainly different (Harry was a terrier, Chelsea a German Shepherd) and the sex of the animal too. But what else could this enforced pet-ownership be, other than a reminder of his life with Harry when he was still a child? Though why his unconscious would have given her the name *Chelsea* was beyond Connors. Tottenham was his team: Chelsea were pricks.

And come to think of it: what his mind was tying to tell him by allowing him to barge in on a scene of wilful sodomy, two nights earlier – surely this could spell out only disturbing consequences. As it was, Connors had apologised and made a hasty retreat back above deck, with the image of the gaptoothed smile of the boy being buggered like a wasp sting in his brain. He had tried to avoid both parties ever since.

This wasn't easy, of course; but Connors had learned of one or two corners where, his shift ended and a rest time imposed, he could lay his head for a few hours – try to sleep his path home to waking… Almost without fail Chelsea found him; she joined him. She slept across his lap, while Connors dreamed of Alannah, or the two boys screwing, and laced his fingers through the German Shepherd's fur or tousled the name-and-address tag dangling from her collar. (It read: 77 Wilberforce Drive, Edlesborough, Bedfordshire.) In his sleep he tasted the sea; he licked spittle over his windchapped lips.

So it was then, while bare-chested and dozing, during one of his off-shifts, that Connors was alerted to a fresh development on the ocean wave. The voice that snapped his sleep was a vibrant shout: '*Land ahoy!*'

Opening his eyes, Connors felt Chelsea's weight, but also the sensation of great velocity. As he pushed the dog off his lap (Chelsea barked), he struggled to his feet and took the full impact of a hard wind, against his face and chest. The ship had achieved a devilish clip. Connors reached for and donned his shirt and jacket (both of which had long since begun to smell). When Chelsea barked again (could she sense his excitement?) Connors leaned down to give her ruff a loving squeeze: he was saved! They all were! For there, off to starboard, a finger-thin strip of land was observable through the mist and bouncing water.

'Thank you, God,' Connors whispered.

Chelsea barked again.

'We're going home, girl…'

'Home?' said a voice behind Connors. The addressed turned; his interlocutor was a boy of no more advanced years than fourteen. He went by the peculiar name of Elvis Leader. Three nights earlier, Connors had helped the kid shave his hair off; the scalp had been ridden with lice. 'That ain't no one's home, Con! But that's our port. That's Toenail Island!'

At first Connors was certain that he'd misheard the boy's words; he tried to make *Toenail Island* into something less bizarre – a corruption of a French word, perhaps, a foreign term. After a few beats, however, Connors simply repeated what he believed he'd heard.

'That's right!' the boy told him. 'Stick close to the port and you'll be fine, Con! The cannibals live mostly in the hills.'

'The what? The *cannibals* did you say?'

'Aye, cannibals, Con! The don't like the water.' Elvis pointed at Chelsea, his fingernail black either with embedded dirt or with bruising to the quick. 'They like dogs, though. I'd keep her tied up onboard, I were you.'

'*Elvis!*' someone shouted.

'I'm wanted. Nice knowing you, Con!' The boy span on his heels.

'Wait!' said Connors. 'You mean we don't get a ride back?'

'Back where?' the boy asked.

'Back to where we started out from!'

The boy's perplexity grew visibly. 'We didn't start out from anywhere, Con,' he explained. 'The ship sails as soon as soon as she's commissioned; she's been sailing all her life. If you're lucky, Captain Carousel will need you. If not...'

'*Elvis, now, boy! Here!*'

'...if not?' Connors prompted.

Elvis hefted his shoulders and showed the brown palms of his filthy hands. 'You volunteer for another captain,' he said, as if this was the most logical thing under the sun or stars.

As Elvis Leader made his exit, Connors fingered a patch of sunburned skin on the back of his neck. He touched it lovingly, though he relished the pain. Maybe pain would rouse him from his slumber if nothing else would.

Chelsea barked repeatedly as the ship made headway for the shore. Birds that weren't gulls – or none the like of which Connors had ever seen in life or on screen – circled and wheeled overhead; their caws were monstrous, amplified crow-sounds; their bodies were long and straggly, the plumage an exotic purple; their beaks a bright green in the shape of the sharp end of scissors. It was mainly these vicious-looking creatures that had caught Chelsea's attention: the bitch was hopping on her hind legs to snap at them, working her way up into a frenzy.

Connors did not try to calm her. He saw no point in the exercise; indeed, her noise, after days and nights of mostly the sounds of weather, came as a most welcome change. Let her bark! He didn't even care who she annoyed; he'd disembark in a matter of what? – minutes? hours? – and as soon as his feet made contact with *terra firma* he had no intention of climbing aboard another fucking boat for the rest of his days. Despite the conversation that he'd just shared with Elvis, Connors couldn't imagine that he'd need to see his travelling companions ever again.

To Hell with it. It was *his* dream.

My gaff, my rules, he thought with a smile that looked crazy and vexed at the same instant.

2.

Connors hadn't been in the port long before he started to believe that he was being followed. While stopping on the quay, for example, to watch a man with a finger missing on each hand gut an example of one of the ugliest fish Connors had ever seen, Connors would roll his eyes left and catch a glimpse of his subtle pursuer as he ducked down behind a large groyne, or a rowboat bulging with fishing nets. So Connors would wait; maybe next time he'd see his follower's face. But no; even if Connors turned quickly, despite the fact that he'd been sure that someone was directly behind him, there'd be no sign of the other, only crowds of men and women, many of them in flowing robes and colourful attire that appeared to Connors's decidedly untravelled eyes as North African... The people he saw in the port were an odd mix. Though their features were vaguely Oriental, their skin was a mixture of olive-European and dark, so maybe Connors's own white face was a reason that he was feeling self-conscious; maybe no one was following, after all. It was only in his head. Maybe...

Then again, it could be the dog that had so fascinated the islanders. Despite what Elvis Leader had advised, Connors had felt guilty at the thought of leaving her alone on the ship; as the ship approached port she had shaken and whined as though beaten. In fact, her actions had made Connors believe – if only briefly – that Chelsea could read his mind and was thus well aware of his plans. So he'd brought her with him. For a leash he had used three tea towels from the ship's kitchen, tied together

and then lashed to Chelsea's collar. It would have to do; but if she
saw something that made her run from him, as Harry had done,
then God help him. She'd vanish as fast as a breeze. At least there
weren't any cars.

No cars. The only transportation on the quayside was the
rickshaw, several hundred examples of which weaved their way
through the throngs, their bicyclists, young and of either gender,
pedalling madly and swearing (it seemed to Connors) in a language that he could not comprehend. For all the good the raised
voices did, perhaps the waterfront strollers failed to recognise the
dialect as well: there was certainly no hurry among them to move
out of the rickshaws' way. These vehicles were mostly transport-
ing catches of the ugly fish; Connors assumed that they were *en
route* to market or straight to a restaurant's baking tray.

That's a point, thought Connors. Food… Apart from rice
and figs, he hadn't eaten anything since… Jesus… since his last
supper with Dorman, and even then Dorman had done most of
the eating. Connors pictured the older man slurping on chicken
wings. At the time he had thought Dorman's table manners disgraceful; now (he realised) he would do anything to watch the
man violate a plat of greasy poultry one more time… A nauseous sadness rode up Connors's body, using his organs as a
ladder. Grief belted through his brain; in order to stop himself
before he started crying, Connors hiccoughed. The memory of
Dorman's decapitation returned with force.

Food.

Where and what could he eat? As they'd filed onto the
gangplank, Captain Carousel had handed them all five coins –
three that looked like silver, two that looked like bronze, but Connors doubted that either metal was in these coins' constitution
– and Connors had thanked him and let Chelsea lead him down
to dry land. These five coins were in Connors's jeans pocket,

jangling stiffly as he walked against the other coins therein. The *English* coins. The four pound coins, the three fifty pees, the seven twenty pees, the six tens, the five fives and grip's worth of shrapnel – twos and pennies. This was in addition to the notes in the same pocket, the notes in his wallet: all he needed was a *bureau de change*. He was minted. Maybe it was this money that the follower wanted; if so, could Connors surmise that it was someone from the ship? Foolhardy it might have been (in retrospect) to have counted it so brazenly, so openly, in front of the other men, but if it hurried him back to his dreambed – to his sickbed if need be – then Connors felt prepared for any attack on his person. He would fight till he woke.

No assault was forthcoming, however; just that nagging intuition that he was being tailed. As Connors moved inland, into a labyrinth of narrow alleyways, the protective shadowy cool of which was pleasant after so much sun, he sought somewhere to dine. Did no one *eat* on Toenail Island? This was no nightmare seafront of candyfloss sellers, of stands selling mussels and whelks; in the alleys' storefronts, on the contrary, the displays were of jewellery, fashioned from what looked like bone, and of ornaments, and of wristwatches with blank faces and no hands.

Eventually, after what seemed like twenty-or-so minutes of walking, Connors found himself trailing the aroma of meat cooking. Chelsea's bark suggested that the dog was identically ravenous, and Connors allowed her to lead him down passage after passage, the light above dimming with every corner they rounded, moving deeper into the maze. Then they were up on it. And if it had been in England it would have had the Devil's own job of attracting customers. For a start, it was filthy; flies the size and colour of sugar cubes – they hummed and buzzed on both ceiling and walls: a lively confetti. For another thing, the establishment was plainly more than a simple eatery: blood was splashed up on the walls; red-brown footprints crossed the mucky packed-dirt floor, as if more than one pair of feet had walked blood in on their shoes. The heads of animals that Connors didn't recognise hung from fireplace-wide joists in the roof; in fact, some of these hunts were so fresh that they still dripped blood – drip! – and unable to hold herself back, Chelsea began lapping hungrily at a pool of gore. It was a butcher's shop. But with three sets of tables and chairs. And a tantalising smell of roasting meat in the air, but neither customers nor any sign of a proprietor. So Connors called:

'Hello? Anyone home? Hello?'

The man who emerged from behind a curtain made from a rust-coloured pelt had to be the butcher. Wearing nothing but his birthday suit and a blue-and-white striped apron to cover his modesty, he was slapdashed from head to foot in some poor creature's life fluid. He even had blood on his lips. But his serial killer get-up was not what Connors noticed first and foremost: the man had half of a second head attached to the right side of his ordinary head, the features on this unfortunate addition drooping as if this part of his physiognomy, and this part alone, had suffered a stroke. In total he had three eyes: two blue ones on his ordinary face, one brown eye on the half a head latched on; and though his whole-head was clean shaven, the half-head sported half a moustache on the squashed upper lip, and it was this, the pursed half-a-mouth that spoke to Connors.

'*Survan-dam?*' he seemed to ask.

Instructing himself not to stare, Connors said, 'English? Do you speak English?'

The butcher made no reply but scratched an armpit. Connors mimed bringing food to his lips, then rubbed his belly and hummed appreciatively, hoping that the culture of Toenail Island extended to food appreciation. Still the butcher appeared nonplussed, but now his eyes were drawn to Chelsea, who was muzzle-deep in some scraps she'd found on the floor. Once more Connors rubbed his belly and smiled, before remembering a language greater than that of love. From the back pocket of his jeans he pulled out one of the Captain's silver coins, unaware of its denomination or value.

The translation was instantaneous: though the full mouth remained straight, as stoic as that of a figure on a Grecian urn, the half-mouth twisted up in a grin made wry by the absence of its complementary half. Oh, this wanker understood all right! Had Connors offered too much?

The butcher stepped forward, one of his bare feet sliding in a patch of blood and silver feathers. '*Sloon-yik serl-lul fran,*' the man said, talkative bell-end that he was, Connors thought. *Just lay the table, knobcheese!* This was the lexicon, he understood – angry and belligerent – of his empty stomach. Connors watched as the butcher stooped and stroked Chelsea's brow. Chelsea drank up the praise like an infant.

His stomach gargling, Connors assumed mission accomplished. It should only be minutes before he tucked the paper napkin into his shirt collar...

'He thinks you're selling him your dog to eat.'

The voice came from behind Connors; cross-legged, Connors span, his fright tuned and revving.

The speaker was Elvis Leader.

'Have you been following me?' Connors demanded.

'To protect you.'

Connors frowned. 'I don't need your *protection*, son.'

Elvis sniggered. 'Your dog wouldn't agree with you. She was nearly on a skewer with a bowl of bread and corn-dip.'

Connors paused. An ally at this moment sounded agreeable; perhaps this could work. 'Are you hungry, Elvis?'

'I could eat a penguin's sphincter.'

'A penguin? You have *penguins* here?'

'Not here,' replied the boy. 'The sun should've been your clue. Penguins prefer ice.'

Chelsea yapped.

'Enough of the backchat, son,' said Connors. 'Just tell him we're hungry and have cash. We want an animal's flesh on a plate, with some green bits for balance. And a beer of some description… Can you manage that?'

Without further hesitation Elvis gabbled; after ten seconds the butcher laughed, using each of his mouths. Then, bowing both heads, he indicated a table and retreated into the back quarters.

Connors asked, 'What do you fancy?'

'There's not a lot of choice, Con.'

'Okay; so what are we having?'

'You don't want to know,' Elvis told him.

HOSPITAL PATIENCE

1.

'Don't worry, Nurse Jones, I've asked the patients not to be sick on your busy schedule. I know you're busy.'

Bernadette had expected something similar. 'I'm sorry I'm late,' she said; 'you won't believe what happened at home last night. Or this morning, I should say.'

But Margaret seemed in no mood for forgiveness. 'To be frank, what happened last night,' she answered, '*or* this morning, ranks low on my list of must-knows. You are a nurse and you have patients who depend on your ability to set an alarm clock correctly.'

'I *did* set it correctly!'

'You slept through it then.'

'With good reason!' Bernadette argued. 'There was an accident in the village – I was awake until three helping.'

Margaret crossed her arms over her sturdy bosom. 'Mr Williams, in bed seventeen, for example, has also been awake since three o'clock. I suggest you see to him first.'

'Yes, Sister.'

'And don't *sigh*.'

'I didn't.'

'In which case my ears are deceiving me. Maybe *I* need a lie-in!'

'No, Sister... I'll wash my hands first, if I may.'

'I insist. And don't *sigh*.'

It was going to be a long day, Bernadette decided. Only while scrubbing under her nails did she experience a burning sense of ridiculous injustice. The *hours* she'd spent, damn it! And to be spoken to like this! It wasn't fair. Even by the standards of a normal nursing day, it wasn't fair.

Two hours and a dozen patients later, Bernadette entered the Staff Room, a strong cup of tea on her mind. She was exhausted... Two women were already inside the room: a young Malaysian nurse on the same grade as Bernadette (they swapped hellos) and a thick-set police officer in her forties. Using a spoon, the latter was squeezing the life out of a purple teabag in a departmental mug. 'Hi Bernie,' said the police officer, turning. 'Good night's rest?'

'Very funny, Mo.' Bernadette flopped onto one of the sofas; suddenly it was like her legs wouldn't do their job for one more second. They'd called in the unions. 'You couldn't make me one while you're there, could you? If there's anything left in the kettle.'

'Sure,' answered Sergeant Maureen Tennan. 'Which is yours?'

'The pink mug with March for Cancer. Teabags in the middle tin, Say No To Biscuits.'

'This one? Oh yeah I see... How's your morning been so far?'

'Diabolical. What brings you to my shores?'

'A drink driver brings me to your shores. Doing the school run with a litre of vodka in her system. In her *nightdress*.'

Bernadette nodded. 'She banged it up?'

'Write off. BMW, six months old. One of the yummy mummies near the airport. And hubby *won't* be pleased when he comes home from golf.' She passed a steaming mug to Bernadette, who nodded her thanks. 'Why's your morning been diabolical?'

'Oh, the fun we had last night. And managerial bullshit.'

Tennan nodded. She'd been there. 'There's a squad at the house right now. Environmental scientists, the Water Board... the works. But no one's coming up with a decent explanation.' She sipped and smiled. 'Don't blame it on the sunshine. Don't blame it on the moonlight.'

'I blame it on the boogie,' said Bernadette, silently resolving at this moment to pay another visit to the war zone on her way home, fatigue or no fatigue, police barriers or no police barriers.

2.

Accident scenes (of which she had seen many) and crime scenes (of which she had seen far fewer) never failed to remind Bernadette of ant-farms. This evening's activity was no exception. Her neighbour's house and small front garden were surrounded by police tape, inside which a small plague of uniforms buzzed... Bernadette parked on her own driveway and walked back. If she walked confidently enough, perhaps she could slip under the tape before anyone noticed her.

She was stopped.

'You can't come in, I'm afraid, madam,' said the officer on the neighbour's drive. 'There's been an accident.'

'I know. I'm a nurse.'

'I can see that. There's no one here for you to help.'

'What about the owners?'

'Not here.'

'So I gather... Kyle, isn't it? What I mean is, where are they?'

'They're safe... How do you know my name?'

'I'm a friend of Maureen Tennan. You were at her youngest's birthday party, about a year ago. Northall Village Hall.'

The officer snapped his fingers. 'I *thought* I recognised you. Well remembered!'

'So where are Bill and Lucinda?' Bernadette asked, pressing her advantage and smiling thinly.

The officer frowned. 'Do you actually know them?'

'I actually do. I live up the road. Number 77. I was here last night.'

'Give a statement?' Kyle asked.

'Most of it.'

'I don't understand.'

'I asked you first.'

'Mr and Mrs Riley were attending a funeral yesterday, in the north of the country. Instead of driving back down last night they'd decided to stay at Mr Riley's brother's place in Durham. They're still there, as far as I know. They were told there's nothing much to come home to for a while.'

It sounded like a prepared statement; but the important facts had been conveyed – Bill and Lucinda were not coming home straightaway.

'You were saying?' the officer prompted.

Knowing that Chris would be furious with her, Bernadette fessed up.

'Two guys came to our door last night – very late. One of them was the man who lost half his head. When the explosion happened, I was one of the first in the back garden.'

'And this is in your statement,' said Kyle.

'No, this is the part that's off the record.'

'I see. Why did they come to your door?'

'They were burglars. They were checking us out,' Bernadette lied. If Chris was going to be furious that she had said anything of this to the police *at all*, he was going to go bug-eyed if she mentioned that they had been burgled an hour or so earlier. *They were checking us out* was close enough. But she hadn't given Kyle what he needed, she was certain. She had given him some fresh information but nothing more – and the tidbit didn't add much. So what if she could identify half the head of a dead man? It was the same guy who had come knocking. Big deal.

What happened to the younger guy? Bernadette wondered. How had he escaped?

Had he escaped?

In Bernadette's mind an approximate timeline had been drawn up. The two thieves had done Number 77 first, and taken items that could be replaced – things with a monetary value. And because Chris was terrified of the police, and because there'd be no claim on the insurance, the police were not called to the scene of this first burglary. But the *thieves* didn't know that the police would not be called. Having got away with the theft, what on earth had brought them back to the same street? If they'd been feeling punchy with success, why not go at least as far as Eaton Bray or Dagnall? *What had brought them back?*

They were looking for something specific, thought Bernadette. We weren't the intended target; we were only convenient – the building was empty. But they made a mistake. They went to the wrong house.

What are Bill and Lucinda hiding?

Kyle was asking Bernadette something. Bernadette tuned in.

'But they didn't actually steal anything?' he said.

'No, they didn't actually steal anything,' Bernadette replied. Immediately she felt strange. It was the first time in her life that she had deliberately lied to an ambassador of the law. There was something liberating about it.

Vowing that she would get inside that house, one way or another, Bernadette trudged along to her own. Chris was waiting for her.

'Where've you been?' he demanded.

'Don't I get a kiss?'

'Okay, kiss.' He kissed her. '*Now* where've you been?'

'To the Quatermass Experiment down the road, as if you need to ask… Have you done dinner?'

'There's a chicken in. I thought we *agreed*, Bern.'

'Well I didn't have much choice,' Bernadette lied again – the second fib in five minutes. 'They saw me driving past, they waved me down…'

Chris followed Bernadette into the kitchen. 'Who did?'

'Smells *lush*. Rice and peas?'

'*Mais oui.* But *who* did, Bern?'

'Some colleagues from work. They waved me down so I parked and went back. I thought they were gonna tell me something new, but it turns out they wanted the goss from me. Of which there is *nada*.'

Chris remained silent. Nervously expecting more questions, Bernadette glided around the cramped cooking quarters, filling the kettle and dropping teabags into two mugs. It wasn't until her partner said, 'I have a game tonight' that Bernadette knew that she'd got away with it. For now, at least.

'Where? And what?' Bernadette asked.

'Luton. Texas Hold'em.'

'Oh dear.' She smiled. 'You always come back from Texas Hold'em sounding like Boss Hogg from *The Dukes of Hazzard*.'

'Hey babe, what can I say?' He held his arms wide. 'I'm *trying* to get the Rosco P. Coltrane down pat but it ain't easy.'

'I suppose not.' Bernadette waited. The water in the kettle continued to boil. Then she added: 'I think we should consult the Object.'

'I've been dreading you saying that.' The man sighed. 'But I agree with you.'

Relationship Problems

1.

At first they had been kept apart, and that had been rough enough: cuffed to a radiator in a room that sang with echoes every time you raised your voice (suggesting there was no furniture). For the last two days, however, they had been kept in the same walk-in wardrobe: and this was proving tougher than ever. It had got to the point where they had little left to say to one another. And sometimes hours passed when Nero would not so much as look at Jess, in the hope that when he next turned in her direction (perhaps as a way of straightening out a cramp), he would find her less repulsive to regard. But it hadn't worked so far.

The hats didn't help, of course. One day (or thereabouts) into their abduction, the podgy little fuck who had disabled them on the railway platform had come breezing into Nero's room and had told him that from now on he would be wearing a hat.

At that juncture, before he'd been sodomised for the first time, Nero had still been full of rage and fear at having been abducted in the first place. Accordingly, he had struggled violently against his handcuff and the radiator to which the twin cuff had been attached; and he'd told Charlie Eastlight that he could go fuck himself, he wasn't wearing no stupid fucking hat. And he swore and he spat and he tried to get up off the carpet.

Eastlight had urinated on Nero's left leg. *Let's try this again,* the jailer had said.

Go fuck yourself! Nero had shouted. *You filthy fucking pervert!*

Yes, I thought we'd established that at the train station. A pervert is quite right. As for fucking myself… I wish I could, mate! And so do you, believe me! If that kind of thing was possible – well, you and your girlfriend might not be in such a fix right now… Put the hat on.

'Nah, man,' Nero had said, though he'd sounded a lot less sure of himself than he had a minute earlier, before the ammonia aroma of Eastlight's urine had had a chance to waft through their confines.

At that point he had yet to be raped. At that point he had not even been stripped. And to think he'd kicked off about wearing a silly hat! How green he'd been, how green…

Silently he had agreed to wear the hat. The decision had seemed like a caving-in, a rock-slide; it had felt like a failure. But at first (at least) he had been able to pretend that he wasn't wearing it. Even when the two men had taken turns with him the first time, Nero had tried to grip hard to the lie that he had refused to wear their hat. It had meant something: a way of holding on to his sanity, perhaps.

Back in the days when he and Jess had been held in separate rooms, Nero had counted his breaths between sexual assaults. Tried to teach himself not to struggle: the perverts enjoyed a fight, and besides, it was useless to test his strength against the radiator pipes to which he'd been cuffed. Practice had made this clear enough: he was not the equal of metal, strengthwise.

As soon as they'd moved Nero and Jess into the walk-in wardrobe, Nero had guessed that things were soon to get worse, for a hat had perched on Jess's head too.

The hats meant that Jess and Nero had become property. When Nero had been alone he had maintained a miniscule store of inner strength: he had thought of himself as merely a prisoner. Now that Jess had joined him, he knew exactly what status they had been relegated to. This was one of the reasons why Nero had found it hard to look at her.

She was stirring now.

2.

She slept a lot, did Jess. She gave in to exhaustion in the same way that Nero fought it: with enthusiasm, with quiet vigour. Reading into her frequent departures, Nero saw a place of refuge that she would find; a space of healing. For Nero there was no equivalent: his sleep was wrecked by dreams in which he spoke the wrong language, in a place where no one could understand him – his fears, his panic, his predicament. And in these dreams he was always walking, never still; as restless as fleas on a hot plate. An ocean dreamstained burgundy; a dog that read his mind and yearned for language of its own; a wall made of a vast toenail…

Nero envied Jess, her ability to stay away from whatever place that was – or any like it. Her sleep (to Nero) felt pure and refreshing; she would send her memories away, bobbing perhaps on that same wine-hued ocean, in a boat made of folded paper. And her memories were taken from her; they didn't haunt her… or so it seemed to her teenaged lover. So it seemed to Nero, who could not help despising her a tad more, every time that she closed her eyes to escape this.

But she was stirring now; twitchy; her nose wrinkled swiftly, tasting the air, to make sure that it was safe for her to return.

So Nero looked away.

3.

'I'm hungry,' Jess muttered eventually on another day.
Five days in? Six?

Nero ignored her. Never had the phrase 'same shit, different day' meant so much or been so apposite; and no longer did he care to tell her to change the record about her hunger pains. She was hungry. Like, *yeah*? Well, the *world* was hungry, rah? *Stop whining and that...* Try as he might not to move, however (an attempt to pretend that he hadn't heard a sound), a left thigh muscle twanged and a spasm shot through his torso. He'd been seen.

'I said: *I'm hungry*, Nero.'

He turned to her. 'I'll pop out and get some fried chicken, shall I? You dickhead.'

'No, *you're* the dickhead,' Jess spat back.

'Like rah,' Nero added wearily. As usual he was cuffed to the radiator, which wasn't turned on, but this time the cuff was only on his left wrist. His right hand was free... not that he could do anything with it.

Unlike Nero on the carpet, Jess had been given a narrow camper bed. She had been restrained so that she could sit up slightly – her right hand cuffed to one of the bed's pole-like legs – but so that her legs remained widened, with two sets of cuffs securing her ankles to the legs of the bed at the other end. As was Nero, Jess was now naked: if he glanced her way, she had been positioned so that he stared directly at her vagina.

4.

More days had passed. Nero was getting muddled up.

To begin with, Nero hadn't seen a reason why they'd positioned Jess like that: positioned her so that her legs were open on the camp bed. Positioned her so that any time he glanced in her direction, the first thing he saw of her was her widened vagina. The point was what exactly? He'd seen it before and this new, fresh torture – with Nero still cuffed to the radiator in the walk-in cupboard and Jess cuffed to the camp bed by one wrist, tied the ankles to the bed's legs so that her thighs were kept parted – was nothing more or less than weird.

But it hadn't taken him long to learn a grim secret about your girlfriend – one of those secrets that rap or porn didn't much cover.

You could get too much of a good thing.

Now that the light was left on around the clock, Nero's only view was of Jess's labia (the walk-in cupboard had no windows, and he couldn't stand up anyway), so the new game seemed to consist of artificial light and the sight of sore flesh.

The jailers were not teasing Nero. They were punishing him.

On balance, he had preferred it when he and Jess had been left in the dark for days on end. The artificial light screwed with your body clock. And the company had seemed better... But then, one day, while he'd trembled through a troubled doze, the two men (or at least he'd only heard or seen two so far) had stripped Jess down to the skin. They had probably fucked her as well. And they'd stripped Nero too, the cunts. Left them naked as the day, Adam and Eve in chains.

Nero was sick of the sight of it. Probably Jess thought something similar about the sight of his penis, Nero imagined; but at least he could lift up a leg to block her view; he could shuffle around on the carpet, although the damage done to his rectum made some sitting positions uncomfortable or downright painful. He could show – he could exhibit – some dignity. That was what it boiled down to. *Dignity*... Which seemed an odd ambition in the circumstances – to be dignified, given everything – but it was the only thing that Nero believed he had left.

Suddenly he started crying. Fury went through his body like volts; he expelled a cry of impotent rage and kicked repeatedly at thin air. Putting everything he had into the action, Nero tugged at the pipe, the bracelet of the cuff chewing into his wrist

The pipe did not move.

He had known that it wouldn't so why bother? Because he had to do *something*, that was why. Because he had formed opinions, and plenty of them, about their captors.

The fit passed quickly. Nero leaned against the wall (the same creamy off-white colour as the other three walls, and the door) and hunched himself together in a shaking bundle. The tears were gone; they hadn't lasted long – they never did. It was anger that he felt now, not sorrow, not grief: anger at his own helplessness. Anger at being in this so-called room. Anger at Jess.

I will kill them.

Nero was as certain of this promise as he was of the disgust and shame that he had experienced, the instant the fat man's semen had leaked out of his anus that first time, and dribbled between his buttocks, on to his scrotum.

I will kill them. I will do it.

In his mind, Nero said the words slowly, testing them for weight and plausibility. Not only did they seem right, they seemed inevitable: they were the future. Not only would he find pleasure in making them suffer (or so he believed), he would sense that there was no alternative anyway.

'You finished?'

Nero sighed. Wearily he asked, 'What now, Jess?'

'Your little paddy. You had enough?'

'Yeah.' Nero didn't want to face her. He knew that he would though. 'Yeah, I've had enough. Enough of a lot of things.'

And he faced her. She had sat up as well as she could; their eyelines simmered.

The beanie hat she wore said BE MY BABY. So did his.

Hers was pale blue. His was pink.

'And what good did it do?' Jess demanded.

'No good at all.'

'So you might as well've saved your energy.'

Nero sighed again. 'Yeah, I might've,' he admitted. 'For what exactly?'

And he turned away. 'Close your eyes,' he added as he reached for the slops bucket. He needed to urinate. Without bothering to check if she had closed her eyes (or had lain back down to stare up at the ceiling) Nero did his business while experiencing the twinned emotions of hope and panic. Both of these emotions concerned a visit from one of the two perverts (but probably the fat one; the Italian-looking one appeared less in control). Nero hoped that the fat bastard would come soon to empty his bucket. And he panicked that while he was here he would think up something new to do to his prisoners involving their waste products.

'Nero?'

'What is it?'

'I know this is my fault.'

'You bet your *arse* it's your fault. How do you feel about it?'

'Rancid, boy.'

'Yeah. And you're not the one who's been buggered. Imagine how *I* feel!'

'I've been wondering about that,' Jess continued – so carefully and slowly that the words did not sound like hers to Nero's ears. The tone made him face her once more.

He waited.

A few seconds passed before Jess said, 'About a year ago, my mum and dad were having problems, right? Mum was gonna leave him. And she wanted me and Vanessa to go with her. So at the weekend we had to go with her to see all these houses on the market – she wasn't gonna live in their house when the divorce came through, she said.'

Nero waited.

'And I can't tell you how many we saw, and Mum going *Yes, yes, this is the one,* all excited, and me feeling bad when we drove home and Mum told Dad all about what she decided. *The girls and I,* she kept saying – as if Nessa and me had any fucking say in it. I started to hate her for that. But the point I'm making is – most of the houses looked just like this.'

'Like what?'

Jess waved her free hand around to take in the confines of the walk-in cupboard, but at the same time she also meant the bedroom to which it was attached – the bedroom in which both of them had been raped repeatedly after they'd been drugged. The bedroom without any furniture - just a porridge-grey carpet of a hard-wearing fabric and heavy blinds fitted over the window. The bedroom with the locked door… through which both of them had tried to escape when they'd been teased that they could run away. Or when they'd thought they'd got lucky; when they thought their captors had got attention-sloppy after orgasm. (*What's stopping you, fuckhole?* the fat one had asked one day near the beginning. And she had tried the door handle. Behind her back he had held up the key, just below the bulb blazing in its ceiling fixture. *But you'll need this first, won't you… Get on your cunting knees. Now.*)

'Painted cream walls, beige carpets,' said Jess. 'No bed or chairs. Probably one of them fireproof doors… It makes me think this house is for sale or rent.'

Growing interested, Nero said, 'And? Assuming you're right, what of it?'

'Well… Sooner or later someone's gonna make an appointment to view it, to look around. And when they do, fucking Tweedle-Dum and Tweedle-Dee will have to move us out of sight.'

Nero snorted. 'If they haven't killed us first,' he answered.

'We're *already* out of sight! We're in a fucking cupboard!'

'*Killed* us?'

'...Don't say the thought hasn't occurred to you.' As he spoke, the sense of panic won out over the hope that he'd harboured. 'They haven't even bothered to mask their faces or covered our eyes, apart from a few days at the start. You think they're gonna let us go back after this? *Grow up.*'

Jess paused. A little breathless she said, '...I wouldn't tell.'

'You'd have no choice,' Nero informed her. 'They have police psychologists. You say yes and they know you mean no. And besides, if they move us, what? We escape *then?* They'll drug us up, Jess, or brain us or something. It's a stupid plan.'

'Well. At least it's *something*, Nero. Least I'm *trying.*'

'Well don't. You're getting on me nerves.'

'Tough shit,' Jess answered sulkily.

'We're an experiment to them,' Nero added, closing his eyes. 'The pink hat on me, the blue hat on you... but it's pink for *girls*, blue for boys. Why are they doing that? An experiment, that's why... And they're trying to get you pregnant, is my guess. They want a baby to fuck up.'

'God...'

'So the good news is you've probably got nine months left. The bad news is...' Nero chuckled with surprising warmth. 'I probably ain't.'

I will kill them, Nero's mind repeated; but this time the promise did not sound anything like as certain as it had before. It more or less concluded with a question mark. The thought crossed his mind that they would want him to kill Jess... in time. The worse thought crossed his mind that by then he would probably do so for a slice of bread.

The worst thought was that he knew there would be no one to start looking for him – not yet. He was not supposed to be in the UK; no one would know that he was missing. But what were Jess's people doing, that's what Nero would like to know.

WHIPPING BOY

1.

Having eaten an extra portion of fried rice for the purposes of tonight's sex games, Phyllie had no difficulty at all in defecating on Roger's chest. Sometimes she struggled: she'd be straining like a toddler on the potty, her temples throbbing with the exertion, black marks flitting across her vision as she almost passed out, and all for what? A fawn-coloured, thumbnail-sized Richard, and the perfume of sin and sewers. But not tonight: tonight Roger was treated to a veritable *omelette* of ordure, which he smeared across his nipples while Phyllie fisted him with one hand and yanked him to a surprisingly copious conclusion with the other. It was only while loading the bedsheets into the washing machine that Phyllie mused on the salad days of their courtship, back when simple urination had been as far as they'd dared to go. How sweet they'd been! How green! But what did it say, she wondered parenthetically, about their marriage, that these days even watersports weren't enough? On the night after Vig and Dorota's barbecue, Phyllie had timidly suggested a session of vaginal intercourse, and Roger had looked at her as if she were mad. 'You mean *retro*?' he'd asked. 'Not even Virginia?' (Virginia was Roger's preferred codeword for anal sex, after the broadcaster Virginia Bottomley.) 'Well, let's see how it goes, shall we?' Phyllie had replied, and warming to the theme Roger had grinned and told her that old school might be fun, *outré* even, and that a minge was as good as a rest. But after ninety minutes he had faltered – the 'skinhead' had let him down – and Phyllie had felt obliged, in a spirit of *quid pro quo*, to pretend to be a rapist again and cuff him to the radiator pipe with the pink fluffy handcuffs that they usually employed only on birthdays or anniversaries. Even then Phyllie had needed to tongue his rectum before he ejaculated… and now it was over again for another evening, with Phyllie setting the machine to a spin-rinse cycle and smiling nostalgically about their early days together, when it had usually consisted of Virginia and watersports… and the odd bit of whipping.

The washing machine hummed; water drenched the drum. Phyllie left the utility room and walked into the study, where the phone was ringing. From upstairs she could hear Roger singing 'Uptown Girl' in the shower, and with another smile (she loved him so: Roger, not Billy Joel) she picked up the receiver and said, 'Hello?'

'Hi, it's Vig.'

'Oh hi. How are you, Midas Boy?'

'Good. Sorry it's late.'

'No problem. I just finished having sex.'

'Oh. Anyone I know?'

'Some bloke at the bus stop.'

'Again? And how was he?'

'Cock like a workman's shovel.'

'I was calling about the other night. You didn't leave a bracelet here, did you?'

'No, it's not mine. What does it look like?'

'Hippie-ish. Little blue triangles hanging off it. Quite nice, but not really Dorota's taste – not even as finders keepers. Someone left it near the aviary – it might have been one of the kids.'

'Oh. Talking about the aviary and kids: Roger told me a funny thing that night…'

'The crying in the woods?' Vig ventured.

'Yeah!'

'I heard about it. But I didn't hear it – to tell you the truth, I even went into the trees myself, see if I could catch an earful; but no dice.'

'Spooky. Do you have foxes?'

'No. I haven't *seen* any. Dorota swears she saw a deer – but I've got my doubts.'

'Where is she, by the way? Phyllie asked.

'Having a bath. She's trying to decide on her favourite bathroom and she's taking a bath in a different room each time she has one.'

'Blimey. How many have you got?'

'Seven.' Vig laughed again. '*Seven bathrooms.* I mean, who needs seven bathrooms? Seriously… She's in there for two hours at a time. Takes a book and a radio; makes an evening of it.'

'You're not tempted to join her?'

'In the bath?'

'Yes! Be an incorrigible romantic!'

'No, I don't think so. Dol's rather grabby about her privacy.'

'Shame. Well, if you're ever tempted away from her loving bosom and want someone to surprise in the bath, you know where to find me, Vig.'

Vig paused. 'One of the few things we never tried, as I recall.'

'Are you getting all misty-eyed with nostalgia?'

The question remained unanswered. Changing tack, Vig asked, 'And where's Roger, by the way? With you talking so candidly.'

'He's having a shower, funnily enough,' said Phyllie. 'Case of snap. He likes to have a thorough soak after sex. He's treating me to Billy Joel's back catalogue as we speak.'

'I can't hear him. You mean you really *were* having sex?'

'Of course! You thought I was lying?'

'Well, *exaggerating* anyway.'

'Not at all. I mean, he's always been a once-a-day man, ever since we got together; but recently, with my bump showing, he's got this fresh new fat chick and he's like a rampaging army!'

'…Hell's bells,' said Vig, after another pause.

'Come and watch some time,' Phyllie added, 'you'll see what I mean. Roger would love that.'

'We've been through this, Phyll.'

Phyllie smiled. 'I know, I know. Dorota this, Dorota that. Bring her along! More the merrier.'

Vig chuckled. 'I wish I could see your face,' he said.

'Only my face?'

'To see if you're having me on.'

'I'm not, I promise you. Or you could borrow one of our films, as long as I watched it with you… Oh, hang on a minute.' Phyllie's ears pricked at the cessation of singing from the first floor. Enjoying the conversation as she was, she was reluctant to hang up, but if Roger was finished in the bathroom… 'It's okay: he's started again. He was obviously choosing from his repertoire. He's on to 'Tell Her About It' now – ironically enough.'

'Anyway. It's not your bracelet, then.'

'It's not my bracelet. Have you got tired of the big boy table talk?' Phyllie asked, momentarily confused to hear her own name breathed down the line.

'Dorota says hi,' Vig told her.

'Oh she's *with* you now,' said Phyllie. 'That was a quick bath, I must say. Evidently… not enough sin in her soul.'

'I'd better go.'

Phyllie laughed briskly. 'You're great to tease – and one of these days…' she began.

'G'night, Phyllie.'

'Night, Bill Gates. Think about my indecent proposal, won't you? One of you in my bum…'

The phone line died. An hysterical pitch to her laughter now, Phyllie raced up the stairs to startle Roger in the shower and to tell him verbatim how the conversation had gone… Who knew? Perhaps it would be enough to turn him on once more.

2.

It *was* enough to turn him on once more, and Phyllie collapsed into a satisfied slumber before the semen had had a chance to dry on her forehead. The satisfied slumber, however, was not set to last. Strange dreams pursued her: strange dream that *started* promisingly enough – Roger and Vig holding hands, naked, on a zebra crossing; teaching tomorrow's class on the subject of igneous rock while stark naked, to a room full of kids (also naked) and her much-missed parents, fully dressed and frowning their combined disapproval – but which morphed into unrecognisable shapes, loud noises, bad aromas. When her unconscious woke her at a little after two a.m. she felt packed out – stuffed – with an answer, or set of answers, that she couldn't read, to a question that she couldn't remember.

Her hand on her pregnancy bulge, Phyllie padded downstairs, into the kitchen. Although she was not experiencing cravings (she hadn't since the first month), and although she wasn't hungry, she removed some celery from the fridge and ate it sitting on the edge of the table. Her bottom was sore; she fancied a glass of the white wine in the fridge door. She didn't dare: but she wanted to. Munching celery and thinking about her ragged and roughed-up catflap, then, Phyllie experienced a flash of what had come to her in her sleep. Not so much a dream as a premonition – a solution… Jessica Olney, the missing girl, had entered her classroom, nude, and had beckoned to Phyllie, saying *I'll show you where.* Hand in hand they had floated up Vig's driveway, but not as far as the house: they had crossed the wide lawn to the right and gone into the trees. *Can you hear me crying?* Jess had asked her.

Yes.

I'm in the birdkeeper's house, aren't I?

And Phyllie had nodded her head. *Yes you are, Jess.*

'Yes you are, Jess,' Phyllie said aloud. So long did she stay motionless, rearranging snippets in her mind, that a bite's-worth of celery turned to mush in her mouth, the flavour leaking out into swallowed spittle.

Could it be? *The quiet ones*, she heard her father say to her from two decades earlier, *are the ones you have to watch out for.* But Birdkeeper Don... a *kidnapper?* It sounded preposterous.

Spitting her mouthful of celery into the bin that swung out on the door under the sink, Phyllie tried to free her mind of these silly night notions. But the thought persisted; in fact, it flourished – it flew. It carried her on wings of fear and deposited her into her room. From the next bedroom came the rattle and hum of Roger's snoring. She wanted to wake him and tell him what she'd concluded, however fanciful or lame it sounded: she *wanted* him to tell her that she was being ridiculous. Perhaps it would break the spell. But she didn't wake him. She didn't have the heart.

3.

'Roger Billie,' said Roger into the phone.

'It's me. Can you talk?'

'Sure; I've got a meeting at ten.'

'It won't take a minute. I've been thinking about Jess – it came to me in a dream, if that doesn't sound pretentious enough.'

'What did?'

Phyllie recited her theory and asked her husband if she was being a wet. Roger hissed a sigh into her ear. 'I don't know,' he admitted.

'It might be worth a call to the police, do you reckon? I wouldn't want them to laugh at me but if I don't say anything and I'm *right*...'

'Have you spoken to Vig?' Roger asked.

'No. I wouldn't know what to say.'

'You'd say what you've just said to me... Where are you calling from?'

'The Head's office. His secretary let me in; it was too noisy in the staffroom, and I didn't want anyone...'

'No, I see. Let me think now... Can I call you when this meeting's over?'

'What time?'

'About twelve?'

'I'll be with 8G then, and I'm teaching all afternoon. This is a bit now or never, Rog.'

'Okay, I'll go,' Roger told her.

'Go where? To Vig's place?'

'And see for myself. Why not? I've an offsite assessment to do at one-thirty. A G.P. referral: she's threatening to cut her wrists if she runs out of milk – a new case on the book.'

Phyllie interrupted him. 'Charming as I find your enthusiasm for your job,' she said, 'I need to be quick. Breaktime's nearly over. So you'll do what? Go out to Vig's after you've talked the crazy bitch down from a ledge?'

'Something like that.'

'Okay, thanks. And I'll apologise in advance if this is a wild goose chase.'

'Apology accepted. Do you have his number?'

'Whose? The birdkeeper's? No, I –'

'No. I meant Vig's. To let him know...'

'No, don't call Vig. He might say something to Don, even if you ask him not to. And that gives Don a couple of hours to do whatever he needs to do. To cover his tracks.'

Roger paused. 'Do you suspect *Vig?*' he asked.

'No, not at all. But think about it, Roger: if someone said to you there's a certain thing hidden in our house, the first thing you'd do is go and look for it, wouldn't you? I think the element of surprise is best.'

'Then how am I supposed to get in?' Roger protested. 'They've got a big fuck-off gate, and I forgot to put my pole-vaulting stick in my briefcase this morning.'

'My simple darling,' said Phyllie in her very best patronise-the-class tone. '*You ring the bell.*'

'And what if no one's home?'

'...Then you'll have to be punished,' she answered.

'Oh goody gumdrops. I was rather thinking a spot of *spanking* this evening. Leading to a course of Virginia.'

'I'm afraid Virginia's off the menu for a couple of nights, Rog. We didn't use enough baby lotion – I've been bleeding like a butchered *baboon*. I've got jamrags front and back at the mo. I'm padded like an American football player.'

Exiting the office and intending to thank Sandra for allowing her to use the Head's phone, she was shocked to find the Head, her manager, right outside the door in the outer office.

'Alistair! You made me jump!'

'Not half as much as you've put even more white hairs in my beard, Miss Reydman.'

Phyllie suffered a churning in her stomach. Trying desperately to sound light and breezy, she said, 'I hope you didn't have to hear too much of that phone conversation.'

'Only the last part, Miss Reydman,' Alistair replied. 'You

told Sandra you had a plumbing issue, but that wasn't *quite* the sort of thing I pictured.'

'Oh Christ. Sorry. It's not what…'

'It's not what it sounded like. I'm sure it's not. I *hope* it's not anyway. But I can't interfere with *that*: nor would I want to. But what I *will* say is this: make personal calls on your own time, Phyllie. Do I make myself clear?'

'As crystal,' Phyllie told him, a blush surging north, up from her chest to her face.

Alistair entered his office and slammed the door.

4.

Dorota was waiting at the head of the steps leading up to her front door. She gave Roger a crisp wave as he drove closer; Roger waved back and a few seconds later shushed the engine. Stretching out of the Saab, he thanked her for letting him in.

'Vig's off shooting with Curtis,' she informed him.

'Shooting? With a gun?'

'Presumably. I can't think of a better instrument, can you?'

The thought of a gun appealed to Roger. It wasn't so much that he wanted to use one, or even that he knew how (he did not); it was more that if Don cut up rough, the presence of a firearm might take some of the wind from the man's sails.

'You have guns?' Roger wanted to clarify.

'Not yet; I think Vig'll get one eventually. They're at Broomfields – the shooting club… Roger, what's this all about?'

As mindful as possible of any sense of loyalty that Dorota might have towards Don, Roger explained the reason for his visit, there outside the house, with a turbid sky scaly with clouds overhead – a cosmos-sized fish that had evolved to speak one word: *rain*.

'Let's go,' Dorota decided. 'Right now.'

'...You don't want to wait for Vig?'

'Why? Don Bridges is an old man – between the two of us? He won't know how many different *ways* his arse has been kicked. And Vig might be hours: he only left at two. And if there *is* a girl in there – Jiminy Christmas! He might be starving her!' Dorota took off at a fair clip. Calling over her shoulder she added: 'Besides, it might be pissing down in twenty minutes and I'm a girl who doesn't like to get her hair wet.'

For a split-split-second, Roger's heart hastened; he wondered if he might be in love. As Dorota galloped away from him, Roger locked in a memory of her (for future masturbatory material) – her buttocks mounted and muscular in a pair of tight white jeans; the bagginess of a lumberjack shirt (probably Vig's originally); the rippling zigzags of her strawberry blonde hair – and then he was in, if not exactly hot, then at least lukewarm pursuit. He wanted to stay behind her to watch her Khyber.

They entered the woods, and immediately the quality of sound was different: pressed, harried, anxious. The light too: something squinty, horrid and ancient. Or such, at least, were Roger's initial impressions. And in truth he was far from comfortable. The ground underfoot was springy; it made him think (absurdly, surely) of the misdemeanour of squashing frogs. With every single step he was pulverising a rotund amphibian – into the ground. The thought was hideous; it made Roger grin. He pressed his muscles on, picking up the pace in Dorota's slipstream.

The cabin was small, weather-whipped and incongruous (Roger thought) – out of place among all these spruce and poplars, the elevated bonnets of which sponged up what existed of the afternoon's sun. For the first time it occurred to Roger that Don might not be inside, and he had no appetite for kicking down the man's door or breaking a window. 'Innocent until proven guilty' was literal, beanshoot-eating anorak-wearing bullshit, as everyone knew, but Roger had no intention of bruising a shoulder or earning himself so much as a hangnail. He'd go home. If Don wasn't home, *he'd* go home.

Don was home.

Dorota knocked: small pale fist to brown-painted wood (streaked with white wormy lengths of bird poop): and Don opened the door, something quizzical and perturbed on his face.

Declining the opportunity to sweeten the pill by one granule, Dorota asked, 'Do you have a child in there?'

Don blinked. 'A *child*, Miss?'

'A child. Do you have one?'

'Well no, Miss. The wife and I weren't offered the Lord's grace on that score, though it would've been a blessing, sure and true... May I ask what you and Mr Billie would be referring to?'

Impressed that the birdkeeper had remembered his name, Roger said, 'A couple of kids the other night – they heard crying from in here. A child.'

When Don smiled, his face cracked into a twoscore of isosceles triangles. 'I heard about the twins' spirit of adventure, sir. I can assure you it was nothing in here, but you'd be welcome to take a look if it would soothe the itch on your skin. It wouldn't take long.' As a gesture of goodwill Don stepped aside from the doorway. 'A small lounge, a small bedroom, a small khazi, a small kitchen: take you all of forty seconds to explore my domain, it would, sir.'

'That won't be ness –' Roger began.

'Thank you, Don,' said Dorota, stepping over the threshold and wiping her heels on a mat that read IT AIN'T MUCH BUT IT'S HOME TO ME.

The estimate of forty seconds proved conservative. The inspection conducted by Dorota and Roger took half that. And was fruitless. Less than two minutes after arriving, the two of them were back on their way through the woods, towards the house, their tails not wagging, their voices muted.

5.

'I think some things were said that we didn't mean.'

'Not by me, sir.'

'Well, allow me to refresh you memory, Don. You said, quote unquote, if I called you Donald Duck again you would shatter my knees.'

'I did indeed.'

'You *did* say that? You remember?'

'Sir, it wasn't me who was drunk that evening. I remember everything.'

'... Well, this is a turn-up, I must say. I had it in mind that you'd be grovelling for an apology.'

'To a cunt like you, sir? You must be drunk again. There's not a chance.'

'All right then... Donald Duck.'

Don sprang up out of his favourite chair and grabbed the mallet from the table. He bounded into the kitchen and swung the mallet at Eastlight's knees.

The effect was remarkable. Not only did the bones in his victim's left knee disintegrate, *the entire leg exploded.*

Blood, bone and remnants of trousers formed a blizzard in Don's home.

Don swung again, this time at Eastlight's head. The head was knocked clean off the shoulders. Then the torso caught fire – and Don woke up.

'Bloody hellfire,' he muttered; and the dream's sticky burrs stayed with his brain as he unlocked the back door and bare-footed it bollock naked across the clearing to his spot to piss.

Looking up as he peed, he saw the moon in tortured frag-
ments, cracked open by branches that were still in a rare absence
of breeze. Sometimes he fancied that he could hear the moon:
he could hear it as it sang, as it wept. Tonight, however (or this
morning, to be accurate) it was as silent as a tomb; it was keeping
mum.

Don had thought of telling Vig and Dorota what he'd said
to Charlie Eastlight at the barbecue – the threat he'd made. Such
was the guilt he felt at having made the threat, and at not apolo-
gising in the aftermath, that his sleep was being affected. Not
badly; but a bit. (He had never been a talented sleeper, not since
his stable boy days – and certainly not since the halcyon days of
his first big wins in the saddle.) Days later, would a full confession
be helpful, or would it rake up old ground? If Eastlight had intended to retaliate, wouldn't he have done so by now?

No, Don answered himself; not if his style of retaliation
went further than a ratting phone call to Vig and Dorota. And
Don couldn't help thinking that a grassing-up was not Charlie's
style.

Don could not remember if he had thought Eastlight capable of wrongdoing from the *very first* second he'd met him, but
it wasn't long afterwards, if not.

It takes one to know one, Don thought, slipping back into
the cabin for the purpose of dressing. It didn't matter that the
luminous hands on his alarm clock said 3:25: the Devil made
work for idle hands; there was always something productive to do.

6.

Don closed his eyes and lifted the little girl out of the emergency hideyhole: not her regular hole under the rug in the kitch-
en, but the hole that enveloped the septic tank. He had sensed

their approach. After all these years, if he didn't know the woods, what *did* he know? Their arrival had silenced birds; it had created its own sounds, its own energies. So Don had removed her from the kitchen, taken her outside. For the little girl, perhaps it was a day out. Don might hide her with the septic tank more often, even though he remained confident that no one else would come to pry.

NIGHT PURSUIT

1.

Pretending that he was working on another assignment for college, Yasser had spent every available minute on the internet, researching how to be a private detective. Was he worried? Worried wasn't the word: Yasser was terrified. He thought it ironic that he had driven into a travellers' camp and taken a baby away with him, suffering held-in-check but nonetheless minor discomfort; yet the thought of handing Maggie back her financial retainer broke him out in the night sweats. And not just because he'd already spent it: Yasser was frightened of the sense of failure, true, but in an acknowledgement of a rare racial slur, he was also frightened of being looked down on by a people over whom he felt ethnically and morally superior.

The very real problem, however, was that he didn't have a clue how to proceed. Aware that sulking in his bedroom wouldn't cut it, Yasser had spent time and petrol (and chewed-up, spat-out fingernails) on interviewing people around the camp, fishing with the least nutritious of bait, against Maggie's explicit wishes and advice. She told him he'd learn fuck all there: and he had! He had learned a great big handsome *pile* of fuck all.

In addition he had interviewed people in Hockliffe – or he'd tried to. At least the residents of the camp had got wind of the fact that Yasser was present for a good reason, and had more or less cooperated with a suitable expression on their faces. (A message about not stealing his hubcaps, letting down his tyres, scratching his paintwork, or setting fire to his vehicle seemed to have gone around as well.) The residents of Hockliffe were of a different stripe. Suspicious, for one thing: wary that this Asian lad would want to know anything more than directions to one of the pubs – or even to Woburn, to Milton Keynes. For another thing, they were largely clueless about the abduction anyway. While standing outside the CostShop, in the rain, willing neighbours to have an inkling of what he was talking about (and urging himself to formulate a better interviewee selection process), Yasser thought that there must be more to life than this. More than several times he had almost phoned Maggie: to tell her to sod it, she could have back the wonga: it wasn't worth catching his death of cold for.

Capping each of these moments of doubt, however, had been a picture in Yasser's mind: an image so clear that he might well have seen it in a photograph sometime. A baby in a dimly-lit room, was what he saw. The baby cried. Hungry, dirtied and visibly ill, Maggie's child had been stolen and then – apparently – abandoned, the deed completed, the action performed. Left to weep alone.

He had to find Maggie's child. It had stopped being anything to do with choice.

As Yasser closed down the machine, there was a knock on his bedroom door. The caller could only be one person (because Mum rarely knocked, and Dad never climbed the stairs, he just bellowed out Yasser's name from the front door when he needed him). Yasser said, '*Entrez-vous*' and one of his cousins, Shyleen, opened the door.

'Not interrupting anything, I hope,' she said.

'I was working,' Yasser told her.

'At least you kept your trousers on.' She sat on the edge

of Yasser's narrow bed – the very same bed on which they had undressed one another during Ramadam two years earlier. Shyleen was the second cousin who had helped Yasser with Maggie's address when he gave her the licence plate number of the truck belonging to Maggie's father.

Yasser resisted the urge to argue with Shyleen, as they had as children and even as adolescents. A petty argument was what had led to the removal of one another's clothes, and to the subsequent pregnancy scare that had turned to smoke but which had felt real enough – *dangerously* real enough – at the time. 'How's it going down there?' Yasser asked her. 'Am I wanted?'

'Only by me… Oh your *face*.' Shyleen laughed. 'I'm teasing. They didn't send me to fetch you, Yass, don't worry. I just couldn't deal with any more *sympathy*. It's like too much chocolate.'

'Yeah. About that…' Yasser started.

'Don't. I know.' The young woman held up her hands but she was not looking at her cousin.

Yasser nodded. He was grateful that she had turned away. He had never been good with news of the illness of others; and he was no more competent now than he had been, two evenings earlier, when Shyleen's mother had phoned to inform the family that her daughter had been diagnosed with an ovarine tumour of a polysyllabic name. Hearing that Shyleen had already sickened of sympathy made Yasser feel guilty but relieved.

Directly after dinner, when his mother had asked the girl's parents a question involving the word *prognosis*, Yasser had excused himself from the table, saying that he had homework to complete in his room.

'Is there any other topic of conversation?' he asked. 'Or are they…'

'It's all me.' Shyleen laughed again.

'…So what do you wanna do, while they're otherwise

engaged?'

'You wouldn't dare!'

'You reckon? You wouldn't *believe* what I've done in the last fortnight.'

'Is that a boast, Yass?' Shyleen asked, turning to face him with a distant smile on his face.

Yasser considered the question. *Was* he boasting? Certainly it didn't feel that way; but it *did* feel as it had felt while talking to Tim Branston in one of the college's cafes – as though he would be glad to unburden himself of the story so far, to find a new witness; and as though, once he'd reached a particular point in the telling, he would become frightened to finish what he'd started. The weight of that untold would crush his chest; it would spill his innards everywhere.

So he told her.

2.

And something nagged at Yasser while he told her. Something plucked at Yasser's consciousness, time after time, as sentence followed sentence.

Tommy.

Tommy the so-called Brazilian.

Yasser could not shake the opinion that Tommy was involved – was, in fact, knee-deep in shit when it came to this project and its prospects – and when at last, a fortnight having elapsed, he confessed this suspicion to Shyleen on the phone, his cousin's predictable and refreshing resourcefulness arrived like a cool breeze on a pig farm.

'Why don't you follow him around?' she suggested. 'Hey, I'll come with you! When I'm not at work, of course... We'll have a bit of fun on our stakeout!'

'…Every night?'

'Or every day. Depending on our busy social schedules.'

'But he'll see us!'

Shyleen sighed into Yasser's ear. 'Oh *do* grow a pair of balls, Yass,' she concluded.

3.

Were it not for Shyleen's illness, the confession might not have happened; but by spraying a jet of Yasser's anti-perspirant into her face, she managed to acquire two red eyes that gave her parents (and Yasser's parents) the impression that she had been crying. When she announced that she and Yasser were going out for a drive, she was not so much as asked where. If the children had something to discuss, they deserved a bit of privacy with which to do so. 'But no pubs!' was Shyleen's father's parting shot – his only word of counsel.

'Are you sure you don't want to go in mine?' Yasser asked her, on the pavement.

'What good would that do?' Shyleen replied. 'They *know* your car.'

'Who do?'

'The gyppos!' She got in the driver's side and gunned the engine.

Yasser got in on the passenger's side.

'Belt up, boy! Clunk click for every trip innit!' Shyleen barked at him in an impersonation of his own mother's heavily-accented English. Then she laughed. And accelerated.

'Slow down, Shy!'

Shyleen was doing fifty by the end of the road.

'Oh *grow* a pair for fuck's sake,' Shyleen told him. Without checking for oncoming traffic, she pulled them out onto the main vein through Bury Park (a late bus honked its horn). 'Or I'll turn my lights off as well. That'll shit you up!'

She laughed as she ran a red light.

4.

Nor did appeals to common sense or rationality find a favourable ear.

'They'll expect us back,' Yasser tried, having lost faith in his own courage for the moment. 'We haven't got time, Shy.'

'Oh *we* haven't got time!' Shyleen chuckled. '*I'm* the one with fanny rot! *I'm* the one going under the knife! They'll allow us a moonlight flit.'

'It's not a moonlit night,' Yasser countered, sounding grumpy.

'And don't sulk. Or you won't see it again, boy, or wiggle your wand…'

'Not in my mum's voice. Please!'

Shyleen laughed once more, and she gunned her car towards the roundabout. 'Dunstable or Houghton Regis?' she asked. 'Which is faster?'

'Same difference.' Yasser sighed. 'But there are speed traps going into Dunstable.'

'Houghton Regis it is!'

Earning a beep from another driver, Shyleen lanced over into the other lane and indicated right (a rare courteous touch for the road's other users); with the speedo showing seventy, she barrelled the two of them down Poynters Road. Then she turned on the CD player. Shaggy was halfway through 'Mr Boombastic' and Shyleen joined him on the chorus.

5.

'Now what?' Yasser asked her.

'Are you still sulking?'

'No… I wasn't *sulking*.'

'You're sulking *now*.'

'I am not sulking now,' Yasser retorted. 'I happen to be a worried man.'

Shyleen snorted. '*You're* worried!'

'I know. But we shouldn't be here, Shy, it's not safe.'

She turned to him in the car and widened her eyes in mock-horror. 'Do those cows get a *bloodlust after dark?*'

'Yeah they do, actually. It's like *Dawn of the Fucking Dead* around here. Except with cows.'

When Shyleen laughed, this time Yasser joined her; he couldn't help himself. Joking aside, the road outside the camp was eerie by night, but this was a fact that his laughter suppressed for a few seconds.

'Do you think they'd be welcoming,' Shyleen asked, 'if we went in?'

'A moot point,' Yasser told her, 'because we're not *going* in. They'll all be asleep anyway, just like we should be.'

'Do you have work to do tomorrow?'

'No.'

'Or college?'

'No.'

'Then cultivate a growth of *cajones*, ho. We've only just got here.'

'Please, Shy – not the voice. Let's go back, eh? I mean… what's in it for you? Sitting in a layby in the middle of nowhere…'

'With no one to watch us, eh Yass? Does that put any thoughts in your head?'

'Christ… Well we'd have to be quick.'

'Now don't start getting sentimental on a poor girl…'

Yasser looked to the left and right. The empty road was black as soot; there was no one and there was nothing, and that was all.

Nevertheless, Yasser remained cautiously nervous. 'They'll know,' he said.

'Our parents or the gyppos?'

'Our parents. Please don't call em gyppos.'

'Oh sorry, I forgot all the *friendships* you've made.' Shyleen leaned towards him. 'Tell me, Yasser,' she whispered. 'Are my words of sarcasm getting you motivated?'

Yasser smiled. 'They are, a bit,' he admitted. He lowered his jeans zip. When he produced it, he was about halfway hard; and this was good enough for his kissing cousin. She lowered her mouth onto him, to see what she could do about the shortfall.

But then Yasser saw Tommy the Brazilian's truck.

6.

The vehicle turned out of the camp, its headlights bleaching the plants and hedges until it had straightened up. Now it approached Shyleen's car, and the lovers within. Yasser tensed. Shyleen wouldn't be seen – her head was below the windscreen – but Yasser's face was in the Brazilian's spotlights. With no better option available, Yasser ducked slightly and raised his hands to cover his features.

The Brazilian drove past.

Yasser relaxed.

'What is it, Yass?' Shyleen enquired from his lap.

'That was Tommy.'

'Hurrah for Tommy.'

'Well, where's he *going* at this time of night?'

Shyleen sounded indignant. 'Maybe he's going to get a blowjob. You *could* pay me some attention, you know, Yass.'

'Sorry.' But he felt his erection dwindle.

Shyleen sat up straight. 'You've lost that loving feeling,' she announced.

Tucking his slim pickings back into his jeans, Yasser said, 'The pub? A pub somewhere?'

'Us or him?' Shyleen was angry. She started the car and be-gan an accurate three-point turn, not speaking for a few seconds.

'Well, this was kinda your idea,' Yasser told her.

'Can't believe I lost out to a pikey thug,' Shyleen muttered.

'*What?*'

'I'll follow him,' she continued.

7.

If the journey out of Luton this evening had been marked (for Yasser) by a fear of the maniacal travelling velocity (and the shadowing terrors of car crash and speeding ticket), the journey back in the direction they'd come, trailing Tommy, was marked by alternative slabs of disquiet. Stay too far behind and they'd lose him. Get too close and he'd know that he was being followed. For Yasser, the perfect trailing distance (a wholly unknown qual-ity) kept changing in his mind; he was a mile past being surprised that Shyleen could drive at a sensible velocity, and the nerves were playing havoc with his gut, with his groin.

Why was Tommy driving towards Luton? This was the question uppermost on Yasser's mind: posing it aloud had not helped one bit. 'Maybe he's going to see *you*,' Shyleen had told him. Huffily Yasser had informed her not to make jokes, and she'd replied that she wasn't joking.

Maybe he was. Maybe Tommy the Brazilian was *en route* to

Bury Park, with one thing on his mind: to use that drum of petrol in an act of arson, once and for all. On Yasser's car? On Yasser's *house*? Where else could he be going but Luton? He'd already passed the turnings off for everywhere else...

'He's going to the motorway,' Shyleen seemed to promise.

'He's going to the airport,' Yasser hoped.

As it would turn out, Tommy was leading them to neither destination, although for the moment, with the right-hand indicator blinking as the truck pulled up to the Tesco roundabout, the second possibility still appeared valid. The airport was in this direction.

'There are no flights after ten,' said Shyleen. 'We signed the petition.'

'It might've landed already. He's picking someone up.' Yasser fidgeted in the passenger seat. 'You'll have to pull back a bit – there's not enough traffic.'

Indeed, the bypass road was hardly being used. If Tommy hadn't noticed them so far, now might be a good time for him to start. There were only so many headlights, surely, that he could ignore.

Neither Yasser nor Shyleen said much when Tommy led them onto the ring road, away from the train station (a third option that neither of them had taken seriously). The airport remained plausible as a destination: both of the pursuers, by this point, had all but taken for granted that this was where they were headed, when Tommy turned left and used the bus lane to move closer to the High Street, the shopping centre, the church, or –

'The University?' Yasser wondered aloud.

'Yeah, one of those midnight lectures they're so famous for.'

The ludicrousness was not lost on Yasser either... but this *was* the way they were going, and beyond the University's main building, what was there?

'Hang back a bit,' said Yasser. 'I think he's onto us – he's taking us in a circle.'

'What circle, Yass?' Shyleen answered. 'He could've done that around Dunstable.'

'He wasn't *sure* around Dunstable.'

'We've come this far,' Shyleen added in a defiant tone. 'I'm not going home without an *answer.*'

Yasser half-sighed and half-chuckled. 'Had a feeling you were gonna say that,' he told her.

Surprising the cousins, Tommy pulled into a small parking area outside an eight-storey block of flats that displayed the University's logo. It was student accommodation.

'About that midnight lecture,' Yasser said quietly.

Shyleen did not pull into the parking area. On the off-chance that they had been lucky so far, she did not wish to stretch that streak of good fortune until it twanged. She parked by the kerb and killed the engine.

'What's he want with *students?*' Yasser wondered.

'Here.' Shyleen handed him the keyring. 'Keep the engine running, and if *I'm* running when you see me next, get us the fuck out of here.'

'You're winding me up, Shy,' Yasser told her with a shake of the head but little conviction. 'You're not going in there on your own.'

'What, a student dorm? You think they're killing goats in a pentagon of chicken feathers?' She opened her door. 'There's no time to argue, I need to see where he's going – and he's never met me before.'

'I don't know, Shy…'

'Neither do I, but what could happen? He asks me if I was following him, I say no… I *live* here for all he's aware.'

And she was gone. Yasser's vision followed her plump backside across the car park and towards a doorway crowned with a sign reading B Block. The door was still closing slowly and Shyleen caught it: Tommy had gained entrance to the building by buzzing up – he held no key but he did know someone inside.

Suddenly Yasser was alone; it felt strange. He walked around the front of Shyleen's car and got into the driver's seat; he inserted the ignition key and turned the stereo that they'd soon turned off at the start of the chase back on again. The volume was too high for stationary listening, but as a genre selection modish R&B would do. Lowering the volume, Yasser settled down to wait for Shyleen's reappearance, his eyesight locked on the B Block front door. When he checked his mobile he found that he had missed no calls – so far he and Shyleen had not been classed as missing or out too late. He wasn't sure if this made him feel better or worse. He decided on worse.

8.

The distance between Shyleen's parked car and the entrance to B Block was not great – a matter of fifteen metres, tops – but it was sufficient, at night-time, for Yasser to have been unaware that Tommy had made a sartorial effort to dress up for his evening out. While he might not have hit the town booted and suited, or with a tux and tie, he had at least donned a better class of smart-casual dress than Yasser had yet to see him in; and because Yasser had not said anything along these lines, Shyleen had formed a mental wardrobe for Tommy that did not match the clothes worn by the man leaking cologne in the Student Hall entrance foyer. Additionally, in the darkness of the car park, Shyleen had been unable to fix the man's physical dimensions either. The man in the foyer, his back to her approach as he waited for the lift, was shorter but broader than she had made him from

Yasser's story, and Shyleen wondered if this was a different man altogether. If the real mark had slipped into the lift in the few seconds that Shyleen had needed to cross the car park, he might have reached any of the six or eight storeys by now; those seconds could have spelt the end of it, and this guy in grey slacks and a navy blue jacket, with his permafrost-hued hair slicked back and with a bucket of aftershave seeping in and out of his pores, could have come from any of the rooms on the ground floor.

Shyleen came to a halt a few metres behind him. Smiling over his shoulder in a reptile fashion (she conjectured), the man offered her a good evening, then went back to perusing the strip of lights above the lift's doors. He didn't give a toss who she was. In Shyleen's mind this meant that he didn't live here. Having lived all her life in the Bury Park terraces, the knowledge of one's neighbours was in the blood; strangers wore extremely different clothes.

The doors opened and two male students – a black boy in a wheelchair and a white boy in a perm – came out. With a slight bow and a theatrical flourish, Tommy indicated that Shyleen was free to proceed him into the soup-smelling box. Standing by the buttons, Tommy asked Shyleen, 'Where to?'

'The eighth.'

Tommy pressed 3 and then 8.

'I hope you don't mind me saying,' said Shyleen, 'but we've had a burglary – we've all promised to question any visitors.'

'Oh?'

'If you don't mind, of course.'

Tommy faced her. 'I'm a thief, is that it?' he asked, a smirk decorating his features.

'We've promised to question any visitors,' Shyleen repeated. She hoped that she didn't sound as nervous as she felt.

'Well go on then. Question away.'

Shyleen took a breath. 'Do you mind telling me who you're here to see?' she said.

'The name's Flowers. Joseph Flowers – Joe to his friends. A little *game* going, see?'

'A game?'

'Texas Hold'em… Poker. Is that okay with the welcoming committee and the sentry box?'

Shyleen shrugged. 'Sure. What room does he have?'

'Shouldn't I be asking *you* that?'

'Why?'

'Because *you're* a visitor too.'

Shyleen stiffened. 'What makes you say that?'

Tommy smirked. 'You'd never pass for male in a thousand years,' he told her. 'Block B is a male-only establishment. So perhaps you might say where *you're* going. For reasons of security, like.'

'To see my boyfriend.'

'The name being?'

'Wafiq,' Shyleen plucked from the air.

'Oh Wafiq. Like Yasser's uncle.'

'…Who's Yasser?'

'Never mind, Miss.' The doors opened at the third floor. Tommy took a step out onto the corridor, the smile he wore both victorious and oleaginous. 'Don't play poker yourself.'

'I won't.'

'No poker face, see, Miss. There's no such thing as a male-only block on this campus. That's just me chatten the bollocks. And if you're going to follow people from their home to a hand of cards – this is just a tip – have the good sense not to park *outside their fucking camp*… Tell the boy I'm disappointed, and so will Maggie be, I'd guess. We'd asked for a pro.'

The lift doors closed.

9.

'He's in there gambling. He's playing poker.'

Yasser nodded.

'And he knows it's you in the car.'

Yasser flinched.

'It's time to go home, Yass. The Pikey's winning or losing, but he's not doing anything wrong. We might as well call it a night. Besides, I'm hungry and I've work in the morning.'

Yasser did not need to tell her how much she'd changed her tune. He was busy trying to plan what to say to Maggie the next time he saw her.

'This is all going tits up,' he said.

'Drive me home, James,' Shyleen answered in her poshest voice. She ran her fingers through her hair; a second later she expressed disgust at the harvest that they'd gathered. 'My hair's falling out already,' she said. 'I haven't even started my treatment!'

Yasser drove Shyleen back to his parents' house and let her in. Shyleen and her parents left ten minutes later (Shyleen declined the offer of a fifth cup of tea), and Yasser announced that he was turning in for the night. In his room he sulked and brooded; he lay on top of the duvet, with flies buzzing in his brain. He had not undressed. He tried to talk himself out of going back to the camp, to talk to Maggie; the urge to drive, however, was upon him, despite the hour. Tommy the Brazilian would be tied up with his poker game for hours: so Yasser decided. This was his overwhelming impression of card showdowns: that they lasted for ages. Maggie would be asleep, or at least in bed. Would her father be present? Why wouldn't he be? It was where he lived, after all...

Yasser sighed and sat up. He could hear his father snoring in the next room. Clutching his car keys, he crept across the landing and down the stairs. He unlocked the front door, and the air outside was cold and smelt of diesel.

10.

Yasser may have paid visits to the camp in the course of his investigation, but they had made him no friend of the dog called Excalibur. As Yasser walked the driveway, having left the car in the lane outside, he fantasised that he'd be able to creep along without awakening the hound that slept chained to its master's caravan near the entrance. He was wrong. His assumption was loudly incorrect. Yasser could not help kicking up gravel – he'd banked on this much as inevitable – but he'd imagined it preferable to the noise of his engine waking up the camp's residents at this hour. Excalibur, however, had but one important task to perform: to protect the camp; and Yasser had scarcely set foot on the travellers' land before its highpitched barking began to shred the fabric of the night. Yasser flinched – and ran.

He ran as fast as he could towards Maggie's home. Behind him, straining against its shackles, the dog all but throttled itself as it yapped and snapped out at the invisible intruders: Yasser had already sprinted past.

Some of the caravans and trailers had lights on within. But were they switched on now, or had they been illuminated *before* the dog's protestations?

No way of knowing.

Yasser ran until he felt distanced and nauseous. Up ahead was Maggie's caravan, with the blue painted moon on the side the same size as the pollution-pastelled mauve one overhead, to the rear of the camp. Yasser ran. Two moons drawing him on: a duel of orbits. No shouts. No bellows from behind… *Piece of piss… make it…*

And this was when the bullet hit him on the left side of his forehead.

Yasser was knocked to the right. Although his momentum carried him for a few more strides, the blow to his temple had been considerable and his knees and thighs weakened. Stumbling like a drunk, Yasser tried to yell Maggie's name; he collapsed to his knees. Not only could he sense blood pooling down the left side of his face, he could smell it too; the aroma was stronger than that of paint, chip fat and diesel, which perfumed the camp customarily, Yasser had long since discovered.

The stars that he saw were not in the oxblood sky; they were in Yasser's head, leaking out for him to see. The word *concussion* echoed around his skull on a sound like bird wings flapping. The problem was, right at this moment Yasser did not know what concussion meant – not the word and not the condition. He was aware that he'd been shot, but he was too busy reeling from the pain to be aware of anything else. The fact that he had heard no gun report – no bang – seemed irrelevant: he'd been shot in the head and he would die on these filthy wankers' soil; this was all that he was sure of.

He fell forward. *Yet...* he tried to think; *and yet...* His hands splayed out before him, to soften contact with the road. And *yet*: he *had* heard something. Not a gun... Yasser fell onto his front, the palms of his hands scraped and scratched on the road's surface. A sound of something metal as it had hit the tarmac... Something dropped. Something *thrown?*

Breathing huskily, shallowly, Yasser educated himself at speed. If someone had shot him, there must be a shooter. Behind him. *Turn around.*

'Get up, you cont,' a voice demanded, close to the soles of the expensive trainers that had made this entire escapade seem such a tickle. 'Get up!'

Yasser's right foot took a kick.

'I won't tell you again, boy,' the voice impatient.

I'm not dead. I can roll over. If he's talking to me, I'm not dead.

The pain in Yasser's temple had turned effervescent, but Yasser had preferred the solid blast. Pain was information. A solid blast of pain he could read. This *fizzing* he didn't know what to do with.

As he rolled over onto his back, the voice spoke again, almost merrily, triumphantly.

'Helluva focken shot, eh son? Trew it like the dagger guy at the circus: you know the girl on the wheel, in her spangling focken gymslip.'

And the cunt started laughing.

Yasser objected to his assailant's merriment even more than to the assault itself. Sitting up in one movement, he waited out his vision as it swam through uncertainties, blurred lines and milky haloes to solid objects; and in a few seconds he squinted to see who had addressed him.

The light was only so-so. Moonlight helped, naturally, and there were patches of orange illumination spilling from makeshift streetlamps and from caravans. It was far from perfect. Nonetheless, Yasser recognised the man who was speaking.

'Max.'

'Helluva *shot*, eh?'

Yasser dared to prod his wound with a cautious forefinger. He inspected the tip: an apple core of blood, nothing more. The blood streaming over the hillock of his cheek had been in his imagination.

'The fuck d'you do that for?' Yasser asked.

'He comes rattling onto our land and asks a bollocks question like that! Maybe you'd like to ask your girlfriend that question.'

Yasser examined the state of his palms. 'Maggie's not my girlfriend,' he said.

'I don't mean Maggie. I mean the Paki girl in the car with you. Chasing Tommy as the man does an honest evening's work, if you don't mind.'

'He's playing cards. Jesus. That *hurt*, Max.'

'The sting's your pride. Now get up, y'cont.'

Yasser struggled to his feet. 'He phoned you.'

'Of course he phoned me. Are you under the impression that we're still in the seventeenth focken century and don't own a phone? Or is it the Pikey Telekinesis you'll be chatten?'

'What was it? What did you throw?' Yasser asked, rubbing his head.

The man called Max was the third man who had met Yasser on the latter's first visit to the camp. Max, Tommy and Maggie's father had stood near Yasser's car and tapped tools into their palms.

What had it been *this* time?

Max held out his right arm. In his fist was a spanner.

'*Devil* of a focken shot!'

'There was no need,' Yasser complained.

'He said you'd be coming.'

'The cunt's a psychic. There was *no need*.'

Max shrugged. 'Uninvited on a man's land? *I'd* say there was a need… Now tell me what you had in mind with Maggie.'

'Surely that's between me and her,' said Yasser.

'She and I,' said Max. 'And I won't ask you one more time. Evan a man like me gets hungry for his bed eventually.'

Yasser smiled. 'What was the question?'

Max stepped forward. 'Don't play me for a cont, son,' he warned.

Some more lights twinkled on around them, and suddenly Yasser felt more scared than he had in a long time. The dog had ceased barking, he noted.

They were waiting for me.

Now they emerge from their caravans.

However, nothing of the sort occurred. Fingering the place where the chucked spanner had struck his head, Yasser turned on his expensive heels and continued to walk towards Maggie's caravan. An instant of worry about the car flashed briefly (it would surely be trashed) but he ignored it. He moseyed on and Max said nothing.

But the cunt was laughing. Like a man with a bellyful of gas, he was laughing, a jolly, mirthful Santa for the tourists – the wanker. His laughs were like bullets into Yasser's arse. Not even into his back: straight into his muscular butt.

Nerves awash with adrenalin, Yasser knocked on Maggie's door, and it opened in less than five seconds. *I've been expecting you,* Yasser anticipated Maggie to say; but he didn't hear this.

'What the hell are you up to, Yasser?' Maggie's father asked, tying up the belt on his dressing-gown.

11.

Responding to a silent cue that Yasser did not intercept (a dart of Maggie's eyes, perhaps), Maggie's father had dressed and taken his leave of the caravan straight away. Or nearly: he had taken the precaution of informing Yasser that he was an inconsiderate twat before he'd pulled a leather coat on over his dressing-gown. He'd completed the look with a long red scarf and a pair of muddied wellies. The door had slammed; and though he had not said where he was going, Yasser had guessed that the destination would be Max's. They would want to review tonight's welcoming procedures.

Now, Yasser was alone with Maggie. The lights were on and two windows were ajar, and yet it felt close, cramped and hot

– closer, more cramped and hotter than it usually did.

'Would you want some tea?' Maggie asked him. She was filling the kettle.

Despite the fact that Yasser knew Maggie's tea to be on the verge of undrinkable – a wholly discredited brew – the offer at least felt like an invitation to a normal party. A mug of the foul stuff would at least seem friendly.

Yasser nodded his head. As he had on a score of occasions, he sat down near the table, but on this occasion the back of one chair had been reclined and was strewn with a sleeping bag, a pillow and a couple of ratty grey Fire Brigade blankets. Evidently this was where Maggie's father laid his head of an evening. Partly out of respect, partly for a reason that Yasser failed to decode, he made sure that he did not sit on the bedclothes.

He watched Maggie as she prepared their tea. She was dressed in a purple dressing-gown of her own, cinched tightly at the waist. Her hair was a bedraggled nest of snoozy vipers, and about her was a faint aroma of curdled perfume; as she poured steaming water into two cups, Yasser attempted to deduce if she was wearing anything under the dressing-gown. She certainly had nothing on her slightly sooty feet... And perhaps it was an after effect of the hormonal tug that contact with his cousin customarily provided him with, but Yasser experienced the thrill of a horny recognition of Maggie's rough diamond appeal. Unless it was relief, pure and simple: a half-hearted erotic reaction to having made it here tonight.

Then again, it might be brain damage.

Whatever the impetus, as Yasser allowed himself to relax, he was conscious of the inspissation in his boxers.

Maggie handed him a mug. 'You're gonna have a shiner,' she told him. She pointed to the left side of her brow. 'A black eye.'

Yasser knew what a shiner was. All he could do was nod his

head, and Maggie sat on the opposite side of the table.

'Nice of you to call,' she said softly; she sipped her tea.

Having nothing to offer of his own, Yasser sipped as well. The wound to his temple throbbed on the offbeat to the pulse in his groin.

Maggie wanted to talk, however. She test drove another elicitation. 'You were bacon bushed, boy,' she said, grinning.

It worked.

'I was what?'

'It's an old joke. Soldiers in the jungle somewhere, and they're warned: Don't go to the bacon bush, lads. But boys will be boys, as you well know; and two go out to find the bacon bush. And of course it grabs em and drags em in, never to be seen again. So two more venture out to rescue the first two – and they're grabbed and pulled in. Munch munch. And so it goes... until the squad commander enlists some sort of local expert, who says: No. That ain't a bacon bush. That's an '*ambush*.'

Yasser wrinkled his nose. 'Yeah.'

'A *ham* bush, you see...'

Yasser nodded. 'Yeah, I get it, Maggie. What the fuck's going on?'

'You're asking *me*?'

'Yeah, I'm asking you, because I've got doubts going through me like shit through a sieve.'

'Nice image; thanks.'

'I'm serious. I'm not getting anywhere finding your child, and what's worse is I can't get any – enthusiasm from anyone, yourself included.'

'I'm paying you, aren't I?'

Yasser looked away. Once more the cat had lost his tongue. Balanced against the deadening notion of there being nothing more to do (his penis had shrunk), the action of sipping a vile beverage seemed delightful. It was something to achieve. And in fact… didn't it taste somewhat better anyway? Could it be that he was getting used to the flavour?

'Is this different tea?' he eventually asked.

'No. Yasser, I don't know why you're here, unless it's just to see me.'

'Then maybe that's it.' Yasser shrugged. 'What time's Tommy likely to be home?'

'He's my neighbour. I don't control him.'

'But based on previous experience.'

Maggie copied Yasser's shrug. 'Four, five… Depends if he's winning. Depends how angry he gets if he's losing.'

'What does that mean?' He gets angry?'

'Well, what do *you* think?' Maggie replied, a little sharply. 'You've seen him.'

'I thought it was a pose. Largely.'

'Well it isn't, largely or small-ly, I can assure you of that. I've seen him do damage, Yasser. Don't make him a friend, whatever you do.'

Yasser smiled. 'Not much chance of that.'

'Well, no; not after your shenanigans tonight, for which he'll want words, by the way… Who was the girl?'

'My cousin.'

'And your cousin's been given the gift of a name, presumably.'

'Shyleen.'

'Pretty name. Pretty girl?'

Yasser nodded. 'She's all right, yeah.'

'Kissing cousins, are you?'

'Once or twice.'

'And you'd like to make that twice a thrice, don't tell me.' Maggie's eyes twinkled with mischief. 'It's all got you going tonight, be honest. You don't think I saw what you boasted in your pants a moment ago but I did. So you're either dreaming of her or me. Tell the truth.'

Yasser made sure that his eyes met Maggie's. 'I was wondering,' he said, his nervousness at bay for the instant, 'what you were wearing under that bathrobe.'

Still smiling, Maggie answered, 'Have you ever been with an older woman?'

Yasser shook his head. The answer was a lie but he believed it would be what Maggie wanted to hear.

'I don't mind if you think of her sometimes,' said Maggie, standing. 'But not now, okay?'

'Okay.'

'The answer's nothing.'

Maggie opened her dressing-gown; she was naked underneath it. With her fists bunched on her hips she was able to keep the gown open for Yasser's eyes.

Less than half a metre from those eyes, Maggie's breasts bobbed in midair, or so it seemed; miniscule rises and falls, in time with their owner's breathing. Her groin had been shaved to a coconut-coloured stubble.

Only a few seconds passed; to Yasser these seconds were feasts of time – he could watch her forever. The stiffening of his penis told him so; the sweeping tingling that sugared the coating of his scrotum during moments of excitement (and not only sexual excitement) told him so too... And yet... And yet her father was who knew how close. Max as well. For all Yasser knew, even Tommy could be outside the front door, fresh from caving in Yasser's windscreen and ready for the next challenge in his diary.

'Give me your hand,' said Maggie.

They all know I'm here, Yasser told himself; in the small hours of the morning. Who'd believe a visit to carry on talks in the abduction summit?

This was one side of the argument. The other side said (firmly): She's a grown woman, Yass. Coming on to you…

Yasser held out his left hand; it trembled only slightly.

Maggie took her hand, twisted it gently at the wrist so that it was palm up, and then, having stepped forward, pressed the palm and fingers up against her vagina, her legs wide apart for a more productive contact.

Her lips felt hot on Yasser's hand; she was damp; she pushed his hand a little harder. When she looked up at the ceiling, Yasser, still sitting, followed the sight of her body skyward, attracted by the undersides of her breasts, the sweep of her throat. All the time his erection drummed in his trousers.

Did she know this? Suddenly she looked down at him, scary-eyed (hopefully) with longing, and said, 'Let me see.'

Yasser made to stand up, but Maggie indicated that he was to remain seated by placing her free hand on his shoulder. Rubbing her wet lips with his left hand, he went through the difficulty of opening his zip with his right. What he produced was three-quarters ready.

'Show me how,' Maggie instructed.

Needing no further invitation, Yasser tweaked his helmet slowly, taking care of that pesky remaining quarter. A light fuzz of sweat had appeared on his brow; it made the wound to his temple sting. His heart was going at it like a Sufi drummer.

'You'll be real man for me, won't you, Yasser?'

'Yes.'

'Good boy.'

And Maggie bent at the waist. The angle was right for her to take his tip into her mouth, but she didn't do so. Instead she teased him with a couple of licks to the underside of his glans.

'But not out here, though, eh? Not where me da sleeps,' she continued.

She led Yasser into the bedroom.

He *had* had a reason for coming here, after all.

UNPATROLLED BORDERS

1.

By telling the tale, Connors had reasoned, he would be led to a border, the crossing of which would take him back to the world as he knew it; where *exactly* he'd end up he was not fussy. Where was possible? Soaking wet in the garden of Number 11: this was fine by Connors. Drugged and addled but otherwise of sound mind, in a hospital bed somewhere: this would do equally as well. Gorged on faith in the logical, to Connors it had seemed like a workable plan: tell it all to exhaust it; tell it all to *make it go away*... So it was that on the second night after shoring up on Toenail Island, with his belly full of unrecognisable berries and his temples ringing under the pull of a few cups of liquor that would put his usual pint of wifebeater lager to shame, he had said to Elvis Leader (also to Chelsea) that he wanted to tell a story. And the three of them had perched by the fire that the human contingent of the trio had built, and Connors had started talking while Elvis kept a nervous eye out on the silently grinding shadows encircling their makeshift camp.

It hadn't worked. The following morning, Connors had woken up confused and alone; the boy and the dog were else-where. Light was thin, and desperate streaks of rain clutched hard to the wind gusts teasing his face. It was cold; and for the first time in as long as he could remember – possibly the first time ever – Connors had screamed. He had screamed until his lungs felt bruised; the only sight that had stopped him was that of Elvis and Chelsea, returning from over a rise, where they'd gone to evacuate their bowels.

Now, once again, they were walking. Mid-morning (as Connors calculated it) had since been and gone, and his stomach complained for sustenance; it was time for some sort of lunch. At the shack on the edge of the harbour township, where they'd eaten the gas-inducing berries, Connors had purchased more of the same, but he had done so in the sure belief that there would be alternative foodstuffs to buy before long. However, up to now, this had not been the case; and Connors had been forced to admit that as they plodded on, stride after weary longing stride, it was looking less likely that an oasis was waiting over the next hill. But what choice did Connors have, but to continue on foot? Another mile. Another five miles... By this point his feet were sore with blisters, his calves burned with the exertion; and yet... Connors could think of no better way than to stroll on in as straight a line as he could manage, in the hope of locating the next township, or the coast on the far side of Toenail Island – whatever materialised first. And if the boy insisted on keeping pace, despite Connors's warnings that he himself had no idea what he was doing and was made of no leadership material, then whose fault was that exactly. Not Connors's.

All the same, Connors remained uneasy about Elvis's presence. When Connors had announced, that first night on the island, that he intended to walk out of town until he was too tired to walk any further, Elvis had lost no time in making his opinion plain that it was a bad idea; and yet, now seeing that Connors meant what he said, the boy had added *I'll come with you.*

Why?

The boy had shrugged and said, *I'm tired of the sea. It does you good to get your land legs every once in a while.*

My sentiments exactly, mate.

When Connors had broached the subject, as tenderly as he was able, of Elvis's parents, the boy had turned away from him and muttered that there was no one special in his life. An odd response, Connors maintained; but the kid was entitled to his privacy – if he didn't want to discuss his back story, that was his prerogative, surely. But what *was* Connors's business was why Elvis seemed determined to venture deeper into land that was riddled (by folklore or fact) with cannibals. It had taken Connors a night to realise that Elvis had not answered the question at all. Not wishing to board another ship, and wilfully pacing your way into imminent danger – these were two different matters altogether.

'Time for lunch,' Connors decided.

Their picnic spot was halfway up one more in a seemingly endless succession of wet-lead hills sprouting tufts of orange-red vegetation. Their witnessing sky was a patchwork of shades of brown and beige; the air, charged and still, was spoiling for a fight. 'Feels like a storm,' Connors mentioned; but the boy ignored him. Silently Elvis busied himself by gathering some of the vegetation, leading Connors to the conclusion that the boy longed to start another of his beloved fires (they knew that the orange leaves ignited); and although they didn't *need* a fire – not at midday, and not to eat their feast of berries – Connors could not find the heart to instruct the boy to desist. Let him have it. What was one more blaze, after all? If Connors's prediction about the weather turned out to be correct, they wouldn't even need to dampen the fucker down when they'd finished with it. Sighing wearily, Connors sat.

Chelsea barked.

For a second Connors imagined that she had barked *at him*; but no – and she had not barked at Elvis either. As taut as a railway line now, she stared up the hill, a thin grumbling rumble leaking from her jaw.

'What's she heard?' Elvis asked.

'I have no idea,' Connors admitted; but the thought occurred to him that whatever it was that Chelsea had been made aware of, it was close. Her bark had been the first since yesterday.

She barked again.

Connors scrambled to his feet. 'Come on, Elvis,' he said. 'Let's see what she's got in mind.'

A few metres away, Elvis replied, 'What about our berries?'

'Fuck the berries.' And Connors resumed their path up the incline, sticky with perspiration, guided by hope.

Had they managed to cross the island? Was it the sea that Chelsea had sniffed out? Was it meat? Was it people?

'*Come on!*' Connors repeated. Although his breathing was laboured, he set his party a new pace within a few strides. He was excited. For Chelsea to have barked, after such a monastic silence, there must be something at least to *see* from the crown of the hill they climbed... The bag containing their provisions – the bag given to them *gratis* by the shack-owner who had sold them the berries and two canisters of water – bumped against Connors's backside as he ascended. He could hear the water sloshing in the canisters; his throat was sore and dry – he had needed their pit-stop – but the tease of what lay beyond was too alluring for him to stay and rest. A rest could follow later on...

Almost breathless, Connors reached the top of the hill... and then he waited to believe his eyes. He wanted what he saw to be something else. The more he glared, however, the more stubbornly the picture held steady.

It wasn't any sort of ending that Connors might have anticipated, but as he remained fixed to the spot, taking in the sight of the vast wall in the milesaway distance, he could not lose the fear that this was the end nonetheless.

He waited until Elvis had caught up, and then said, 'And what the fuck's *that*?'

'Wow. That must be the Nail,' Elvis answered. 'I didn't think…'

'You didn't think what?' Connors prompted.

'I didn't think the stories were true.'

'And what stories would they be?' Connors asked, sensing his own impatience.

Chelsea barked – but not from beside them. The dog had not moved from her original spot.

'There's something here she doesn't like,' said Elvis, quietly.

'There's something here *I* don't like, Elvis! What *stories*?'

'I told you!'

Chelsea barked.

'Told you on the first night! You asked me why it was called Toenail Island.' He pointed at the wall that sliced across their vista from left to right. 'There's your answer. That's the Nail.'

Having already been grabbed by a breathlessness that now receded, Connors fell into a silence from which he was not certain he wished to emerge. Very little more than a breeze was in motion – the progress of any wind perhaps buffeted by the Nail – and were it not for the touch of this breeze to the sweat on his face, Connors might have imagined himself dead. He was dead. And this was a hell-dream… Then Chelsea barked once more, the smell of something rotten fetched his nostrils, and Connors was back at the top of a hill, with a child companion, a dog, and a pocketful of change that he was tapping addictively, while remembering what Elvis had taught him about the origin of Toenail Island's peculiar name.

The story goes, the boy had said, *that God lay down wounded, on a rock. The seas that formed around him were the tears of a billion generations. And they submerged him, as sure as bathwater submerges a bather. But just*

like when you're in the bath — some of you sticks up above the surface. Your
toes, for example.

Folklore and superstition, Connors had believed at the
time; but now, in context, he was less sure of his determination.
Why *shouldn't* they be on the very tip of God's toe (*which* toe?) especially if the inward face of a colossal protruding nail was really
what it was that they faced? Why not? Nothing else made sense,
after all. Why should this?

'I have literally no idea what to do next,' Connors announced.

Chelsea barked.

The sound was like a shot of neat adrenalin, a bolt to Connors's heart. What was near? What was it that the dog didn't like?
Connors swivelled at the waist, on the lookout.

Nothing.

Something else rancid on the breeze, but nothing to see;
just the stink of what lived between toe skin and Nail... It occurred to Connors that an assailant — invisible and light as the
wind — was approaching, skirting rather than treading a close-by
incline.

Connors slapped his knees. 'Come on, girl!' he called to
Chelsea.

The bitch was not for moving.

'It's one way or the other,' Elvis reminded him. honesty

Although Connors resented the intrusion, he knew that the
boy was right: it was back the way they'd come, or onwards towards the Nail in the water.

Then the dirty man appeared to Connors's left.

2.

With him, from foot to brow, he brought a stink of death

and sweetshops. At first glance he appeared to be buzzing with flies; it was only as he strode closer to Connors that the latter realised his mistake: the man was *made of* flies. From head to toe: the shape was humanoid, but the solidity was down to compressed insect life. Although hundreds buzzed free at the silent thump of every footfall, they recollected on shoulder, on forehead. Only the eye sockets were empty – a wrinkled moving black – and the mouth writhed with an expression that seemed reluctant to settle.

Connors released a held breath. His hands shook.

Halfway back down the hill, Chelsea barked madly. She rocked from side to side, her tail lowered, her teeth bared, as Elvis said, 'I dig the threads' calmly.

And the insect man stopped walking.

The drone of flies was this arrival's sole communication, at least for a few unworded seconds. He had ceased his advancement four metres from where Connors stood (with Elvis now clutching at his arm). The flies that formed his mouth made the figure grimace; and a voice emerged, so high-pitched and squeaky that it was like that of a cartoon gopher. It said:

Are you lost?

The timbre surprised Connors; it amused him too, though he tried not to display his mirth. If this was an offer of assistance, honestly provided for all its unconventionality, he did not wish to offend this would-be guide. He nodded his head.

'More lost that you can imagine.'

Where do you want to go? the insects buzzed.

And this was a killer question. Where indeed? Connors and the party he'd adopted – they were not off to see the Wizard of Oz; they were not in Never-Never Land; they were not bearing the One Ring that would bind them all.

Shrugging helplessly, Connors said, 'Home, mate.'

Home?

More specific, Connors decided; this was the best chance they'd had to date.

He swallowed a gulp and said, 'Beds. Bedfordshire... I started in Bedfordshire.' It sounded lame; it sounded desperate.

The man made of insects hummed, as if in pensive consideration. *Across the water?* the voice peeped in query.

'Yeah. That's one way of putting it... How come you speak English?'

The pitch of the drone rose higher. For an instant Connors was concerned that he had asked something insensitive.

What is English?

'Never mind. Where do you go from here?' Connors replied. Elvis's pinch on his arm had grown tighter and more uncomfortable; and still, from down the hill, the dog barked. The compound effect was to set Connors's nerves more on edge: very badly and *right now* he wanted to be away from this place; but with no other markers – not even place names in this dream – he was wildly lost. Suddenly the insect man's original question struck Connors as sublimely humorous.

His not-quite rhetorical question having elicited no further response, Connors tried another tack. 'What's beyond the Nail?'

Beyond?

'Yes, beyond. Further than. On the other side of.'

Ocean, the insect man answered simply.

'And what's on the other side of the ocean?'

Nothing. We all live here, the insects buzzed.

Were they communicating among themselves? Connors wondered briefly. He looked down at Elvis. 'Do you wanna come with me, son?' he asked, his belly contracting at the sight of tears in the boy's eyes.

'Where?'

'Past the Nail. Or did you intend to stay on God's Big Toe

until you hit puberty?'

'What's puberty?'

'It's when your knackers… Never mind. Are you willing?'

'I thought you said no more ships.'

'I did. Bloke can change his mind, can't he? Or we can swim.'

Elvis took a step back. 'Swim the *ocean*?'

'Why not? It's *my* dream: if I drown I'll wake up properly – I probably got a lungful when that flood…' He was staring at a quizzical expression. He stopped talking. Intending to ask more of the collection of bug life, he noticed that the shape had moved slightly: not only had it taken a few steps closer, it had also altered its shape visibly. Where before it had appeared stocky, now the overall form was tall and thin, long-legged like a spider. 'Where are you going?' Connors inquired of this new stranger in their midst.

The answer was soon revealed, though not in words. The humanoid set off down the hill that Connors and Elvis had climbed, his speed a matter of future legend.

It headed towards Chelsea. At the sight of the thing it so feared screaming closer, the bitch turned tail and ran off in a straight line at an obtuse angle to the approximate path they'd travelled. From where Connors stood with Elvis they could hear Chelsea whimper as she retreated.

Shouting out the animal's name, Elvis ran in a pursuit of his own; his velocity, however, was only a fraction of that exhibited by the insect man.

'Jesus,' Connors whispered. He in turn joined the chase, huskily bellowing the boy's name, and painfully aware within a few strides of how unfit and undernourished he'd become. His legs felt rubbery.

By the time Elvis reached the point on the hill where

Chelsea had stood barking, both the dog and her pursuer were some seconds out of sight; but their absence seemed to reignite the boy's fire for the chase... Several metres behind, it struck Connors that if Elvis vanished, he might be gone forever. As he pounded down the slope, trying to keep control of his steps, Connors suffered a pang of pre-emptive loneliness; this was abolished by another attempt at calling out Elvis's name.

As if the boy had seen sense, he slowed his pace. With a flap of both arms against his sides, Elvis stopped at the top of a minor hillock. In due course Connors joined him, panting.

Both of them knew that it was too late for Chelsea.

The dog had been right to be afraid, right from the beginning.

3.

Millions of insects had flown on from Chelsea's corpse but small clouds remained among the spoils. They had stripped her almost to the bone. On a picnic blanket of fresh shining blood the skeleton lay on its left side, the spine and skull gleaming with digestive fluids. She had not so much as barked when they'd caught her: Connors hoped that her heart had burst – that she hadn't been eaten alive – and an image of Dorman bloomed in his mind. At last the poor sod had had his revenge, not that revenge was any sort of valuable commodity where he'd gone.

'I feel sick,' said Elvis.

'Me too.'

'And scared, Con.'

'Yeah, me too.' A snap decision was needed. 'We'll wait until they've finished; then we're going back to the harbour. All things considered, I think it prefer it on the water.'

Elvis smiled thinly. 'Me too,' he whispered.

The swarm of flies was twenty metres away from Connors

and Elvis; the swarm had not reassembled into the shape of a human being. There was no need perhaps, for any more deception, not with their tiny bellies full.

Then, in midair, the black cloud turned; an increase in the volume of their buzzing could be heard. And the sight and sound combined rolled a chill along Connors's spine.

Elvis said, 'They're coming back.'

'Yes.'

'For *us*, Con!'

'Yes.'

But Connors couldn't move. His legs were not cooperating, but more than this, his brain was not telling the truth. The fact that the insects enjoyed flesh was incontrovertible; and yet Connors, now with Elvis pulling on his left arm, felt suddenly less sick and scared than angry and thirsty. *Thirsty* of all things! It was time for a drink of water. Let them have him if that's what it took to wake up, once and for all…

'*Con!* We have to run!' the boy screamed.

Was this shock? Connors pondered the question carefully. Shock seemed likely: first Dorman's decapitation, then the dog butchered down to her bony frame…

Shock.

Shock sounded *nice*.

'Come on, Con!' The boy had started to run in the direction of the Nail. 'They're coming!'

So they were: the swarm had widened the breadth of its net; darkness had snuffed much of the light from the sky.

Once more following the boy, Connors started to run. Every footfall arrowed aches through his shins and inner thighs. And behind him, he could hear the insects squeal.

He wanted to stop. To give up. To accept defeat and let nature – of whatever form – take its course. And were it not for

Elvis in the lead, he might have done so: but the boy's ragged pelt was working wonders for Connors's instinct of self-preservation. So on he ran, a self-defeating sprint, he was certain; but the Nail, as a ribbon across a finish line, spurred him on.

The boy had slipped into an easy lead – the distance between Elvis and Connors had increased to ten metres now, and was rising – and yet Connors could not move any faster. Years had passed since his last sprint, even including swift exits from premises that he had been burgling at the time, when the owners had arrived home ahead of schedule. There was no more gas in the tank.

Midway up a hill two hills on from where he had addressed the insect man, Connors pounded to a gradual halt. The ascent had proved too much: his leg muscles burned with the uncharacteristic exercise.

The Nail was at least four hills away in the distance.

It was over.

To Hell with it.

Connors dropped loudly to his knees.

4.

Then Dorman came to Connors in a dream.

Not the Dorman who had shed larcenous advice like a sloughed skin; nor the Dorman who had wanted the dog made extinct. Not even the Dorman of doubtful table manners in chicken outlets. No. The Dorman who patrolled Connors's dream had half a head: the top had been sawn off by a flying slice of conservatory glass. Not that this incapacity was enough to stop him conversing. The mouth was present, after all.

'Connors,' he said, 'a proposition for you, mate. I've been thinking. Shall we give this fucking Number 11 lark a wide berth?'

And Dorman laughed: his body spasmed and a geyser of blood erupted from what was left of his head. 'To tell you the fucking truth, son, I've got a bad feeling about the whole thing. What do you reckon?'

The younger man could not help but laugh as well. 'You might have a point,' he said wryly. 'Fuck em, right? Fuck Massimo. And fuck Benny.'

'Yeah. Do you wanna go bowling?

Connors took a second before answering. '...Bowling? Now?'

'Why not? What else you got on?'

Connors could not think of an answer to this question.

The air around them was liquid, in violent motion. They were in a bubble. Vision pointed in any direction, and all that could be seen was milky, cataract-smeared.

'The dog's dead,' said Connors, conversationally.

'Good.'

'No, *not* good. It was horrible, mate. And a child had to see it too.'

'It's a child's job. To see things you imagine a child wouldn't want to see. It breeds a race of supermen,' said Dorman.

'...You've lost me.'

'No. You've lost yourself, Connors,' Dorman answered. 'Where are you? At this moment.'

'On Toenail Island.'

'Maximum points. And where's *that* exactly, cunt?'

'I don't know.'

'You don't *know*? Where's your SatNav?'

'Don't take the piss, Dorman. Are you here to help or not?'

'Not. Why should I? I found *my* route. You're on your own.'

Connors sounded sour. 'Well bully for you, prick,' he told his mentor.

'Yeah, bully for me. You want my help?' Dorman demanded.

'What have we been –'

'*Do you want my help?*'

'Yes.'

'Then open your eyes.'

5.

Connors opened his eyes.

Not five metres from where he knelt, Dorman's ghost fluttered and lingered; then it was gone.

'I can't.'

The milky fluid outside their bubble was stirred into yet more agitation. Fist-sized bubbles popped; the temperature had risen.

'This conversation,' said a now-invisible Dorman, 'it's just not happening, mate, is it?'

'You're telling me!'

'No, Connors: *you're* telling you. My life's ended and I can't do no more for you. I tried me best. Believe it or not. For our short acquaintance.'

Connors nodded. 'I know you did, Dorman. I don't think I said thank you.'

'You can say it now. Not in words.'

'How then?' The memory of the fly-storm struck. 'I'm covered in bloody insects, mate. That want to eat me. I'm not in much of a position to dole out favours.'

Dorman smiled. 'All you have to do is open your eyes. Surely even a twat like you can manage *that*.'

Once more, Connors opened his eyes…

6.

...and the noise was the worst he'd ever had to endure. Were there flies in his ears? In his brain? There were certainly flies on his eyelids: he felt them nibbling his skin and yanking out his lashes. But they wouldn't have his eyes: Connors was determined on this matter, and he squeezed his eyelids shut tighter. His mouth too; he pressed his lips together until they ached. At the same time the bites that he was receiving either stung or itched. They were on his upper lip, his jawbone; they writhed in the contours of his cheeks, asserting their right to ingress. The warm meat inside would be tastier.

Remembering the fate of the dog, Connors knew that he did not have minutes; depending on how long he'd been with Dorman in that vision, he might not have seconds left either.

When he climbed to his feet he seemed to have gained weight – and not a pound or two either. The insects on his body, their progress slowed but not halted by the clothes that protected his skin, weighed a stone, or so Connors calculated. As he swiped at his face to clean his skin of his attackers, his arms felt heavy – and he wondered if he was simply transferring one legion of insects into the place of the predecessors. But all doubts aside, Connors knew that he had to do *something*. Despite his earlier pseudo-deathwish, he would not lie down and give up, not just yet. He only hoped that Elvis had escaped to the Nail...

This thought gave Connors strength. Not the thought of the boy making good – not exactly – but the thought that the Nail – the end of the world, after all! – might offer a form of salvation... Towards the Nail, then? Yes. It had to be worth a try. Connors possessed no better plan; and so, having taken one quick peek to establish the correct direction, he set off as quickly as he could, with his eyes closed. Accompanying every step was a movement that involved sweeping tiny vandals from his features;

stamping heavily to dislodge his trousers of the flies he now wore; and shaking his rump like a hula-hoop champion.

The journey was a torment. The slopes were killers, their inclines made more of a travail by the extra mass that he carried; and he feared tripping up on a piece of vegetation, or his foot sinking deep into the entrance-hole of some animal's lair, and twisting his ankle. Only rage and terror kept him fresh; only the notion of Elvis's welfare provided Connors with a scintilla of hope... The next time he winked open an eye to check his whereabouts, he caught a glimpse of Dorman's ghost on a subsequent hillock. The older man was waving him on with one hand; with the other hand he was petting the ghost of Chelsea.

The two spectres fizzed; they fluttered like candle flames in a strong breeze; then they were gone. Connors vowed to make it to the Nail in their memory. As best he could he ducked his head into his jacket and tried to pick up the pace. By this point his face and hands were sharp with agony: it was like they'd been set alight. But all he could do was attempt to fight through the pain, including the fierce dull aches in his legs; the husky sick feeling in his lungs; and the fact that the sum of his life's ambition would currently seem to be... to vomit on a hillside. It wasn't enough. *Fuck it*, Connors thought; *being sick in the open air – it's not enough.*

He surged forward.

And was it his imagination, or was the noise in his ears slowly lessening? Connors hoped that this evaluation was not a by-product of hope. He wanted it to be real. Wanted it to be the case that the insects had realised he was made of sterner stuff than the poor dog had been.

Connors inhaled though his nose (the insides of his nostrils had been bitten too: they were raw and bleeding) and he made another forward thrust.

It was like receiving an electric shock. Head to toe: a mas-

sive thump along the length of his body. The opening of his eyes
was by instinct alone. He had reached and walked blindly into
the Nail.

Did this arrival make him safe? Certainly the flies were retreating: Connors could feel their mass strip away as they buzzed
back the way they'd chased him. There was something about the
wall that they didn't like. Perhaps the smell. Connors was partly
grateful for the taste and aroma of his own blood, for at least it
masked some of the cheese scent – overpowering and ripe – that
assailed his senses. Within a minute he was alone, in the shadow
of the Nail; a few flies ticked and hummed on the ground nearby,
and Connors found some comfort in squashing these stragglers
underheel. Then he took stock.

His eyesight remained unimpaired; the flies had failed to
nibble through his eyelids. But his face was awash with blood:
when he wiped at his skin, blood streamed off in sheets. The
flesh was excruciating to the touch. With his back against the
Nail, Connors sat down and breathed out some of his exhaustion for nigh-on two minutes, during which time he also drank
water from the canister in the bag. His system soaked it up like a
sponge. His throat was sore.

Ten metres away from where he sat, Elvis lay. Connors
tried calling the boy, though his voice was weak.

No response.

He tried again. Panic surged in his belly, in his gut. Was
the boy alive? He would have to venture forth to find out. Like a
brick on a wave his heart sank.

'*Elvis!*' he shouted – almost screamed.

The boy did not so much as twitch. Some of the insects
that had lingered on the boy's brow fluttered away; while Connors could not believe that their scattering was due to his voice
alone, he was relieved all the same. Anything to save the kid from

further consumption.

Go out there!

Connors used the Nail as leverage to prop himself up. For the first time he noticed the state of his hands and wrists: as bloody as a hare freshly butchered. Halal digits. Kosher knuckles. When he flapped his arms, Connors saw drops of blood swing out in a scarlet arc. Crimson arrows.

Before he could give the matter further consideration, he sprinted towards Elvis, his throat newly ragged with the screams that he offered. Unwilling to accept the evidence of his eyes, Connors grabbed hold of Elvis's bony wrists – his *wet* and bony wrists – and tugged him back towards the Nail in a halting, shuffling manoeuvre. Residual clusters of flies claimed their places; but Connors shook his head and spat blood and dragged on. The removal of the boy's body was a matter of minutes: and it was only when Elvis had been delivered into the Nail's shade that Connors was forced to accept the obvious.

The boy was dead. A hole the size of a coffee mug was embedded in his left temple. Half of his nose was absent; his lips had been kissed to the bone. His neck was perforated, and still bleeding.

They had eaten away his eyes.

With no choice in the matter, Connors flattened out on the ground. The vomit he'd fought before would not be fought again, and his body shook.

Wish Fulfilment Vignettes

1.

Nero sank to the bottom of something that felt like paint.

On waking, he was exhausted. On waking, he needed a sleep; and when he heard her voice – 'Are you there?' – and looked over at the striplit vagina from which it had been ventriloquised, Nero wondered what the question actually meant, so accurately had the dream breathed.

He tried to remember the voice he'd heard – the man who had addressed him by name – and he knew that Jess had broken the spell. It was as gone as perfume.

'Yeah I'm there,' he whispered, the defeat conceded. 'Here,' he corrected. 'That was a weird one. I was dreaming of a bloke called Chris. But I don't *know* no one called Chris!'

'You sound drunk,' said Jess's vagina.

'Wish I was.' Nero twisted his upper body, one ear open for those satisfying cracks that signified his bones shifting back into realignment… or some shit like that. And it took a beat of time before he realised that he was free.

He was no longer cuffed to the radiator in the walk-in wardrobe. And it felt like a long while that he stared at his wrists, at his fingers. The lingering moment felt spiritual.

The door was still locked (he would discover a few seconds later) but this was progress.

I will kill them, he thought once more. *I will kill them.*

'What's so funny?' Jess asked him.

'...Was I laughing?'

'Like a nutter, mate,' she answered.

'...Can you move?'

'Move?'

Nero held up his arms. 'They've undone me.'

'Well, undo *me*. Oh God, Nero. Undo *me*!'

2.

Nero's vision skated across an acre of packed ice. He was not physical. He was not purely sensual either: he was something else. Ahead of his vision and to the side, mountains loomed. Ugly mountains, black as doom in the patches seen beneath the rags of melting snow that they wore. Was Nero to climb? He didn't know. It was as if he were following... following something more than simply his own eyesight. A glance back down the icy slope that he'd travelled so far – a slope that appeared longer than miles – made Nero realise that he was not the owner of this journey; it was not his. The reason that he did not remember the ascent so far was because it was not he who had made it. And in an instant Nero realised once more that he was not physical or purely sensual either: he was something else. *He was memory*. In this ice-clogged passway between ugly mountains – where no wind gnawed at his temples, where sound had yet to resolve itself into something recognisable, where the very nature of the pink-blue balance of the sky was in philosophical doubt – Nero was somebody's memory of this same trek: a memory catching up with its owner.

Hurry!

Inside the dream's fragile skull, Nero was aware that time was limited. As soon as he understood this, the temperature dropped: one reality had sneaked in another, and surely further sensory impressions would be swift to follow.

Hurry!

I'm hurrying! Nero answered back, willing a fast-forward up the gentle gradient of the passway. The willing worked. The resulting velocity propelled his vision into a thickening confusion of falling snow. And it was quite a blizzard: certainly Nero had seen nothing like it in his fifteen years. Indeed, the flakes were so thick in the air – falling faster as Nero continued to accelerate up the incline – that his breath pulled up short in his lungs. It was hard to breathe.

Why had the man come here? Nero wondered.

There was no doubt that he was following a man... but why had the mad bastard climbed this passway?

This question was on Nero's mind as the snow coalesced and congealed; as the temperature dipped, the blood in his veins drumming against the chill. The damage to his lungs was bound to be longlasting, Nero feared; and as his eyelids opened, the question was flipped open for him to see through the storm of coughs rising from his chest and throat.

Jess said, 'Drink some water.'

Nero jumped up to his feet, still coughing. He'd been holding his breath, in his sleep. Now he bent at the waist and picked up the water jug. Instead of pouring from it, however, or even drinking from it directly, he tipped what remained of the water over his head. Then he shook like a dog emerging from the sea. Water ran down his brown back, his lightly-muscled chest.

Lying on her campbed, Jess was evidently not impressed by Nero's actions. 'You're in a funny mood,' was all she had to say on the subject, however.

'Weird dreams,' Nero told her.

'Change the mix.'

'I'm point blank. Like I'm chasing this guy through the hills. All snowy and shit…'

Jess looked scared. 'I've been having something similar again,' she admitted. 'Do you know who he is?'

'Nah. But I know one thing, Jess. Following people in times of trouble is how religions start. Following the Prophet and all that.'

'…So who's he following?' Jess asked.

Nero shrugged. 'Maybe I need to get back to sleep to find out. Nothing else to do… Maybe it's God. Or maybe he's just one of them nutters who likes extreme sports.'

3.

But he wasn't, Nero knew. The man he was following was no sports fanatic – extreme sports or otherwise. The longer Nero spent on trying to tune into his leader's consciousness, in fact, the more he came to believe that this leader loathed his own trials. He was certainly not travelling for the good of his health – or not specifically at any rate – the element of personal survival was at stake.

For him as it is for me, thought Nero; and he surprised himself with the vaguely Biblical-sounding construction of his own sentence – as if it had been passed to him from a source other than his own word pool.

'Jess?' Nero asked into the darkness.

No response.

Probably best. Nero could hear her breathing: she was still alive. Best he could shoot for, though. Alive or dead's the options, innit. She's alive – so that must be good, I suppose. Anyway: what am I gonna say to the girl? *Jess, what do you remember about Jesus from R.E. lessons?* She'll think I've gone nuts. *Did Jesus have to climb some fucking bare high mountains? Snow on the top…*

'What is it?' Jess answered.

Either personal desperation or the shared visions had made Nero brave. 'You know the guy we're chasing?'

'Who said it's a guy? Could be a girl,' Jess replied. 'Nah, you're right: it's a guy.'

'Can you see him?'

'No. But I can feel him, I think.'

'In what way?'

Jess cleared her throat. 'You won't laugh?'

'I'll try not to,' Nero assured her – or tried to.

'My *feet* get cold,' Jess told him. 'He's up in the hills, moving north, right?'

'Right…'

'Well, he ain't wearing the correct footware. Gonna get frostbite. Lose his toes.'

'I agree with you.' Nero closed his eyes; in his head he searched for the leader.

Jess continued speaking. 'I get the impression,' she said carefully, giving Nero the impression that she was choosing her constructions with defiant deliberation, 'he's been *placed* where he's at. It wasn't his *choice.*'

'Yeah, I agree with that too. He's a stranger.'

'In a strange land,' Jess finished.

The two of them fell silent.

Why me? Nero asked himself – immediately amending the question to *Why us?* Why was it he and Jess who could see the man in the mountains?

'Do you think we're the only ones who see him?' he asked.

'Doubt it.' Jess paused. 'Probably anyone in a world of pain sees him.'

The possibility was one that Nero had considered, and it

pumped him full of hope. Two reasons for this show of optimism pertained.

The first reason to be cheerful was surely that they'd be able to get in touch with their new leader at will… somehow. And if the transmission was two-way, perhaps their leader would have some words of wisdom. What other use were leaders for, anyway? If the mad prick was capable of shimmying fucking barefoot across a glacier (or whatever), surely the cunt was capable of getting his disciples out of a locked room!

The second reason to be cheerful was the chance that he might reach out to other observers. If the mad prick was the focal point, couldn't Nero think his way *through* him? Couldn't he form some sort of… some sort of *network?*

Once more Jess cleared her throat in the darkness.

'His name's Chris,' she said.

Nero did not respond.

'That's a lot like Christ,' she added in a dreamy tone of voice.

WILD NATURE

'Do you know what the crocodile bird is, Mass? Well, it's name gives you everything once you know it, but the concept's weird. It's a bird, right, that lives in the crocodile's mouth! So why don't the croc eat it, you may ask. Because the bird cleans his teef. The bird's his fucking dental hygienist! Pecks all the shit from the croc's nashers, mate! And that's nature that is. That's evolution. That's cosmic harmony, mate.

'And then there's the fish that lives on the ocean floor, where by all accounts it can get a bit nippy, right? Female says to the male: Let's have a cuddle, warm ourselves up a bit. So the male gets cosy and lovey-dovey, and do you know what the squaw does to him? She *absorbs* him. She absorbs the cunt, right into her own body… Wish I could remember the name of that fish, but there you go: I'm closer to seventy than sixty these days, and forget about bladder control and so forth: the *real* problem after forty is the memory.'

Benny tapped the side of his head, helpfully reminding Massimo of where the memory was stored. Massimo said nothing. With men like Benny, sometimes it was better to say nothing.

'Do you know, Mass, there is literally no point to a wasp. No biological or etymological – is that the right word? – *point* to the cunt. He plays no part in the food chain. He's full of spite. And he loves to kamikaze into me warm pint of flat lager at The Dreadful Doris. He's just a *wanker*, Mass. Not even wasp so-called experts could give two tin shits about wasps. If they died out to-morrow, *nothing would change*. Apart from you'd have safer picnics.

'What do these three creatures have in common, you may well be wondering. Why's old Benny giving me this flannel? Well, I'll tell you, Mass. It's about environment. *Environment*. The crocodile bird could live anywhere theoretically, but he don't. He risks it all perching in a killing machine's mush. The male fish just wants a nosh off his missus, if fish go in for that sort of thing. But instead of getting fucked by his wife, he gets fucked by what? He gets fucked by what, Mass?'

Benny waited.

Oh, the man required an *answer*, Massimo realised. 'By his environment?' he ventured.

Benny clicked his fingers.

'By his environment − precisely. And then you've got the wasp − that natural irritant; that prince of chaos. Who demands an environment larger than ours. And who will be squashed by its natural enemy − man − who is four-and-a-half million times larger than he is, the cunt. But what does this make *us*, mate? Am I supposed to feel *brave*? That I've killed a tiny creature with my beer glass? What does this tell me about *my* environment?'

Massimo shrugged.

Benny waited.

Massimo shrugged again and said, 'I don't know. What?'

'It is my solemn duty,' Benny answered carefully, 'and my moral responsibility, to do everything in my power to control my environment. Do you follow me?'

The answer was no, but Massimo said, 'I'm not sure.'

'In the examples I've given you, Mass, you might think of yourself as the bird to my crocodile…'

'I don't know about *that*.'

'Well, you'd be wrong. The truth is, *I'm* the bird − that's how it feels. *And* I'm the male fish getting absorbed into something much more powerful than I am.'

The female fish, Massimo deduced. This was all about a *woman?* 'What's her name?'

Benny shook his head, a line of impatience ploughing vertically through his muscular brow. 'You might even say,' he went on.

'You're a wasp,' Massimo interjected, believing that he was finally on the other man's wavelength.

'That's right. I'm an irritant – to you. I love chaos.'

'Well, that's good, considering how much there is around.'

'Considering how much there is around that's precisely of your own making.'

'Me? What did *I* do?'

'You hired imbeciles to burgle the house,' Benny answered simply. 'One of them lost his life and half his head...' Benny chuckled. 'The other one's been sending me messages.'

The news came as a surprise to Massimo. Knowing Benny's preference for old-fashioned faxes over emails (Benny made no secret of the fact that he didn't 'do the Internet'), Massimo asked: 'He sends you faxes?'

Again, Benny shook his head. 'Not faxes, Mass, no; not faxes. Messages.' He touched the side of his head once more. 'In here... In me dreams.'

'...Are you serious?' Massimo said.

'Serious as herpes, mate. What I said to you, if memory serves – and I'm sure it does – is to find two blokes who've never worked together.'

'Which I did.'

'Which you did. Full marks for recruitment. And to enter Number 11, in the full awareness that they'd know what it was I wanted them to find. They'd know it when they saw it.'

'Yeah… about that…'

'You wanna know what it was.' Benny grinned: two rows of pearlies, as flawless as a dolphin's, giving rise to Massimo's query-to-self as to whether or not they were dentures. 'I've been waiting for this. Fair enough. You've been patient on that score – more patient than a cunt like me would be in your size nines. The honest answer is: I don't know. Do you wanna see me snakes?'

What Massimo wanted was a beverage. He'd been in Benny's Ashridge home for thirty minutes and he hadn't been offered so much as a glass of water. Coming here, he was starting to believe, had been a mistake. This could have been done on the phone. And the traffic back was likely to be murder… The only consolation would be the crate of knocked-off Shiraz that was waiting for him in the shed. A nice pint of red would do the trick quite nicely right now.

'I have several vivaria,' Benny elaborated.

'Are they poisonous?'

'No, Mass. A vivarium's a place where you keep and nurture the cunts. Do you know, the boa constrictor is one of the few creatures on the planet that we refer to by its official Latinate name? It's interesting that, don't you think? Why'd *he* get preferential treatment?'

Massimo could not suppress a sigh.

Benny chuckled. 'Sorry, mate, am I keeping you awake?' he asked. 'I'm digressing a tad, aren't I? That also comes with age.'

Massimo held up a hand. 'I'm not an educated man, Benny; you're losing me a bit. I'm struggling with the relevance.'

'I am explaining my personal philosophy, Mass – me system of values if you will.'

'And that's cool. But the traffic's a fucker at this time of day…'

'Of course. In that case, I'll come right out and ask you a

question. Do you know what an intra-rationalist is?'

'Jesus. A reptile?' Massimo guessed.

'No, mate. I'm one, for one. Intra-rationalism is the commonsense in my view opinion that separate realities exist in balance side by side. And most people in either reality are unaware – their whole lives – that the other reality chugs on.'

Forced to change mental gears, Massimo struggled with the clarification. 'Are you... are you talking about alternative timestreams?'

'Not exactly; but you're getting the idea. And it's my contention – bear with me on this – that your man Chris Connors was taken to an intra-rationalist existence when the seam between the two worlds split.'

The words hung in the air like Agent Orange. Benny snickered.

'And don't even ask if you heard me right because you did. And I'm point blank on the level, Mass. Cunt *went* somewhere. Somewhere we don't understand. Somewhere *I* wanna go, mate. And *that's* what I wanted your boys to check out for me. Whether or not the gate's open.' Benny shrugged. 'Turns out it is.'

'...You set him up.'

'Not in the slightest. I had no idea what you'd find. You might've found a gold-plated hairbrush, or a toilet bowl full of worms and blood-riddled stools. But the rumours said – the rumours said, Mass, it was a place to watch.'

Sitting forward, Massimo demanded: 'What fucking rumours?'

'Like attracts like. There are newsletters, groups. *Conventions* if you don't mind.' Benny sniffed a single nasal ingestion that lasted a full four seconds. 'Between you and me, you've never seen drinkers like Finnish intra-rationalists.' He smiled at the recollection. 'Convention in Winnipeg. These Finnish cunts doing half pints of absinthe and reciting scripts from *The Two Ronnies* for some reason. Word for word.'

'Spunky. So you wanted my boys to open your portal to another dimension.'

Not knowing if he was being mocked, Benny sniffed again. 'In a manner of speaking.'

It was time to go. The warhorse had lost his mind.

'Are you under the impression,' said Benny, 'that you owe me something?'

'No. I'm under the impression,' said Massimo, 'that you owe *me* something.'

'Explain your reasoning.'

'I did what I was asked to do.'

'Well that's debatable, but okay. I thought an explanation might suffice. And I've offered you me snakes, which I don't do for everyone, stand on me, so what...'

'I don't care about your bloody snakes!'

'Careful.'

'They belong in the Arizona desert. You're sitting there sipping green tea that smells like an operating theatre and you haven't offered me so much as the sweat off your prick. I'm thirsty. I'm hungry. I'm hungover and I want to go home.'

'No one's stopping you, Mass.'

Massimo rose from his chair. 'These *messages* that Connors sends...'

'Yeah?'

'What's he say?'

'Well. He don't know me from Adam, does he? So it's not like he's speaking directly to *me*. It's more like a broadcast. You could probably tune in as well.'

'Thanks; but I've lived without it so far.'

'Fair enough. Are you a betting man, Mass?'

'Yes.'

'Good. I'm reluctant to fully trust a man who doesn't gamble. It shows a failure of ambition. So would you take on the following wager, I wonder. I bet you a month's salary – your average
month's salary against *my* average month's salary – that you visit
the Edlesborough house before the end of the week.'

'And why would I do that?'

'I've piqued your interest. You can't be sure I'm talking bollocks – I'm not, by the way, and I'll go toe to toe with any cunt
tells me I am. Hear me out. You'll go to that house because you
want to know what happened to Connors. Well, I'll tell you again.
He was taken away and landed on a ship at sea. Don't ask me
why it happened at precisely that moment: I've no idea. But you
can bet your arse the word's gone around the intra-rationalist
community, like the pox in a monastery. And some people get the
dreams and some people don't. The two kids you've got locked
away in a big house – *they* get em.'

Massimo sat down.

Benny waved a hand; his wedding ring caught a beam of
sunlight and sent a fairy to climb the wall. 'Don't look so worried,
Mass. I won't interfere with your business – you've got your reasons. None of mine. I'm merely illustrating the fact that I know
what I know.'

'But *how* do you know?' Massimo asked.

'I had you followed... Now now. Don't take umbrage, mate.
Simple business insurance from my point of view. I had to know
what I was getting, didn't I? Even if you did come highly recommended. So I had one of me boys go into the house and have a
poke around... and there's two kids chained up in the walk-in
wardrobe! In the nuddy!' Benny laughed. 'Frit the life out me boy,
that did! Thought they was dead. They was snoozing.'

Massimo nodded.

'So here's me proposal,' Benny said. 'Go to the house yourself; try to get in. Bring me back something I can use and I'll give you a grand for your night's work. Can't say fairer than that.'

Chewing his lip with bovine gestures, Massimo worked up some saliva. He was close to spitting at Benny's crotch – but he'd never been a very good spitter, and he reconsidered the act of insurrection.

'I'm not a housebreaker, Benny,' he said.

'No, but I am. Or I was at least, in the early days. A younger man's game. But I did my share as I built me empire, and the principles haven't changed.'

'…You wanna come with me?'

'No, mate. Too old for that now. I wanna teach you what to do and what not to. See, I don't need you to farm this out to a lackey – no offence. If the house really is a road to God knows where, I need a bloke with a sensible head on his shoulders.'

'Well, that rules *me* out.'

'Don't be so modest. Hubris is an underrated expression in my book. I had to break a man's fingers once for being too self-deprecating to take my thanks for a job well done. Kept thanking his *team*, if you don't mind – or even if you *do* mind. Had him in tears in me Jag on the way over to the hospital, begging me to do the other hand as well for being so shallow. Funny bloke. Anyway. If you can hold it together, you and your… friend? Partner?'

'Partner.'

'If you can hold it together in a hostage situation like you are, you're more than responsible enough to break a fucking door lock without alerting the neighbours… though there's one you need to keep an eye on, apparently. A nurse. I've had a boy take a look at the place – drive-by, you understand. She lives down the road at Number 11, where your boys went wrong the first time. Probably just a nosey squaw, but it's good to know the full picture, I believe.'

'Benny...' Massimo leaned forward: an intended show of sincerity. 'I've also driven past that house a couple of times. There's filth on duty, I'll never get in.'

'Not at night there's not. They knock off when it gets dark and go home for a mug of Ovaltine. That's when you make your move.'

Massimo sat back in his chair. 'All right then, try this one. That house has been explored and examined by all sorts of people. Not one of them's disappeared.'

'And how can you be so sure of that?'

'Oh, come on!'

'All right. *They* don't know what they're looking for.'

'Neither do I.'

'They don't *believe*.'

'Neither do I.'

'Yeah you do,' Benny answered dismissively. 'You just don't know it yet. You wouldn't be sat there listening if you didn't believe. Where else did Connors go? Where did all the water come from? It's not rocket science, mate.'

Massimo had gone back to remaining silent: as various constables had instructed him over the years, he had the right to do so. His mind was full and plump: ideas were curling around one another, feeding one another.

Talk about a long shot, he thought. But if what Benny had said was true, what was to stop them using the *intra-rationalist existence* to dispose of the bodies of Nero and Jess? It was beautiful. There was a *poetry* about it. If Massimo or Charlie could get the door open to the other world, the problem of corpse-disposal was solved. As it was, they had talked loosely of dismembering the bodies; had even joked about *eating* as much of the teenagers as they could manage (comparisons with too much turkey at Christmas had been drawn); however, no firm plans had been hatched… and time was moving on. Soon the teenagers would be dead.

Massimo nodded.

'I'll do it,' he said at length.

'Yes, I know you will,' Benny answered.

THOUGHT FOR FOOD

Connors had meant business. His plan had been to sleep for as long as his body dictated, and then to explore the length of the Nail.

Best-laid plans!

He had awoken sick and convulsing, his face as stiff as papier-mâché with dried blood, his limbs like heavy metal plumbing.

His mouth was like a nomad's flip-flops and there was no water left in the canister. He was dry. Alone and dry. The thought of walking seemed worse than impossible: it seemed terrifying. It meant that he'd have to leave Elvis behind, and a part of him couldn't bear to dish out such an indignity. Yet what else could be done? Connors had found no makeshift tools that he might use to dig a hole for the body to rest in; what was worse was the fact that the more he regarded the corpse, the hungrier he felt.

The night had passed in a fever: and something sweet had ridden his dream. The sweetness of pain; the sweet vision of ripped skin. In his nightmares he had eaten the boy's face.

There was no choice: he must follow the Nail. In fact, it was logical to do so. If he followed the Nail, eventually he would arrive at the skin looking over the sea: the skin adjacent to the cuticle. And then…

And then he didn't know.

Just walk.

So he walked. And he was walking now, with the light on his bloodied features feeling like sunburn. More than anything else he desired a bath: he wanted to wash off the dried blood and crisped skin. Half of his body weight would be lost, he reckoned.

Such was the pain in his legs that Connors didn't notice at first that he had a stone in his blood-soaked trainer. It was only after he'd stopped and removed the article that he understood that it wasn't a stone. It was a bone. And removing it made Connors feel queasy... Bending over to retch, he wanted to know where the bone had come from.

All the while the Nail was to his left.

Navigational reasons were one thing; also relevant was the ongoing terror of the insects. As far as he knew, Connors remained safe while he walked near the Nail; and while he wasn't in a frame of mind to be cocky, he believed that the smelly wall would work to his advantage.

For now, at least.

He plodded on. Shuffled on. Nightmare images of eating Elvis returned to haunt him, and he thought back to the boy's early warning about cannibals living in the hills. Before long Connors had managed to twist the admonition to such an extent that the boy had been talking about *him*. He was one of them. He was starving. The berries and the water were gone, and the next dead thing he saw he would cook and eat, be it human or not. Except...

There was nothing to find. Slow mile after slower mile passed, and the only matter in Connors's path was dust and greying petals, blown from the close-by hillsides. Only once did he imagine the smell of a fire, but he could see no smoke. Imagination.

The third night had almost arrived when he reached the final stretch of the Nail. To his left was the ocean, perturbed and acrobatic. The smell of it was as wholesome as that of a Sunday roast. Connors itched with a wild desire to bathe; but most of all he wanted to drink it. To drink it all up and burp loudly, the king now of all he surveyed.

To these ends he picked his way down to the waterline.

The water was cold. It felt like magic. Connors splashed in the shallows like a kid with a bucket-and-spade: a self-absorbed distraction from the main events. Within seconds he had ripped himself down to his Reg Grundies; and then, with little more thought, he had whipped off his bags and gone skinny-dipping in the ice cube tide. Laughing like a corsair. He didn't even care that his jewels shrank to punctuation points, to an emoticon. The water chilled his pubis, and the sensation enchanted. And though the taste was too salty, Connors drank from his cupped hands, scoop following scoop, till his belly groaned full.

Then he was sick.

However, there was little to regurgitate; a few strips of tendon-like residua left his gullet, nothing more. Connors had sat down in the place where the waves broke, believing himself to be the luckiest fucker alive.

Carefully as he could, he doused his face and hands and washed away brown blood. And thought about his position.

If he was bathing in the waters surrounding the very tip of one of God's toes, then the voyage he had taken part in had been on the wild sea that covered the rest of God's foot. No? Where a toe existed, a foot must be attached; and then a leg, if he sailed far enough. The ankle-bone's connected to the – shinbone... or something like that, if he remembered the song correctly. With nothing better to do with his time, Connors took the mental trip further: he tried to imagine God's genitals (he assumed male). Was God the type who liked to play with himself in the bath? Perhaps he was engorged at full throttle at this very moment: an erection the size of Mount Rushmore! His imagination keening, Connors followed God's body: he travelled a whole summer on the slopes of His chest. He lost breath climbing God's throat (he bivouacked on God's Adam's apple) and remaining full of fire, he moved closer to God's lips. But the quest was not for the purpose of kissing Him. No. The quest was for the purpose of *talking* to him. Connors wanted some answers. And he wanted them fast. However, the best he could hope for was a long journey – the labour of years, perhaps – in order to speak directly to the Source. If *God* didn't know what was going on, then who would? He'd crawl into the cunt's ear for a look at His brain if need be.

The journey would be the work that might see Connors to the end of his days: he was aware of this. Having no better plan, on the other hand, his mind was made up. Just as soon as he recovered...

Dusk was spreading thickly. Thinking about what might live in the ocean, Connors decided to get out while there was still enough warmth in the air to dry his skin. He collected his clothes from where he'd shed them, and climbed back up to a point where the tide was unlikely to reach him. Maybe sleeping near the Nail was a good idea – it had protected him so far – but he was sick of the sight and smell of it; tonight he would rest under a spray of stars only, near a fire he'd build. Parenthetically he wondered if he'd seen a moon since leaving the back garden of Number 11, way back when. He couldn't remember. If it rained tonight... well, it rained. He'd get wet. A little rain had never hurt anyone.

His dreams did not stand on ceremony. Shortly after he'd closed his eyes (fully dressed once more) his mind played its usual nocturnal tricks; but the images were fanciful, colourful and violent. One moment he was on the ship, incising Chelsea's teats with a broken bottle to drink the milk that she lactated, while the tide tossed them hither and yon; the next he was interrupting those two boys having sex and begging the alpha male for a turn of his own, even going so far as to display his naked rump in the ritualistic manner of a baboon. He saw Dorman, searching on muddy grass for the top of his head, then attaching it in place with a length of clothesline torn from the garden's whirligig. And he dreamed of a face so vast that it was impossible to travel between its eyes without aircraft.

When he woke, he believed the dreams still had him. A child stood nearby, her skin as black as the sea itself; she watched him as he sat up, not breathing a word… Connors's first thought (rapidly discarded) was that she was Elvis reincarnated. 'Do you understand me?' Connors croaked, then said again — the first time he had scarcely understood himself. He guessed her to be about six, but then again he had never been good with estimations of people's ages. Even though only a few metres separated the two of them, Connors struggled in the darkness to make out her features with any confidence; however, his gut instinct convinced him that she appeared stern. Her hair was either tied back or cropped close to her scalp; she was wearing a light pink dress, with sandals on her feet.

Connors put a hand on his chest and said, 'My name's Chris.' He opened the same palm in the girl's direction. 'And what's *your* name?'

She didn't answer.

Well, fuck the introductions; there were more important questions that needed answers. Pointing at his mouth, Connors asked, 'Do you have any food? I'm very hungry, I've been walking… Oh never mind. Do you have any *food*?' Wearily, Connors clambered to his feet.

The girl was as fast as a tumbling gymnast: the knife she produced from a scabbard attached to her back was at least as large as the span of his hand. She held it at head height, in the stance of a javelin thrower.

'Woah there!' Connors said. 'Chill your boots! Just stretching me legs!'

The girl watched him. She said something in a language that he couldn't understand; couldn't so much as recognise. He stepped closer to what lingered of the fire: tiny embers glowing and a modicum of warmth expelled.

'Only asked if you had *food*,' Connors muttered. 'No need to cop an attitude and a fucking *knife*. Why'd you even stop and wake me, eh? That's what *I'd* like to know…'

'Ruth.'

Connors faced her. 'Your name's Ruth? Put the knife down, eh? You're making me nervous. It's nice to meet you, Ruth. Now moving on to my second question…'

'No. No I don't have food.'

Connors grinned sourly. 'Well that's just pie and gravy, that is,' he said. 'What use do you think you are to me, then? Eh?'

'You're hangry.'

'You bet your life I'm angry!' Connors shouted. 'I've been stuck on a boat and attacked by some pretty fucking hardcore midges. *You'd* be angry!' He paused. 'Did you say angry or hungry?'

'You're hangry.' Ruth mimed a spoon to her mouth.

'Yes! Do you know where I can find food? Are you *with* people?'

Are you a cannibal? was a question that flashed through his head.

The knife was either for protection or to hunt, Connors reasoned as she lowered it and reholstered it behind her back. Perhaps she'd popped out for a bite to eat herself.

She said, 'Come.' She turned her back on Connors and walked away from the Nail, inland. At least it was in the direction that he'd planned to travel in anyway. So he followed her.

Familiarity with the terrain, and her youth, made Ruth light on her feet; before they had covered half a mile she had increased the distance between them by ten metres or so. Connors kept losing sight of her, but sirened on by a warbling, ululating song that she had started to improvise, he was sure that he was proceeding the right way. Every now and then her pink dress flashed in the starlight.

Up ahead, more singing. Although Connors wondered why they couldn't decide on one tune between them, he was grateful for the sound of the tribal choir that he could hear. Grateful too for the smell of something cooking. The fragrance seemed Sundayesque (it made him homesick): if it wasn't pork roasting, they could twist his nipples and call him Patricia.

(It wasn't pork roasting. No pig had been slain for this evening's feast, but Connors would have to wait another thirty minutes before learning this fact.)

By Connors's arithmetic, there were thirteen or fourteen mud huts gathered around a waist-high fire in a central clearing of a twenty-metre radius. Probably twenty-five people, some with skin hues as dark as Ruth's but others as pale as bone, sat in the dust near the flames; it was their collected voices that Connors had listened to. Nor did they stop singing when he approached with Ruth; if anything, the volume rose exponentially with every half-metre that they covered. As if they had been waiting.

Connors was welcomed warmly. Quickly finding the tribespeople's smiles contagious, Connors was offered a sweet hot drink, something like chicory, which he sipped gladly. Over his pained shoulders they dropped a blanket made of hide, to keep him warm. He sat on the ground near the fire, shaking slightly, his brain fuzzy as he tried to learn the harmonies of some of the songs. Singing along, perhaps, would demonstrate his amiability and his thanks.

In a greedy manner he consumed three bowls of a spicy broth, only later learning that its chief ingredient had been a dead boy that they'd found, marinated in stock brewed from the skeleton of a ravaged dog.

CONFESSIONS AND ACCUSATIONS

1.

'Roger? Do you think we need to talk about this?' Phyllie asked.

Bluffing more than somewhat, her husband replied: 'About what?'

'Is it because I'm getting fatter?'

'No.' Thereby acknowledging that there was indeed a problem worth discussing.

'...Then what is it?'

'Something bugging me,' Roger answered curtly.

'Yes I know that much, Rog. My question is what. You've hardly so much as touched me for three nights. And I'm starting to think you're not ill, which was what I thought at first.'

'No, I'm not ill.'

'Then *what?* What have I done?'

Roger turned on the bedside lamp, rolled onto his side, and took Phyllie's hand. Over the following few minutes he confessed his suspicions ('crazy feels' he called them) about Don the Bird-keeper. His concluding summation was tense.

'We missed something,' he said. And then he made a long confession. And then he waited for Phyllie's disgusted response, which did not arrive.

'To phone Vig.' Naked, she exited the room, her legs un-steady in that familiar way that Roger loved (she was always un-steady on her pins after she'd been lying down for a while).

'It's two in the morning!'

'He'll be awake.'

Roger followed her out onto the landing. 'What makes you say that?'

'He can't sleep in that big house. He told me.' Phyllie lit the landing and descended the first of the stairs.

'He told you when?'

'On the phone. You know we talk. I'll call him while you get some clothes on.'

Roger remained on the landing. 'Now? You wanna go there *now?*'

From the hallway Phyllie called: 'If it stops you being a monk. No time like the present.'

2.

Roger's confession went like this.

Emotionally bruised by the weird altercation with Don Bridges, he had entered Homebase a few minutes after it opened on Saturday morning. In his left hand, the grease from the bacon butty that he'd bought from the van in the car park seeped slimily through the shopping list he carried. (Roger was a great one for lists. He believed in lists.) The shop was empty: just the way he liked it, and he allowed himself time to linger. A keen aisle assistant, spiffed and polished in the black-orange uniform, asked Roger if he needed a hand. Though the phraseology used amused Roger, he didn't smile; he just said no thank you to the boy and dropped a coil of washing-line into his basket. By the time he had reached the checkout, the basket contained two drums of fence paint, the washing-line, and a packet of ten sheets of rough grade sanding paper. The paint was for a long-overdue job on the back garden shed and fences (a chore for tomorrow morning, weather permitting); the line and the sandpaper were intended for tonight's bedroom shenanigans. He'd got the idea off a Latvian bondage website to which he expensively subscribed.

The problem was, he remained troubled by the visit that he and Dorota had paid on Don Bridges. Despite his wife's questions on the subject, he hadn't revealed the reasons for his unease; in truth, he didn't know the reasons himself. But there was something: it was something he'd seen in Don's cabin; something that hadn't quite rung true. And the knowledge that it had been there – just beyond his mind's reach – had been putting him off his game. His erection was less sure of itself; he had trouble concentrating in the bedroom.

He pocketed the till receipt and offered his thanks for the Saturday girl. Parenthetically considering what her teeth braces would feel like on his scrotum (would he know they were there?), Roger placed his purchases in the boot of his car. His memory had snagged on a case over which he had presided, three or four years earlier. In a gathering drizzle he stood stock still to the rear of his car, squeezing his keyring. When a hopeful fellow motorist pulled close, eager for a space so near to the store, Roger was conscious enough of his surroundings to wave him on with a regretful shake of the head (he wasn't leaving just yet); but other than this action, Roger was back there, climbing stairs in his present memory that had felt much harder to climb in reality. Oh, he had seemed to climb stairwells *for ever!* What a tough old day that had been, that case...

The sales assistant's braces were what had brought the memory clambering back: the girl in the Bedford tenement – Louisa – had worn braces as well. And he'd ascended to her flat in a thickening drizzle: maybe the weather was partly responsible for the recollection too... Roger continued to squeeze his keyring, in much the same way as he had on the morning that he'd walked up through the drizzle, expecting to find Louisa and her daughter dead.

It would have been impossible to work in psychiatric crisis assessment for as long as Roger Billie had without having encountered death, or at least an awareness of the same. An awareness of death − of what human beings might conceive to do to and with their own bodies − was nothing more than the air that Roger breathed, professionally speaking. In fact, for some years now he had been preparing a paper that (in his imagination) he would deliver at some hypothetical healthcare conference at the end of the universe: a paper that would triangulate the subjects of psychiatry's expectations of high-risk suicide; the erotic and spiteful transference process by which the high-risk patient loves and hates her care-provider; and the erotic countertransference inherent in the discovery of the patient's dead body. The paper that would get him struck off the medical register; possibly prosecuted. At the very least *investigated*. And then − Good Lord! − what would the authorities find out about him!

The truth was, nothing much that would *definitely* incriminate him. Or rather, nothing much recently. Go far back enough and you'll locate a ball of yarn that began its journey as one of a different colour; and Roger's past was not unstained. In his salad days in particular, he had made no bones about accepting the occasional sexual favour that was more or less (he quickly learned) little more than a perk of his job. And while he had never failed − not once − to make a patient aware that he had noticed the scratches on her arms, or the faint whiff of brandy on his breath at ten in the morning − or the soapy pupils and goaty sweat of a patient's mental indigestion that the patient himself could not pronounce; the freshly shy character of a six year-old girl who would not go to school on the days she had Gym − Roger had been guilty in the past of using these observations as *tools*, as helpful leverage – rather than as punishment for the patients that he feared would clam up from him from that point onwards. He had told the patient that there was no need – no *absolute* need – for him to record what he'd noticed in the casebook… provided he heard a solemn pledge that he would not notice it on his next visit. And although, as a tactic, it was limited (it rarely acted as a cessation of the self-hostilities), it had at least served to get patients on Roger's side.

It had been working with Louisa for four months. Tough love, if you wanted to call it that. Roger had made it clear that he knew of Louisa's fondness for inflicting cigarette burns on the skinny belly that she imagined was too fat, but that if she ever performed something similar on her baby's flesh – *ever* – she would be receiving a visit from employees with greater authority than that wielded by the social services. She'd be going to prison; she would lose her daughter. Did she understand?

I've done it, Roger, she had told him on the phone that morning. *I've really done it this time.* And she had started crying.

Standing in the rain by his car, Roger could bring back that phone call with a clarity that chilled his scalp. He was certain that he'd never forget it, and good luck with trying to do so.

Done what, Louisa? he had asked her in the office he had shared at the time, before his promotion. *What have you done?*

But she wouldn't stop crying at the other end of the line. Neither in his private life nor in his professional had Roger ever been good with tears (apart from his own, which he enjoyed shedding). Louisa's lament had only made him cross; his reserves of empathy had been low that day.

What have you done, Louisa? he'd demanded.

I've hurt her, she had answered in a gluey voice that had sounded neither drunk or normal. Pilled-up, possibly. *And I've emptied the medicine cabinet. How long will it take?* She had seemed genuinely curious.

For what? For death to arrive? For the ambulances to get there?

I'm on my way, Louisa, Roger had told her. *Don't lie down.*

I'm already lying down.

Then get up. Call an ambulance. Keep moving and talking to Billie. Do you understand me?

Yes.

I'm angry, Louisa.

I know you are. I knew you would be. I couldn't take it anymore. I wish I were sorry. I wish I could feel *something.*

One law of the universe that Roger had observed was that traffic worsens in direct correlation to one's anxiety. The journey had taken twenty minutes (it was ten on a good day) and he had expected to find two bodies when he kicked down the door. All the same, as he'd marched along the fifth landing walkway, a weird sense of calmness had enwrapped him. They'd be dead – he was sure of it – but his anger had evaporated; he'd felt ready.

What he *hadn't* been ready for was Louisa opening the front door for him when he arrived. But she did. And what was worse was the smile on her face: the smile that said *Gotcha!* The smile that showed her braces, and the braces that caught the light.

I just wanted to see you again, Roger, she'd said. *I've bought new bed linen – just for you.*

And he'd slapped those braces hard. He'd knocked her over.

Roger stared into the cave of that much-regretted morning, seeing it as clearly, as colourfully, as he saw Homebase through the shiver of rain: one reality as the palimpsest of the other, but which was which? Dodging idling cars sharking for a free space, Roger walked over to the supermarket, intending to browse in the baby aisle, as he often did. But not to buy for their germinating first; nor even to perve over the pregnant women buying things for their own. No: Roger wanted to check what colour boxes Pampers nappies were sold in.

In his mind it had all come together. Remembering Louisa, as he'd pushed her backwards into her kitchen; as he'd slammed her door shut; as he'd moved towards her, down the narrow hallway… On her small kitchen surface, next to the toaster, had stood a large box of Pampers. Roger remembered it clearly, this box. Even when Louisa had sunk to her knees in front of him, he had not wished to look down into her crybaby eyes; he had kept his gaze on the Pampers. He had focussed on that box while he lowered his fly, and while she did what they both knew she must.

Pampers nappies.

Funny the things you remember, Roger thought, knowing that he had seen a box of an identical colour in Don's front room.

Why would an old man be buying nappies?

3.

Phyllie was sceptical.

'That's it? A box of *nappies?*'

'In the lounge of a man who takes care of birds for a living. Who has no children and especially no grandchildren…' Roger argued (silently congratulating himself on his bowdlerised version of the confession: it had ended with the slap to Louisa's face and then a talking-to in the young mother's kitchen. There were some things that even Phyllie might not forgive).

'But how do you *know* he's got no children, Rog?'

'Dorota said.'

'And how would *she* know? She only met him ten minutes ago! She's not exactly his *biographer.* Maybe he's met someone! And she's married or something, and she brings her child – or why not *their* child? – to the gingerbread hut in the woods. And while the baby's sleeping, Don treats his new flame to a hunka hunka birdkeeper love...' Phyllie laughed.

Roger didn't. 'You get a feeling,' he tried to explain.

'Oh I know all about your *feelings*, Rog...'

'I'm serious.' His frown and the muscle-knotted nub of flesh at the crown of his nose confirmed this. 'I mean, how many homes have I entered in the line of business over the years?'

'You tell me.'

'Hundreds! That's how many. And you look for clues, Phyllie: it's not a million miles away from being a private detective.' Roger waited to be contradicted; failing a contradiction, a furtherance of the interrogation would suffice. But nothing came. 'The man's hiding *something*,' was all he could think of to add.

They had finished a snack of cheese and crackers during the conversation and were sitting at the kitchen table, their elbows to either side of their completed plates. Now taking her husband's hand, Phyllie said, 'So what are you proposing, Rog?' Her voice was soft and understanding. 'You already went there and found nothing. And he did well to keep his temper, by the way. But he's not likely to be so sympathetic a second time.' She waited; she squeezed his fingers. 'Is he now?'

'No.'

'So what? Sneak in when he's not there? It's not impossible, Roger, but ask yourself why you'd be doing it. It's not against the law to own a box of nappies, even if he *doesn't* take care of a baby. It's not as if he's done anything wrong, and if you remember, the reason we suspected something in the first place – it had nothing to do with a *baby*. It was a missing schoolgirl.'

Roger sighed. 'Yeah I know. I know it *logically*. But I can't stop wondering why a man of his age would be hiding –'

'Or storing.'

'... a box of Pampers in the sideboard. And if it wasn't for Dorota and I on the floorboards at the same time, or the draft we made – or whatever it was – the sideboard door wouldn't have swung open half an inch and we wouldn't...'

'Okay, Rog. Would it make you feel better if we managed to get Don out of his cabin and you could have a proper rummage?'

'And how would you do that?'

'I'd talk to Vig.' Phyllie shrugged and let go of Roger's hand. 'He owes me one for refusing my well-intentioned sexual advances.'

Roger chuckled. 'I'm not sure it works like that, Phyl.'

'Oh he knows the rules. He's *German*, for Christ's sake. And speaking of refusing my sexual advances...'

'Don't. I didn't *refuse.*'

'All right then. Speaking of sexual advances, it's been three nights. I must admit, it was nice to have a rest on the first night, but I'm starting to worry you've gone off this fat girl.'

'I haven't,' Roger told her.

'Good. So prove it. Then I'll call Vig.'

4.

As Phyllie had predicted, Vig was awake – and awake for the reason that she had given Roger. He couldn't sleep. The truth was he had simply not taken to the house. The space he found constricting, of all things. He was trapped by all of this extra room. It wasn't natural; and it was playing with his biorhythms. While Dorota slept soundly, it was Vig's new hobby to wander around the house; to read in his library – his library! – and to stroll out into the chilly pre-dawn air.

Sometimes he went to see the birds.

His footfalls on the path away from the house (or on the

lawn, if he was of a mood to feel wet grass through his slippers) would trigger the security light on the patio; and enjoying the cold, perhaps with the moon on his back, Vig would stroll out to Don's aviary, his shadow as stretched out before him as a bad dream of being chased, or of chasing. The threat of rain in the air had been known to be a comfort.

Rarely were the birds pleased to see him. They did not wake and squawk; they did not fly around within their confines. Quite often, in fact, they slept peacefully while Vig spied on them on their perches, and fantasised the contents of their dreams. It was peaceful. For Vig, it was like… like being invisible. If he could cause no fuss, then surely he could not be present physically.

A childish logic, of course. But it kept him calm, sometimes. Kept him calm until, inevitably, one bird or more woke up and raised the aviary alarm. At that point, it was time to beat a hasty retreat… or to wait for Don.

Sure as night followed day, Don Bridges came running when he heard a commotion in his birdhouse. And as richly as he respected the birds for their enclosed spaces and parameters – even envied them the same – Vig respected the fact that Don responded faster to a cat among the pigeons (as it were) than ever he would, say, to news that the main house was burning down.

If you wanted to witness Don at full pelt, you could do a lot worse than slide a snake into one of the cages.

At the moment, however, Vig was alone. While he thought it through, he was struck by its undeniable poeticism: *it was Vig and the birds, by starlight.*

And so it was. The rain that had threatened earlier had not materialised, and the wind had taken the pancake clouds away with it. The sky was a held breath; it was flawless… Feeling about the size of an ant beneath it, Vig watched the birds behind the mesh – as well as he could by starlight and security beam com-

bined – and added to his pondering of what birds dreamed the
predicament of why he felt so ill-at-ease.

No, he knew why. The question was unfair (on himself).
There was no doubt about it.

It was Don who unnerved him.

Didn't matter that the accusation was unreasonable; didn't
matter that Dorota's search of Don's hut had come up with not a
small thing to show. The seed had been planted in Vig's imagination; and in the absence of anything workmanlike or profitable to
do with his day, he had become a noodler and a brooder.

Vig could call himself pathetic until his back stung with
whips and self-absement, the truth was that he didn't want Don
on his land. The sheer scale and space that he owned was not a
solution. In fact, his acres were part of the problem. Wherever
Vig stood on the estate at any time, he knew that Don was out
there somewhere – a secret known only to himself – and doing
precisely what at that moment was anyone's guess.

No evidence.

It's not important.

They searched.

It's not important.

He's a harmless old man who loves birds.

It's not important.

When the realisation struck Vig that he walked out to see
the birds on insomniac nights for the *purpose* of meeting Don,
it was sufficient to make him come over queer and giddy. The
sensation – help me God! – was not far from a pang of love, a
strobe of longing.

'You can't sleep again, sir.'

Vig turned. Don had a habit (and an ability) of creeping
up on him.

'Evening, Don. Are you well?'

'Fair to middling. And you?'

'I'm exhausted,' Vig answered honestly.

'Same here.'

Nothing in the older man's tone – not now, not since – gave any indication that he'd been put out or chagrined by the search of his modest home. Incredibly, the man had behaved impecca-bly. However, if he'd intended a good grace to indicate humility, the ploy had failed. As far as Vig was concerned, Don behaved like a man who had got away with something and was currently surfing the waves of relief.

They chatted for a few minutes, Don rolling, lighting and smoking a cigarette as they spoke. It felt natural. Calm. Two strangers at a bus stop, perhaps. Two men queuing. Vig realised that he knew nothing more about the birdkeeper – not one single thing – than he had when he and Dorota had moved in. Had he expected the old man to reveal all about his past in bite-sized chunks? Well, kind of. No, not kind of. Yes. Yes he had. *Exactly* what he had expected, the man living on his land and so forth…

'Thought I saw foxes earlier,' said Vig, this time not so hon-estly. Rather cackhandedly, in fact; but Vig imagined it to be a good idea to get back to the subject that had been abandoned: the subject of unexplained noises in the woods.

'Couple of families-worth,' Don agreed. 'You can hear them when it's still.'

The two men fell silent. Vig heard nothing but the wind combing through branches, ploughing the trees. He did not even hear the phone ringing in the house.

3.

But Dorota did.

She swore in Polish, and eiderdowned in a thick night-dress, she swung her legs out of bed and shuffled along the corridor to a spare room that housed one of the property's phones.

'It's Phyllie Reydman.'

'...Do you know what time it is, Phyl?'

'Yes. Do you know where your husband is?'

'No,' Dorota admitted. 'What about him?'

'Roger's on his way over to you. I'm about to follow in the other car.'

'Why?'

'You might not be safe, that's why. Not in the long run: reputations and all that...'

Dorota shook her head. Maybe she remained gluey with slumber; maybe this was really making sense after all.

'What's up?' she asked.

And Phyllie told her.

4.

When the Berlin Wall splintered and cracked, Vig had been thirteen. He was old enough to remember hatred and forgiveness, easily, and knew more than he wanted to know about the spastic death throes of Communism, about witch hunts...

Much of it came back to him now.

Having finished shooting the breeze with the birdkeeper, Vig had been crossing the lawn in a gloomy slouch when Dorota burst out onto the patio, actually waving her arms as if she'd expected to have to use semaphore to attract his attention from a distance. Running out to meet him, she had called: 'Roger's coming!'

'Roger who?' Vig had called back.

'Roger Moore! Who-do-you-think Roger!'

'Sorry! What's he doing?'

In the space of this interlocution, their strides had brought them closer, almost to a collision point. Then Dorota had swept him up in her aura of energy and purpose, now striding blokeishly, and had collected Vig along with her, like a relay baton.

'I've opened the front gate,' she said, not answering her partner's question.

'Dorota. What's going on?'

'We're going to see Don.'

'I just saw him. What about?'

'You just *saw* him?'

'By the birds. We had a chat.'

'Roger swears he saw baby milk in his hut.'

'Slow down, will you? So what if he did?'

'Why would he have it?'

'I don't know. For the birds?'

'For the *birds* now!'

'I *don't know.* What are you suggesting?'

'It's what Roger's suggesting.'

'Then what's *Roger* suggesting?'

'You *know* what he's suggesting!'

'Shouldn't we wait for him?'

'Surprise is the best form of attack, Vig.'

And it felt like a witch hunt. It was hateful, creative in its cruelty – and to Vig it resembled a witch hunt. He didn't know whether to feel guilty or appeased.

DELIVERY

1.

How do you know when it's time to stop work for the day, Tim?

Well, Victoria (or was it Virginia?) *it's like asking a high-jumper why he doesn't try for his personal best for the eighth time that afternoon. You always want to be doing your best work, whatever you do. In life, I mean. And just like the high-jumper won't get his magic.*

What?

Three metres?

How high could an athlete jump?

...two metres sixty, or whatever his best happens to be, I know instinctively – it's like an instinct – that whatever I do at that point is likely to need to be redone in the morning. So it's time to put down the pen.

That was a laugh. A pen now! Since when, Tim? *I ply the scrivener's trade,* eh son? And all that wind.

Branston was interviewing himself again (old habits died hard; he had tried to quit but self-interest had proved too heavy an anchor to ignore); but for this particular interview, on the compositional process of film scripts, the subject had brought along with him an annoying punitive superego of an interruptive smartarse. Who would not keep it zipped. Who wanted its own thoughts on the record. Who wanted in.

It had come to something when a man could not conduct a conversation with himself without fearing an interruption by a third party!

Branston lowered the weights. A *monologue interieur* was one way of sublimating the dread and rage that he directed towards physical exercise, but he could taste rust on his lips and this was his usual sign that he'd benched enough.

Rising to his feet, Branston performed a tight boxer's two-step in the full-length reflection. As ever he had exercised nude. Exertion had drawn his penis into itself: it was all but smothered in a nest of auburn curlies. If the whim took him, he could reverse that situation in the bath in two minutes flat; but he knew he must wait. Work before pleasure, Victoria. (Or was it Virginia?) Having reached for a towel, which he used to mop his shoulders, Branston crossed the landing and settled down at his desk to mark some of his students' work.

It was Saturday morning. Branston could not recall the last time that he had not marked students' work on a Saturday morning.

The task he had set was to write between one and two thousand words on an inspirational film- or documentary-maker of their choice, paying attention not to the artist's *oeuvre* but more to the qualities that made that person inspirational and what the contemporary budding filmmaker could learn from them. The low word limit had been intentional: Branston had imagined that without it he would see novella-length hagiographies about Lynch or Tarantino. What he'd wanted was for his students to analyse, not to gush.

By the third essay in, the tactic seemed to have worked. These were better than he'd expected. So far, so good: even if he had needed Google's help with the identity of a Finnish epidemiologist that Sammy had chosen to concentrate on, for reasons of her own.

Midway through a minefield of exploded punctuation on the first page of an essay on Jim Jarmusch, Branston jumped when the letterbox flapped shut downstairs. For decency's sake (and just in case) he pulled on a pair of jogging shorts and skipped down to collect his mail, thinking: *Early for a Saturday.*

The package was the size of an electrical plug. It had not been delivered by Royal Mail: there was no stamp on the packaging; there wasn't room for one.

Branston tore it open. A memory stick was inside. Intrigued, he bounded upstairs and turned on the computer.

2.

Half an hour later, and Branston perched on the chubby wing of his old-fashioned sofa, thinking back to the class in which Yasser had shown the film he'd made about the kidnapping. That film had been hard enough to watch. But this new one – delivered by hand to his house, he reminded himself – had been even worse... Branston's arms felt tired, though not because of his workout. Anaesthetic-like tiredness had closed in on him. What to do?

Branston knew. And because of that first film he also knew where Yasser worked for his Saturday job.

High Town Market.

Branston got dressed quickly and left his house.

3.

Yasser was changing a twenty-pound note for a customer when he saw his teacher approach on foot. So surprised was he that it took him two glances before he'd confirmed that it was indeed Branston coming his way.

Transaction completed, the customer pocketed his change and sloped off, clutching a pair of hedgetrimmers to his considerable chest.

'What do you do for lunch?' Branston asked. 'Usually.'

'Go to the bacon van, Tim. Usually.'

'I'll treat you.'

Yasser cocked his head. 'What's the occasion? Is this about college?'

'I wish it was. Can you leave your post?'

'In a minute I can. My uncle's gone for a coffee. When he gets back.'

In due course they walked away, Yasser and Branston, but they did not tarry at the former's favourite stop for breakfast and lunch. They carried on walking along High Town Road, saying little after Yasser had earned from Branston a brisk nod of the head with the question: *Is this about Maggie?*

They repaired to an alehouse called The Green Child. In the workman-clotted back garden, Yasser waited for his large chilled orange juice, wishing that he had a paper to read, while Branston ordered at the bar. But Branston wasn't long. He emerged back out into the lunchtime sunlight, blinking, with an orange juice, a pint of bitter and a thin cigar. As Yasser sipped his drink, Branston tore the cellophane from his smoke and lit up.

With his other hand he slapped the memory stick on the table.

'What is it?'

'It's you, Yasser,' Branston told him, reaching for his beer. 'And your ladyfriend Maggie.'

'...I don't understand.'

'I deliberately didn't bring my laptop to show you, and it wasn't something I wished to discuss at Barnfield.'

'What wasn't? I'm confused, Tim.'

Branston rinsed his mouth with bitter. 'You may or may not know that you are on digital record – you and Maggie, sitting in a tree. It's all there, Yasser. And while it's none of my business, of course, what you get up to with whomever…'

'You mean *sex*?'

Branston nodded. '…what I *do* have to ask myself is why someone – Maggie presumably – thinks it's a good idea to take a copy to my house, for me to see.'

'You mean she *filmed* us?'

'That's exactly what I mean. Or someone did, anyway. And then she – or someone – thought it was a good idea, it seems, to show me your performance.'

'Christ. But how does she know your address?'

'That was one of the questions I had for *you*.'

'Well *I* didn't tell her. Why would I? And I don't know where you live anyway.'

Branston took a long swig. 'I had a feeling you'd say something along those lines.'

'It's true!'

'I believe you. Which means someone's followed me home.'

Nothing to argue with there. 'But why?'

Branston shrugged. '*Keine Ahnung.* That's why I'm here.'

Noisily Yasser exhaled. He could not conceive that Maggie might have done this to hurt him – not deliberately. No. It had not been Maggie's idea. It had either been her father's or it had been the brainchild of Tommy the Brazilian.

And one of them was going to pay.

4.

Having brooded for the rest of Saturday, and having slept through storms of difficult dreams, Yasser showered and got dressed on Sunday morning and walked out to the car. With the engine running and the wipers moving, he took a few minutes before he engaged first gear and pulled away. This was it: the last time. He could not imagine that this trip to Maggie's could be anything but the final visit. Done. *Finito.* How could it be anything else, now? All the same, it surprised him to note that the understandable emotions of anger and disappointment had been joined by that of regret. As he calmly drove through Dunstable, he regretted the fact that he had been unable to handle the commissioned task. He had failed. And if the signs had been clear for weeks – the signs that he was *going to* fail – they had not prepared Yasser fully for the reality of the bust that had followed the boom. He had failed to locate the missing child. And he felt lousy. If this was the last time that he'd see Maggie, this morning was their break up. Something had shifted, not only in the universe, but also in Yasser's heart: he had had no choice but to come to realise that he cared for the woman… and he had never been good at transforming a girlfriend into an ex.

Not that he'd shout her down, of course: that wasn't Yasser's style. She would be allowed to explain herself. (*That's big of you, Yass,* Shyleen had told him sarcastically when he'd confessed his plan to her in a postcoital moment of their own, last night. *Oh the women you use and discard!* She had laughed. The comment had left Yasser reeling. Urgently he had asked himself: Is it *me* doing something wrong?) Yasser found that he was looking forward to hearing Maggie's reasoning. And then, afterwards, perhaps she would blow him – an apology fuck, *non?* Just a quick one for the road – then *adios, sweetheart, it's been as much fun as an anal pimple, but I can't say it hasn't been an experience.*

Something like that, anyway. This was what Yasser had planned for his parting shot, and Shyleen had even dared him to go through with it. She claimed that Yasser's lovemaking style improved when he was in a state of anxiety. I'll give *you* an anxiety in a minute, Yasser had replied, wiping himself off with the wanksock that he kept behind the chest of drawers – the sock that resembled a Womble's toboggan.

It was only as he pulled onto the camp's driveway that Yasser experienced the full force of his nervousness – its rich extent and pull. Excalibur's manic barking was nostalgically welcome (if not welcoming): Yasser went so far as to imagine that he might miss the vicious wanker when all of this was over. Was there even something valedictory in the fact that the dog had been allowed off its leash for a change? It chased Yasser's car, yapping all the while, until it grew tired or bored.

Yasser pulled up outside Maggie's home.

Frantically inflating a rear tyre on his vehicle – his foot pumping up and down with real welly – was Tommy the Brazilian. On seeing Yasser get out of the car, the man smirked with a matchstick between his lips. The smirk appeared spiteful.

'She ain't home,' Tommy called.

Yasser took the half-dozen necessary steps to Maggie's door.

'She's out over the doctor,' Tommy added. 'Getting the morning-after pill.'

Yasser turned to face him. 'Morning after what?' he demanded. 'I wasn't *here* last night!'

'What cont said you were?' Still smirking, Tommy took a break from inflating the tyre in order to make his point. 'You think you're the only blade in Maggie's life, do you, boy? The only one she shares her sheets with?'

'I have no idea.' Yasser felt queasy.

'No, well *get* an idea.' Tommy laughed. 'Quite an adventuress, our Maggie. Even her pa agrees.'

Yasser grimaced. 'You're disgusting,' was the best he could manage.

Tommy held up his hands in mock surrender. 'Don't beat me no harder, sir!'

Yasser returned to his car. He was about to get in when

Tommy said: 'And compared to the others, boy, by the way…'

What others?

'…your performance was *languorous*.'

Languorous? Yasser had encountered the word before but he could not define it now. The meaning was probably irrelevant. What Tommy was saying was that he'd viewed the sex tape.

Or more.

'*You* filmed us, didn't you?' Yasser demanded.

'That's between me and my conscience.'

'You haven't *got* a conscience.'

'Between me and this slow puncture then,' Tommy answered, kicking the tyre in question.

'…Where is she really?'

'Well, pardon me but I've misplaced her focken social diary.' Tommy was growing bored with the conflict; he was drifting away – his energy ebbing like that of a ghost.

Maggie had once told Yasser that she only travelled on the 61 bus, but that didn't help him much. In what direction had she headed? He couldn't spend the morning scoping out all points on the Luton-Aylesbury continuum!

Maybe she's gone to see me, Yasser imagined with a sudden panic. She's taken a copy of the sex tape to show to my parents!

5.

Tim Branston, meanwhile, had made a decision of his own.

He had smelled a story on Yasser's clothes from the moment the student had brought the film assignment of the kidnapping to class. Instinct had told the tutor that the end of the film was unlikely to represent the end of the *story*; that more would play out; that the sum total of what had been recorded marked no finale.

Overall this impression had been confirmed on Branston's receipt of Yasser's sex tape... although Branston had perhaps not seen this bigger picture at that time. Not quite: at the time he had been frightened and furious that someone would have followed him home from work in order to deliver the memory stick by hand. It had made him feel violated; he had gone through a period of post-trauma depression (one which he soon regarded as ludicrous), simply because a would-be pornographer or two had proved themselves cleverer than one of his students. Oh, and cleverer than Branston himself, as well: let's not forget that he had been shafted along with Yasser.

The ramifications being what?

This was one that Branston had demanded of himself, time after time. In fact, it had grown into his favourite puzzle to solve while working out; the sort of conundrum that he had long since stopped regarding as an odd thing to work though while performing one's physical jerks. (It was what got you through the sweaty session that counted. Some delved no more deeply than adding up repetitions; some grunted and thought of nothing at all; some claimed to visualise sexual encounters; and Branston even knew a guy who recited the value of pi under his breath while benching his one-twenties and holding for the strain and burn.) And it was during a workout, a few days after he'd viewed the sex tape the first time that Branston had experienced his epiphany.

By watching the film of Yasser with Maggie, he was part of the story himself. Up to that juncture, true, he had been no more than a bit-player, a victim; his ascension up the ladder of closing credits would depend on what he did next. Participation was the passport to a starring role: for this reason, he had vowed, he would strive to learn the backstory and to introduce a few twists of his own. Why, by the time he had completed his session, his shins aching, a dull throb shining in the small of his back,

Branston was halfway convinced that he could smell the polishing lacquer on the statuette that he'd win for Best Short Picture at the next Cannes Festival.

Branston had begun two activities simultaneously. The first was a journal – a Word file that he simply called *Yasser and Maggie* – and the second was to follow Yasser wherever the young man went, within the obvious boundaries dictated by the laws of temporal, physical and ethical discretion.

At a stroke, it seemed, he had become Yasser's shadow.

6.

The new working week began, and on Tuesday evening, when he arrived home in the middle of the afternoon, Yasser sensed change in the air: something hard to define; a tension. Trying to remain as optimistic as possible, Yasser held tight to the possibility that his parents' bad mood was down to a rapid deterioration in Shyleen's uterine health. Not that he wanted his cousin to suffer, of course; it was more that he disliked being the focus of their negative attention. Maybe she'd died in her sleep. Though it shamed him to consider this alternative, briefly he hoped it was so. It did not take long, however, for that fag end of possible good fortune to be pissed away along the long urinal trough of an already bad morning.

'We've had a visitor,' his father told him, shortly after he'd sloughed off his coat.

Yasser sighed. 'I better sit down innit.'

'Don't you innit me, boy.'

Yasser sat down anyway: the settee cushion pumped out a farty acknowledgement of his tensed body mass. Then he saw his name in bold type: a headline in a Sunday tabloid, perhaps. Banged to rights. Guilty. *I feel so ashamed*, purrs Bury Park's Paki

D'Amour. The lounge's dark and treacly shades had rarely felt so oppressive. It was the like the walls had inched in over decades, only now the film had been speeded up.

'Did you play it?' Yasser asked.

Although his father had remained standing, his eyeline was not much higher than his son's. In the past he had used this resultant eyeball stare to his advantage; indeed, he did so now.

'Play what?' he demanded, goggled.

'The film, man!' Yasser shouted back.

'And don't you man me either! What the dickens are you discussing, boy?'

Yasser frowned; his belly gave a quick squeeze. 'She didn't give you a memory stick?' Yasser knew that his father knew how to use one: the man had taken Barnfield College up on its offer of free computer training for the over-50s, a few years earlier.

'Now what nincompoopery? What *she?*'

Yasser took a breath. With an effort he was able to keep his eyes open.

'Who was the visitor?' he asked softly.

'A boy! He says his name's Fonehacka. He even spelt it to me, like I don't know my ruddy English!'

And who the dickens is Fonehacka when he's at home? Yasser wondered.

'He wants you to help him find his brother! You! Apparently you've got a reputation in High Town for finding people, Yasser. You found a stolen *baby.*'

'I did,' Yasser admitted.

'So why didn't I know nothing about this?'

'About what? It was a college project I caught on film. It was a fluke, Dad. I'm not a *detective;* I got no *talent.*'

His father's eyebrows writhed. At length.

'Well *he* thinks you have, and it transpires half of bloody

Luton thinks you have! So what you gonna do?'

Yasser repeated, 'About what?'

'About finding the bloody boy, boy! His name is Nero – or Neil in real money. He's fifteen and he's trotting out with a white girl, the child reckons. I want him found by the end of the week.'

Yasser waited for a different interpretation of the mini-speech to emerge, but no different interpretation was forthcoming.

'You want me to *what*?'

'Find the missing Nero! And don't shilly-shally about it, fart-arseing on your bloody laptop!

Throughout this direction, Yasser had shaken his head. Now he tongued his lips damp, the better to produce his flat re-fusal.

'You've got to be joking,' he said.

'Joking? You've got a new reputation for something useful, finally! And all the Fanny Adams with your college –'

'Dad. I'm not about to start a business locating missing people. Period.'

His father wiggled a finger. 'Don't you period me, boy. You'll establish a profitable sideline by the time I say Jack Robinson or you'll regret the day you were born! How else are you buying your expensive shoes?'

'The stall.'

'Billy Bollocks. You take me for just off the banana boat.' His father stretched up to his full height, adding an inch or two to the total: he was preparing to leave the room, Yasser guessed, his words delivered as a *fait accompli* – and lo, it shall come to pass...

'And one more thing,' the man added. 'You'll marry Shyleen too if you're so keen on plugging her weak spots with your little man's didgeridoo! And if she's pregnant... you'll name your son after me.'

7.

Naturally, Shyleen was the only person with whom Yasser felt comfortable discussing the matter and these latest developments. As usual, she suggested a drive: she thought better when she drove, or so she claimed.

'When you drive,' Yasser answered, 'you don't think *at all.*'

'Then *you* drive. I'll pout and look pretty as your Asian babe. Maybe tickle your *didgeridoo* if you're lucky. You can always go back to the Pikeys tomorrow.'

Yasser smiled into the mouthpiece. 'I've got a better idea.'

'Impossible.'

'We're going to see those students – the ones Tommy played poker with,' Yasser replied.

'Why?'

'Because he might've said something. People say all sorts of things to strangers.'

'How do you know they're strangers?'

'Well I don't. But I don't have any better ideas.'

'And what makes you think they'll talk to you?'

'I don't. But I don't have any better ideas. And I have to get out of my room.'

They met outside the Galaxy Centre, and had a coffee in the work-dodgers' pub before heading up the High Street on foot, with the smell of that establishment – disinfectant, hops and curdled hope – scorching their nostrils.

Ten minutes, and they were standing outside the student Halls of Residence.

'And now you're King Kong,' said Shyleen.

'Do one,' Yasser told her reflectively, staring up at the oxtail-coloured brick. Then he turned to her and added: 'Do what?'

'Climb the walls? Or do you surprise me with the announcement of a *plan?*'

'No, no plan. Heaven forbid! I could pretend to be pizza – a pizza delivery.'

'Like in a porn film!' Shyleen was beaming. 'Then I share you with all them eighteen year-old Nursing undergrads from *Hull*. Ooh, you know how to turn a girl on, Yass. I'm like the Grand Coulee Dam in me thong!'

'Shut it, Shy, I'm thinking. Or dare I ask you what *you* suggest?' said Yasser.

The beam on Shyleen's face burned brighter.

'You *suggest*, dear boy, what abuses of my position in car insurance I might've committed since our phone call, and what evidence of those abuses I might've printed out using work time and work ink.'

'...The fuck?'

'Well, students have cars too, you know.'

'So?'

'So. I can do address searches, and I did.'

'*So?*'

'So a student in this very Hall of Residence owns a Mini with oh-nine plates. Her name is Melissa Claybridge – and I'm just about to tell her I saw a black guy tying to steal it. And not *just* because she's an overprivileged bag of foxshit either, driving a car her daddy paid for when I had to pay for my own. No. In order, my Yasser, to *get in your pants*.'

'You've got her *number?*'

'Well, I have. But how would a passing member of the public have her number? No. It's the intercom blackjack for us, Sunny Jim. Then when I panic her into coming out... you go in.'

Yasser grinned. 'Not bad. For that,' he said, 'my didgeridoo is yours for the blowing.'

'Always was. Come on. I'm feeling like that bird off *The Killing.* Don't want to lose my mojo.'

8.

Shyleen had seen Tommy pressing a button less than half-way up the panel, and this at least gave Yasser a clue where to start. The building was eight storeys high, after all.

Third floor. By the time he'd stepped out of the lift he'd rehearsed his door-knocking speech, truncated though it was.

The fifth door that he tried was already ajar, and heavy metal throbbed within. A tangy incense of hash smoke snaked out into the corridor. The gland problem who opened the door wider – twenty stone in his khaki beach shorts and faded Fields of the Nephilim t-shirt, his features foetal and his scribble of beard less philosopher than mouse turds on a Welcome mat – appeared to have partaken of more than his fair share of the latter. His eyes were like the Roadrunner's.

'*Buenos noches*,' he piped, '*amigo*.'

It was three forty-five in the afternoon.

'*Buenos noches*,' Yasser answered, and then offered his real name. 'I'm a friend of Tommy's. Here for the cards the other night?'

'Sure, *amigo*.' The glandjob nodded his head.

'Says he might've left his phone here.'

'Yeah? Well, come in and look, *compadre*. My igloo is your igloo.'

'Cheers.' Yasser stepped over the threshold, yanked by the dizzying silver fog. 'Jesus.'

'Yeah, it's pungent, I grant you.'

'It certainly is.'

The apartment was filthy. Clothing and food competed for space on every surface. There was no sign of a carpet anymore: it was covered with newspapers.

Making a show of looking for a mobile, Yasser spied egg-shells on a bookcase; and such was the volume pounding from the music centre that a pizza – an entire cooked *pizza* – bounced and wriggled with the bassline, upside-down on a sofa cushion.

Yasser expected to see a mouse. Or catch a throat infection.

'Oh wait a minute, bro,' said the glandjob. 'It weren't here – my mistake.'

'What weren't?'

'The poker game? It was next door.'

'Jesus.'

'My memory, eh? Too much voodoo. It were next door: Paul Physics.'

'That's his name?'

'No, man, that's his subject he's studying – I don't know his surname. Or maybe I do. To tell you the truth – I hide it well, I know – but I been doing a lot of Class C. I mean, like *wheelbarrows* of the fucking shit. I tend to live a lot in the American Sixties and Seventies. A speedball was –'

'I know what a speedball is,' Yasser interrupted. 'Heroin and coke.'

'…You wouldn't have one on your person you'd be good enough to sell, would you? My folks are well rich and money's no object, *compadre*.'

Yasser laughed: a bark. 'I don't tend to carry em around. The five-oh ain't so copacetic round here, man. Street hassle, you dig?' For the occasion of this satirical pisstake, Yasser had even adopted a chiffon-light American accent.

'My *brother*. Ain't *that* the truth.'

So Yasser stepped out into the corridor and knocked on what he reasonably hoped was the relevant door. At least the student who answered it appeared student-normal: long, rodent-colour hair, parted in the middle; a lively culture of spots on an angular chin; John Lennon spectacles, darkened glass. He spoke with a Gallic burr, and listened in a manner that suggested a slight deafness, as Yasser explained his predicament.

The man was hurting. On Cards Night he had lost heavily; he had taken, in fact, a thorough spanking, to the tune of three hundred quid. For this reason alone he was happy to talk – to analyse his play and his misfortune – in the loquacious manner of all breathing victims the world over.

Yasser could not believe his luck. (It was about time.) Midway through a recital that was italicised by emotion, the student started framing thoughts on how he would report his lack of funds back to his father. And Yasser said, 'I have a few pounds I could help you with.'

The man's face glowed softly. He couldn't believe his luck either, but he was wary with it, not used to getting his own way, perhaps. 'Yeah?'

'Yeah, that's right. Twenty pounds – and twenty pounds only – for the names and addresses of the people you played poker with the other night. Any information appreciated.'

The student nodded.

GOODBYE TO THE CARNIVORES

No more fire.

These were the words that Connors repeated silently to himself.

No more fire.

A tattoo as he marched along, as best he could.

Although he was now three days away from the village (and by his own reckoning, out of danger), there was to contend with the fact that his cigarette lighter had run out of gas the previous evening, and if he didn't make it back to the harbour town where he'd landed on Toenail Island today, he would most likely freeze in the absence of a remarkable blaze.

No more fire.

Was he going the right way? To his eyes all the landscape looked the same, and he had long since grown to distrust his inbuilt instinctive compass. All he could hope for, as long as he wandered in a vaguely straight line, was that he'd encounter civilization sooner or later.

And then what?

The hell of it was… he didn't know. After dining with Ruth and her extended family (but before he had learnt what he'd eaten) he had sought opinion on the subject of his proposed journey to God's mouth. In no uncertain terms he had been told that the voyage was impossible: if it had ever been attempted, the reckless sailor or crew had not returned home to tell the tale. It was suicide. Thus, it was right up Connors's alley: something suicidal sounded good, about now.

Ruth's father had fed Connors well, and had sold him provisions for his onward travels – something herbal and spicy, he had had to insist on it. It was filling but samey, and Connors couldn't wait to find the butcher's shop-cum-restaurant where he had dined with Elvis on their first night on the island. Couldn't wait to blow the rest of his wages on a big pile of something bloody... as long as it had once owned more than two legs. A new golden rule.

Several stories had been told that night, interspersed with the singing. The tribe consisted of cannibals, but as they were at pains to convey, this did not make them murderers: in a spirit of waste-not-want-not, they ate what died naturally. They ate the elderly deceased, tumours and warts and all; but they didn't kill, and Connors was informed several times that he was in no danger of routine execution.

So happy and tipsy had Connors become that he had almost believed them. And now he missed their company. Eventually hobbling into the outskirts of the harbour town was one of the loveliest activities that he'd ever taken part in. When he knew where he was, he sat for a rest on a bench near a yard where some children were playing basketball. The tears that flowed down his cheeks were copious... After Connors had rebuked himself for the outpouring, he told himself that he should have bottled what he'd shed. In *this* fucking nut-house, he had no way of knowing when he'd need to drink his own tears. He stood up.

Connors headed back through town, towards the harbour, having pulled from his bag a small bouquet of plant life wrapped in grass – an analgesic that Ruth's father had also sold him. As he walked he plucked a stalk free and popped it in his mouth. It tasted foul; but chewing it made him feel better almost on the instant. Some of the pain retreated; some merely dulled, ready for the next time that Connors was unprotected. Good shit they packed here, the man mused. He wondered if he could smuggle some back to the real world. Sell it in Marsh Farm or High Town. Make a killing. Despite everything, Connors smiled.

Near the harbour where he'd first arrived, he sat again. Not once in his life had he been more depressed. He had nothing left. Thanks to the flies that had attacked him, he scarcely had skin on his palms; a grand total of five or six coins jangled in his pocket – coins of a lousy denomination. All but worthless, Connors reasoned. And all that he'd done was circle an island, like a tourist with time on his hands, starving the flesh off his rump… and eating boy soup.

This time, when he cried, he did not stop so easily. After a few minutes, in fact, it seemed as though he would never stop crying ever again. It didn't feel good: but producing the tears felt marginally better than not producing the tears.

It was all he had.

PROPERTY VIEWINGS

1.

Throughout the ordeal, Nero had endeavoured to stay physically fit, though he'd discovered, as the days ploughed on, that it wasn't the case that he had less and less energy for his exercises: it was more that the thought of exercise crossed his mind less and less often. Things that had once been second nature to Nero were falling from him as the weeks passed: things like an awareness of the need to exercise; things like his (already limited) vocabulary. Indeed, there were times – notably in the hum of the long afternoons – when he had to grasp and make the effort to recall events before he and Jess had come to live in this bedroom. He had to chase his own memory – hunt it down and hold it – while reminding himself (occasionally, when he forgot) of the colour of his skin, or that the burgeoning blimp of activity about his lower body was a signal that he must defecate soon. It was only when he remembered to exercise – some lunges, some push-ups, some sit-ups, but he didn't count his rounds or even his reps – that Nero also remembered the rage that went with them. And the reasons for the rage in the first place. It was only while gunning his body temperature higher that Nero pictured the faces and the penises of Eastlight and Massimo... and how he'd once believed that no man should ever see another man's erection in real life (in porn was fine).

It was only while engaged in callisthenics or aerobics that

Nero recalled that he intended to kill them. And yet… even this urge was less pronounced; and less pronounced; and less pronounced… as time went on. Nero knew this for a fact because he was doing his exercises now. And very little in the way of revenge was playing in his head.

He stopped exercising.

A few days earlier, he had awoken from one of his many daily naps to find that the door to the walk-in wardrobe had been left unlocked. Still naked as the day, he and Jess had crept out of the wardrobe and into the unfurnished bedroom, the carpet comfortable beneath their bare feet.

It had felt like a treat – a reward, perhaps – to have been entrusted to the run of the bedroom; at first they hadn't wanted to try the door handle. It had been locked. But the bedroom was better than the wardrobe; and under its bare light-bulb, Nero surveyed it with something like self-respect. He had arrived. He'd been promoted. This was his and this was Jess's. And he would do whatever he could not to enrage his captors, in case they wanted to tie them both up again.

Such at least was his opinion *this* hour. These opinions changed often, and Nero had long since realised that he (and possibly Jess as well) was suffering from a sort of captive madness, a cabin fever; he had long since doubted that his mental health was entirely cloudless.

By way of avoiding more painful decisions, Nero wondered once again if they – Charlie and Massimo – actually *wanted* him physically fit? Should he exercise again, right now? Or was he simply deluding himself and killing time? (Why would they require him to be physically fit?)

Confusing.

The thought of more activity stirred a memory in Nero's mind – but also in his upper arms and shoulders (muscle memory).

Underaged in the HeartLines Gym (he remembered), Nero had worked out with his older brother, crashing weight after weight – curling, shoving – bending those muscles and wanting the fuckers to twang. And now, sitting down on the carpet in the bedroom, Nero thought again about Molecule: really *thought*. With effort he framed the young man's face; then he watched an old film of the two of them, in the gym, with Molecule daring him on and calling him pussy for fearing the addition of another half-kilo on the stack.

Nero smiled.

But now he was puffed out and aerated as the result of two minutes of squat thrusts. Sweat ran off his (twitching) shoulders in a steady trickle.

Why hadn't Molecule found him?

'Who's Molecule?' he heard through his highly laboured breathing.

'My elder brother.'

'What about him?' asked Jess.

Had Nero misheard the original question? Turning in Jess's direction, he saw the girl squatting, leaning against the wall, an inquisitive expression on her face. Odder than this look, however, was the query that Nero held in his head.

Who's Molecule? and *What about him?* had been asked in two different voices. While the second had belonged to Jess – no question about it – the first had sounded… masculine. Through the exercise-heated breathing it had seemed normal enough, but now that he examined it, the voice had sounded like a man's. And Nero hadn't said his brother's name out loud anyway. Had he?

'Did you ask me about Molecule?' Nero wanted to know.

Jess shrugged. 'Who's Molecule?'

Yeah, who's Molecule? Nero heard in the original interviewer's voice.

'Woah!' said Nero.

'What?' said Jess.

'Did you hear that?'

'No. What?'

'Someone said *Who's Molecule?*'

'That was me.'

So who is he? said the man's voice. *You've told me your brother, but gimme something else. I need a story!*

Jess looked worried. Inasmuch as she 'sprung' anywhere these days, she sprung to her feet. She crossed over to Nero, taking careful steps, as if a layer of black ice had formed on the carpet.

'Are you all right?' she asked.

'Yeah I'm peachy. Apart from this *voice* in my head.'

A beat.

Jess considered the information and chose not to challenge it.

'What's it saying?'

Nero bent a little at the waist; he cupped his hands over his ears – like Molecule used to do when wearing headphones, mixing beats. Nero found that he wanted the transmission: he was urging it on. And it didn't take him more than a second to wonder why: it was contact with the world outside this room. It smelt of freedom.

'What's it saying, Nero?'

'*Ssshhh!*'

But there were no more words in Nero's head – not for ten seconds, twenty…

'Shit,' he whispered, gradually becoming aware of Jess beside him but not wishing to acknowledge her. By allowing her back into his reality (or trudging his way back into hers) the connection would be cut, the spell broken. Nero did not want to hang up just yet: there was *something* there, wasn't there? A small sound using his skull as a pathway; a noise of weather – the wind? Yes! It was wind! Nothing drastic, nothing heavy; maybe wind stirring through trees, a light patter of misty rain on leaves. The sensation followed – still in Nero's head – that the weather was chilly. Not icy, but chilly. Where?

Nero gambled. Surely the signs had been strong enough, these last days. It wasn't as if it mattered if he ended up looking like a fool. There was only Jess to judge him... and *she* had been made to watch while he was raped. The aggressors had taken turns to hold her head still. As a result, there wasn't much further he could fall in her eyes. So he said:

'Are you there, Chris?'

Nero waited for an answer – as if he'd shouted next door to one of his brothers (if he'd been shouting for one of his parents he would've had to have shouted *way* loud).

No response.

'Nero?'

'I said *ssshhh*.'

Nothing in words... but that sense of cold present, which Nero attempted to picture. What he saw was the inside of a hut, where Chris had taken refuge. If not a hut, an equivalent haven. Comparatively warm – compared with the outside. Wind like a tongue round a lolly.

Where was he?

'*Nero*. I *hear* something,' said Jess.

That same wind? The rain?

'They're here,' Jess continued. 'That was a door. They're downstairs.'

'Who? Oh yeah. You ready?'

'For what?' she asked, panicked.

'Jesus,' Nero sighed.

'Is it Jesus Christ you're hearing, Nero?' Her tone was hopeful and large.

'No. I meant Jesus-I-don't-fucking-believe-you. Are you ready to fight them?'

'No.'

'No, nor am I,' Nero confessed; 'but I'm not sure they'll give us much of an alternative.'

Footfalls on the stairs.

'I can't do this,' Jess confided.

'Do what? Do what comes natural.'

'That's what I'm scared of doing.'

One set of footfalls or two?

Nero wasn't sure. Almost before he knew what he was doing, he was praying to his new leader, to the distant man named Chris, for guidance and strength. For the wherewithal to know how to brain his captors if the chance was presented.

He heard Jess hold her breath. Good idea, thought Nero, doing the same thing (but he didn't know why). Depleted of oxygen, he waited.

The next thing would be the key in the lock. *The door will open...*

Pounce and strike.

But there was no key in the lock. The handle turned and the door swung inwards.

How long had it been unlocked? Nero wondered, bewildered.

And who were these people?

For neither of his rapists – not Charlie and not Massimo – stood on the landing, peering into the bedroom. In fact, Nero had never set eyes on any one of these three visitors in his life.

The shock was enough to make him cover his penis with one hand.

2.

'Anyone know where Charlie is?' asked Jean, holding one hand over the mouthpiece of her receiver.

There were three other people in the office, two men and one woman – all of them wearing black suits and lighter-coloured shirts with the necks wide open. Towards the end of the working day, and there was little going on: a bit of filing, a bit of appointment planning. When the phone rang, three of them had gone for the call.

'Gone home early, I think,' said one of the guys. 'Something about an anniversary. I wasn't listening.'

Jean relayed the news to the caller; what followed was a long period of silence in the office, but with the caller's words buzzing in Jean's ear.

'Hold the line, please.' To the remaining crew she added: 'Charlie's dropped a bollock. He was supposed to collect a Mr and Mrs Murphy and take them to the Eggington property for a viewing. They've been waiting outside the gate for half an hour and can't get in.'

'He cancelled,' said the second man present – a man named Joe, who was arranging appointment notes on his computer. 'I heard him call and leave a message when I was having a smoke.'

'Well, they're still outside the house and they're pissed off. I think they've told me four times that it's started to rain.'

'I'll take it.' Joe stood up. 'It's on my way to the farm shop – I said I'd pick up some carrots for my neighbour's Shetland.' When he crossed the office, the floorboards protested and groaned. He flicked open the key safe and checked the chart.

'One of Charlie's colleagues will be with you in twenty minutes,' Jean continued into her phone. 'Sorry about the mix-up... Okay. Bye.'

'The key's not here,' Joe called. 'Maybe he's gone there after all.'

The other man – the one who had answered Jean's first question – looked up from his filing. 'No, he definitely said he was getting something ready for his anniversary.'

'Well, it's not here!'

Jean unlocked a safe near her desk – it was where the master keys were kept. She asked for the reference of the house in Eggington; the first man clicked a tab and brought up all of the properties on the company's books. He read Jean the code and she fished out the relevant key.

'Don't lose it.'

'No, Mum.'

3.

The drive to Eggington took Joe twenty minutes, as Jean had promised the potential house-buyers. Preparing to leave the car, Joe brushed crumbs from his jacket's lapels – he had eaten a sandwich *en route*.

Mr and Mrs Murphy were waiting in their vehicle near the house's front gate. They did not appear happy to see Joe.

'I'm sorry about the mix-up,' the estate agent repeated on behalf his firm, and of Charlie Eastlight. 'Let's get you in to have a look around.'

He unlocked the gate.

4.

Already shocked that the gate had been left open, Eastlight was horrified to recognise one of the two cars parked on the driveway. It was Joe's. And seeing as the other car was not a police car, Eastlight was forced to accept that his work colleague was showing someone around the house.

The panic that he felt was rich. It warmed him throughout, then it turned to ice in his organs. There was no conceivable good way that this could go.

'I cancelled you fuckers,' Eastlight breathed into the rearview, steaming up the glass with his poison and fear. Didn't anyone check their voicemail anymore?

To Hell with that. What was he going to do? They were here, that the was meat and potatoes of the fact: *they were here*. And nothing that Eastlight could do would make them *not here*. One way or another they would find the teenagers in the unfurnished master bedroom; and sooner or later the teenagers would finger him and Massimo for the kidnapping, for the sex games... even if he drove away now.

Think!

But it was difficult to think (he had discovered) with sweat running down into his eyes. It was difficult when his bladder felt fit to burst.

Eastlight dialled Massimo from the dash. Get him over here, perhaps: it was *his* mess as well. Actually it had all been his idea! So let *him* come up with a solution.

The answering message cut in. Eastlight killed the call and thumped the steering wheel. Seconds were passing.

Now. Do it now. There's no choice.

In a fatman flurry, with no sign of his customary concupiscence, but with movements that read desperate, Eastlight rolled out and opened the boot. He'd been shopping. What he'd bought for Massimo (for their anniversary) lay there in a nest of car blankets and supermarket bags.

He had not expected to need it so soon, but was sure that his partner would understand.

5.

This was work on top of the normal day's requirements, but Joe was content enough to put on a decent performance and to do a good job. Even though the property was not on his own books, he was certain that Charlie would be grateful if it sold. Despite Charlie's faults as a human being, he had always been fair when it came to money.

So let's sell the fucker, Joe told himself as he led the couple through the rooms on the ground floor.

In due course they mounted the stairs. The tiniest trace of something in the air, as if someone had been smoking up here… It took Joe another second or two before he recognised the aroma from one student party or another, way back when. It was dope smoke.

When he opened the master bedroom and saw the two naked youths – the boy dark-skinned, the girl as white as alabaster – Joe wondered if the smoke had really got to him. This had to be an hallucination, after all. They were just standing there…

'My God,' said Mrs Murphy.

…the boy with one hand over his particulars, the girl with her wrists by her sides.

'What?' started Joe.

'Who are you?' asked the girl.

'Who am *I?*' Joe challenged. 'Who are *you?* What are you doing…?'

'We live here,' the boy answered.

'No you don't.' Joe felt the viewers back away across the landing. 'This house is for sale and you're trespassing.'

'Maybe we bought it,' the girl answered. 'And *you're* trespassing.'

'Don't muck me about. Get your clothes on and get out before I call the police.'

'We haven't got any clothes,' the boy told him.

Odd that they'd stay in the middle of the floor, not retreating, not advancing. Shameless, thought Joe. They seem shameless and even innocent.

'What do you mean, *no clothes?*'

'They were taken,' the girl added… and was it Joe's imagination or was there a note of pride in these words?

'Who by?'

'By me,' said Charlie Eastlight, below at the foot of the staircase.

By taking a few steps back, Joe was able to peer over the banister. He saw his colleague ascend the stairs in a dash. And what was Charlie holding?

'Get in the room with them,' Eastlight barked as he rose higher.

'Charlie?'

'Don't Charlie me, Joe! Get in the room or I'll use it, so help me God.'

It was shaped like a truncheon, but the handle boasted buttons and controls.

Mr and Mrs Murphy moved closer to one another and Joe held up his hands.

'What's got into you, Charlie?' he demanded.

'Get in the fucking room!'

Eastlight had reached the landing; he was waving the weapon like an orchestra conductor. 'Don't make me use it, Joe,' he warned. 'It shoots between ten and a hundred volts at a pop, and it's fully charged up and set to sixty. That's enough to make you soil your cheap suit twice over. So I won't tell you again…'

'Okay!' said Joe, stepping into the bedroom and breathing the fug within – a room left unaired for too long.

Silent but shaking, the Murphy couple followed Joe over

the same threshold.

'Into the wardrobe.'

Murmuring stunned protests, all five made a twitchy move for the other door.

'Not you two.'

Five pairs of eyes now on Eastlight.

'*You* two can guard them,' Eastlight instructed.

The boy straightened up, just in the left field of Joe's range of vision. 'What makes you think you can trust us?' the boy asked – a peculiar question, Joe thought.

Eastlight smiled. 'The door's been unlocked for three days,' he answered, 'and you haven't tried to escape. I can trust you.'

By the time Mrs Murphy had entered the walk-in wardrobe, she was blubbering uncontrollably. Her husband and Joe followed her in.

'Now pretend you're in school assembly,' Eastlight went on. 'Cross-legged on the floor, please; hands on your heads.'

For the first time Mrs Murphy spoke. 'I have arthritis,' she said, 'in my right knee. I can't cross my legs.'

'You'll have worse if you disobey me, dear,' Eastlight informed her.

'I'm serious! The doctor prescribed Pilates but I couldn't I couldn't…'

'Oh all right, stop whining. Just get on your arse and we'll call it quits.'

'Charlie? Like what the fuck?' asked Joe. 'If you're having a bad day, we can talk.'

'Shut up, Joe,' Eastlight interrupted, a note of sour fatigue in his voice. 'It's got nothing to do with you, okay? It's unfortunate you're here but there you go. God's bowled you a googly. It happens. Now we've got to think of a way out of it.'

Joe grinned. 'That's what I'm talking about! We can talk it

through!'

Eastlight fired a bolt of electricity at the wall. A spiky ribbon of blue lightning bounced off the cream paintwork with a sound like a power outage.

Mrs Murphy squealed.

Without another word the three new prisoners dropped to their haunches and assumed the requested position. A smell of ozone hung in the still air.

Jess started chuckling.

'Don't breathe a word,' Nero told the people in the wardrobe. Then he closed the door and raised his left eyebrow at Eastlight, as if for praise.

6.

Eastlight was whistling by the time he arrived home. Whistling past the graveyard, he had joked to himself in the car. It was a nervous whistle.

The house was dark and silent. No burnt offerings sizzled in a ruined pan; no smoke bustled in the kitchen. Massimo had not started on their evening meal. The house was cold.

Has he left me?

Calling his partner's name as he prowled the ground floor, Eastlight paused only turn on the stereo and flick PLAY. The music was a two-decade-long project: a selection he'd made of his favourite songs from the annual Eurovision Song Contest TV programme. As Eastlight climbed the stairs, Cliff Richard sang 'Congratulations' – a tad ironically, Eastlight spent a second thinking.

Although it wasn't Massimo's way to pass out on the bed, it was not unheard of either, and Eastlight wanted to check to be sure. The bedroom was empty. So was the bathroom: Massimo had not fallen asleep in the bath. He wasn't home.

Back in the lounge, the selection had moved on to 'Puppet on a String' by Sandi Shaw. (Was anything free from coincidence?) Whistling along, Eastlight called Massimo's mobile. When he heard the peculiar dialling tone he turned down the music in case he'd heard it incorrectly: it was not the usual tone, it was the tone he had heard when calling someone overseas – longer beeps – and Eastlight's immediate thought was that Massimo had absconded to Naples. He'd had enough. He'd got scared. He'd run away to stay with his sister Violet, perhaps.

Just when I need him most.

No; perhaps this was –

This dial tone died. No connection. No answer service.

– perhaps this was for the best. With Massimo back in Italy – back in the motherland – Eastlight was free to do what he needed to do with the five prisoners in Eggington. Might be a blessing in disguise.

Eastlight turned up the music. Now it was his favourite: 'Diggy-Loo Diggy Ley' by the Swedish band of brothers, The Herreys – the song of which he was always reminded when he saw or thought of Vig; the song that had lent Vig the nickname Viggy-Loo (which he was more than reasonably certain that nobody else comprehended). The thought of Vig made him smile and stop whistling. He sang along to the tune about the golden boots; as ever, he pictured the lead singer and imagined the man beating him off while wearing nothing more than the eponymous footware. Then the singer's face melted into Vig's… and an idea dawned.

If I'm quick… Eastlight thought.

As he usually did, he changed the song's chorus to 'Viggy Loo, Viggy Lay/Let's all bum and be gay' – and he continued the recital at full voice as he stepped outside and unlocked the car. Wouldn't matter that he'd left the CD running. By paying a call on Vig he would buy himself an alibi, however flimsy. At the very least his unannounced appearance would annoy that haughty slag Dorota. And with any luck he'd be able to frustrate Don Bridges too – the old fool. He was not about to forgive Don's crack about shattering his knees, irrespective of what happened in the meantime.

He slipped into the car.

7.

When Eastlight arrived at Vig's pile, the front gate was open; he drove in behind a car that he didn't recognise, wondering if Vig and Dorota were expecting guests for a party of some sort. If so, why hadn't he been invited? *Had* he been invited? Perhaps the invitation had gone to the house and Massimo had accidentally buried it beneath a stratum of gas bills, fliers for laser eye treatment, waterways holiday brochures, and Council Tax final demands. But this was good! If more than a few people witnessed Eastlight's presence at Vig's do, how could he have been in Eggington? He'd only been home for ten minutes! So he'd gone to the rendezvous in Milton Keynes, picked up the weapon, and driven straight here.

No. He'd gone *shopping* in Milton Keynes – an anniversary present for Massimo.

No. He hadn't bought anything – that wouldn't work. He'd need a receipt.

He'd gone *browsing* in Milton Keynes; found nothing appropriate; then decided to drop in on Vig and Dorota, as a good estate agent will, to ensure that they'd settled in nicely. The party was a surprise…

Party?

Probably not, Eastlight concluded. Not enough cars. Or too early for the main event?

The vehicle ahead splattered gravel in its wake. Some of it pinged against Eastlight's bodywork, so Eastlight decreased his speed: he was all but tailgating the twat in front.

The cars drew up to the house. Eastlight recognised the man who got out of the other vehicle. He had met him at Vig's barbecue. Eastlight flicked through his memory files.

'Good evening, Roger!' he called, having exited.

The man looked angry and preoccupied. Because of the tailgating?

'Charlie Eastlight,' Eastlight continued.

'Yeah, I remember.' Roger Billie set off on foot – to Eastlight's surprise – away from the main building. 'Are you with the mob?'

What mob?

'Need to straighten this out one way or another,' Roger continued.

He was walking in the direction of the woods, as if towards Don's hut.

Eastlight said, 'I agree.'

'Well come on then.'

Eastlight followed him.

THE EDLESBOROUGH HOUSE

1.

Massimo turned off his phone; then he silenced his car's engine and killed the headlights. And breathe, he told himself. He had parked coincidentally close to where Connors and Dorman had parked on their return visit to Edlesborough, on the night in question; but even if he'd known this and had read something of an omen into the coincidence, he would not have re-parked. He wouldn't have been able to. There *was* nowhere else. Two schoolboy football teams were slugging it out on the floodlit pitch on the village green. The match had attracted a good audience, and the players' parents had been forced to park up wherever there was space. It was here or half a mile away.

Keeping his mood as chirpy as possible, Massimo experienced the tickle of rain on his bald spot, and set off up the road on foot. In the five minutes it took him to walk to the house, the atmosphere made up its mind: a light shower commenced; a wind shoved at his shoulders. Nervousness had provided him with a semi.

A woman left Number 11 and crossed the front lawn instead of taking the path. If she hadn't fitted Benny's description so adroitly, her uniform would have given Massimo all the evidence required. She had obviously come straight from a shift and hadn't changed.

The nurse. Bernadette.

Had she been inside the house? How had she got in? What had she found?

Bernadette turned left out of the drive and walked on, towards her own home.

Massimo watched her. Then he walked around the side of the building, into the back garden, where it was dark and awash with shadow.

The field at the bottom of the garden was grey and beige. No life was evident: it might have been a field on the moon. Massimo paused. That field was probably where Connors had been washed away; where Dorman had lost half of his incompetent head… The deduction was sufficient to engender a certain emotion in Massimo: it was a second or two before he understood that he'd just experienced empathy. *Empathy* of all things! And then something else flooded his system, something much more recognisable and familiar.

Hatred.

And telling himself that he would do this for Connors – but especially for Dorman – he strode to the conservatory, feeling empty of belly but charged up.

Much of the glass had been boarded up; very little of it had survived the explosion, or the clearing-up process that had followed. This would be easier than he'd dreaded… Massimo pulled from an inside jacket pocket the small hammer that Benny had loaned him. Without a further thought he set to. Using the hammer's claw, he tugged at a board that he chose at random. If the noise alarmed a neighbour, he would have to deal with that on the spur of the moment.

The board popped free of the structure with little resistance. Such was the feeling of achievement that this produced that Massimo attacked a second board, directly above the first, with flat-out gusto and determination. This one clung a little more tenaciously; but Massimo was on a roll, and no sheet of fucking plywood was going to thwart his plans tonight. Not now: not now that he'd made his decision to get in. After two minutes of grunting and under-the-breath insults, Massimo felt a rivet pop and give: it shot past his body and bounced on the patio with a *tink*.

And then Massimo turned around quickly. Breath crammed his throat.

'Mind telling me what you think you're doing?' the woman who had crept up on him said.

It was the nurse. Well, Benny had advised him that she might be trouble, but Massimo had not expected to have been so easily outwitted or cornered.

The hammer was heavy – nice and heavy – in his left hand. Three strides in that interfering bitch's direction, a quick swing of the arm… It could all be done efficiently enough, Massimo reckoned. No different from what he had planned for Nero and Jess. Drag her into the house and *Open Sesame*.

Suddenly the ludicrousness of what Benny had told him returned – with a punch. His body was wet with panic-sweat; his bladder felt full to bursting. He scarcely dared breathe.

'I'm going in,' Massimo told her, tripped up and forced to state the obvious.

'So I see. I'm coming with you,' the nurse replied. 'Hurry up and make us a door.'

2.

Inside, the house stank of mould. If any fresh air had made it past the plywood slabs and through the spaces where once there had been glass, it hadn't been enough. The smell was dense – a fog of stench – but there was something else in the miasma, was there not? Risking his lungs' safety (or so he imagined), Massimo inhaled deeply and searched for a memory. The underlying aroma was one that he knew.

Bernadette recognised it too. She found the file in her databank first.

'Do you smell seaweed?'

That was it! Seaweed on a beach – a holiday – any number of holidays – the sea gone out, having deposited its cargo of rotting strands.

'Yeah I do,' said Massimo very quietly – his voice so low *why*? Did he fear that he and his new compatriot would cause the disruption of something that had settled? 'Why would that be?'

'I have no idea,' Bernadette replied.

'Medically speaking.'

'This isn't a medical matter.'

'But if it was. In your professional opinion, is there anything that might account for a sea smell in a landlocked village house conservatory?'

Bernadette snickered in the darkness. 'Yeah. The sea… Let's find some lights, eh?' She flicked something that she held in her right hand and a narrow beam of light poked out.

'Good thinking: a torch,' said Massimo.

'I went home to get it… when you thought I didn't see you outside. I have a feeling the electricity'll be off, but let's try.' Bernadette used the torch beam to locate some dimmer switches on the wall. As she'd predicted, no light was forthcoming when she turned the dials. 'Dead.'

The carpet underfoot was marshy; their footfalls squelched as they stepped carefully through the debris, following a line of torchlight like passengers exiting a plane in an emergency. All evidence of human life was in their path. Swollen cushions like undersea plants; a disembowelled television; a broken-spined electric guitar... Massimo acknowledged that old devil called Empathy once more. The sight before them – made better or worse by the limited illumination he could only guess – was tragic. Full-on heartbreaking. Someone's *home*. That old couple who'd gone to the funeral in the north of England...

How had *Benny* known that they'd be away at that funeral that evening?

It was a question that Massimo had meant to pose but had forgotten to do so. Why specifically that night, from an intra-rationalist point of view?

Filing the question away for a later opportunity, Massimo led Bernadette from the conservatory into a dining room. Reflex-ively he reached for a light switch; the lights were in the same in-operational state. It made sense that the power would have been turned off, Massimo supposed. Lot of water around.

In fact, the room had been drenched. If anything, the dam-age in here was worse than it had been in the conservatory. A sideboard had been pulverised in the deluge, its chinaware in-nards smashed to pieces and scattered with such force that shards were embedded in the wall like rock formations. Wedding photo-graphs lay trampled in muddy pools. The table was upside down, a gesture of defiance or submission. A display cabinet had been made ovoid with wood-warp, its glass front nothing now but an owner's memory.

'What's your name, by the way?' asked Bernadette.

'Massimo. And you?' the man asked, keeping up appear-ances.

'Bernadette. Are you connected in any way with the two men who came to my door the night this happened?'

'Came to your *door?*'

'I'll take that as a yes then,' Bernadette said behind Mas-simo's shoulders. 'Just for my own curiosity... was it also them who burgled my house?'

Massimo walked from the dining room into the kitchen. Underfoot he crushed crockery into smithereens, his hands reaching out for the light switch once again (the light was dead) and then for anything else that he might be able to identify by touch alone.

'Do you think you can keep that torch steady?' he asked.

Bernadette turned off the torch.

The room darkened and expanded; though the kelp-smell (or whatever it was) was less pungent, the room had the same density of soured atmosphere. Without the torchlight it went on forever, and simultaneously closed in on Massimo's chest.

'I asked you a question.'

'Turn the light on, Bernadette,' Massimo ordered. He spun quickly and lashed out with the hammer… which whistled through empty air. She had either kept a step or so back from him, or he'd spun too far or not enough. Deprived of any solid point of physical reference, Massimo was disoriented and wrong-footed.

'Please,' he added gruffly. Or I'm going to kill you, he added silently.

'Were they the same men who burgled me?' asked Berna-dette. Her voice came from a slightly different place, as if she'd managed to creep further into the room, past where he stood. Of course. She had a house up the road; she'd be familiar with its layout if she'd spent any time there longer than a week or so.

'Yes. They went to the wrong place. You were a mistake.'

'My dog bit one of them on the arse,' Bernadette said.

'That was Dorman. A dog bite's the least of his worries, believe me.'

'I know. He was decapitated… Was he a friend of yours?'

'A colleague. Bernie, please: the torchlight. I don't like this…'

Bernadette thumbed the torch back on. It wasn't much but it was better than nothing. 'I appreciate your honesty,' she told Massimo. 'You didn't know they came back to me that night, did you?'

'I had no idea.'

Bernadette positioned the torch so that it beamed up from underneath her chin. Her face patched in shadows.

'You gave em a bollocking and they came back to this house. What were they looking for?'

Massimo paused and calculated.

'If I promise I'll tell you when we're out of here, would that be good enough?'

Bernadette had kept the light on her own face. Her 'No' came out ghostly and cold.

'Why not?'

'Because my dog has never been seen since that night. Wherever your other man went – the younger one – my dog went too.'

This did not feel as much like being caught out as Massimo had imagined it would. The fact that someone else knew something of what Benny had discussed – or seemed to at any rate – was uplifting.

'So tell me what we're looking for,' Bernadette went on. 'I want my dog back.'

'I can't promise you anything like that.'

'I'm not asking you to promise me anything. What are we looking for?'

'A gateway… or a door. Something tells me you know what.'

'I don't.'

'Are you an intra-rationalist too?'

Bernadette turned the torch on Massimo. 'A what?'

'Never mind. It's a door – a hole. I don't know exactly. My

informant says it goes to another... dimension. Now get that light out of my eyes.'

'Sorry. Do you want to take the upstairs and I'll finish down –'

'No. We stick together,' said Massimo. 'It's too weird to be alone. What room's through that door?' He pointed to his right.

'In my house, that's the larder.'

'Well are you ready to open it?'

'As ready as... Yes, I'm ready.' Bernadette pointed the beam at the door in question, the one that Massimo had been able to make out in the torch-created shadows. And then she added, 'Do you dream of that place?'

'No. You do, I take it.'

'I don't. But my partner does.'

'And where's *he* right now?'

'At a game. He's a gambler.'

'Did you leave him a note?' Massimo asked. 'Saying where you might be.'

'Do you think I should have?'

'If I didn't believe in something I wouldn't have come: that's what Benny said.'

'Who's Benny?'

'It doesn't matter.' Massimo reached for the door. 'Take a deep breath...' *in case there's another surge of water,* he did not need to explain.

He pulled open the larder door...

3.

Apart from some jars of preserves shattered on the floor, and a few bags of pasta slit open, their contents disgorged, the larder was the least-harmed room so far. Most of the shelves still groaned with washing powders, cleaning products, canned good, pickles, teabags… and wine. When Massimo reached for a bottle at random, Bernadette said:

'You're doing that now?'

Massimo unscrewed the top. 'I am *not* being sucked into a timewarp on an empty stomach. I refuse to.' With which he took a couple of nips, then a sharp tug.

'What about a clear head?'

'It's overrated. Do you want a belt?'

'Yes. God, I'm scared.'

The bottle trembled in her other hand. The light went up and down the larder's shelves like a stroboscopic effect.

'Just don't drop it.'

'What? The torch or the wine?'

'I meant the torch… but actually the wine as well.'

'Yeah, it might spoil the look of the place,' Bernadette answered sarcastically.

'I was referring to the noise – and the neighbours,' said Massimo.

'I promise to drink with confidence, in that case. Red wine's a bugger to get out once it stains.' Bernadette laughed. Then she raised the bottle to her lips.

It did not take them long to finish drinking the wine, and Massimo was about to suggest opening a second bottle when Bernadette reminded them that there was the rest of the ground floor and the whole upper storey still to search.

They moved through the house, the carpets so wringing wet in places that it was like trudging over prairie grass after a storm, and their socks and tights respectively were soon wet through.

Everywhere the carnage was the same, the chaos identical and total. Belongings broken if not atomised; a television sliced horizontally in half, its lower segment now full of water, like a fishtank. Books spread-eagled on every surface, like birds that had fallen to the earth and stayed there to die. Compact discs embedded in upholstery, as if fired by a novice assailant...

'There's nothing here,' said Bernadette.

'Upstairs, then.'

'Upstairs.'

Here, the mess and confusion were even worse. Three of the four doors had been yanked half-off their hinges, and now hung at crazy-house, trippy angles that didn't fit the doorframes. The carpet on the landing was less marshy than swamp-like, to such an extent that Massimo formed the fear (with remarkable ease) that the two of them would slip through, as if into quick-sand.

'I hate to say this, Bernadette, but I suddenly need the toilet. Which one's the bathroom?'

'I don't think it necessarily matters where you go, Massimo.'

'This is someone's house!'

'Not anymore, I doubt. It's that door.' And she flung the beam in the relevant direction, at one of the doors that hung off its hinges.

Massimo squeezed past one of the lopsided doors, thank-ing God that at least the light in here was better than it had been downstairs. With no boards covering the windowpanes that had remained intact, a dreamy mix of streetlamp and moonlight gave off something better than the black hole darkness. Massimo was able to make out the shower stall, bath, the sink... and the toilet.

'I'll be as quick as I can,' he called out. 'Please don't go anywhere. No pun intended.'

'I don't exactly want to hear your noises, but okay. I can't even say close the door!'

'You're a nurse! You've heard worse!' Massimo assured her, pulling at his belt tongue and unsnapping the poppers at his groin.

'Yeah yeah. Less explaining and more straining, please.'

'Don't worry – I won't ned to strain.' Massimo sat on the seat.

'Nice image – many thanks for that,' Bernadette called. As well as she could while still holding the torch, she inserted a finger in her ear. She really did not like hearing the ablutive noises of others. At the same time she could not deny that the wine they'd drunk, on top of a few cups of tea in her last break of what had been a busy day at the hospital, had given her a full bladder as well. She'd hang on, though, she resolved.

In the bathroom it was hazy and strange: it was like his early-morning pee-trips, when he'd sit in the gloom (always sit, even for a pee) because he'd worry that turning the light on would wake him up too thoroughly – and he wanted to go back to sleep. So he'd sit, as he sat now, in surroundings that the darkness had rendered unfamiliar. Or like the times when Charlie borrowed the keys to a nice big property on the sales or rental market.

Sometimes it was fun to pretend that they owned a place as grand as that, especially if it was fully furnished, like the place where Massimo enjoyed receiving stolen goods. A bit of class. The oiks respected it. In fact, with the wine leaving his system but with it having done its job on his brain, if he tried he could almost imagine Charlie had simply borrowed this very house for the evening… Yes. They'd borrowed it and they'd hired a rent boy from Milton Keynes…

'Am I safe to take my fingers out of my ears yet?'

Ah, there he was now, bless him! Massimo chuckled.

Then the bath gurgled.

The shock to Massimo's system was sufficient to send his sphincter into spasm. While it was fortunate in one way that he was sitting where he was sitting, the following couple of seconds were pure torture as he struggled to rise and pull up his pants and trousers.

The bath gurgled again – louder this time. No mistaking

the noise: a drainy rumble, in a bathroom's clear acoustics.

'Oh I smell you haven't,' said Bernadette on the landing. 'Thanks for the bouquet... just when I was getting used to the smell of rot...'

Shut up, woman! thought Massimo, trying to voice something – voice anything... If the bath was the gate to Oz, then he wanted Bernadette in here with him. A solo voyage sounded horrendous.

The problem was, he couldn't speak.

Clutching his trousers high (no time to refasten the poppers), Massimo stumbled forward in the darkness – and misremembered the angle of the lolling door. His right shin spanked into the wood – he yelped – and he fell forward, over the rest of the door, and onto the sopping carpet on the landing. Though he ended up on his left side, he had no intention of remaining in this position for long.

The torchlight burst into his face.

'Massimo,' said Bernadette's voice behind. 'What the fuck?'

Massimo pointed back into the room. 'It's in there...'

'What is?'

'The doorway – in the bath.'

He must have sounded scared enough for Bernadette to take him seriously: for the next beat of time, while Massimo breathed incompetently and struggled to his feet, she kept the light on his features as much as possible.

'Get it out my face!'

'Sorry!'

Bernadette pointed the torch at the flight of stairs that they'd climbed.

'Not there!' Massimo screamed at her. '*In the fucking khazi!*'

She pointed the torch at the available space between where the door hung wonky and the doorframe. Following Massimo's collision with the door, and its subsequent reshifting, this space was now a triangle of about the same area (but different shape) as a dinner tray, and into it she and Massimo peered, both of them aware of changes in the atmosphere. It wasn't the smell of Massimo's passed stool that hung in the air; it was a sudden chill so acute that it burned the insides of their nostrils and paralysed their nasal capacities. They smelt nothing at first; nothing at all.

Heard nothing either… until gradually a sound, one that seemed to emanate from the bathtub, came to the ear: a sound of winds blowing hard from outside somewhere safe.

The chill intensified – another dramatic drop in temperature. Without knowing they had done so, Bernadette and Massimo had taken hold of one another's waists, side by side.

'God, it's freezing in there,' said the former, feeling the skin pinch on the hand that was holding the torch closer to the aperture.

'It wasn't…' said Massimo.

The light inside the room was changing too: it was brightening far more brilliantly than could be accounted for by a simple pocket flashlight.

'Getting bright,' Massimo murmured, but he was not sure if he had spoken. The cold had seized his synapses. If he didn't move now, he vaguely taunted himself, he would freeze solid in a matter of minutes.

Gripping his waist, Bernadette said, 'Don't let go of me. Please.'

Freeze together, would they? Massimo tried to smile: the gesture broke a film of ice that had formed on his upper lip.

Cold…

And he remembered what Benny had told him about the deep-sea fish, where the temperature was oh-so low. The male fish cuddled up to the female… and she absorbed him into her own body.

No!

Massimo struggled and wriggled – he would not allow Bernadette to absorb him – and he wondered if they could be at the bottom of the sea.

How would they breathe?

And why was it getting so bright, if this was the ocean floor?

Still he struggled. Not getting anywhere.

The noise of winds howling, louder now – louder, it seemed, by the second; but *outside*. And they were *in*side – or were about to be – safe from those gales, but without the adequate clothing... in a place as bright as a snowfield in summer.

'Hold me tight,' said Bernadette... and her command fed Massimo's fears of assimilation – of being absorbed – as thoroughly as he himself and his own words (and actions) must have preyed on Nero and Jess.

As the light from inside the bathroom brightened, as the freezing temperatures dipped still lower, Massimo thought of those two teenagers. How ironic that he'd considered dumping their corpses into the very same wormhole into which he would be dragged!

Once more, he tried to smile; but the process of freezing had been so rapid that he could not move more than a couple of secondary muscles that served no purpose here.

His heart... slow... slower. No smile muscles available. Eyes... Ah! He rolled his eyes in their sockets, and he saw that the house that he and Bernadette had entered illegally was all but disappeared. Fading fast. Everything around him – *cold* – was bright white, but he was *in*side – *cold* – and the winds outside – *cold*...

Bernadette screamed.

Like inside an igloo, was Massimo's last conscious thought. But he heard the voice: it reached him. The voice that said:

'Well, *you* took your fucking time, cunt.'

REUNION

1.

Massimo and Bernadette were not permitted to sit down: they were made to walk around in small steps to keep their blood circulation active. Rugs and shawls that smelled of beasts were wrapped around their torsos and laboured onto the quivering racks of their shoulders; and the people who administered these extra layers onto the freezing travellers were short, stocky, muscular, dressed in similar protection against the cold. There were seven of these helpers. Their skin was toast-coloured, their teeth short and yellow; the men wore barcode beards, the women had wide eyes, flattened noses...

And then there was Connors.

It was Connors who had addressed Massimo and Bernadette: *Well,* you *took your fucking time, cunt...* although the apostrophe had been for Massimo's benefit mainly. It was Connors who had barked his orders to the walls of the iceroom, and in from the cold and the winds had streamed his assistants with their furs and their busyness. It was Connors, it seemed, who ran the show.

The better part of half an hour elapsed before the visitors became comfortable with the new temperature. The shock to the system had been conquered, but more work was needed. Neither Italian brogues nor hospital-regulation flats were suitable footware for the environment; and once they had been allowed to sit (in chairs fashioned from bleached bone of indeterminate origin), the assistants set to wrapping the travellers' things and feet in more applications of aromatic fur and hide.

Throughout this operation, conversation had been kept at a minimum, and this wordlessness suited Bernadette fine. She was used to the professional company of practitioners going through the medical motions – she was a nurse. And so was the young man helping her to keep warm. They all were – they were nurses... with Connors the watchful surgeon – the doctor on his ward rounds – calling the shots. Yes. This was something that Bernadette could comprehend. To be a nurse required patience (and living with Chris required patience): Bernadette would wait. She could and she would. She would listen to the mad wind throttling the building from outside, and be grateful that she was not in its grip... and she would wait.

Massimo, on the other hand, had some different ideas. He was edgy and restless; as he found himself able to speak, more and more questions – some of them fully formed and sensible, others dreamy gibberish – spilled from his voicebox. He was scared. He was livid. He writhed on his seat, a steady flow of who-why-where-how hissing in the supercooled oxygen.

It was not Bernadette's place to tell the man to shut up – not in someone else's home. No. It was *Connors's* place to tell Massimo to shut up, which he did as the assistants withdrew one by one, their functions discharged for the nonce.

'Zip it up, Mass,' Connors said eventually and simply. 'You don't come in here shouting the odds in front of my new friends.'

Massimo lowered his head. His breath was a balloon of steam in front of his eyes.

Taking this unexpected cessation in the hostilities as her cue, Bernadette said, 'Do you mind if I ask a few questions?'

Connors nodded. 'Sure.'

'Do you know where my dog is?'

'Not *Where are we?* Not *What do you do for food around here?*'
Connors appeared amused by Bernadette's directness.

'I know where we are, and I'm not hungry,' Bernadette told
him. 'So how about some dog news?'

Connors nodded again. 'I'm really very sorry about your
pet,' he began.

'Oh God.'

'I looked after her's best I could, swear I did. But there were
things –'

'All right. She's dead, you're telling me.'

'I'm afraid I am, love. Sorry.'

Bernadette looked away. The walls of compacted ice
claimed her attention. Her eyes prickled with tears.

Connors asked: 'Were you in the house? When you made
it across?'

'Yes. Number 11,' Massimo answered. 'So what have you
got here, mate, then? With those pygmies running around after
you. Is this *The Man Who Would Be King* bullshit? You their fucking
leader all of a sudden? King Chris? Lord Chris?'

Connors smiled. 'You sound a tad envious, Mass,' he said.
'But as you've asked so nicely – yea, I suppose there's a certain
kowtowing from certain quarters. My reputation...' He laughed.
'...it grew a bit as I travelled north. *Prophet* Chris is more like it.
Holy Traveller Chris.'

'Bollocks.'

'Yeah, that was my own initial reaction, funnily enough. If
you want me to, I'll tell you all about it in a mo. But just tell me
first... were you *upstairs* in Number 11?'

Bernadette faced Connors again. Slipping her hands free
of the furs, she wiggled her fingers to test their condition of
numbness and spoke.

'Thank you for trying to look after my dog,' she said. 'May

I ask why the position in the house is relevant?'

'It's a theory I've developed. The higher you are in the house, the further north you are up God's body.'

'Excuse me?'

'When I came here I was outside the house, as I'm sure you must know. And I landed on a ship at sea. See, the house is the body, I reckon. If I'd been in the basement, I would've come here in the far south, right by the Toenail.'

'By the *Toenail?*' asked Massimo.

'Toenail Island. You see, all the scale's to cock... How long have I been away?' Connors asked.

'Couple of weeks.'

'You see? Here I've been travelling for nearly eighteen months. That's why I've picked up a bit of word of mouth as I moved along.'

Bernadette interrupted. 'You're talking as though this makes sense to you.'

'It does! It didn't at first, I grant you that, but you get used to it.'

'Well, our houses don't *have* basements,' she continued. 'We do have attic space, though.'

'Right. And that's what's further north... if anyone's mad enough to go somewhere even colder than this godforsaken territory... What's your name, by the way?'

'Bernadette.'

'Chris Connors.' He stood up and slid across the ice like a skater; his feet were wrapped in fur and cloth. He extended a hand... and after a momentary hesitation, Bernadette shook it, gratefully and at length. A sharing of warmth. 'I really am sorry about your dog – she was quite a faithful companion to me, especially considering.'

'Thank you.'

'And while I'm dishing out the apologies, I'm sorry we robbed your house.'

Bernadette dropped Connors's hand.

'It was nothing personal,' Connors tried to assure her. 'Massimo's probably told you: we went to the wrong house. Which I *still* think was your fault, Mass, by the way.'

Massimo snickered. 'Hardly the point now, though, is it? How the hell do we get back?'

'Get *back*? There's no going *back.*'

'Well I'm not staying *here.*'

'The door's there. Mind it don't slam on your arse on the way out.'

The three of them fell silent. Outside the walls, the wind picked up a gear.

'What time is it here?' asked Bernadette.

'There's no such concept in the north. It's seen as blasphemous.'

'The *time* is?'

'Yeah. We're in a place called Gadshin, which if you say it after a couple of hypothetical whiskies, comes out exactly as what it is: God's Chin. You have to picture – don't matter if you believe it or not – you have to picture God lying down in the sea, most of the body underwater.'

'Speaking of whiskies,' said Massimo, a note of hope in his voice.

'You already reek of booze.' Connors withdrew and slid back to his seat.

'So would you if you'd known what was about to happen.'

'Fair enough. What did you do? Go to the pub first?'

'We had some wine in the kitchen,' Bernadette answered.

'*And* I went to the pub first,' Massimo added.

Connors sat down. 'Well, you gotta get your priorities right,

I suppose. But where's me manners?' He shouted something in a foreign tongue. 'I can't promise you a perfect single malt, but it's a local preparation at'll get you good and pissed for bedtime.'

One of the women who had helped dress Bernadette and Massimo entered the room. She did so, not by opening a physical door, but by leaking in through the compacted ice like a mist and reforming in front of their eyes. Fully materialised a few seconds later, she awaited her orders like a servant.

Connors spoke to her in her mother tongue. To aid what might have been a problematic pronunciation, he held up three bare fingers on his left hand.

The waitress stepped backwards towards the wall. It claimed her, and she reverted to mist once again, bowing gently as she disappeared and left the room.

'I can't believe I saw that,' said Massimo.

'A day or two in this place,' Connors replied, 'and you won't believe you ever thought it amazing.'

Bernadette shook the image from her head. In the past, in the course of duty, she had witnessed the remarkable – the dead man's feet dancing a full two hours after his heart had stopped beating; the baby on the operating table, barely five months old, who had clearly said *Try not to hurt me too much* – and she had learned not to question sensual evidence. And of course she owned The Object, which defied its own explanation.

'Why would telling the time be blasphemous, even on God's chin?' she wanted to know.

'Do you hear them winds?' was the answer. 'They're said to be His breath... Cold as arseholes, right, but that's what they believe. Some say He's *snoring*.'

Bernadette waited. When nothing more was forthcoming, she added: 'But what's that got to do with blasphemy?'

Connors shrugged. 'God's breath should be timeless, right?

But who knows? Who *knows* what goes on in the mind of Johnny Foreigner? Ah! Here she comes! Come in, girl!'

The local woman entered by a door in the ice. Although *she* did not need the door, the steaming clay mugs that she carried most certainly did: the *mugs* would not vanish into the air.

Wind spat snow into the room – a violent flurry – and the local woman handed out the mugs, filled as they were with what looked like forest mud raised to boiling point. Bubbles popped on the surface.

'Tastes better than it looks,' Connors promised.

2.

'You travelled north up God's body.'

'That's right. Go on – ask.'

'…It's hard to put into words.'

'No it ain't, Mass. You're dying to ask, so ask. One of the things I respected about you from the first was your directness and candour.'

'Is that right?'

'Yeah that's right.'

'All right then. Ready?'

'When you are, mate.'

'What…'

'…*Yes?*'

'What was it like in God's bollocks?'

3.

Bernadette stomped out into the snow. It was morning. Or it was morning by her body clock, at any rate. She had even managed to sleep – six hours by the watch on her wrist, if that meant anything at all. A long shift at the hospital had been enough – plenty! – to ensure that as soon as she and Massimo had been led to their sleeping quarters, irrespective of any residual anxiety, her eyes had clicked shut on her second heartbeat.

If the concept of morning meant anything – if the pale sky was anything to go by, given that it had looked the same when they went to bed – then a beautiful morning was where she'd landed. Undeniably beautiful, but cold and blustery: the sort of climate that Chris would have described understatedly as 'a bit nippy' – or as 'fresh' – when what he meant was an entire half-degree above authentic physical system collapse. When what he meant was *bloody freezing*.

Thinking now of Chris back at home, Bernadette followed an icy, snow-covered path down a gentle descent. The direction was unimportant: she appreciated the burn in her lungs, the sense of freedom; every stride shook a kink from the muscles in her shoulders and lower back. She'd been tenser than she'd thought. However, continuing to imagine Chris in the house brought back some of this tension. He'd had a game last night (Bernadette had forgotten where), so unless he had done spectacularly well or badly he would have arrived home late. He would have seen the made bed and would have figured that she'd been required to extend her shift. An accident on the motorway, perhaps. Either heavy-of-heart or amiably resigned (depending on how the game had gone), Chris would have crashed on their bed, knowing that these things happened in a nurse's day. But perhaps he would have tried her phone first…

The idea of owning a phone made Bernadette twitch. It made her reach for where she knew it wasn't: in the handbag that she wore on her left shoulder when she was out (as she was now); but the spasm of hope faded as quickly as it had sprung into life. The phone was in her handbag all right, but her handbag she'd left at home when she'd popped back to fetch the torch.

Parenthetically wondering if Massimo carried a phone, and if so, what the reception was like, Bernadette strolled on down a track about three metres wide, which was lined with purple bushes that gave off breaths of warmth, and house after house made of snow. Outside a few of these houses, the inhabitants worked at splitting wood or hanging furs on a line. Beasts resembling mules tugged at their tethers; ate from buckets of orange mush that were fixed into the sides of the houses.

A few women said something like 'Hello' – closer to *Hulloo* – and most of the men that she encountered nodded politely. *Probably wondering where I'm going,* thought Bernadette.

Good point. Where *was* she going? Down, down, down was the direction; but the destination could only be a guess. The foot of this hill? Of a mountain? It was impossible to predict: if the sun-on-snow was not sufficient to dazzle and disorient, the wind knew how to play with the freshest fall. Scooping flakes up by the kilogram, the wind tossed it around like a drunk with confetti at a favoured niece's wedding. The snow danced in front of Bernadette's eyes, part-dervish, part-waltz, part-tarantella.

Bernadette thought back to what Connors had said about God's breath. The notion was temporarily intoxicating: that she, a nurse from the Home Counties, could be breathing the holiest of holy carbon dioxides! It was enough to quicken her pace.

However, the extension of her stride brought a problem – immediately. Her right heel skidded on a well-worn patch of ice, her legs spread, and it was all she could do to remain upright by whirling her arms. Equilibrium restored, she could not help but notice the twanging pain that she'd caused herself in her groin. She winced. Bloody snow, she breathed. A least no one had seen her...

Wrong.

A child had seen her: a boy of twelve or thirteen, dressed snuggled up in the protective cattle by-products of his people… and bent at the waist laughing. Bent at the waist laughing *at her*. And just so that there was no doubt about the source of merriment, he even pointed Bernadette's way.

Bernadette failed to see the funny side. Quick to her lips were a couple of nasty conditional clauses; after all, slips, trips and the common variety of household accident were what she had to deal with at work on a daily basis. *She could've this, she could've that…* But it was hard to stay riled with the kid for long: his laughter was too infectious.

'Where are you going?' he asked at length, his accent heavy, his tone hormonally deep. (He made Bernadette think of someone speaking Russian.)

'I don't know. Just walking.'

'You shouldn't go much further. It'll be difficult to come back… if you intend to come back.'

'I do. Why would it be difficult to come back?'

'It gets steeper,' the boy said; 'you need equipment, a guide – some proper clothing, resources…'

Bernadette held up her fur-mittened hands. 'I'm not running away. I only just got here.'

'I know.'

'But what's down there?'

'Bears.'

'Oh my!'

'…Do you want to see the lizards hatch?'

'Not… Yes, I would. Thank you.'

'Take my arm, Bernadette.'

'You know my name. I will.'

'It's a village,' the boy explained the name-awareness.

'So what's yours?'

'Atchoo.'

'Bless you.'

'I haven't heard that before,' the boy answered, a trifle bitterly. 'Maybe I should change it to *Simon*.'

4.

'So what do you intend to do now?' Massimo asked.

'I intend to finish my breakfast,' Connors answered. 'Funny. I never had much of an appetite in the real world. Here I eat like a piglet.'

'So I see.' While Massimo had dithered over his own bowl of red-berry potage, Connors had tucked into his third, which he had all-but completed.

'The mountain air helps.'

'I didn't mean now as in after you've stuffed your face, I mean now as in the general future.'

'Oh *that* now,' Connors answered. 'Well, I keep moving north, don't I? The rumours are, if you get to God's eyes you see through them – you see everything ever existed, multi-dimensional.' He spooned in another portion of blood clot; Massimo winced. 'Wanna come?'

'Sure. I'll fetch me coat.'

'Are you not enjoy your brekkie, by the way?'

'It's all right, I suppose. I'm a bit hungover. And not only because of the drink.'

'I know the feeling. It's the weirdest jetlag you've ever had.'

'That's one way of putting it.'

'Well, think yourself lucky you didn't land on a *ship*. We were arse-over-tit for two weeks on the ocean wave!'

Massimo nodded. 'I accept that me and Bernie have had it better.'

Connors smiled. 'She's Bernie to you now, is she?'

'Unofficially.'

'Forgive me asking, Mass, but are you banging her?'

'No.'

Connors nodded. 'Good-looking bird... man gets lonesome. You wouldn't mind if I tried, would you?'

'Fill your boots, mate. I'm queer.'

'Ah! But I thought you said – when we was in your house, I think you said to Dorman to be careful where he pointed Percy – because your missus is a devil for cleanliness and hygiene in the bathroom.'

Massimo laughed. 'I probably *did* say that,' he admitted, 'but I'll tell you something else for the record, now that it don't seem to mean much, one way or another. That weren't my house.'

'Eh?'

'My other half's an estate agent. House I called mine was one of the places on his books.'

'It was fully furnished.'

'That's how he sells em. Well, some of em, anyway: fully furnished for rich fucks with no time to waste on painting and decorating. Year-long leases. That game.'

Connors laughed. 'You fooled *me*.'

'Thanks.'

'You fooled *us*.'

'Yeah. Poor Dorman.'

'...We have work to do,' Connors announced, laying down his spoon.

'What sort of work?'

'Planning. I was absolutely serious about moving on north.'

'I don't doubt it.'

'And about you coming with me.'

'...I wanna go home.'

'We've discussed this, Mass. No point in being petulant about it.'

'I'm not being *petulant*, Chris. I'm homesick.'

'You haven't been here a day!'

'Don't matter. Things I gotta do.'

'He won't've missed you yet, probably. You've only been gone five minutes, your time, or whatever. What's his name, by the way?'

'Charlie.'

'Well, Charlie can uncork his own wine for a couple of nights. He won't starve.'

But Jess and Nero might, Massimo thought. No one knew that they were in the Eggington house. What if Charlie forgot to feed them, as he sometimes did? It was worse than having pets.

Connors summarised his position. 'I'm going north to God's eyes, to see the whole of Creation, living and dead. Can you imagine? Only a handful of mystics have come back alive.'

'Did they bring chocolates?'

'Their brains were fried. They were made imbeciles by the experience.'

Massimo shook his head. 'Put it *that* way, Chris, where the fuck do I sign up?'

'Well, I can't get anyone here interested in accompanying me.'

'Fancy that.'

'But with you and Bernadette...'

'What makes you think *she'll* go?'

'She's a nurse.'

'...So?'

'Honour-bound to help the medically needy.'

'In a *hospital*. I doubt her contract includes mountain ranges or hippie religious clauses.'

Connors shrugged, resuming his breakfast. 'Won't hurt to ask, will it?' he said. 'Where is she, talk of the Devil?'

'Went out for a breath of fresh air.'

'Mmm. It don't come any fresher.'

'I suppose not.'

5.

Massimo filled two wooden buckets with snow and used them as weights to work out. After a few reps, while experiencing the familiar bicep burn, he let his mind trot away to pastures new. God's eyes? What about God's *brain?* Why limit themselves to *seeing* everything, when a trip to the Big Man's noodle would allow them to *think* everything, *remember* everything? God's first steps as a toddler in the cosmos. Playing bricks with entire constellations. Swatting alien spaceships down like flies…

The thought developed. How did deities reproduce? What was the godlike equivalent of a one-night stand? Imagine the Cunt fucking! There He is, in some intergalactic nightclub somewhere the size of Venus… and – hello hello! – who's *this* Goddess? *Bonjour, darling.* All things being equal in the Heavens, she clicks over on Milky Way-sized high-heels and asks Him to dance. 'Calling Occupants of Interplanetary Craft' by The Carpenters is in a mash-up with Bowie's 'Space Oddity'. The DJ's augmented bass is causes tidal waves in Honolulu… They go back to His place: a black hole south of Neptune (the universe-cab costs a fortune at this time of Existence; the driver is not keen on going south of the time stream). Using a frozen planet as an ice cube for Her glass, He pours Her a drink…

A century later, both of Them climax. 'Did the Earth move for you?' They quip in unison… but Massimo could not picture Their celestial congress, try as he might, as he flexed his biceps.

God's dick was simply beyond his comprehension.

He put the buckets down in the snow; the workout was over, and he felt peculiar. Not sick exactly. The hangover had passed uneventfully enough; no ghosts of pain haunted his muscles, synapses, or clogged up the back of his throat. It was more like jetlag, as Connors had suggested. Or more like one of those dreams where you could see that the bus on which you were travelling was about to hit a pedestrian. The inevitable hung in the atmosphere – like a restless calm before a storm. And he did not see Bernadette until she was three metres away, approaching him from behind.

'Hi.'

'Hi there. Nice walk?'

'Apart from slipping everywhere,' Bernadette answered. 'I went to see some lizards.'

'Was it fun?' asked Massimo.

'It was a distraction, I suppose. A small boy introduced us – they were hatching.'

'Have you eaten anything?'

'Yeah, the kid gave me some bread and jam. You?'

'You did better than I did. I had slop… What's the plan for the day, do you think?'

Bernadette shrugged. 'The boy seems to think we're travelling north. Connors has been thinking about it for a couple of weeks at least, apparently – the news is on the psychic front page. I asked him why he didn't seem surprised to see us and he said they've been *waiting*. For us. Or for some people like us, anyway. Apparently the… the prophecy is, three people – two men and a woman – travel north to become part of God's brain.'

'Christ. Just been thinking about that.'

'Yes, I felt you thinking about that,' said Bernadette, 'as unlikely as that sounds.'

Massimo exhaled. 'I don't think *anything* sounds unlikely anymore,' he admitted. 'So we're going then – it's decided.'

Sidestepping the question, Bernadette started walking; Massimo followed. 'I've got to keep moving,' she explained, 'or I get frozen toes.'

'That's fine. Let's stroll.'

Neither of them said anything for a minute. Aimlessly they strolled in the snow, each of them scarcely daring to believe that this was the same place that had hosted the violent wind storms of the night before. The air was Alpine crisp; the winds were boisterous, but no more so than they would be at the top of any mountain.

Massimo longed for conversation. 'I didn't know lizards could stand the cold,' he said. 'Always picture them on a Brazilian tavern or something. Diplomats in white suits sipping cocktails.'

'I know what you mean, but the boy told me – this is what I've been thinking through. He said they were bred for the purpose – get this. By someone from *Eeeng-lan*.

'England?'

'Presumably. He didn't know for sure, but there's at least one man who's made the voyage across… and guess what he had in bags when he marched through Customs. Fucking lizards!'

'But why bother?' Massimo asked.

'I don't have a clue… except if you think about it, say there are animals here we don't have at home. And say you happen to be fascinated by these reptiles – maybe you breed them, sell them… Imagine your good name in the professional lizard fraternity, if you so-called discover a brand new one. You'd be famous!'

Massimo stopped in his tracks. He raised his mittened hands to his head, as if to hold the thoughts in before they flew away.

No.

Couldn't be.

No, he insisted silently.

'What's wrong?'

'Did the boy describe this traveller? This reptile-fancier?'

'No. I didn't ask him to. Why?'

'Where does he live?'

'I asked you why. Do you know him?'

It *couldn't* be, could it? But Massimo heard Benny's voice loud and clear. *Do you wanna see me snakes?* he'd asked. Then that bull about intra-rationalism. And knowing that he couple at Number 11 would be up north for a funeral…

Benny?

Massimo felt cold - a cold that had nothing to do with the air temperature. *I've been bamboozled,* he thought – *bamboozled* being a word he'd picked up from Charlie.

'I might do. Will you take me there?'

6.

Connors went with them. He told them that he was intrigued, and besides (he joked) it was good to get out of the house every now and then. It was a fifteen minute walk away. They made it in twenty due to the minor injury that Bernadette had sustained slipping earlier.

Atchoo was waiting for them, knotted into a yoga position on a patch of cleared dirt the size of a picnic rug. He had one ankle behind his head. His eyes were closed, the calm expression on his face all but catatonic.

'It's nice to see you again, Bernadette,' he said with his eyelids still down. He sniffed the air and opened his eyes. 'And welcome to your friends.' He unhooked his ankle and floated upright.

'You're gonna do yourself a mischief, son,' said Massimo.

'I can't believe it,' Connors whispered.

Experiencing a tightness in her back – possibly a result of the almost-tumble that she'd taken – Bernadette prevented herself from being too amazed. Sure, the kid did something like yoga and could elevate. Big deal. Had *he* ever known a patient who worked as a ventriloquist, who could make his voice emerge from his own penis? No, he hadn't (most likely); but Bernadette had. She had also nursed a man with a saxophone reed embedded in his rectum. Bizarre things happened all over, and she would have to keep an open mind as to what might be commonplace in these parts.

Connors said again, 'I don't believe it,' at a normal volume this time.

'I'd like to ask you about the man who brings the lizards,' said Massimo.

'Can it be *you?*' said Connors.

Massimo and Bernadette regarded their colleague; the boy's eyes were bright, his expression now mildly quizzical.

'It *is* you, isn't it?'

'Chris?' said Massimo, his tone concerned.

'This is the boy I told you about,' Connors replied, excited. 'When I first got here! I thought you were dead! I saw you eaten… by those flies…'

Atchoo smiled.

Connors stepped forward, arms wide.

Copying the gesture, the boy hovered half a metre off the ground and wafted backwards, in the direction of his snow-and-wood dwelling.

This action stopped Connors where he stood.

Atchoo stepped down off the air and also stood still, a full two metres back from where he'd been a second earlier. The clear message was: keep your distance.

'Elvis?' Connors pleaded.

'My name's Atchoo.'

'But you…'

Massimo took hold of Connors's right arm. 'It's just a coincidence, mate,' he said. 'They just look the same.'

'No. No they *don't* look the same. Or sound the same,' Connors argued. 'But it's him. I swear it is.'

'He says not,' said Bernadette.

'Who was Elvis?' the boy enquired.

Surprising everyone, Connors started to cry. The alteration about him was dramatic: from one second, cock of the walk, almost a lord of the manor; to the next, a blubbering wreck, fallen to his haunches, his arms folded over his head, in as near to the foetal position as was possible while his feet stayed on the ground.

'His son?' the boy persisted.

Nobody knew what to say – or do.

A long time passed before the boy invited the three of them inside his home.

NUMBER 77 (AND THE CAMP)

1.

Yasser pushed the button and heard 'Greensleeves' from within the house. A light came on in the hallway. The door opened with a great hurried tug.

The man who answered had a half-clean air about him; the air of someone feverish, someone who hadn't slept much in the last few nights. Dressed only in a dressing gown, he was scruffy about the face and hair, with a ratty expression and an exudation of stale wine b.o.

'Thought you might be Bernadette,' the man said. 'Lost her keys.'

'Are you Chris?'

The man nodded. 'And you are?'

'Yasser. You were at a card game three nights ago. You won handsomely.'

'So-so. A hundred up. Are you a copper?'

'No. I'm a detective, though. Sort of.'

'Yeah?' The sentence seemed to cheer Chris up. 'Like the *Scooby Doo* kids. Your age, I mean. What is it you want exactly? It's cold.'

'To talk about the game.'

'…Well, what about it?'

Yasser plunged. 'How well do you know Tommy?' he asked.

'Well as anyone on the circuit, I suppose. Played him a few

times.'

'Successfully?'

Chris shrugged. 'You win some, you lose some… Look, it's getting colder, I think, and I'm a bit worried about my partner; so if you could arrive at your point I'd be grateful.'

'He lives not ten minutes from here,' said Yasser.

'Tommy? So what if he does?'

'So I wonder if you know him outside the occasional game.'

Chris grimaced. 'As a detective, son, you're getting close to having your face filled. Just what is it you're insinuating? If anything at all.'

Yasser stood his ground. He was halfway of the opinion that he hadn't a lot to lose. Unlike the students…

'The students lost a lot. You two won a lot,' he summarised.

'So what? You don't send a boy to do a man's job. It was a game.'

'You sharked them.'

'Now you're the gambling police? We sharked them: what does that even mean?'

'It means you paired up to fleece them. Split the winnings afterwards.'

'Is that right. Well okay, son, you've had your say. But I'd like to remind you, in the absence of clearly defined rules of engagement, what we did was no different from the genius mong who counts cards. Okay? It's how I earn a living. And if I blur the lines occasionally, it's between me and my conscience. So *if* you'd excuse me…'

Glass broke, somewhere behind the resident. Balletically he span. As he headed off along his hallway, Yasser hissed in a breath… and followed him in. If Chris found Shyleen in his kitchen – the most likely place where she would have broken glass accidentally – there was no telling what he might do. It's a man's right to protect his property from intruders.

This flashed through Yasser's mind; and if he hadn't been unsure enough of Shyleen's plan to gain entrance to Chris's house by the back way before, he was now. She had obviously managed to get *in*. (She had guessed that a back door would be open; maybe she'd been right – Yasser couldn't imagine her climbing through the utility room window.) Only clumsiness had let her down.

Chris stormed into the dining room, Yasser a few strides behind. The patio doors were open, and the parquet floor was sprinkled with the shards and contents of a broken white vase that must have stood in front of them. So... Shyleen had tried the doors, knocked the vase over... and run away?

She was not in the room, Yasser noted with relief. Even if she'd only got as far as a retreat to the garden shed, she was out of harm's way for the moment. Yasser stood on the threshold between the hall and the dining room; his heart told him that he should contemplate a retreat of his own.

A gust of chilly air from the garden, and Chris seemed to wake up. The flowers scattered at his feet, as if as an act of devotion, were not as engaging as Yasser's presence was.

'I don't remember inviting you into my home,' the man stated.

'It's about a missing child,' said Yasser – the time for deftness or subtlety had surely passed.

Chris cocked his head. 'Is this *your* doing?' he snapped.

'How could it be? The wind must've caught the doors. Stranger things happen at sea.'

Yasser could tell that Chris remained unconvinced (and reasonably unimpressed)... but there was a flicker or two of something on his features. Was it doubt? Suspicion? The reflexive spasm of concern produced by anyone hearing the words *missing child?*

Crunching pieces of vase underfoot, Chris stepped out onto the patio. Yasser watched him take a look around, then he entered the dining room again.

'What missing child?' he asked.

'Her mother's name is Maggie Earl. She lives near Tommy on the Travellers' site.'

'Hang on. How did you find me anyway?'

'One of the students on the ground floor,' Yasser answered. 'Likes to think of himself as Mr Security; keeps a record of licence plate numbers of all the vehicles that visit. There were only four unfamiliar numbers on the night of the game. Two of the cars belong to women. One was Tommy's truck. One was yours… I got lucky. I traced your address through your car insurance.'

Chris exhaled. 'Fuck me. I underestimated you, son, but I'm going to disappoint you now. I don't know any Maggie. And I definitely don't know nothing about a missing child. What do you take me for, son? I'm a gambler, pure and simple.'

'I'm starting to believe you,' said Yasser.

'How blessed I feel. Now if you'd kindly vacate my premises… I have to make some calls, see if I can find my partner.'

'She's missing too?'

Chris closed the patio doors. With a long stride he attempted to hurdle the wreckage on the floor; he moved into a brightly-illuminated kitchen. 'Yeah, she's missing too,' he admitted.

Perhaps he was going for a dustpan and brush. 'How long?' Yasser asked.

'One night.'

Yasser followed as far as the threshold between the rooms. In for a penny, he decided.

'Did you argue?'

'That's none of your business, son.' Chris reached for a shelf above the stove and pulled down the chinaware container in the shape of a cute pig. He removed the pig's head, took out some keys on a leather band, and strode back towards the dining room.

Stepping out of his way, Yasser asked, 'Did you call the police?'

'I don't do police,' Chris answered on automatic.

'What's her name?'

'Bernadette.'

For a fraction of a second, before he'd completed the first syllable, Yasser had expected him to say *Bid* or *Bridget* – the name of Maggie's cousin. How beautifully neat that would have been! If all roads led back to Maggie somehow; and if the two women were messing with this guy's mind as well... How beautifully *neat*.

The name Bernadette, however, meant nothing to Yasser. If there'd ever been a square one, he was back there now.

Retreat with dignity, he decided. It was time to find Shyleen; time to give up for the night. He was tired.

While Chris was locking the patio doors, Yasser's phone beeped. Yasser was back in the hall, on his way to the front door. He thumbed the keys: it was a text from Shyleen.

'Let me know,' Yasser added as an afterthought, 'if she doesn't show up. Finding people's my business, Chris.'

The man turned, a smile on his face. 'A business pitch?' he asked.

'Opportunity knocks but once.'

Yasser thumbed open Shyleen's message.

'What are your rates?' Chris wanted to know. 'Out of curiosity, like.'

'Oh I'm reasonable. But I should go.'

The front door had not been closed; Yasser stepped out. His heartrate had increased.

'At least leave a card,' said Chris, still standing at the patio doors.

'I don't have one.' Yasser pointed at a notepad by the phone. 'Can I write my number?'

'Please do.'

Yasser's hand shook as he printed his contact details on the pad's top page.

Shyleen's message had been simple but chilling. *I'm in the house*, it had said.

2.

It wasn't an accident – wind pulling at the patio door, for example – that had broken Chris's vase. No. Shyleen had broken it on purpose. She had heard but a snatch of the trouble that Yasser was having at the front door, so she'd picked up the vase – not intending to smash it so *thoroughly*, granted, but intending to break it *a bit* – and she'd done the business.

Then she'd skipped through the kitchen, to hide.

Several years earlier, Shyleen had had a friend who lived in this village: a girl called Amanda Cleveland. Although Shyleen had envied the girl her ledge of bust and her pony, they'd bonded because of a mutual (but as it turned out for both of them, fleeting) fascination with Amateur Dramatics. Once a week, after school (different schools), they attended an AmDram group in a church hall in Dunstable, pretending to be a sandwich – to *get into the character* of a sandwich – or playacting Eugene O'Neill for laughs, depend on the caprice of their Group Leader, whose first name, oddly, was Chamber. As a result of this term-long friendship, Shyleen had been invited to Amanda's house. She had got to know the layout well.

The house that she was in now had the same layout.

Shyleen had tiptoed through the kitchen, smelling faintly – very faintly – cigarette smoke in the air. This aroma made her intuit that Chris took his fag breaks outside – he certainly didn't smoke in the house – and if he was anything like her father, he didn't bother to lock doors to the outside until bedtime. Sure enough, the door was unlocked; in fact, it had been left ajar. So Shyleen had crept into the utility room.

It was a tight fit. And the disguise would not survive any serious examination. But Shyleen had curled herself up and wedged herself into a small space between the end of the sink unit and the room's far wall. From the door she would not be seen; but if Chris came into the room…? To use the tumble drier? The washing machine? Or to reach into the cupboard for some shoe polish or toilet detergent? It would be finished.

Peculiar as it was, however, Shyleen felt no fear. She was not afraid of being discovered, and the absence of emotion made her query her mental condition. Surely it wasn't normal to feel fine as an uninvited stranger in someone's house…

Scrunching herself tighter into the hole, she fiddled with her phone and sent Yasser the message that she was in the house. She made certain that her phone was set to silent and no-vibrate, and then she tried to prepare herself for a long wait. However, after seconds – no, it must have been minutes – she began to feel both bored and cramped.

Call Yasser?

No, not yet; what would she say anyway? *I'm still in the house?* Waste of a call – or a text. And besides, she wanted to remain sharp: if not observant then tuned in, alive to the house owner's every movement – every squeak, fart… every phone call. If she concentrated on her own business, how would she keep tabs on Chris's?

The screen lit up. HOME, it said.

Bismillah!

Shyleen felt her shoulder muscles clutch together; immediately her scalp beat with a fresh temperature. The fact that she couldn't hear the phone ring made it worse; it was an age before the answering service picked up, with Shyleen weighing up how she would explain a missed call to her parents – especially to Papa. A missed call was as bad as a confession of lesbianism, more or less.

3.

Yasser waited until his boredom had turned panicky; then he started the car engine, engaged first gear, and swerved a long glance across the length of the empty park. In his head he had set the whole stretch – the grass, the swings, the slide – alight, in a blaze of petrol-ignited fire. Why? Because he was that pissed off, that was why. Pissed off with Chris and with Shyleen.

Fuck this noise, he breathed. *She can wait.*

He was referring to his cousin, but he was not being mean-spirited. As far as Yasser knew, Shyleen had sneaked into Chris's house, and now she was not answering texts. Having got it into his head that Shyleen would be all right for another half-hour if she had survived this far, he pulled away out of the car park with his credit card throbbing in his wallet like a badger's heart.

At the station he bought ten quid's worth of petrol in a green can meant for lawnmower engines. And a lighter. With a head crammed with rage he crossed the forecourt and got back in.

Then he drove the five minutes to the camp, all the time part-believing that he was in a pantomime. *He's behind you!* All the time waiting to be caught out; to be pinched; to be *rumbled.*

Yasser was buoyed up by indignation. First he wanted some answers from Maggie, and then he was going to burn down her caravan.

And the Brazilian's.

4.

When Shyleen stood up in the utility room, her joints clicked with gratitude and her spine stretched like a cat's. She felt like she'd been sitting in the same position for half a year, and it was good to move. She checked her phone for the time (the light illuminated the small room drowsily, lending it the appearance of a Cornish cave) and she was surprised that it was nearly midnight. Now that she felt restless and in need of something to do, the reality of hour growing late spurred her mind on. Iin fact, it raced... but it wouldn't settle. One of the very real flaws in her and Yasser's strategy to get into Chris's house had long since become clear: they had no idea of what they were doing or what they were looking for. So she checked her phone for messages, intending to ignore the discomfort in her bladder, and again read 4 MISSED CALLS. Probably Mum or Dad, Shyleen reasoned; Yasser would know better than to ring. She opened her texts.

WHAT U DOING? Yasser had texted.

U OK? X, he had thumbed a half hour after the first message, at 10:37.

I'M IN CAR PARK, NEXT TO MECHANIC, read his last words on the subject. TEXT ME U OK.

The house was silent; probably Chris had gone to bed – she had minutes to spare to let Yasser know that she was fine so far. The problem was... she *wasn't* fine: she really needed to urinate. Her body wasn't joking anymore.

In the darkness she fingered the cold sides of the utility room sink. There was no plastic bowl in the sink; her stream would not make much noise... would it? Shyleen unbuttoned her trousers and lowered them to her knees along with her thong. It took her two attempts to hop backwards on to the sink unit; when she managed to do so, she could not kill a sigh that poured out with her pee.

And that was when Chris found her.

5.

'I want some answers,' said Yasser.

'Well, aren't *you* the man.'

'I'm serious, Maggie.'

'I don't doubt you. Do you want some tea?'

'Not the shit tea you serve. Are you serious?'

'Yeah. Yeah I was as a matter of fact.'

Maggie grinned like a dolphin; there was nothing lovely about this smile.

'Take a seat why don't you.'

'I'd rather stand,' Yasser answered.

'How Oscar Wilde. Well, suit yourself. I'm brewing up.'

Yasser took a look around the well-familiar environment. 'Why did you film me?' he asked.

Dressed in a tightly-wrapped dressing gown, with slippers on her feet, Maggie stood still at the stove. Water in the kettle was already boiling; steam mingled.

'For fun?' Yasser demanded.

'Yeah, why not for fun? Do you feel you've been disadvantaged in some way?'

Yasser coughed and cleared his throat. 'How did Branston get hold of it?' he managed to say.

'Who's Branston?' Maggie poured milk into two hefty mugs.

'My film teacher.'

'I have no idea.'

'It was Tommy then. Or Max.'

'Or me da,' Maggie added, pouring water from the kettle into the mugs.

'…Do you know what I came here to do, Maggie?'

'Confess your sins? Declare your undying infatuation?'

'No. Burn your caravan to the ground. I even bought petrol.'

'Good riddance to the dump,' Maggie answered. 'Here's your shit tea. Just the way you don't like it.'

'Thanks... But *why*, Maggie?'

'Jesus. You assume *choice*?'

'Well, who forced you? The Brazilian?'

'Me father forced me, that's who. Oh do sit *down*,' Maggie added as she did as she'd instructed. 'You're making me a bag of nerves.'

'That's rich.'

'Which is more than I can say for this brew.'

Despite himself, Yasser laughed. 'Maybe I should burn Tommy's down instead,' he said.

Maggie raised her free hand and said, 'Your funeral!'

'Yeah that's right.' He sipped his tea; it was woefully familiar – as bleak as a weekday hangover. 'Do you want to help?'

'Can't say I'm not tempted.'

'Go on, live a little. You should be getting out of this shit-hole anyway.'

Maggie smiled: a nicer, more genuine smile this time, it subtracted a dozen years from her weary façade. 'Now it's *career advice* you'll be giving, eh Yass? Well, that'd be fine from anyone other than a bloody market trader living with his parents.' And she laughed like a faulty cistern.

'Thanks.' Yasser had believed himself to be unprovokable; to be indifferent to another further slur. He had thought himself coolly professional (of all things) in his intentions to perpetrate arson. After all, he had endured the initial threat, then an actual physical assault, and the embarrassment of his brown arse bopping by camera light... not to mention the wealth of verbal insults that he'd taken in fairly good grace in the weeks since he'd first entered onto the driveway of this godforsaken camp. He'd nearly been savaged by that bastard hound Excalibur; he suspected that he'd had his petrol siphoned; he was certain that the whole experience had taken years off his lifespan in worry alone, and that was before he stopped to consider (he tried not to but sometimes in the night, when the dark thoughts crowded, he couldn't help himself) the irreplaceable amount of time that he'd misspent on Maggie so far… And now *this?* And now she was teasing him for the fact that his life seemed to lack prospect and direction?

Well, to Hell with her.

'Who are *you* to criticise *me* for living with my parents?' Yasser said as calmly as he could manage. 'Unless this is all a big show, you're hardly a high flier yourself, babe! And who is it you share this box with, again? Oh that's right: your fucking *father*. So don't come the Lady Muck with me, Maggie. At least I'm *trying*.'

Maggie's eyes had turned flinty. 'Trying what, exactly?' she demanded.

As Yasser answered 'I'm studying, aren't I?' in a tone of voice that made clear his frustration, he could not help wondering what it was – what it was exactly – that Maggie was attempting to goad him to say or do. What was he missing? he wondered for the thousandth time. What he been missing all along?

Into the ensuing silence Yasser repeated softly, 'I'm studying,' but this time there was something different in his voice. It tasted like shame. Or defeat.

Maggie's tone was more understanding; she had melted a tad. 'Yes, you're studying to be a home porn video maker. I'll bet your ma and da are's proud as focken peaches, right?' And then she turned away from him, all passion spent.

It took a few seconds before Yasser understood that she was silently crying.

He did not attempt to comfort her. Rather than inspiring his sympathy, Maggie's softly shaking shoulders provoked a sense of distant disgust, like something unpleasant viewed not at the time but through the lens of memory. Inexplicably Yasser found himself thinking of a legion of bluebottle flies feasting on a lump of dog crap on a pavement. So strong was the connection that the first shake of his head was insufficient to rinse the image away; it took him another two goes before he was successful. And even then he felt unclean.

Tick tock goes the clock, he heard his father say into the part of his brain that nurtured guilt. He had to be getting back to Shyleen. Say the man was more than a gambler. Say he liked a bit of rough. How would Yasser's conscience ever recover? He had to be leaving...

And yet.

Where's the camera man this time? he wondered. If Maggie was playacting for another taste of his penis, he wanted to know at what angle he would be captured. (He was aware of his best side.) But somehow he did not think that tonight a fuck was on the cards.

'I'm not going to say anything to hurt you, Maggie,' Yasser explained.

'Well that's a relief.'

'Not deliberately hurt you, anyway.'

'Thanks for the warning,' Maggie muttered, now turning to him once again. 'Sorry about that. I must be pre-menstrual.'

'I was going to suggest exactly the opposite.'

Maggie smiled. 'You think I'm pregnant?'

Yasser shrugged.

'Oh I see,' she went on. 'You think I borrowed you to *get* pregnant. What a focken charmer you are, Yass, really. Cuz we're all the same, all us focken Pikeys, so we are. Why buy it if we can steal it, right?'

'That's not what I meant,' said Yasser.

'Then why don't you make me a *film* about what you meant, because as God made little apples your spoken word is a dismal bloody failure, so it is.'

Yasser sighed. 'I'm trying to be civil.'

'Comes with an effort, does it?'

'So why can't *you* be?'

'Be civil?' Maggie laughed. 'Oh you poor lamb, you wanna see me when I brew up a *real* head of steam – or rather you don't. So listen. For clarification, if for nothing else, okay? I did not take you into me bed in order to squeeze a child out of you, Yasser. In point of fact, you have *no idea* quite how racist some of the people are on the land, and you make it from me that a child with an Asian boy wouldn't do me immediate prospects any focken favours. Or me long-term prospects either, for that matter. Chances are I'd be out on me arse. So no: I did what I did because I *wanted* to; because I fancied a bit and I was fairly certain you liked me too. I could've been wrong, of course, but as it turned out I wasn't. So take it as a compliment.'

'I do.'

'Good. Of course – if you didn't pull out in good time then we'll have to cross that particular bridge when we reach it. Okay?'

'Okay,' Yasser answered. 'But did you know it was being filmed? Be honest.'

Maggie shrugged and sipped her tea. 'Naturally I did. They film me every night.'

Yasser raised his eyebrows. '*Excuse* me?'

'You heard. They like to keep me scared – under their thumb, like.' She paused; exhilaration and relief at finally confessing something had made her a little breathless. Her bosom swelled, as if on waves of lust.

The need to hear more was strong in Yasser, but pictures of Shyleen formed colourfully, vibrantly. What was she doing right now? Was she safe? Yasser fought an urge to remove his phone; he wanted to text her. Ideally he wanted to produce his phone and read a message from his cousin that read: I'M PERFECTLY FINE. DO AS YOU WANT FOR A COUPLE OF HOURS – as unlikely as such a communiqué happened to be.

Nothing seemed more likely to destroy the mood, however, than producing, in front of Maggie's eyes, the one non-human material link to Shyleen that Yasser owned: the mobile phone. So he sat where he was, still wondering if he was on camera somehow, and tired to think of good words to offer… The problem was that every time Maggie opened her mouth, Yasser's only plausible response was a question to put to her: and Q and A took *time.* Too much time (thinking again of Shyleen); but how could he stop this now? It was like being in a maze, and everything that Maggie told him took him to ever-greater numbers of pathways to choose from.

Despite any intentions that he might have had to clear things up tonight (including arson), it was apparent that he wriggled, more pinned down than ever before.

At great length his brain showed him the next question to ask… although a bigger question loomed above all of the others. *Why are you telling me this now?* From Maggie's point of view, what had changed? What had put her in the mood for confession?

'Why do they want to keep you scared?' Yasser asked.

Maggie's eyebrows flattened: she was serious. Whatever she was close to saying would make her miserable, but at least she was being serious.

'To punish me,' she said at last.

6.

So engrossed had Shyleen been in the transient satisfaction of micturation that she had not so much as heard him move through the house. Dressed only in boxer shorts, he had come downstairs for a glass of water and had heard Shyleen clambering onto the sink unit... and then the sound of water drilling against the basin.

Chris turned on the light. When he saw Shyleen perched on her unlikely throne, he did not gasp, but the girl side-on in front of him did. And then she turned away from him, faced the beige wall, and said, 'Do you *mind?*' But Chris did not move an inch: his vision feasted on the girl's left buttock, crushed on the lip of the unit, her brown thighs, and the pubic hair that she had shaved into the shape of a question mark (for Yasser).

'Wanna tell me why you're pissing in my sink?' Chris inquired.

'Can't you wait?' Shyleen demanded, still facing the wall.

'Couldn't *you?*'

'No I couldn't as a matter of fact.'

Chris took a step into the tiny room, for a better view. A smile flickered on his features when he confirmed that it was indeed a question mark, and he watched the top of her legs as they opened slightly, any further movement impeded by the trousers throttling her knees.

Shyleen asked, her voice softer than before, 'Good show?'

'Yes,' Chris answered.

'But what if your wife comes home?'

'She's gone,' was the simple response; and as the last drops of Shyleen's urine tapped against the sink, with the aroma a cloud in the air, Christ bent at the waist and pushed the trousers and thong further down to the intruder's ankles. And then over one foot. The clothing hung from her right foot, and Chris stepped up against Shyleen's perched body while she opened her thighs wide.

The erection in Chris's boxer shorts was all but ready; he was hard enough to ease his penis into Shyleen's warmth, which he accomplished with the girl leaning back against the taps.

They both felt feverish and strange (and would later query if it had indeed happened) but Chris answered Shyleen's shaved question mark with a subvocalised 'Yes.'

And thrust against her.

7.

'Why do they want to punish you?' Yasser wanted to know.

Maggie stood up and took their mugs to the sink. 'For losing me child,' curled in her wake.

There really *had* been a child? Yasser had all but discounted the very possibility. He had long since concluded that Maggie had lied about the abduction; but now his function − that of baby-finder *extraordinaire* − returned to focus all that he'd learned up to now into one amorphous lump.

'The truth now, Maggie.'

Maggie displayed her empty palms. 'I've been all about the truth from the very beginning.'

'Now *that's* not even true.'

'You insult me, sir. Well, a bit. I can see your point, I suppose. All I can say is, some of it you'd've found harder to swallow than a focken prune stone, so I might've smudged some of the lines a little squidge.'

Nodding his head, Yasser suggested: 'How about you unsmudge them now. I want a full frontal close-up shot, Maggie.'

And the woman laughed − momentarily. 'You've already had one, you greedy bugger.' Maggie sighed. 'I'll sit down − I'll *need* to sit down.' Her eyelids closed, and quietly she said, 'There was a child – there really was. I used to work in the police station in Bedford – ironically enough, you might say. Tea-making was not one of me duties.' She smirked. 'Basically, I was there to chop onions and carrots, all that bullshit. You might call it prepping and you might call it donkey work; all I know's, it was an honest job, and I look back on it fondly because it was the last time I was free...

'You can probably guess the next bit: I met a bloke – a grocery delivery guy who came to the kitchen. A mouth-breathing shit-eater, it turned out, but at the time I thought the world of him... Anyway. Night followed day, as they say, and then one month I didn't get me period. So that's the end of that then, I thought; that's me life, I thought, over – and me barely in me twenties. Cuz I was pretty bloody certain he wouldn't stick around – how right I was about *that!* – but I had worse troubles to care for. First one being: the wanker's name was Ali and came from a strict Muslim family, ho-bloody-ho. The second being, I'm not exactly from the kind of... ancestral stock that puts much faith in chasing irresponsible fathers down via legal channels and bloody paperwork. I was more worried I'd get home one night and find the tips of the bugger's fingers in a decorative sash... Tommy likes a bit of mutilation if he thinks he's on the side of the righteous, you know? The point being, how was I gonna pay for a *baby?* There'd have to come a point when I wouldn't be able to work – and then what?'

Maggie did not answer her own question straight away, which led Yasser to the conclusion that he was expected to participate. 'And then what,' he agreed more than questioned.

'Then my son came along.' Maggie shrugged, as if to say: *what else?* 'And then one day... he wasn't here anymore... Well. To say that Tommy suddenly took an interest in me is a bit of an understatement, Yass. The fucker was absolutely *obsessed*. Imagine. Up to then he'd hardly given a damn about the child, one way other to be honest – I didn't even get the stick I was expecting for the boy being mixed race. Which I suppose was understandable – we were never, you know, really close like some siblings are.'

'Siblings? You mean Tommy's your *brother?*' Yasser asked.

'Of course he's my brother. Why else would he take such an interest in you, the over-protective sod?'

'Well, that's one way of putting it. But taking dirty pictures of his *sister*. That's well perverted.'

Maggie chuckled. 'Oh he's done a lot worse than that in his time, all in the service of what hangs between his legs.'

'I can imagine.'

'No you can't.'

'You see, I thought he was your ex.'

'As I say… he's done worse than take mucky pictures of me.'

Yasser's back straightened. 'Are you serious, Maggie? Hand on heart time.'

Maggie put her right hand on her heart. Her eyes were wide open she fixed Yasser with an earnest stare. 'But not recently. When we were younger.'

'Jesus. He should be in prison.'

'Nice try. Not if your da won't believe a word you say,' Maggie answered; 'or if he believes, doesn't really give much of a toss. Don't forget, we have… we have different rules on the land. Different from you.'

'But it's incest! It's a crime!'

'It doesn't happen anymore, Yasser.'

'You're missing the point.'

'No I'm not. I'm trying to tell you a story.'

'Christ,' Yasser interrupted. 'Was it your father as well? I mean, if he's aware of the filming…'

'*Aware* of it? He *sells* it.'

'…I feel sick.'

'That'll be me tea. Shall I go on?'

Yasser sighed. 'You'd better, I suppose.'

8.

'You'll probably notice, there's not a lot left behind to steal – we were burgled a couple of weeks ago,' said Chris. And he watched Shyleen carefully, conscious that the comment might be offensive.

Shyleen took it well enough, however. 'I'm not here to steal anything,' she told him.

'I take it, though, you and the Asian lad I spoke to are in it together.'

'In a manner of speaking.'

'So what's going on then, if you'll forgive my nosiness? Is he your what? – your boyfriend? Your brother?'

'Cousin,' Shyleen answered. 'Sometimes boyfriend,' she added. 'Maybe we should get him in here, assuming he hasn't gone home.'

'Yeah why not?' Chris chuckled. 'Invite the whole street, why don't you.'

With the sex tour of house having taken in only the ground floor, the two of them had made it into the lounge for Chris to finish on Shyleen's face. That had been twenty minutes earlier – since then they'd been talking – and now Chris stood up from the sofa.

'Would you like a drink?' he asked.

'Do you have any Baileys?'

'No. I've got vodka and some grass. A smoke's always nice

with a Bloody Mary.'

'Sure. What don't kill you makes you stronger,' Shyleen told him, and she watched dimples form on his buttocks as he slouched from the room.

What had she hoped to find here? Or more to the point, what had *Yasser* hoped she would find here? As Chris had pointed out, the electrical appliances had been taken from the room; the TV stand seemed naked without its wide screen, the CDs on a rack above the fireplace an almost surreal touch in the absence of a player... Every bit as naked as Chris was, Shyleen crossed the room in her birthday suit, in order to see what music he shared with his absent partner. As she skimread the sides of the boxes – jazz, acid house, Madness, ska – she absentmindedly chipped at a beauty mark of dessicated semen on her left nostril with a painted fingernail.

Chris returned carrying a tray. They sat on the carpet, in the middle of the floor, with Shyleen wondering how late Yasser would wait, and Chris rolling two thin joints with equal measures of tobacco and marijuana.

'This is French,' he said. 'You've probably had stronger.'

'I probably haven't.'

'But it's a mellow enough smoke for this hour of the morning.'

The lighter flared.

A minute or so later, Shyleen repeated her opinion that Yasser should be present. After what she and Chris had done together, it could not have been fear of the man that made her want this. Indeed, in her new lover's company she felt assured, confident – she felt good. The fuck had invigorated her mind and cleared her system; but if she'd hoped that he would spill the beans as comprehensively as he'd spilled his sperm, she was out of luck. Orgasm had made the man no more trustful; no more open. Perhaps he had nothing to tell; perhaps he'd been telling

Yasser the whole truth when they'd talked at the front door. Perhaps Chris had nothing to do with anything at all.

'You've gone quiet,' he said.

'Thinking.'

'Do you know what *I* think? I'm wondering why you didn't let him into the house when you had the chance.'

'And what chance was that?'

'When I was asleep.'

'I didn't know you *were* asleep. I must've fallen asleep myself.'

Chris laughed and exhaled smoke. 'You occasionally read stories about people like you,' he said. 'Burglars who get so pissed in the family's wine cellar they forget what they're there for, and then the pigs arrive with the sirens flashing.'

'I told you: we're not burglars. So I didn't let him into the house.'

'Then what *are* you? Apart from feisty.'

Shyleen sipped her Bloody Mary. During the period of consideration she shifted her position, so that she sat cross-legged, her question mark curling down to her cock-swollen lips. Sensing her agitation, Chris asked if the question had made her uncomfortable; she shook her head. 'No it's not that. Angry, is the answer.'

'Ah! Was that why we…?'

'Why we what?'

'Why we − why you were happy for me −'

'Spit it out. Don't be coy.' And she laughed. 'You think it was a revenge shag, don't you?'

Chris had inhaled and was holding it down. Shyleen had to wait for his answer, which she did gladly − she was enjoying the company, the careless guilt-free nudity, the stripped-down room. She was comfortable. Although she remained angry (no sense in denying *that*; why not embrace it? she wondered), she was comfy;

she felt at home.

'The thought had crossed my mind, I must admit,' said Chris.

'Well it wasn't. But you're right to… to um… to what's the word I'm, fucking. Christ my *memory*. Where the fuck – something's stolen my fucking *brain*.'

Chris giggled. His laughter had changed pitch suddenly.

'I'm not sure I should smoke any more,' Shyleen slurred.

'Fair enough, but trust me. The booze and the grass are jibbing. Your cranium is the casserole dish. And you wouldn't fear a lamb casserole, would you?'

'No.'

'Then wait it out. You are either getting,' Chris taught slowly, 'or you have already got – high. Let your brain sort it through.'

'ASSUME!' Shyleen shouted, remembering the word that she'd struggled for. 'You are right to *assume* my kissing cousin has spread his seed.' She lifted her half-emptied glass. 'And with a Pikey bird no less! A filthy – fucking – Gypsy Fucking Rose Lee. Beautiful! Oh it makes me feel so *special*. The cunt.'

Chris was nodding his head. The nod said *I understand, I understand.* The nod said *Smoke and drink, sweetheart – I don't need your war stories.*

Or so Shyleen inferred – in her altered psychic state. She handed Chris the remains of the joint; she'd had enough of it, she was starting to feel sick. She did not need to say as much.

What she said instead was more shocking.

'Besides, I'm dying.'

The words expanded.

'…How come?' Chris asked at length, nubbing the joint out on the inside of his glass.

'Growths. Downstairs,' Shyleen explained, nodding perfunctorily at her vagina.

'Nothing catching, I hope.'

'No. Nothing catching… About inviting Yasser in.'

'Go on. Call him.'

'Thank you.'

'But aren't you going to dress first?'

Shyleen shrugged. 'He's seen me naked.'

'Well, he hasn't seen *me* naked,' Chris said; 'and blokes don't show each other their cocks.'

Shyleen grinned. 'Not even in a threeway?' she asked.

9.

Together with Max and a handful of vigilantes from the camp, Tommy the Brazilian and Maggie's father went in search of Ali, the delivery driver who had impregnated Maggie; but as soon as the reluctant father had been informed, he had been on his toes, abandoning his job in the process.

The lynch mob couldn't find him.

The search was hindered, of course, by the fact that he'd delivered fresh veg and frying oil to a police station: it was not as though anyone could wait in a van outside a cop shop without attracting suspicion; not make enquiries – with or without menace – of the uniforms who worked therein, for that matter. And owing to the Asian lad's reticence to take Maggie anywhere close to home (what with racism being rich, with so many suits to wear), the paramours romantic entanglements had taken place at The Charity, a nudge-nudge-ask-no-questions flophouse B&B near the A6. (Cash payments encouraged. Rooms available by the hour.) However, the stakeout in The Charity's car park had not lasted long. While Tommy had expressed confidence that the cunt would be back with another bird to giblet, the bearded fuckpad owner (with his physical resemblance to the wrestler Giant Haystacks) had expressed a similar confidence that the man parked outside for the last three nights in his blue van was peddling pills: and this he expressed to the local constabulary. Max, on watch that night, was lucky to escape, wheels spitting mud from the wrecked path up to the building, without a caution – not so much as a *conversation*.

They couldn't find him.

But one day they would: this was a pledge that Tommy made at the time, and Tommy was not a man to swear pledges aimlessly: so he proclaimed.

The baby was delivered on the camp by Bridget, Maggie's cousin – the woman who owned a dog-grooming parlour in Hockliffe. Even at that time, she was already a horny veteran of the washing-up bowl of scalding water, the oven-fresh steaming wet towels. She had already delivered twenty-three babies in the name of family favours, for sixty quid a pop.

'And then one day… he wasn't there anymore,' said Maggie to Yasser.

'Yes, you've said.'

'No. I mean more than just simply not present physically. I don't care if this sounds fruit loops, but ever since he went away… I could glimpse him every now and then. Not in dreams – or not only in dreams. I'm talking about a sense of him. A chuckle, a bubble of snot from a nostril, the touch of his fingers, maybe – so much that… I didn't really think of him as properly gone. Not really. I might've been alone n my bed and I could *feel* him, wriggling on me breasts, draining me to *sacks*.

'It was like he was with me and not with me – at one and the same time.'

Maggie stopped talking. She rose to her slippered feet again and heavy-stepped it to the bedroom. 'I'm gonna fetch something stronger.'

'I can't drink. I'm driving.'

'All the more for yours truly, then.'

Maggie slipped away, and Yasser felt the pull of the phone in his pocket. The time he refused to fight it: he checked his texts. But before he did so, he turned away from the direction of the bedroom door and showed his back to it.

There was nothing from Shyleen.

Why not?

What could have happened to have stopped her answering his U OK? What might have possessed her attention to such a degree that a simple OK was disadvantageously time-consuming?

Once more Yasser was worried. It was time to leave, by the love of God – it was surely *time*. Hearing Maggie on her reapproach, Yasser pocketed the mobile and twisted to face his hostess. She was carrying a bottle of colourless liquid.

'Bootleg,' she announced. 'There are no coppers here anyway. Fuck em. Have a drink. Only a few months before Christmas.'

Although the mood swing was obvious, its reason was not so apparent; and Yasser was baffled. Was this the result of the unburdening of a secret? If so, he himself should unburden the breast more often.

'The coppers are not the point,' said Yasser. 'You were telling me about...'

'He disappeared. I know, I know.' Standing near the sink, Maggie used her teeth and pulled the cork jammed between the lips of the bottle; with a violent toss of her locks, she spat the cork in the direction of the bathroom door, and giggled. '*Patience*. Or do you have somewhere else you need to be, I should be asking?'

Perhaps some honesty of his own would not go amiss at this point, Yasser thought. 'As a matter of fact, Maggie,' he said, 'there *is* somewhere I should be getting to.'

'Oh. Another hot date?'

'Are you teasing me again?'

'Would you love me any other way?' Maggie poured generous – if not gluttonous – measures of the moonshine into two plastic beakers, one pink, one yellow. 'Is it your kissing cousin again waiting for you with a hot water bottle on her breasts to keep herself warm for you?'

'In a manner of speaking,' Yasser admitted.

'Well, in a manner of *speaking*, you're going nowhere until you've had a shot with me. Take it.' Maggie was holding out the yellow beaker, swirling the liquid within with a curl of her wrist, like a wine connoisseur releasing the aroma.

Yasser took it. Placed his nose at the rim and thought: *Surely there's been a mistake.* She must have taken a couple of inches from the petrol can in the car. This wasn't a *drink*; it was a *fuel*. People powered mopeds on lower specific gravities.

Maggie sipped and sat down. 'That'll put hairs on your chest.'

'I've already got hairs on my chest.'

'Not many. Put hairs on *my* chest then. Where were we?'

'The disappearance. Your punishment,' said Yasser.

Maggie nodded – and Yasser sipped his hairshirt cocktail. Predictably vile.

'They blamed me, naturally: I shouldn't have been surprised and I wasn't,' Maggie said. 'But when he went away completely – out of range, you might say – I felt a mother's *hollow rage*… the like of which I dare say you won't have encountered in any of your twenty innocent years. And it was then I realised – wherever it is the kidnapped children go… not physically, where their *souls* go, you might say… it has slipped away. And not only for me: Bridget had been spying him at his various ages as well, which I didn't tell you before. Others too, more than likely. So

Da hatched the plan I would steal the kid from High Town –
the one you caught on film. To redress the balance was how he
put it. He was deadly serious. I know. It sounds like a madness
now: a group whadyamacallit. A group delusion. The madness
of crowds… and all that guff.'

This was ground that Yasser and Maggie had covered before; ground that spoke to Yasser, though no psychoanalyst he,
of a deep-seated psychosis – of problems still festering from the
father's own childhood. More than a sense that the world owed
him a living: a sense of fear of imbalance. *Do unto him*, etcetera.
Tit for tat. What goes around comes around… The man was sick.
Clearly and inoperably malfunctioning. And now that Yasser
knew that Tommy had sprung from the same identical loins, it
was no surprise that the offspring shared a portion of the same
demented chromosomes and characteristics.

But what of Maggie? Was *she* entirely right in the head?
Yasser wondered as he managed another sip of the masochistic
brew (the fumes twanged his nostril hairs; he almost sneezed).

Was anybody? *Am I?*

Having drained her beaker, Maggie stood up and returned
to the draining board to pour a refill. Yasser guessed that her
need to drink was symptomatic: she was reaching the hard part,
he surmised. *But what if she's still lying?* Though one obvious diagnosis remained that his storyteller needed booze to get to the
heart of the tale – some food for the journey – he could not shake
the clammy sweats that he had committed to the laptop's camera
two evenings earlier (in lieu of penning his notions in a journal),
at which time he had used phrases like: *I'm just a game to play for
them… I think I'm their new sport.*

Yasser wished that he could tell when people fibbed to him.
It would make life a damned sight easier.

'Where's your dad now, Maggie?' Yasser asked. 'How come

he's never home when I call? He can't be working *all* hours?'

'He's not working at all.'

'You told me…'

'Not working in the sense *you* mean,' Maggie clarified, returning to her seat. 'I suppose it *is* work though – he certainly comes home tired enough, so he does. He's out travelling.' And she took another bolt of the mad dog liquor.

Out travelling? What on earth was *that* supposed to mean?

'You see, Yasser, you might call us Gypsies, you might call us Pikeys.'

'*I* don't.'

'Not you personally. *One* might call us those names, and quite frankly I've never had a problem with those descriptions. Some of us don't like "Pikeys" but me,' said Maggie, 'I've never given much of a fuck about it. Bigger fish to fry… I *know* we don't help ourselves when it comes to community relations sometimes, but if you understand our culture…'

'Your culture of flytipping and spitting in pubs, would that be?'

Maggie smiled; she knew that she was being teased. 'That's the culture I mean. Then you get some… primitive comprehension. Of us. At least.'

'Well, you can't say I haven't tried, Mags. I've even gone for interbreeding.'

Fortunately for Yasser, Maggie took this in the comic spirit in which it had been intended. She smiled again. 'As have I,' she replied. 'The gifts we give to the gene pool – I don't know. But why do you think we prefer the term Travellers, as a general rule?'

'No idea. You never *go* anywhere,' Yasser answered. 'Your caravans don't have wheels!'

'Some of them do, but I take your point… You not drinking yours?'

'I've had enough, thanks.'

'So two for two on undrinkable drinks, then.'

Inside Yasser's jacket, the phone beeped; he had received a message. His torso stiffened.

'Oh the agony of bad timing,' Maggie said, fingering one of the bracelets on her left wrist. '"Will I stay or will I go now?" What *will* the boy do? This is Act 5 of the tragedy, Yasser: it's time to make some decisions. "If I go there will be trouble. If I stay there will be double." Or is it the other way around?'

Not knowing what Maggie referred to, Yasser said, 'Shut up.' Near the opening on his jacket his left hand twitched. Should he? 'It might not be Shyleen,' he added.

'Sure. It's your film teacher texting you an emergency assignment for tomorrow's class – at focken midnight… or whatever the time happens to be.'

Later than midnight, was the answer: this Yasser discovered when he pulled out the phone and read 00:13 and 1 NEW MESSAGE. He thumbed for the text and read it. 'I have to go,' he told Maggie. 'Tell me quickly.'

'No. I'll do no such thing,' Maggie replied. 'You'd better go while she's still warm, Yass. Honey doesn't spread from the fridge and all that.'

'Shut up, Maggie,' Yasser repeated. 'Just tell me.'

Maggie laughed. 'You'll have to beat it out of me, *Monsieur*. I'll give you name, rank and serial number – and that's all.'

Was she drunk already? The bootleg was certainly potent, but was it strong enough to account for this fresh development? How many shots had she had before he'd arrived?

'I will in a minute,' Yasser threatened, referring to the beating.

'Big man.'

'Where's he travelling to? Or from. I don't understand what you're saying.'

Through another storm of laughter Maggie added: 'Maybe you should get the two of us together! Girl on girl action, Yass! We'll do a show for you and take turns to lick your toolbag. How about that?'

'I'm warning you, Maggie.' Yasser rose to his feet: to leave the caravan, mainly. But entirely?

'Ooh. You *are* going to beat it out of me!'

'I might at that. Travelling, you said.'

'"*You are travelling through another dimension,*"' Maggie quoted. '"*A dimension not only of sight and sound, but of mind. A journey into-*"'

Yasser slapped the left side of her face. Though negligible in terms of weight behind it, the blow was sufficient to silence Maggie's ramblings. Adrenalin poured through Yasser's upper body; it added weight to his right arm, as if he'd lifted dumbbells; and squeezing the phone in his left fist, for no other reason than to prove that the one strike had not been a fluke, he slapped the side of her head again with his open right palm.

'You *will* take me seriously, Maggie. I promise you you will,' he said as calmly as he could manage. His breath was laboured.

Looking up at him with cow-eyes piled high with tears, Maggie uttered one single word.

'More.'

This time Yasser used the back of his hand, sideswiping his knuckles into the right side of Maggie's face. The impact must have been more powerful because her head rocked to the side.

'Harder,' she instructed him. 'In the face.'

Although he did not strike her in the manner that she'd specified, Yasser did slap her once more for good measure, employing his original style: the right palm, the left temple.

Maggie licked her lips.

Yasser pulled her up from her seat, and as soon as she was upright he pushed her backwards, using his free hand and her breasts as bumpers. She toppled onto the surface of the table, knocking Yasser's beaker flying, and Yasser slipped his phone into his trouser pocket. Clutching hold of the dressing gown hem, he pulled the garment open like a pair of curtains… to reveal her nakedness.

Or near nakedness, at any rate. As Maggie lifted her knees, she presented her labia and anus to her attacker. Embedded deep into the latter was an item that Yasser had never clapped eyes on outside of pornography: a contoured butt-plug… Taking rage as his inspiration, Yasser unraped Maggie of this implement, pulling it free with an audible pop and an anal burp… She was open to the size of a ten pence coin, and Yasser unbuttoned his fly to find something to fill in as a butt-plug replacement.

CABIN IN THE WOODS

1.

Don's hut showed all the signs of recent habitation – the lights were on, and judging by the aroma, something was roasting in the oven – but Don was nowhere to be seen. The place was empty.

Roger suggested: 'Maybe he's slipped out for a piss,' speaking as he stepped over the threshold and in. Immediately he was enveloped in a friendly homecooked warmth.

'This is ugly,' said Dorota. 'It'd be one thing if he was *here*… but this is his home.'

'It's your property,' Eastlight reminded her.

'I know that.'

'And we got nowhere last time when he *was* here,' Roger added.

'Last time?' said Eastlight.

'A few weeks ago,' Dorota explained. 'So what do we do? Tear the place up?'

Don's absence had sucked some of the wind from the mob's sails. If they were not careful, they'd be returning to the big house with nothing to show but blood-patches of embarrassment on their cheeks, irrespective of their former bluster and lynch-lust.

'He's cooking a chicken,' Roger said as he stepped into the kitchen area and bent at the waist. A light was on inside the oven.

'It's nearly done, it's brown. He hasn't gone far.' Roger paused. The memory of what he'd seen last time – during their inaugural raid – did not so much return to his consciousness (it hadn't ever gone away) as it did reintensify. It was like a lightbulb, suddenly given too much voltage: it burned with a fierce illumination and would surely explode. In his mind's eye he saw the box of nappies once more, and without another word he started to yank open the kitchen drawers and cupboards.

Eastlight watched him. The memories inside his head were a good deal more problematic than what burned for Roger, but they acted in a similarly inspirational way. Ignoring what felt like a fist – a swollen fist – inside his stomach, he set to dismantling Don's lounge with a ferocity known only to the frightened and the insane. He used his left forearm to swipe a row of framed photographs off the sideboard; they crashed to the floor with a satisfying din.

It felt good to damage Don's property. Eastlight had far from forgotten the old boy threatening to shatter his knees: he had *thrived* on the threat, he realised. He had used it as a fuel, perhaps, even through his dealings in the Eggington house. During the first few seconds of destruction in Don's home, the feeling moved through Eastlight's brain that this was as good a form of exercise as any (he needed to lose weight); it was also likely that he would have continued, riding an identical sadistic wave, until he ran out of breath or his muscles grew heavy and hard… were it not for Dorota's interruption.

She said, 'Stop!'

Eastlight stopped in an instant; breathing like a Bull Mastiff, he regarded what little he'd achieved with the slow blink of a fat man waking from a fair sleep. Guilt shook him by the lapels; his mouth tasted dry – dry and bitter – and he understood that he had been taken. He'd been gripped by the pandemic of mob madness, as contagious as the mumps. Mistake! *Mistake*, thought Eastlight to himself, in a spirit of self-flagellation. He was here to earn himself an alibi; he was not here to fuck up the old prick's belongings. ('Sorry.') Doing damage would be better, after all, when Don was *present*. Indeed, he'd make the sad wanker beg him to stop.

Roger was slower to abide by Dorota's command. Having found Don's front door unlocked – which was hardly the action, he reflected, of a guilty man hiding treasure – he was now determined to find evidence of the child that Don must have taken with him, into the woods. For as sure as night followed day, there was no child here in the hut. No smells of one either: the place was perfumed with nothing more sinister than this season's must-have rolling tobacco, and even this residue had all but been obliterated by the rotisserie scent. So at best, Roger was annoyed and frustrated.

But what had he really expected? What *really?* That Don would by lying, supine, on a bed of duck down, with a baby contentedly suckling at his left breast?

Ridiculous.

Horrendous and bloody *ridiculous.*

His nostrils flared and contracted in quick succession; he was livid. Only the discovery of Don-Acting-Weirdly would have tossed a gallon of water on this specific bonfire. In the second or two that he engaged in his last flurry of activity, before he knew that it would be too late to pretend that he hadn't heard Dorota's *Stop*, Roger longed for the scent of human blood, for the hungry or furious cry of an infant – for *anything*.

And then he found it.

Accompanying Roger's elaborate flourish and his presentation of a box from the tray cupboard under the oven, was a loud 'Huzzah!' And then he said, 'The night has magic colours,' slamming the box onto the draining board.

It was a box of twelve jars of baby food.

'What do you think of that then?' Roger asked, his voice a tad intimidating. The finding of treasure can make you as angry as fulfilled.

Eastlight and Dorota stepped closer. 'Baby food,' they said almost in unison.

Roger's excitement was not forced or acted. 'Which tells you what?'

The kitchen door to the outside opened inward. Standing in the doorway, Don said, 'Yes. Which tells you what exactly?' With a face lined and thundery, he stepped into his kitchen and reached for a smudged glass by the sink. This he filled from the tap, his back to his houseguests; and still in this position he raised it to his mouth and drained it dry.

'I asked you all a question,' he said, turning to face them once more. With the slick movements of one fully familiar with his surroundings, Don produced, in swift succession, a bottle of brandy, a bottle of ginger wine, his pouch of tobacco, a packet of papers, and a saucepan to use as an ashtray. Then, carrying all of these items, he pushed past his visitors and took his place in his favourite seat.

'The cat got your tongues?' he asked, and for the first time he sounded more than angry: he sounded as though he were not only within his rights to shoot those who trespassed on his land, he was also accustomed to doing so, and enjoyed it. He mixed brandy and ginger wine in a 50/50 mix that filled the half-pint glass. Took a swig (silence from the visitors) and rolled a cigarette with the hand not busy holding the glass.

Who would explain this to Don? All *in situ* wondered this; but it was Dorota who said, 'We do at least owe you an explanation.'

'You don't owe me anything, Miss.'

'I think we do. But do you mind if I ask where you've been?'

'Looking in on the birds,' Don answered. 'Sometimes I'm of a mind to just let them go – fly free. And it's times like these I wonder what's crueller: releasing them to fend for themselves, even if they wouldn't have a chance, or keeping them cooped up.' He turned to Dorota. 'What would *you* say, Miss?'

'I don't know how to answer that,' Dorota admitted. 'If you let the birds go…'

'I'm out of a job.'

'You're out of a job. But keeping them enclosed has always seemed…'

'Barbaric?' Don suggested.

Dorota nodded her head. 'A bit.'

'I agree. I *concur.*' Don laughed and took down more of the Brandy Mac. A thin plume of smoke writhed upwards from his cigarette knuckle.

'I've had enough of this,' said Roger, under his breath.

Don heard him. 'Oh *you* have. *You've* had enough of this. Well let me tell you, Doctor –'

'I'm not a doctor.'

'So have I. For the last two weeks I've been waiting for you to come back. Do you know why? Because you're a bully, Mr Billie. And bullies always go back to taunt the same weak person if they can – or if they think they can.'

Sulkily Roger replied, 'I'm no bully.'

'Oh yes you are, sir.' Don took a drag on his roll-up. 'Which is why you let your good lady wife wear the trousers in your home life – and your love life, for all I know.'

'How dare you!' Roger spluttered.

'No, how dare *you*, sir.' Don looked up from his chair, and by twisting his neck he was able to lock Roger in his sights. 'It's almost as though you think you haven't done enough damage.

Would that be right, sir?'

Roger stood his ground, albeit with an air about him of unimpeachable embarrassment. 'I want to know why you keep baby food here,' he said.

'Weren't a crime, last time I looked.' Don raised the smoke fizzing in his knuckle up to his wind-bitten lips.

'No, it's not a *crime...*'

Twisting further in his chair, Don added: 'You'll have my resignation in the morning, Miss. The proper morning.'

Dorota shook her head. 'There's no need to be hasty, Don,' she protested.

'But it's only fair to advise you that in this country we oper-ate under certain rules of employment,' Don said; 'and if this don't constitute a case of constructive dismissal then I'll be a bloody Dutchman.'

'No one's trying to dismiss you, Don,' said Dorota.

'It's not a *crime,*' Roger repeated; 'but I'm asking for an ex-planation all the same.'

'Call his bluff,' said Eastlight to the Lady of the House.

Up to now, Vig had refrained from uttering a word. His stomach felt wrong; his conscience felt diseased. But now he raised his voice and said, 'Charlie, you're not helping.'

Eastlight proffered a grin that appeared both sanctimo-nious and cheesy. 'Sure thing, Viggy-Loo.' And he made the mime of zipping up his lips.

'Don. Please understand: we're not trying to get rid of you, okay? I'm very happy with your work – and so are the birds. If they could talk they would confirm this.' Vig smiled. It had been intended as a joke.

'They *can* talk,' Don told him. 'It's a case of learning their language.'

'Nutty as a fruitcake,' Eastlight said to the room. 'Sorry.' He had received a withering glance from Vig.

'Okay, Don – you tell me you're fluent in their language…'

'I didn't say fluent, sir.'

'…but the matter remains, there are, there are *indications* of a baby or child being here.'

'Look about you, sir,' Don continued. 'Let me know if you find one. And Mr Billie? Baby food contains sources of calcium – for the bones, the development of the bones. My doctor suggested it for me knees. It's as shameful for me as it's difficult for you, I assure you: pretending to be a grandfather every time a checkout girl gets a bit nosey.'

Don sipped his Brandy Mac; such was the confidence with which he had clarified the point about the baby food and its constituent ingredients, that nobody had noticed the time-wasting tactic that he'd employed before answering Roger's question. Indeed, even Roger himself appeared humbled by the calcium reference: it sounded medical, authentic; it sounded good. Which left them where?

'What about the nappies I saw here last time?' Roger asked.

Evidently Don had expected this: the shrug of his shoulders was carefree, nonchalant. 'Got to keep up the pretence, haven't I? For the checkout girl… Besides, I'm an old man with a sixty-year sixty-a-day nicotine habit. You wouldn't *believe* the stuff comes out of my nose sometimes. A nappy's more suitable than a piece of bogroll. Begging your pardon, Miss.'

'Nice image; thanks,' said Dorota, but there was a softness beneath the sarcasm. She was as aware as they all were that this mission would be aborted. There was simply no conflict possible if the other party did not want to fight.

And yet?

Dorota could not escape the sensation that she was being lied to: a thick impression, as complicated as grief. What was it? What was tipping her off? She didn't know; what arrived in her head, unbidden and unwanted, was a memory of her childhood home in Brzeźno, Gdansk. She was four or five. And the teacher from England had rented the room in the basement. He had taught at the Business College... and Dorota had been unable to comprehend that he spoke a different language. She'd thought him ill. After all, if her parents could understand her, and if Smilla (the family Dachshund) could understand her, then the only reason that the teacher had for *not* understanding her was illness. A sickness of the brain, the infant consultant had diagnoses... Even when her parents had tried to explain that the teacher came from another country, it wasn't good enough for Dorota. She'd wanted to cure him: and the only way to do this (she had reasoned) was by being mean to him. By being cruel.

The memory drew to an abrupt end, and Dorota was throwing her food across the table at the teacher, much to the displeasure of her parents; she was shrieking. She was telling them that the teacher had hit her.

'Don?'

'Yes, Miss Dorota.'

If being mean was what it would take, then this was a language that Dorota could recall from a long time ago.

'Tell me the truth right now,' she instructed the old man, 'or I will personally release all of the birds. Do you understand me? Not you. Me. I will do it while you're asleep and you won't even get a chance to say goodbye to them.'

'Dorota, please,' said Vig, who'd been under the (incorrect) impression that he had got somewhere in the summit talks and had had matters under control.

'In the morning you'll be out of a job and a home. And don't bullshit *me* about employment law either. It was only a little while ago you were thanking your lucky stars we'd let you stay. So what's it to be?'

As Don stood up his knees creaked, like staged effects in the fiction of his fib. A wince raced across his features; it looked real. He placed his empty glass on the table, his dog-end in the saucepan; and the shuffle that he undertook past his visitors piled years onto his back. He did not seem the same man as he had even a minute earlier. He moved into the kitchen. Wordlessly he turned down the oven, and then (on further inspection: this might take some time) turned it off altogether. From inside the oven the chicken splashed and sizzled in its juices, tastily noisy.

'Powerful threat, Miss,' Don said. 'You know how to wound a man – straight through the heart. Through the *liver*.'

It was a compliment of sorts. Dorota said, 'Thank you, Don. Now, if you wouldn't mind.'

Don opened the oven door. Heat surged out, along with a fresh scent of roasted garlic from the stuffing he'd knuckled into the chicken's sorry cavity. And then he turned to face the four interrogators. He raised his hand and pointed a finger at Dorota.

'I'll tell *you*, Miss,' he said. Then he pointed at Vig. 'And I'll tell you, sir.' With a nod of compliance he then pointed his finger at Roger. 'I'll even tell you, Mr Billie.'

Don frowned like a pantomime villain. He pointed at Eastlight and added, 'But *this* one. This one I wouldn't give the shit off me arse-hairs. He leaves.'

Eastlight reacted immediately. The other people present were a barrier between him and Don, which was something of a blessing in disguise: he would not have taken three steps before someone restrained him... and hadn't he come here to earn an alibi anyway? He'd intended to show that he *wasn't* a violent man, hadn't he? Well, taking a swing at an old man would do little to confirm that rumour.

'You little cunt,' he said instead. 'What gives *you* the right...?'

'Has anyone apart from me wondered what he's doing here anyhow?' Don asked.

Good question. Don had given voice to a query that once out in the open, appeared nonsensical in its simplicity. What *was* Charlie doing here?

'You'd better go, Charlie,' said Vig. 'You can wait in the Games Room if you like.'

Eastlight spluttered. 'Are you gonna let *Donald Duck…*'

'I warned you,' said Don.

'Charlie, please,' Vig continued. 'Just wait for us in the house. Make yourself a drink.'

'I can't believe this,' Eastlight mumbled.

It was Dorota who said it though: the question was on everybody's lips.

'Why *are* you here, Charlie?' she asked.

'I came to see *you*.'

'And not me?' asked Don, and he laughed. 'Get out of my house, please. I think I've been more than patient.'

Eastlight sneered. 'Or you'll do what, Donald Duck? *Shatter my knees*? Did you know he threatened me, Viggy-Loo?'

Vig shook his head. 'I don't care about any threats right now, Charlie. *I'm* asking you. You can make yourself at home in the house or I can speak to you tomorrow. Up to you.'

'Jesus.' Eastlight opened the front door. To Don (by the stove) he shouted: 'And I'd like to see you try, you little prick.'

'Oh I'll try,' Don told him. 'I promised, didn't I? One more Donald Duck and it's your knees. Now get out.'

'There – you heard him!' Eastlight crowed triumphantly.

'I'll say it again if anyone didn't catch it,' said Don. 'But it seems to be only you, *Charlie*, having a problem comprehending. And if I were Sir I wouldn't let you anywhere near the Big House, but that's Sir's prerogative.'

Breathing heavily with the exertion of frustration, Eastlight hissed: 'You have no idea what I'm capable of.'

'But you're wrong there. That's *precisely* why I wouldn't let you anywhere near the Big House. Personally, I'd rather you froze in the woods and made supper for the foxes. Now fuck off! I feel nauseous just wasting my breath on someone like you.'

2.

It only took a few minutes for the night air to reach through Eastlight's light clothing and diminishing inebriation. He had not come fully prepared, he realised: he was not well enough protected from the cold, not in terms of the right jacket, and not in terms of the right skin-full. However. He did not want to go to the main house; and he did not wish to sit it out in his car, with the heater blasting, either. At any length – the discomfort of cold hands included – he would watch Don's hut. He would know when the others exited. And then he'd pay a call on the old man, a solo visit this time.

3.

Don pulled up the kitchen rug and dragged it into the lounge. The trapdoor was revealed (it coaxed a gasp from Dorota) and Roger felt his pulse quicken. In the absence of a physical captive – a baby, a child – then the revelation of what had been hidden was a fine second choice. In fact, it was his stock in trade. What people chose to show you said as much as why they chose to conceal. Unless…

The thought raced through Roger's belly.

Unless the child was under the trapdoor.

Only mindful of the breath he'd taken but had failed to

exhale when it became a burden on his chest, Roger glanced to either side – at Vig and then Dorota – in an attempt to record their expressions. After all, this was good material: there was a paper in this, for somewhere down the line. Or perhaps an entire conference. But their faces were inexpressive – resilient, even. Perhaps their lack of emotion was of note, in and of itself.

'What's down there?' Dorota asked.

'Would you like to do the honours, Miss?' Don replied.

'No.'

'Just open it, please, Don,' said Vig.

'As you wish, sir.' And Don opened the trapdoor.

The only thing to change about the atmosphere was s slight whiff of damp from the ground below; but even this was swiftly challenged and overcome by the aroma of roast chicken and hot garlic.

'How deep is it?' Roger wanted to know.

'About six foot. Not very.'

'What's the *point* of it?' Vig asked next.

'I'll tell you, but before we go any further, can we agree I'm not keeping any children down there? As if I would!'

'Okay, Don, agreed,' Vig told him; 'but you have to see how for us this might raise as many questions as it solves.'

'Like what?' Don asked.

'Like, why have you got a bloody big hole in your kitchen floor?' Vig cleared his throat and looked to the others for signs of support. 'Like, what do you think? Why is the sky blue?'

'Well, I'm about to tell you, sir – I just didn't want you to go on doubting me.' Don led the way back into the lounge, intending for the others to follow; but Roger, bent at the waist, remained peering into the hole. Something had caught his attention.

'What's down there? I see something.'

Don reassumed his position in his favourite chair. While

rolling another cigarette he said, 'A tape recorder. Some food.'
He licked the length of the cigarette paper and sealed it; he even
held it up to the light, a perfect specimen, a wonder to behold.
'Maybe a soiled nappy or two.'

Vig sat on Don's footstool. Leaning forward, he appeared
monstrous, a grotesque, an ogre at stool, or an adult on kinder-
garten plastic furniture. 'You said you'd explain if we got rid of
Charlie. We're waiting, Don.'

Don nodded. He closed his eyes and sipped on his roll-up.

'I had a daughter once,' he began.

4.

I had a daughter once, back in me racing days. Back when
I felt like a millionaire... before the bad times. Daughter called
Polly. But she got sick when she was one, and I stopped... I
stopped being happy after a while. And so did everyone around
me, I reckon.

The only place I was comfortable – really comfortable
– was in the saddle. Golden days they were, in many ways. I'd
bomb around the country, jockey for hire, and I was riding a winning streak, I tell you. I couldn't fail! Making money hand over
fist, I was. The bookies feared me. Not at first: but eventually. I
cost em plenty, riding three-legged nags in a donkey derby – and
I'd *still* win.

My wife wanted me to slow down. She used to say: you're
doing so well you're bound to fall – she was a great believer in
what she called the cosmic balance, bless her soul, God save her
and shine her.

I wouldn't listen. The funny thing about riding a winning
streak is not the sense of self-importance you feel, where you're
like a king among riff-raff. Which is what you might expect – and

which I *did* experience, I'm ashamed to say. No; the funny thing about riding a winning streak is that you are *totally aware of your surroundings* – and you believe they can be controlled. It's not that you think you can do no wrong; it's more like you think you can make *others* do wrong, and shine in comparison. So when my wife said slow down, I knew that's what they were expecting me to do – that would be the logical response. So I speeded up.

I did more and more; pushed myself, harder and harder. Broke a leg, both arms – the left one three times – then my collarbone. But I didn't care, even when I was in traction: I still thought, if I kept an eye on the opposition, it was my fame to be in charge of. I wasn't even overly concerned when I broke both me knees and me luck began rotting.

Then Polly got sick when she was just gone one. The wife brought her to the stables where we kept our own horses – three of em. And three horses with better manners you're never likely to meet, sir. Lovely temperaments… except on this one day.

There was something in the air that morning – and I don't mean the wind. They'd experienced high winds before – they were nine, six and five, they weren't exactly babies – but something had spooked em. Wouldn't settle. It was too rainy to put em out in the field to graze, and I couldn't ride because me knees were sore with the weather. Maybe it was knowing they'd be inside all day that had got their danders up. I don't know. They weren't talking to me. Sometimes they did. Not that day.

One of em was called Noel Never – beautiful mare. Sixteen hands, grey as sleet on a duck pond. I was in her stable, replacing the hay net… and she kicked me. First time ever, as I recall. Got me straight on the left knee. Agony. I went over on her bed and lay there sweating, too much in pain to even scream, if you know what that might feel like.

Well, wouldn't you know, this was one of the days that the

wife chose to take Polly to see Daddy's geegees. She only did it once in a while, and there I was giving Noel Never a good hiding on the yard – she was tied up, of course – and there was me family. I'm a firm believer in spare the rod and spoil the child, and the same… philosophy goes for pets. Don't matter if they're working animals or goldfish: you teach em who's boss. Same with the birds, even now, though I've mellowed; but if one of them buggers were to bite me, it gets segregated from the others and it don't get no food for two days, sir. So I was teaching Noel Never a lesson, making her understand the concepts of fear and consequences , and the wife carries Polly in behind her, where *she knew* not to walk. Never.

Of course… the mare was angry, in pain: I'd just punched her hard on the beak, where it hurts the most. She mounted up on her front legs – like a fucking mule, she were, pardoning my French, Miss – and she kicked Polly in her mother's arms. A flawless aim.

Her skull was broken. Blood everywhere… it haunts me to this day – never been good with the sight of blood, then or now – and as quick as I could, I bundled her in the Land Rover and hightailed it for the hospital. She was in there for nine days; they saved her life. But she was never the same again. She developed epilepsy. She had trouble recognising her parents – she was severely damaged. Brain damaged.

She died when she was two. There was no recovery.

5.

A long pause followed.

'I want you to know,' said Vig, 'that I'm very sorry for your loss, Don.'

'Very sorry,' Dorota repeated, leaning over to squeeze the

man's nicotine-scented shoulders.

'But I don't understand what that tragedy has to do with what's happening today.'

While rolling another cigarette Don said, 'I'm getting to that… Mr Billie. Would you do me a favour and pour me a drink, please? Half brandy, half ginger wine: a winter drink.

'Sure. Do you always cook chicken this late at night, by the way?'

'Whenever the mood takes me. I don't sleep much.' Don tapped ash into the saucepan and said, 'Why? Are you hungry?'

'No,' Roger lied, unscrewing the bottle of ginger wine. Confrontation often made him peckish. However, he was more than prepared to forego his belly for the nonce, having set his sights on grander professional treasure. A conference? A mere *conference?* What Don was leading up to (Roger felt) showed all the hallmarks of a full-length work of non-fiction: a book. Infant mortality and parental madness was always a good opener for the psychoanalytic publishing masses.

No one pressed Don to continue talking while he waited for his cocktail. As their hunches would have it, as soon as he had the glass back in his hand (Don having made his next cigarette in the interim), he started again.

'I kept thinking I saw her. Heard her, more often. At the strangest times,' he said. 'You see… I think she *went* somewhere, when she was ill. Before the kick. Before the seizures… She escaped.' He drank. He smoked.

'Escaped where?' asked Roger, seizing the reins.

'To a safe place. To somewhere it's safe for children. I'd like to think so, anyway.'

All through the story so far, Vig, Dorota and Roger had remained standing. For the first time Vig considered suggesting that they all repair to the main house. Not because the house was warmer (Don's cabin was like a sauna) but because Vig also wanted a drink… and he was of the opinion that he might wait until Hell froze before Don offered any of that brandy. What was more: if Don *were* to suggest a doling-out, would he (Vig) be allowed to accept, given his status as lord of the manor? Still so much to learn about protocol.

'She knew what was happening and she chose to abscond. I respect her for that.'

After handing Don his drink, Roger had stayed close to the chair. Now he squatted down onto his heels. 'A lot of bereaved parents,' he said, 'think they see and hear their children.'

Don nodded. 'I can imagine so. Why should it only happen to me?'

'This has got something to do with the hole?' asked Dorota, gesturing towards the kitchen.

Don nodded again. 'It's got stronger in recent years,' he answered. 'Like she wants to come home. Don't laugh.'

'No one's laughing at you, Don,' Roger tried to assure him. 'Is Polly getting older as you go along? I mean… wherever she is, is she still a baby, or is she growing up nicely? How old were you when you had her?'

'Twenty-six.'

'And how old are you now?'

'Seventy-two. And no, she's not keeping pace with me, if that's what you're asking. She's going faster. The years go by faster there than they do here.' Don paused. In one single swallow he drained his glass and added: 'She's close to five hundred years old.'

6.

Roger was kneeling on his chair in his home office, facing backwards with his elbows crossed on the chair's leather shoulders.

'So he claims to be trying to lure his daughter back,' he said, waiting for the next blow to his bared buttocks.

His wife obliged. She struck him with a wooden spoon and said, 'And his mental state – how would you describe it?' Disappointed by the absence of a wince or any intake of breath from her husband, Phyllie hit him again, harder this time. Red marks blotched his bum cheeks like an infant's paint daubings.

'Thoroughly delusional, I would say,' Roger answered. 'Harder, please. But with a fully functional internal logic. If I had to guess, I'd say that he really believes it.'

Phyllie, behind Roger's back, changed her cudgel; a selection of kitchen utensils decorated the top of the desk for the purpose of this evening's activities. She had placed them there while Roger was out at Don's place. Holding a spatula this time, she whipped a blow to Roger's arse that made him hiss.

'Thank you. Again, please.'

While they continued to discuss the meeting with Don, Phyllie beat and spanked Roger's posterior until it was disproportionately red. With the versatility of a freeform jazz drummer, she used the spoon, the spatula, an egg-whisk and a frying pan. It wasn't long before Roger had grown tumescent, at which point it was time to sit him down on his raw buttocks and masturbate him with one hand while planing his testicles with the cheese-grater in the other.

At no point, however, did Roger lose himself fully in the moment, despite an appearance to this effect. He could not stop thinking about the pit in Don's kitchen.

And Don's story.

So.

Don claimed that he'd lost his daughter in a tragic accident involving a horse.

Believable.

Two. He claimed that the dead daughter had made contact with him over the years.

Believable. Not checkable in the slightest (did Don keep a diary?); but hearing the voices of loved ones lost was far from uncommon, especially if there was an element of guilt involved. The accident having happened at the place where Don stabled the mare would qualify. The guy was guilty: it didn't matter that it was not Don himself who had brought the baby on to the yard: there was guilty by association... and plenty of it.

Borderline psychosis, too.

If the daughter's ghost was Don's guilt manifest, it was probably psychosis that kept him in his own private darkness, by choice; that kept him blinking too long, way too hard.

Wait.

What if *Don* killed the daughter? The horse is an also-ran: this is filicide.

Creates a story to paint over his own memory: paramnesia. Could be.

'Roger? What are you thinking?'

7.

'He's nuts, Vig. He needs a doctor.'

'I don't know where my responsibilities lie as an employer.'

'Never mind as an employer! What about as a human being? He's a seventy-two year-old man who thinks his five hundred year-old daughter lives on another planet!'

'No, he didn't say *that* exactly,' Vig argued.

Dorota cursed in Polish. 'Near as damn it,' she said. 'I don't want him nearby. I'm serious.'

'I know.'

'He could be a danger. To us or to himself. The best place

for him is in a nice warm secure unit, where he can be treated by professionals who know what the hell they're doing.'

Vig and Dorota were in the bedroom, Vig under the covers and Dorota pacing. 'Not really what I had in mind when I won the money,' the former admitted. 'I feel I owe him.'

Dorota stopped in her tracks; her toes flexed in the abundant carpet. 'You don't owe him anything. He's been paid! *Over*-paid, if you ask me, but that's not for now. He should be resting, if that's not obvious. Resting, Vig. Not being left alone with this time on his hands to dream up stories.'

'I can't sleep,' Vig said; 'not after this.' And he rolled out of bed; pulled on his dressing gown. Dorota followed him along the hall and down the wide stairway.

Vig used the preparation of a drink as a ship to sail through a storm of silence – silence that seemed polluted by static. Watching Don push down the brandies had made him thirsty. Why had he assumed that they'd be able to sleep after Don's story?

'What are you making?' Dorota asked from the embrace of one of the library's large green leather chairs.

Lifting the bottle off the tray on the cabinet and shaking it gently, Vig answered, 'Whisky and coke. Want one?'

'I'd prefer a gin and tonic.'

'Coming right up.'

If Dorota's previous pacing in the bedroom had not been proof enough of her similar inability to grow restful and doze, her squirming in the chair was a further powerful clue to the same. She had ants in her pants and no mistake. As Vig got the cocktails together, she sprung up, crossed the room and checked on the car situation in the drive.

'It's still there. Where could he be?' she wondered.

While waving goodbye to Roger, they had noted Charlie's car and thought nothing of it: after all, Vig had told him to go into the house and make himself at home. The confusion had arisen since then. They had not been able to find him.

'Surely he hasn't tried to walk home from here,' Dorota continued. 'It's a long way.'

But booze had been on his breath went unsaid but was understood between them. Eastlight's breath would have been a hazard around a naked flame; there was no way that he'd been in any fit state to drive in the first place.

Vig repeated what he'd suggested when Charlie's absence had first been noted. 'Maybe he called a cab.' He walked over to the window and handed Dorota her G&T. 'More likely he's passed out in one of the spare rooms.'

Dipped if not deep in thought, Dorota thanked her partner in Polish and took a sip. 'But we checked the rooms,' she protested.

'We took a peek. Or is it peep? We didn't do it thoroughly.'

'No. I will in a moment though. It's not as if we live in a mansion.'

'Yes we do.'

Dorota smiled. 'I know, Viggy-Loo...'

'Oh don't *you* start with that.'

'I was English humour attempting,' she joked in an exaggerated version of her own accent.

'Sorry, I'm tired. Humour's beyond me at the moment.'

'I wouldn't be surprised if he's still out there,' said Dorota, and the two of them strolled back to the leather chairs.

'Out where?'

'Out there in the cosmos. Where do you think?'

'In the woods? He'll freeze.'

Dorota shrugged. 'He's a big boy, I suppose. I don't know why I even mentioned it.'

'Yes you do.' Vig smiled. 'Because you hate him.'

'Guilty... We'd better find him. We don't want a manslaughter charge on our hands.'

8.

His visitors dispersed, Don sloped into the bathroom and turned the spider-leg taps to run a bath. The water emerged in pure white gusts and then cleared; it had been a while since he'd treated himself to anything more than a strip-wash (a slag's ablution, it had been known as in his days in the saddle) and the pipes must have clogged up with chalk. Once the water had turned transparent, Don reduced the force of the output, jitteringly thinking over his next move.

First things first. In the lounge he drained his seventh or eighth brandy (he was wankered) and sipped his roll-up to death. With an elaborate flourish he flicked the dog-end the length of the kitchen; it landed near the sink in a cup half-filled with abandoned cold tea and fizzed satisfactorily.

Then he donned his bodywarmer and slipped out the kitchen door.

9.

Eastlight watched Vig, Dorota and Roger leave Don's cabin. Though the cold had done a good deal of work to slow down his mental responses, a sense of revenge had helped keep him warm in short bursts, and as before he was mindful of his need for an alibi. Whatever happened, he must be able, in the future, to say that he'd been here on the estate all evening.

The other side of this, however, was that he could not longer recall why this might be important. The Eggington house was a distant concern: Eastlight knew that there was work to do there, but it had to wait. The teenagers would keep the home fires burning.

When he stood up, his feet tingled with pins and needles. Eastlight stamped up and down; he flapped his arms. His throat was hot. Something of a burgeoning fever worried his brow.

No time like the present.

Warming slightly with every step, Eastlight approached the cabin's front door. From within came the sound of running water, and this only served to make Eastlight angrier. How *dare* the cunt be so carefree and blithe! A bath *now?* No no no. (Eastlight shook his head.) This wouldn't do. This would not do *at all.*

Conscious of the sound of water falling, he opened the door and entered in the time it took to draw breath. He had hoped for the element of surprise, catching Don asleep in his chair, perhaps (drunk, naturally); but Don was not in his chair, and a look through into the kitchen informed him that the old man was not munching his roast chicken either. Not unless he was doing so inside... a *hole?* A hole in the kitchen floor? What the hell?

Momentarily puzzled by the hole and the trapdoor that had been left open, Eastlight turned with gratification in the direction of the closed bathroom door.

Bliss! The geriatric mouthbreather was in the khazi! On his throne or in the tub: it didn't matter. Oh joy, Eastlight thought, conscious of the need for speed, however tempting it was to remain where he was and warm up. Hoping that his luck was really in and that he'd catch Don on the toilet, Eastlight moved to the bathroom door – and flung it open.

Inside the room the light was on, the bath was filling... but Don wasn't in there. So where *was* the old wanker?

A movement flickered in Eastlight's peripheral vision. Turning toward the kitchen door, Eastlight had a second to take in Don striding closer… and the shovel that Don carried.

Not only had the trapdoor been left ajar, the kitchen door to the outside had as well; and Eastlight understood in a split second that the running water and the trapdoor hanging open had been deliberate sensual distractions. The kitchen door had been open just a crack and Eastlight hadn't thought of Don waiting outside *for him*. The clever bastard.

'Don…'

Don Bridges swung the shovel like an axe. It struck Eastlight's right knee and Eastlight squealed like a stuck pig.

When he didn't fall immediately, however, Don swung the shovel once more.

At the left knee this time.

THE SHREDDING OF SLEEP

1.

Something different, Nero realised; something different about the air quality, about the light…

Nero took stock (a matter of seconds) and then stretched and bounded to his feet. And he stared. The reason it was not so dark, and the reason why the air was a tad fresher, was the same reason. The door was open. And Nero could not stop staring at the doorway, his self-preservational instincts prodding at him to acknowledge the inevitable trap.

To his left and rear, Jess stirred – a bone clicked. Sleepily she asked, 'What is it, Nero?'

'Door's open.'

Jess stood up; Nero glanced to his left and saw her white skin, refulgent in the gloom. 'Are you gonna be a man about it, or are you gonna pussy out like a girl?'

'Shut up, Jess. I don't know what's out there, do I?'

'The real world.'

'Yeah right.'

'Together then, tough guy?' Jess took his left hand and squeezed.

Nero inhaled like a madman. 'What's the worst that can happen?'

'You're squidging me fingers.'

'Come on. What's the worst? It's a landing. It's a stairway

out of here.'

Side by side, they stared at the bedroom door.

2.

Jess could hear them crying behind the door, and it was not just the woman in tears. The sound made her cold. Sitting still on the carpet, she covered her ears with the heels of her hands. The sound became muffled and merged with the drum of her blood: blocking her ears wouldn't help. She stood up.

Nero was awake – his eyes traced her movement across the room – but she treated him as if he was asleep. Pointless to try to explain herself to Nero – not after so much had happened. Only yesterday (she believed) she had asked him if he wanted to go home. His reply had disappointed but not surprised her. *I don't understand the question,* had been his answer.

As far as Jess was concerned, Nero was gone; he had vanished days earlier – maybe weeks. His mind was broken. The will to live had lost him; it had run away, eloped with Jess's respect for the boy. There was no point wasting any more time with him. Without Nero, Jess would be stronger.

This, at least, was Jess's latest theory. Was it because thought and opinion came slower to her than it ever had that she was according the theory such weight?

Maybe.

But she had seen it in Nero's eyes, in his expression, when Charlie gave them the responsibility for looking after the new prisoners, when he'd given them their promotion: she had seen that Nero was *flattered.* He was pleased. He had sailed through the interview and now he had a job to hold down. Unless he was a better actor than she'd ever known, Nero was on Charlie's side… at least for now.

Loyalty was something that they couldn't discuss: they hadn't really discussed it since they'd been brought here. Loyalty to Massimo and Charlie; to the men who controlled Jess and Nero, who made them do the things they wanted, and say the things they longed to hear. Allegiance to the ventriloquists had always felt like a taboo subject... and it felt more so than ever right now.

She didn't trust him. In fact, Jess hadn't trusted Nero for a long time, and she wondered what had happened to sever that bond. The answer probably mattered very little: the bond had been severed. It was a thing of the past. Dead. She didn't trust Nero, and for all she knew he didn't trust her either; and this was just fine and dandy.

'Where are you going?' he asked her.

Jess was standing in front of the door to the walk-in wardrobe.

'To Paris. Where do you think?'

'You're not going in there, Jess.'

'You're not my keeper.'

'That's as may be. You still ain't going in there.' But no anger accompanied Nero's words; indeed, he couldn't have sounded more bored if he'd worked in a call centre. He had taken his eyes off Jess and was re-examining his flaccid penis, a scrutiny that had stopped being habitual and had become obsessive a few days ago, when a virulent rash had flared on his helmet.

She owed him nothing – not so much as a simple explanation – so why did she turn? Why did she place a hand on her naked hip? Why not just defy him?

Because he didn't know that she had their interests at heart. All of them. All of their combined interests; which were basically the same interest. A path out of here. A way back into the sunshine, into the rain; it didn't matter which. The only thing that mattered was the one thing she lacked; the one thing she could get from the woman in the wardrobe, the woman bawling gustily behind the door.

It wasn't difficult for Jess to take stock once again; the information had been collated a hundred or so times already; it was available in a trice. And while she was alive to the fact that it could be a trap – that Charlie might have planted these new arrivals for the sole purpose of testing her fidelity – then it would have to be a trap that she fell into, wouldn't it? Even if Charlie and Massimo were waiting for her downstairs, or on the garden lawn, waiting for her (or Nero) to make a break for freedom, the better to justify a worse punishment than those that had already been meted out, she had to try. She couldn't stay here. Even if the torturers had more loving on their mind. Even if their breath stank of the anticipation of the murder that they were sure to perpetrate.

She had to leave.

Now that she had lost Nero, she had to leave.

But she needed something first.

'Don't go in there,' Nero almost yawned.

'Or you'll zap me?'

'I might. I might at that, girl.' His voice sounded foggy and dreamy; still he did not look up again at her, his concentration locked on his penis.

'No you won't.'

'Why not? Maybe I got an itchy finger,' said Nero, and this time almost chuckled.

'You got an itchy *something*,' Jess told him, 'and you'll need more than cream to sort it out.'

Now, Nero looked up from his infected glans. Could he honestly have assumed that his genital rash had not been spotted? The signs were unmistakeable… and yet he had about him the air of a baby who has seen a first balloon – an admixture of wonder and trepidation.

'What you getting at?' he asked.

'I need to fetch you some antibiotics. And me some, for that matter. I'll be back as soon as.'

Nero scuttled to his feet. 'You can't *leave.*'

'They'll never know, Nero. And if they *do* come back… say you were asleep. It was my watch; I took the zapper…'

'No way, babe.'

He stepped in her direction, poking the air with the weapon. 'I can't have it.'

Pointing at his groin, Jess said, 'Do you know what you've got there? Do you? That ain't no fucking clap, mate. That's genital herpes. And so have I, by the way. It'll eat your bollocks and then it nips into your anus. So when they make you fuck the new prisoners, you'll give it to them.'

Nero harrumphed. 'So what? Sod em!'

'It'll be murder. You'll kill them. You.'

Nero paused.

Jess seized the slender advantage. 'I can be back in a few hours.'

'You don't know where we are… and where will you get the pills?'

'Sex clinic. There's one in Leighton Buzzard – it's a walk-in centre, I've used it before. Very few questions asked.' Jess stopped shy of confessing that the *reason* she had used it before went by the name of Molecule. Now was probably not the best of times to admit that she had had sex with Nero's older brother. 'What do you say?'

'I was asleep,' Nero answered, showing her the wasting muscles on his back, walking away.

The key was in the lock. Jess turned it and opened the

door. She had not warned them to try no funny business: if they rushed her, the results would probably amount to much the same. But they didn't rush her. Inside the wardrobe, all three of the incarcerated huddled – serene and already broken – as close to the far wall as they had been able to get. If an escape plan had been discussed, it was not to be acted on at this moment.

Jess cleared her throat and addressed Mrs Murphy.

'Madam?' she said. 'I need to borrow your clothes.'

Troubled Trances

1.

Snapping out of a troubled trance, Bernadette fought the reality of her environment – claiming that it could not be true because she didn't want it to be true – and disturbed herself to note that she was walking (or trudging) a few metres behind Massimo, who in turn was in step by the same distance to Connors's rear.

Sleepwalking, she almost said aloud. I was sleepwalking.

It was similar to those days when she was on an early at work: she would often pull into the hospital car park and only register her surroundings when it was time to lean out of the driver's side window into the morning's icy pre-dawn breath and pull a parking ticket from the yellow machine. Having driven there on autopilot and yet avoided any accident, she would stand beside the vehicle once she'd found a space, and let the cold fill her lungs, thinking there but for the grace of God...

Because accidents were her bread and butter. Professionally speaking, in a world without heart attacks at eighty miles an hour, without drunken youths using the A5 as a dragstrip, without impatience behind the wheel, belligerence, spite, Bernadette was out of a job. Redundant. And yet (here she was) she had driven through a flirtation with disaster, herself, almost becoming a statistic in the process; and not once, either, but dozens of times – hundreds, probably.

How the hell did I fall asleep walking?

2.

Connors had brooded ever since he'd misidentified the boy with the lizards as Elvis. At times he had acted altogether unapproachably, and after a few hours on foot his mood had spread to the other explorers. Everyone was in a foul temper, belligerent and sarcastic; Connors himself, however, appeared not to notice. The big question lassoed in the rodeo ring of his brain pan was this: *How the hell can I be so wrong?*

It wasn't fair. In Connors's mind he had done everything that Fate seemed to have planned for him; and to the best of his ability and conscience he had done it without complaint. He'd played the game. Without knowledge of the rules (or the trophy at stake) he'd played the game, suffering scrapes and knockbacks along the way with the minimum of fuss or tears. And now this: for the first time that he could recall since Elvis was eaten by the insects, this moment of balance-recorrection, this sniff of something positive, had been stolen from him as well. So no. No, it wasn't fair at all.

The confusion was like a rash for Connors to scratch; and just like with a skin complaint, the more attention that Connors paid it, the more the fucker itched. Principally, how could it *not* be Elvis? How could Lizard Larry be anyone *other than* Elvis?

The physical appearance was wrong; the voice was wrong; there was nothing obvious that linked the two boys, in fact. But it was Elvis all right: of this Chris Connors was absolutely sure, and his surety was as strong as love. It *felt* like love too: a mingling of likeminded souls… which was worrying enough all by itself. Love? As if Connors didn't have plenty to worry about already!

A voice bumped against the walls of his attention, like a gale.

'What's up?' Massimo asked.

'Just thinking.'

They had stopped at a wide spot on the path, snow-covered, nature-strangled with vegetation. To the left and right of the path, such as it was beneath a carpet of frost, came the bellowed commands of creatures that might be bulls or alligators. It was impossible to tell which.

'About Elvis,' Connors admitted. 'It's like... Do you believe in guardian angels? Or ghosts?'

'No, neither,' Massimo answered, but he was not being altogether honest with himself. Ghosts, maybe; the life he'd left behind felt spectral enough. Any solidity that he'd tried to cling on to had long since been lost; when he tried to think back it was like pinning shadows to a wall.

A short period of silence followed. Massimo remembered the house in Eggington, and the tortures that he'd perpetrated therein. Surely being here, however cold it became, however perilous the journey got, was better than being in Bedfordshire, facing the legal consequences of his and Charlie's actions.

Was that really me?

This was a question that Massimo had asked himself times without number since he'd arrived here. Not once had he managed to answer it. What had happened in that house had been the actions of a man who shared Massimo's skin and brain; but that man seemed more distant as time went on. Perhaps (a vain hope, this, and Massimo knew it) he had dreamed those weeks, those times, those tortures. Why not? The idea was no more preposterous than that of visiting God's eyes or moustache (or whatever the hell). And it would certainly be a balm for Massimo's conscience. So yeah: *why not?* After all, there was no doubt that he'd changed since coming here. The very first fluttering of a romantic enchantment with Bernadette was proof positive of *that*.

'I was sick,' Massimo muttered to himself.

The object of his nascent affections overheard the miniature confession, her nurse's instinct engaged automatically by the word *sick*.

'What's wrong with you?' she asked, stepping closer.

Massimo shook his head; then, reconsidering, he posed a question with what he hoped was sly caution. 'Is it possible this is madness?' he wanted to know.

'Not exactly my field – but yes, I'd say it was,' Bernadette answered. 'Either we were mad when we thought we had normal lives before, or we're mad now.'

'I was thinking about the first one,' Massimo told her. 'What if we were never there? We were here all along.'

Connors interrupted in a voice that said: *I'm nipping this one in the bud right now.*

'No one's mad.'

'But how do you know?' asked Bernadette, reasonably enough in her own opinion.

Rounding on her, Connors said, 'I haven't gone through all the shit I've gone through, including the death of your dog by the way, for you two to hatch a madness plot. Okay? Cuz if there ain't some fucking... *plan* behind all this, we might as well kill ourselves right now. Don't think I haven't considered the option of killing myself either, cuz you'd be wrong.' And he turned away.

Massimo and Bernadette exchanged looks. Silently they shared a flask of lukewarm but delicious soup; neither of them tasted it much.

Bernadette said, 'Shall I change the subject?'

'That might be a good idea,' Massimo replied.

'It's about something else I've never really understood – something I've got in the house at home.' She sniffed. 'My partner calls it the Object, with a capital O. He won it in a card game...'

HOMES OF WHEREFORE

1.

His body exothermic, with worms of perspiration wriggling on his brows and into his chevron sideburns, Yasser stepped down from Maggie's home and over his left shoulder said:

'You needn't bother to lock up.'

He had told her to dress warm, as soon as he'd completed into her fundament, with Maggie's ankles rattling around his ears. She had done as bidden. She was now clothed in a thick brown overcoat and a purple scarf; she wore leather boots.

'Why not?' she asked… and to Yasser's ears the question sounded almost hopeful, like someone who already knows that she will receive a surprise present but is pretending not to, to spare the giver's feelings.

'You won't be gone long,' Yasser answered. 'Do you smell petrol?'

'No. Maybe I'm getting a cold.'

Parenthetically querying what *that* might mean, and of a mind to order Maggie not to be so bloody enigmatic, now that he seemed to be on top of matters for a change (for a while), Yasser attempted to unlock the car doors. There was something wrong. The something wrong was that the doors were already unlocked; he was confident that he'd secured the car, as he customarily did, when he'd reached Maggie's caravan.

Are you sure, boy? his father wanted to know. *Are you absolutely certain?*

No. Not absolutely. But fairly.

Spinning on his heels in the mud, Yasser peered into the darkness for Tommy – or Max. There was no one around. None of the caravans close by had lights on inside; for all Yasser knew, the place might have been deserted and abandoned.

So why did the air stink of petrol?

'Where are we going?'

The plan had come to Yasser while he'd been washing his penis in Maggie's bathroom, after he'd withered in her anus and her muscle had squeezed him out. He would drive her to Chris's house. Display her to the man. Just in case he'd lied, perhaps a face-to-face meeting with the grieving mother would finger his conscience; he might spill the truth.

Bringing Maggie and Shyleen together would be a pretty good side-plan as well. Show both of them that Yasser meant business. And if either of them cut up rough, they could *both* walk home. Yasser was not going to take any more nonsense.

Then something else flashed through Yasser's mind. While he'd been cleaning himself up – a matter of minutes while he'd waited for the water to run warm – what exactly had Maggie been doing? When he'd entered the bathroom he had left her spread-eagled on the table; on his return she'd been prostrate in the lounge area, at the other end of the caravan.

Could anything be read into the change of position and location? After all, the table had probably not been comfortable; but still… that smell of petrol. It reminded Yasser of the first time he'd driven here, and Tommy's threat to ignite the car with Yasser inside it. Would Maggie have had enough time to go out-side (in the nude), having taken his car keys from the jacket he'd sloughed off during sex, and then enter the car, get the can of petrol and give the vehicle a good soak? No doubt she was deranged enough to do so (in Yasser's diagnosis), and no doubt he might have planted the idea-seeds in her brain with his talk of roasting Tommy's caravan… but would she have had *time* to do it?

Why don't you check? The can should be in the passenger footwell.

'You get in first,' Yasser told Maggie, not replying to her question about their destination. 'Wait.' Imagine she'd poured the petrol *inside* the car. It would go up like a tinderbox; Maggie the Martyr. 'What's in your handbag?'

'I've no handbag,' Maggie answered.

'Your coat pockets.'

She shrugged. 'Box of fags, matches,' she said. 'Capsule of perfume, emergency tampon…'

Yasser tried to remember if he'd ever seen Maggie light and smoke a cigarette. Quite often he'd seen a packet of Superkings lying around, on a shelf or near the toaster, but he'd always assumed them to be her father's property. *Is this paranoia?* Just because he couldn't recall seeing Maggie smoking did not mean that she didn't have the habit. No law against nicotine. Maybe she'd started up (again?) this very morning.

'I'll turn the car around first,' said Yasser. Quick getaway, he thought. If need be.

Smelling nothing out of the ordinary in the car itself (it smelled of the pine air conditioner hanging from the mirror), and noting with relief the petrol can in the passenger footwell (*Doesn't mean it's still full, though*), Yasser executed a three-point turn, his lights sweeping across the blank walls of sundry trailers like a weird prison break. (*Just check if it's full or empty.*) When he faced in the right direction, he saw Maggie breathing smoke, carefree, into the night; she smoked with her fingers straight and stiff. Hardly a portrait of someone who was about to burn herself alive!

The can might be empty, Yass…

And where had the idea come from anyway? It seemed stupid now (*stupid?*); reckless and masochistic. (*The can's empty. No.*) If anything, a good shag had lightened Maggie's mood a little. Yasser laughed. (*Empty.*) It had taken the plug from her butt.

'Get in. Put out the fag,' Yasser told her.

Maggie slid into the passenger side; she did not extinguish her cigarette. Twisting her head ninety degrees to face him, she cocked an eyebrow and said, 'What are you gonna do? Slap me. *Rape* me?' She widened her eyes in mock horror.

Yasser faced the lane and started his windscreen wipers; a fine rain had greased the glass. 'I didn't rape you.'

'That's what it felt like. So drive.'

Yasser moved off slowly and had only shifted a metre before Maggie cried: 'Stop!'

Emergency break situation.

'What is it?' Yasser demanded.

Maggie opened the box of matches that she'd palmed out of her coat pocket; into the box, which was roughly a quarter full, she placed the unsmoked half of her cigarette.

'What are you doing?' said Yasser.

'*Hana-bi.* Fireworks… Watch.'

It took a few seconds for the cigarette's smouldering tip to ignite the head of one of the matches; then another match combusted with a bright flare and the dirty smell of chemicals burning.

'Jesus, Maggie…'

'Wait.'

'You'll burn your hands!'

'*Wait.*'

Another match popped into fire; then another; and another. Maggie held a miniature pyre on her outstretched palm, and again a match-head flared. The sticks ignited the inside of the box itself, and the heat given off was strong. Too hot to hold, surely.

Yasser said, 'Throw it out the window. For fuck's sake, Maggie! This is no time for games!'

Maggie opened the door, and with a gleeful noise – *whee!* – she threw the ignited handful out into the open air, to the side and the rear of the vehicle.

Whumph!

The noise was immediate. No sooner had the burning matchbox hit the ground than it set fire to something already there. In the mirror Yasser watched a line of fire follow something intensely flammable on the floor.

'Oh my God, Maggie…'

But Maggie was staring directly ahead. 'I think it might be an idea to drive *now*,' she said.

'Petrol? *My* petrol?' Yasser panicked.

'I'll pay you back. Drive, Yasser.'

Still gazing into the rearview mirror, Yasser watched the line of flames split into a forked path. To the right, fire reached towards Maggie's home, quickly. To the left, the race was on towards the Brazilian's.

Yasser's question about whether Maggie had had enough time to take the petrol can from his car while he was washing had been answered. She had gone outside naked and done so.

2.

'I love your outfit, dear,' said Maggie.

'Shy?' said Yasser, in amazement.

'She doesn't *look* too shy,' Maggie replied, chuckling. 'Are you going to have us in?' she asked Shyleen, who had chosen to answer Chris's doorbell all-but naked, dressed only in a man's white shirt, which ballooned at the hem near her knees, teased by the wind.

'I wasn't expecting him to bring you,' Shyleen said to Maggie. 'You must be…'

'*Shyleen*. Why aren't you wearing any clothes?' Yasser asked.

'They're overrated. Come in. The wind's playing havoc with my nethers. Chris has had to go to the toilet. He's had too much to smoke and drink.'

As if on cue, from upstairs came a muffled murmur of retching.

Stepping over the threshold first, Yasser made clear his disappointment. 'I didn't invite you to a bloody party, Shy. Where are your clothes and why aren't they on the outside of you?'

'Relax, Yasser. They're around here somewhere.'

'Somewhere?' Yasser's eyes widened.

'Chris said I should offer you a Bloody Mary.'

'We're going home,' he answered defiantly.

'I'd *love* a Bloody Mary,' Maggie told her, following Yasser into the house. 'Thank you.'

As the two women moved along the hall and into the kitchen, Yasser was left reflecting on this fresh state of wretchedness. From the upper storey came another audio round of Chris being sick in the bathroom; this one was made worse, immeasurably worse, by the woeful groan that followed. (Yasser had a good mind to race upstairs and stick the man's head deep into the bowl, and hold it there.) And what was this sisterhood bullshit between Shyleen and Maggie all about? Yasser had imagined that the two women would hate one another on sight; they'd have antibodies against the natural enemy. I'd *love* a Bloody Mary thank you? What sort of. Jesus. Leave em here, Yasser; let em fend for themselves. Get your arse home before you hear the Fire Brigade sirens…

I'm in shock, Yasser realised. *This is what shock feels like. It should be me up there, kissing the porcelain.*

Indeed, all of a sudden, the few combined swigs of weak tea and strong liquor made a wave in his stomach; it rolled up his chest and made a pass at his larynx. Yasser grabbed hold of the newel post and took three deep breaths. The wave of nausea passed, chased by a swarm of black stars across his vision.

The front door was still half open. He could easily walk back out. After all, did he really want to meet again the man who must have had sex with Shyleen? She was wearing his shirt: they must have. Unless it was one of the worst pasta sauce *faux pas* known to man, they had done something together; and who would cook pasta sauce at midnight and offer some to an intruder?

Yasser closed the front door.

Answers first. Retaliation could wait.

He stomped into the kitchen, where Shyleen was pouring tomato juice into four glasses of vodka, two of which were already smeared with the remains of previous concoctions. For all the world she gave the impression of someone who owned this kitchen, this juice.

Yasser's gut tightened. Shyleen had been fucked into a condition of domesticity: it hadn't taken long. Well we'll see about *that.* Animals could be untrained as effectively as trained: and a human being was nothing more than a sophisticated animal. Right?

What am I going to do? If those caravans had caught light, he was what? – an accessory before the fact? It was his money that had bought the petrol, after all. *Prove it.* Petrol stations had closed circuit television these days (they'd had them for years) *Mum and Dad are going to go mental.*

Without a word he accepted his drink and took a swig. You

couldn't go far wrong with a Bloody Mary, unless the cunt also brewed hooch in the back garden – and grew vines of manky toms. No. The drink was familiar and strong; it tasted like nectar – the first good thing that had happened this evening.

'Oh!' Shyleen remembered something. 'Did you want Worcester sauce in that?'

Yasser levelled his steeliest glare at his cousin. '*Fuck* the Worcester sauce in that,' he replied. 'Go and get your boyfriend. I don't care if he's got half a gallon of vomit on his chest. Fetch him.'

Shyleen looked at Maggie and made a face. 'Hark at Yasser so butch!' she crowed. 'What *did* you do to him?' She laughed. 'No, don't answer that.'

Frowning like a baboon, Yasser took a step in his cousin's direction.

'Okay okay,' she said. 'I'm going!'

As she slipped from the room, her elongated shirt-tails flapping like fins, Yasser said to Maggie: 'And *you* can wipe the smirk from your chops an' all! What were you *thinking* of?'

'What?' Maggie asked, all innocence.

'What do you mean, *what?* You set fire to your home!' His tone was angry and bristling.

'A bit louder, could you?' And hers was as near as damn it *bored*.

'Maggie, don't push me.'

'Oh I dare you. I *dare* you,' Maggie whispered, 'to hit me again in front of witnesses. What are my bruises like, Yasser?'

'You haven't got any bruises.'

'Not yet. But I bet I've got evidence of anal rape if I go to the police, so do me a favour, Yasser: stop acting the hero and acknowledge you've been played like a violin. You did what I wanted. And now, as a thank you, *you'll do what I want a lot more.*

Do you get me? Why would *I* burn down me own house? And me brother's? It was *you*, Yass. It was always *you*… from the moment you started stalking me on me own land.'

The glass of Bloody Mary had stalled on its journey, half-way up to Yasser's mouth. The sick feeling that he'd been experiencing now intensified.

'You conniving bitch.'

'And don't you forget it. Not even a physical… deterrent from Max could keep you away.'

'You were paying me,' Yasser protested – at best this rebuttal was half-hearted, however. He knew he did not stand to win anything tonight. How the hell would he get *out* of this?

'Paying you? In tens and twenties?' said Maggie. 'Prove it, boy. I dare you to try. And you'll feel the full community rise against you. *Accept* when you've been beaten.'

Yasser thought about this for several seconds, in his mind's eye watching the mercury level that measured his happiness plummet further to absolute zero. It was over. Once more (he sighed), it was over: there was nothing he could do. 'Beaten' was only part of it – he'd accept it gladly – but in addition there was filmed evidence of him having sex with Maggie; his tyre prints would be everywhere in the mud; and there was little doubt that a hundred camp-dweller depositions could be swiftly rustled up, all testifying to the unsavoury qualities of Yasser's character. *Beaten?* He was fucked. Royally fucked. He'd been played (as Maggie had said) like a violin; but what was the tune? Yasser did not understand.

'I accept,' he replied slowly, 'that I'm beaten.'

The toilet flushed upstairs. Chris and Shyleen would be down shortly, Yasser predicted.

'My question to you – as ever – is why. Why do it? Why me? Why bother? What's the point?'

Maggie took a long drink of her Bloody Mary, and Yasser had seen this tactic before – seen it recently: it meant that she had a tricky matter to discuss.

'I hired you to find my son,' she said.

'And I tried, Maggie. I've really *tried.*'

'Please, Yasser; please… When I hired you I didn't know where he was. I had suspicions but nothing concrete.'

'Then *tell* me, Maggie! Christ's sake! I'll go and do the work,' said Yasser.

'*Please*. Please, Yasser… I told you I couldn't understand why he would appear to me – and Bridget – at different ages. But me da worked it out. He even travelled there.'

'Where? Where are we talking about? Wales? Europe?'

'Another world, Yasser,' Maggie replied sadly.

'The Far East? America?'

'Another *world*, I said. Think bigger. Where time is different… and me da can be gone for an evening in our time, but in *their* time he's been searching for the boy for weeks.'

Yasser waited. Then he said, 'You're pissed.'

Maggie nodded. 'A bit, I suppose.; but you're going to take me there, Yasser… and would you believe it? The doorway's on this very road! You're gonna be my tour guide.'

'The doorway? What doorway?' Yasser asked.

'To the world where me son is, Yass. To the world you're gonna take me to, now I've got no home left to speak of.'

Footfalls on the stairs: Chris and Shyleen were returning.

Yasser did not understand a word of what Maggie had said, but it was easy to read the bright twinkle in the woman's eyes: she was excited. A little scared, perhaps, but unusually excited. For the first time that Yasser could recall, he was in no doubt that Maggie was telling the truth.

'So in your opinion,' said Yasser, 'we don't need Chris at all.'

Maggie shook her head. 'We do need him, I think. We need both of them.'

Yasser frowned. 'Why?'

'I want some witnesses,' Maggie answered.

3.

Chris carried a rucksack into the kitchen. 'Got something to show you all,' he said, taking in Shyleen, who was a few steps behind. 'Only a privileged few have seen this.' As he unpacked the rucksack, he seemed either unable or unwilling to wipe the smirk from his face; the gesture he wore was irredeemably proud. He placed the Object on the kitchen table.

'Isn't it a thing of true beauty?' he asked, not waiting for an answer. 'I've been terrified of having it stolen for as long as I've had it. Brought us nothing but good luck, Bernadette and me.'

'Until now,' Shyleen observed.

Chris cocked his head to the side. 'Yeah. Until now,' he admitted.

'I don't want to appear thick,' said Yasser, 'but what *is* it exactly?'

What Chris had brought downstairs to show them was the size and shape of a dinner tray, albeit considerably heavier to carry. It was made of a dark grey stone, in which lines corresponding to an approximation of bones had been imprinted and fossilised.

'It's an angel's wing,' Chris answered, proud once more. 'I won it in a game two years ago, and like I say, it's been a good luck charm ever since – though try wearing it around your neck like a pendant! Give yourself a hernia!'

'Am I hearing you right?' Yasser asked. 'An angel's wing. The wing of an angel.'

'There's nothing wrong with your hearing, son,' Chris answered. 'That's exactly what I said. And I was sceptical myself at first, believe me – but I had the guy on the ropes. Texas Hold-'em. Place in Biggleswade, when Bernie and me were still living in Ampthill. Down on our luck would be one way of putting it.' Chris laughed. 'But we were happy, more or less. Hungry but happy. Every penny Bernadette earned at the hospital went on rent and pasta. If there was any left over, she used to trust me to gamble it.'

'And you'd win?' said Maggie.

Chris shrugged his shoulders. 'Some you win, some you lose, right? But on this one night – it was three thirty-three in the morning – I remember that clearly by this crappy digital clock radio the guy had on his mantelpiece… Funny. You put a pistol to my head and I couldn't tell you his name, and his face is a bit of a blur too; but the time I won the angel's wing – that'll be with me forever, I think.'

Shyleen was the next to speak. Wrapping the man's shirt tighter against her skin, she said, 'Why did the other gamble it? If it brings good luck, I mean.'

'Well, he didn't *say* it brought good luck,' Chris answered. 'That's just the way it's worked out for Bernadette and me… until now, as you say. But to answer your question: the guy had nothing else to stake – I'd already taken him to the cleaners, but the guy had the fever on him and no mistake. Gambling was his life. For me, it's a job – and I love it – but it's not my life. And I *think* I'm right in saying I offered him more than one get-out clause, but he wanted to fight on. For some it's a badge of honour: to be taken for everything you've got; to be left with nothing. It's like a scar you show your old war buddies. Remember the time the bullet went through my hip? That kind of thing. Remember when I was totally cleaned out? Built myself up again, didn't I, from nothing.'

'So what does it do?' said Yasser.

'Do? It doesn't *do* anything. It's a fossil,' Chris replied.

'All right. So why are you showing us this?' Yasser pressed.

'I thought you might like to see it… and it seemed important. Three strangers in my house on the same night; Bernadette
lost. You can't tell me that coincidences don't happen for a damn
good reason sometimes.'

Yasser and Shyleen exchanged glances; there was not a
good deal of friendliness in what passed between them, and it
was Shyleen who wanted to prove that she followed her new lover's argument. She said:

'So by bringing the angel's wing out you hope to… bring
Bernadette back?'

Chris nodded. 'Or at least make the next thing happen –
whatever it turns out to be. I can't sit here waiting, night after
night. It's not healthy. And the police wouldn't want to know, I'm
sure of it. Not that I would tell them anyway, on general principle.'

Maggie crossed the room to the door. She looked like she
was about to hazard an escape, such was the perturbation on her
features when she turned to face the rest of the group.

'I hate to bring you down, mate,' she said to Chris, 'but your
angel's wing – if that's what it really is, and I've got my doubts
about that if you wanna know the truth – your wing there is
nothing to do with us. And to answer your earlier question: no
it's not a thing of beauty. It's no more beautiful than a paving
slab that a workman's drawn his initials in when the cement's wet.
But each to his own. It brings you good luck, fair play to you, I
say; who am I to argue otherwise? Though I might venture that
maybe – just maybe – you're getting better at playing cards and
that's why you keep winning. I'll just throw that in there, as an

aside, as it were. But think of this. You don't *always* win, Chris, and you know you don't.'

'I didn't say I did!' Chris protested. 'I said I've had good luck. That's not the same thing at all!'

'You lost a little to a man named Tommy recently, for example.'

'Yes I did. And how would you know that, if you don't mind me asking?'

Maggie was on a roll, and Yasser was confused by the return of her loquacity, which had been assumed missing in action.

'We have lost something dear to our hearts,' she said. 'And I'm going to suggest a child. Yasser knows I lost one of my own, though I dare say he doesn't fully believe me. And I know this is none of my business,' she seemed to be asking.

Chris picked up on the cue but his brow was knitted together. 'A child? We've never lost a child,' he told her.

'Think carefully, Chris.'

'Well I believe I'd remember something like *that*,' the man replied. 'Not that it's any of your business, as you rightly say, but Bernadette's been on the Pill since I knew her.'

'Which is how long?' Maggie asked.

'Jesus. Five years, okay? Give or take.'

'And before that?'

Chris was shaking his head, refusing to believe the evidence of his ears.

'Maggie, where are you going with this?' Yasser wanted to know.

She had remained in the doorway; about her was less of the dog fearing its owner's retribution for a messy misdemeanour than the air of a butler, a second before announcing it's time to dine. Nominally in charge of proceedings though she might be for the nonce, Maggie was also respectfully nervous about present company... or about what was on her mind. All of which convinced Yasser, in an instant, that he'd been played for fool once again; she had manipulated him once more; and when he heard, a second later, the distant siren of what he imagined would be the fire service, he could almost smell the petrol on her hands, feel the smoke that she'd produced carving sculptures inside his lungs.

Maggie smiled.

'It's fine if you don't believe me, Yasser, about any of what we've discussed.'

'Which is what exactly?' asked Shyleen, her voice sounding jealous.

'Come on, I've given you the highlights as we went along. Don't pretend you're in the dark.'

'Well *I* am,' Chris mentioned. 'Anyone for another drink?'

Although Maggie ignored the invitation, Chris stood up at the nodded heads of Yasser and Shyleen. He got busy while Maggie continued speaking, her phrases confident: much more so than the she had sounded (to Yasser) twenty minutes earlier.

'Stop me if you've heard this one...' she began, and then paused. Too glib, her expression seemed to suggest. She closed her eyes; she tried again. Maybe direct was best.

'I lost a child. And I don't mean the child died: I mean the child was taken away from me. By the father.'

Wondering to what extent he could believe her (she'd had time to finesse her lines, to rehearse her fibs), Yasser prickled at the unusual, deliberately-distancing vocabulary. *The child. By the father.* Not a possessive pronoun within earshot.

'My family searched and searched,' said Maggie, turning to Yasser. '*Including* Bridget. And we all thought we saw him from time to time, like a ghost – but older, like he was growing up at a different speed, somewhere else. Somewhere not on what we know of as the planet. A state of mind, perhaps: that's an idea Tommy had early on. Long before we recruited you to find him, Yasser.'

We recruited you, Yasser noted. We.

'But you know that old saying: any port in a storm. While me, da and Tommy were off being travellers – and I don't mean travellers as in gypsies – I couldn't bring meself to believe there was a place made of grief: an actual *place*. That you can go to… but only if you've suffered and believe in the concept of loss, which I do now, but I've only become a convert recently.'

Chris doled out glasses. 'And you think the house at Number 11 is…'

'One place where you can go to search,' Maggie finished on his behalf; 'that's right. Me da's there right now.'

'In the *house*?' said Yasser. 'How would you know? And why didn't you mention it earlier?'

'I didn't *know* it earlier!' Maggie replied. 'Do you honestly think they tell *me* where they're going? Most of the time I don't want to know. But I saw his truck parked outside there when we were coming here.'

'And you didn't think it worth mentioning?' Yasser demanded.

'What good would it have done? You were hell-bent on coming here; and besides, I don't think I can travel there. Or anywhere else. I've tried. A couple of times me da took me to see a guy who calls himself an intra-rationalist. Name of Benny. It did no bloody good and it cost me ten score.'

'An intra-rationalist?' asked Shyleen. 'What's that when it's at home?'

Maggie laughed. 'It's not at home when it's at home, that's what! It's between homes – between realities. Intra-rationalists believe that our perceptions are stitched together in such a way that realities can co-exist side by side without one of them being aware of the existence of the other. But if you can believe your way past the stitching itself…'

'A whole new guilt to explore,' said Chris. 'I'm glad we did some puff, girl,' he added to Shyleen. 'I'm not sure I could've handled this with a straight head.'

'Anyway…' Maggie seemed impatient to continue but Yasser interrupted her.

'Where are the other places?' he asked.

'What other places?'

'Where we can go to this world you're talking about. It can't be just one house, can it? There must be others.'

Maggie looked flustered now. 'I'm sure you're right. They're everywhere. But it's like following the well-worn path through the woods: some of the doorways will be hidden. Not by vegetation exactly – more because we don't want to see.'

'Well *I* want to see,' Yasser countered. 'For the last five years I've had to put up with my dad's disapproval with what I'm doing with my life. And now… now that I'm finding lost people, my dad's proud of me. I've got a purpose… even if I haven't been successful at finding Maggie's child.'

'Yet,' said Shyleen – a supportive comment that arrived as a surprise to Yasser.

He nodded. 'Yet. So what if we *could* find them all in the place of missing things? Does it have a name, this place?'

Maggie said, 'I don't think so – not that I know of, anyway. Once you name a place it can be found, it stops being something you can't find. My guess is…' She sighed. '…the house's days as a doorway are numbered. Too many people know about it, and maybe that's what the explosion was all about in the first place.'

'What?' said Shyleen and Yasser.

'Wow,' said Chris. 'My head's getting battered… You mean it was trying to *destroy* itself?'

Shyleen cocked her head to one side, either because of the coincidence of her sharing a word with Yasser, or because Chris appeared to have reached the solution first.

'Possible. Or someone was tying to destroy it from within,' Maggie answered.

'And why would anyone want to do that?' Shyleen wanted to know.

'Some people have no wish to be found.'

When the dust had settled on this sentence for a few seconds, Yasser spoke again.

'Let's go into the house,' he suggested.

4.

By now, the early-morning air was laced with a thin perfume of smoke. The party of four could smell the results of Maggie's act of arson as they stood in Number 11's back garden. Although no sirens blared, in the camp's direction, the sky was smeared faintly with red and orange light: a visual echo of lights or flames.

While Shyleen pointed at a space between some torn-back boards (the space through which Massimo and Bernadette had entered the house), Yasser considered Maggie's position. She had torched her own home and possibly the homes of others in the camp. She had had no intention of returning, tonight or ever. She had led him to this point; manipulated his interests. She had even made him fall in love with her.

He hated her for this.

Chris shone a torch into the space and asked, 'Who's first? Shall we form an orderly queue?'

'How very English,' Shyleen joked.

'We're not English,' Yasser told her.

'We were born in Luton!'

'Roots, babe!'

'Well *I'm* not English,' Maggie added.

'Christ. I'll do it myself,' said Chris, stepping up the opening. He squeezed through, entering the whiff of damp and ruin and trying to cut through the atmosphere with a torchlight that seemed too feeble to be up the the task. He hadn't been able to find their better torch.

Then he made a mental correction. With the chill inside the house inching into his bones, he waited until everyone had climbed in before sharing his news.

'We have two torches at home, right?' he said. 'This one's not great, the other one's much better. But it wasn't where we always leave it, in the cupboard near the back door.'

'So?' This was Maggie.

'So Bernadette must've taken it, and why would she've done that? To explore an abandoned house, right? I think she was here. For sure, now.'

Maggie asked, 'Can you feel her?'

'*Feel* her?'

'Her presence; her spirit... Can you feel her?' she snapped impatiently.

'...No.'

'You never did remember who it was she lost, by the way.'

'Her dog?'

'Maybe.'

'...So what happens next?' Yasser asked.

No one wanted to answer; the silence lasted until a noise from upstairs made them jump. Something had creaked.

Chris put a finger to his lips and Yasser whispered to Maggie, 'Is that your dad?'

'How the hell would I know that?' she whispered back.

'Does anyone else feel like children?' Shyleen added (weirdly for everyone) in a whisper that might have worked as a Shakespearian aside: however, it was much too loud for the surroundings.

'*Ssshhh!*' she was admonished.

Whoever was upstairs was not prepared to loiter; the sounds that followed suggested that he was moving towards the top of the flight.

The group played a game that was diametrically opposed to Sleeping Lions. When the sounds of movement stopped, they moved: they squelched through the water-damaged tufts of carpet, with Chris's familiarity with the layout of the road's houses (not to mention his torchlight) having made him the leader of the expedition. When the sounds from above came again, they stopped walking; they froze like sleeping lions. Employed in this tango, they soon arrived at the foot of the stairs, at which point Chris shone the light up the flight.

'Who's down there?' a voice asked from upstairs. Torchlight beamed down.

Just as Yasser acknowledged that it was not the voice of Tommy or of Maggie's old man, Shyleen called, 'Police. And you're trespassing.'

The man's voice chuckled. 'I think *you're* the ones trespassing,' the man said. 'I don't care if you're the police or the Boy Scouts. Get out of my house.'

His torchlight preceding him, he started to descend the stairs.

5.

The five of them stood in the rank-smelling hallway. 'But before you go,' said the man who was older than them all, 'tell me why you're here, would you?'

'You don't own this house,' Chris told him. 'I've never seen you before. Mr and Mrs Riley live here.'

'They *live* here, yes; but I own it. One of my business investments, of which there are many. And I'll thank you to tell me what you're doing in my property.'

Shyleen spoke.

'Do you know what this house is?'

'Yes I do. It's fucked is what it is. My experiment backfired, you might say. But you still haven't answered what I asked you.'

'We know some people who went over,' Yasser admitted.

The old man cocked his head slightly. 'Do you now? And when did this happen?'

'You mean you know?'

'Of course I know. I've been waiting for this for years, mate.'

'Waiting for what?' asked Maggie.

'For a demand I could exploit,' the man replied simply. 'But now I need to get out of here. The damp's no good for me lungs.'

Shortly after they'd entered the house illegally, then, they were outside in the back garden once more.

'London's burning,' the house owner mentioned in passing. 'From the gyppo camp, I reckon.'

'Your orientation is flawless,' Maggie told him sourly.

He nodded. 'One of them, are you?'

'Until recently. It was me who started the fire, ably assisted in my getaway by Yasser.'

As Yasser began to protest (even though she had a point), the man who had now sat on a stone bench next to the shed gave a smile. 'I can't say I blame you, girl,' he said. 'A filthy race, the gyppos. Filthy.'

'…I wouldn't go *that* far,' Maggie replied.

The man sniffed. 'A pleasure to watch em burn, you ask me; but each to their own, I suppose. The more camps get ignited the better. Ethnic cleansing. Don't knock it, I say. It's not the bad thing the do-gooders would have us believe, you mark my words. The clue is in the word *cleansing*. Do you know: there's a bird, right, who lives in the mouth of the crocodile, cleaning the fucker's teeth? Straight up. They tolerate each other because each of em provides a service.'

He rubbed his hands together and changed the subject. 'A bit cold tonight. No weather for an old man. Especially one who spends half his life alongside rodents – the heat from the vivaria, I mean. You get acclimatised to it. Now...'

The man slapped his knees and stood up again (the others had remained standing throughout, and had grown more confused as he'd waffled on). 'To business, I suppose – unexpected business, but I'm never one to look an unpredicted gifthorse in the old mush. So this is it. My name's Benny and I'm prepared to be your guide for the right price each. We go in one by one and I take you across. Then I come back for the next one, though I'd recommend one of you stays put here, until we're done.'

'Why's that?' asked Yasser. 'Why does one stay here?'

'To tell the story if you don't come back again,' Benny answered, his words forming steam in front of his mouth. 'Only make up your mind quickly. I was getting piles sitting on that stone bench, now I'm catching pneumonia.'

Clearly still smarting from the racist slur (and baffled by the connection to the bird and the crocodile), Maggie sounded curt when she asked, 'What do you call the right price each?'

'A good question, my dear. Your name is?'

'Maggie.'

'My old mother's name, God bless her and shine her. And your friends?'

'Yasser.'

'Nice to meet you, son.'

'Chris.'

'Another Chris. I've already got a Chris Connors... You wouldn't be the Chris of Chris-and-Bernadette by any chance?'

'I would! Yes! You *know* her?'

'I helped her cross,' Benny replied, nodding a modest bow. 'She was with a bloke named Massimo, who I've done some work with. It was Mass who booked Connors and Dorman to rob this place blind, but they made a mistake and did *your* house instead. A bit embarrassing, that. For you I'll do a fifty per cent cut on the price of admission. I can't say fairer than that. Which just leaves...?'

'Shyleen.'

'A beautiful name. For a beautiful girl... The entrance fee is one hundred pounds each.' Benny pointed at Chris. 'Fifty for you.'

Yasser was the first to complain. 'I haven't *got* a hundred quid,' he said.

'Do you take cards?' Maggie asked sarcastically.

'Yeah, I've got a credit card franker up me arse. Just swipe it in me bumcrack,' said Benny. 'Why don't you return when you're ready to play grown-up games, eh? Now if you'll excuse me and fuck off out me garden...'

'I've got the money,' Chris told him coolly. 'I've been winning big.'

'In cash?'

'Chris...' said Shyleen.

'Well *you're* safely across then,' said Benny. 'Why don't you run home and fetch it before I lose me toes to hypothermia?'

'No, I mean I can pay for us all,' Chris clarified.

'*Chris*,' Shyleen repeated.

'This has been, without doubt, one of the weirdest nights of my life, so if it means I have to pay four hundred quid to get us all through it, it's a price I'm willing to fork out. And not only because I miss Bernadette. I think what you were saying before…' Chris addressed Maggie. '…about us missing someone we've lost… isn't it true? Isn't this what it's all about? For better or for worse, we're all in tonight together, and I definitely won't be the one volunteering to stay behind.'

Benny rubbed his hands together again. 'Spoken like a true intra-rationalist,' he told them all.

6.

No one was prepared to stay behind.

While Chris handed over the money that he'd fetched from his own house (and the other three offered their pledges that they'd pay him back as soon as they returned), he made it clear that he was going first. Dealer's privilege, he called it. 'It's up to you three who follows next.'

'Why can't we all go in together?' Maggie wondered, eyeing Yasser nervously. (Yasser assumed that Maggie had wanted him to chaperone her. He was pleased that he wouldn't have to, and that the choice had been taken away from him by Benny. The reason for not wanting to go with Maggie was fairly simple. It was not simply the ambivalent emotions that he held for the woman – love and then hate in a rapid shuttle – it was more the grief that he'd catch from Shyleen in due course if he chose Maggie over her.)

'Why? Well firstly, it's my gaff, so it's my rules.'

'I appreciate that but –'

'And *secondly*, four people at once will stretch things too much. It's risky at the best of times, just in case I haven't made that clear. Even one at a time puts pressure on the connection. I'd be worried that four at once would snap it all together.'

Maggie nodded. 'Two by two, then?'

'Like animals into the Ark?' Benny chuckled. 'Listen. You might not think it to look at me, darling – I've never worn me wealth on me sleeve or in me clothes for that matter – but I've got plenty of money I don't need. *However.* I didn't get it by backing down from a decision. And I know what I'm doing, so here's the newsflash. One by one is what I said. One by one is what I meant.'

'Okay, okay,' said Yasser. 'Benny, you're holding the cards. One by one'll be fine… but could you at least tell us what we can expect when we arrive?'

'I have no idea, son.'

'No?'

'No. I've never taken the trip, personally. I couldn't risk it if you paid me – which you have. You see… it's me rodents. They're more than pets to me, but even if they were only pets, they'd be helpless without me. At home, you see, they need feeding, temperature control… maintenance, basically. And if I couldn't come back I'd never forgive meself, knowing they were starving as a result of my negligence.'

Maggie said, 'That's twice you've alluded to the possibility we might not return. Are you saying it's definitely dangerous on the other side?'

'Oh it's dangerous all right,' Benny answered. 'But travelling to Paris could be dangerous. Steer clear of the frogs' legs and don't shag nothing near the train stations: that would be my less-than-expert advice. Are you ready, Freddie?'

'Yeah I'm ready,' Chris replied.

'Just one more thing,' Shyleen added. 'You said something about an experiment and it's bothered me ever since. In the house. You said something about your experiment backfiring… I think that's the exact word you used,' she said into Benny's silence. 'Did *you* start this off?'

'That's for me to know,' Benny answered, 'and you to find out. Now. Before I lose the will to live... I'll follow you in Chris. Beauty before age.'

7.

Outside in the back garden, Yasser, Shyleen and Maggie found spots to sit down; they gazed up at the night sky and counted stars, hoping that it wouldn't rain. Cold enough without a midnight downpour... And Yasser invited into his head the notion that he'd be well pleased at this moment to pull a deckchair up beside the burning shell of Maggie's caravan... if indeed the thing was still ablaze. He could not recall the last time he had been so chilly.

Shifting his attention from the constellations (which he wished he could name, or at least recognise), Yasser looked at the upstairs windows. *Fireworks,* he thought; *there's bound to be fireworks* – a discharge of sparks and electricity that could be witnessed on the screens of the windowpanes. A clue, at least, as to what awaited them all.

Nothing.

To all intents and purposes, from the outside the house looked as dead as a doornail. An old blind dog of a house, freezing in the water that drowned it.

They heard nothing. Saw nothing. Said nothing.

And waited.

8.

As soon as they were back in the spore-scented kitchen, their flashlight beams playing tag against every wall and surface, Benny slipped in front of Chris and blazed the trail to the foot of the staircase.

'These steps'll be the death of me,' he remarked as he embarked on the climb.

The treads groaned like tectonic plates.

They crossed the landing, as mute as determined thieves. The tipsy bathroom door they disregarded. The fourth and smallest bedroom was their destination. The air stank of cabbage and peanuts; it was as thick as a storm.

In Benny's wake, Chris had assumed the ascetic air of a devoted monk, and most of this attitude could be put down to nervousness and servility. Although worried about what might come next, he was respectful of Benny's authority, in spite of how much he hated himself for caring more than two tin bollocks for the older man's opinion.

'And breathe. And relax,' said Benny.

'I'm relaxed,' Chris fibbed.

'No you're not. Turn off your light.'

'My torch?'

'Turn it off. Mood is everything, mate.' Flicking off his own flashlight, Benny took a few steps away from Chris and told him once more to relax.

The light in the room had been halved – more than halved. Gravy-thick shadows glanced and danced.

'I said turn it off, Chris.'

Chris flicked the switch. The colours in the room became more cloak and bullet, there was nothing less than a dark grey.

'And turn one-eighty,' Benny instructed. 'Do it, Chris. I'm not exactly renowned for my carefree spirit and I have three of your mates clamouring for my attention outside.'

Chris turned; his feet shuffled in the filthy swamp that had once been a carpet. 'I'm sorry I took half a second to respond,' he said violently. 'Not everyone's earned your experience.'

Behind Chris's back, Benny said, 'Don't get lippy with me, cunt. I don't deserve it.'

'…Did you call me *cunt?*'

'Yes I did, cunt. And I'll say it again. Are you listening? You're a cunt. And you're mine. I'm collecting people for my experiments.'

'What do you mean?'

As Chris turned, there was not enough light to see Benny striding towards him. There was even less light to see what Benny held in his right hand; what he'd collected from the windowsill where he'd left it a few minutes earlier.

He swung it.

Benny swung the hammer and it made contact with the fontanelle on Chris's head. With no time to scream, Chris buckled; he folded like cellophane in steam.

He dropped to his knees and wobbled. Muttered something – gasped something – and Benny swung the hammer at Chris's head once again… Embedded as they were in the near-darkness, Benny's aim was a triumph of experience over fortune.

The sound of bone caving in was a kick. Benny grinned. Although he couldn't actually see Chris toppling forward, he felt it. Indeed, he heard it. Perhaps he even smelt it.

To make sure of the programme of events, Benny bent at the waist and swung the hammer again. And this time he used his torch to make sure.

One down.

Three to go.

9.

In Benny's experience there was no qualitative difference between the thicknesses of the male and the female skull - both examples would cave in when addressed by a hammer. In spite of this earlier research, however, he did not choose the hammer when it came to Shyleen. Partly he was worried that a hammer blow might kill her (and this one he wanted to keep alive); and partly he fancied a change. After all, swinging a weapon like a hammer was very much a younger man's game, and he still had three more to get through tonight.

And what a night! A *bumper* night! Made all the more juicy for being wholly unexpected, these visitors having played into his hands.

'We're going upstairs,' Benny said as he began the climb.

'What happened to the other torch?' Shyleen asked. 'The one Chris had.'

'He took it with him.' Benny grinned. He hadn't thought about his first victim's torch but his position on the stairway meant that he could lie convincingly. 'I didn't expect that to happen,' he improvised further.

'So...' The sound of Shyleen's footfalls on the wet carpet; a jingle of some jewellery, if Benny wasn't much mistaken – a couple of bracelets, perhaps. He'd fence those. 'It was a painless journey. For Chris, I mean.'

'I wouldn't go that far,' Benny answered.

'What do you mean?'

'I mean I don't know, but I doubt it was painless.' Benny had reached the upstairs landing. 'Your body will be disintegrated and then re-fused on a plain beyond our current comprehension as human beings. You can't tell me that's not gonna sting a bit.'

Shyleen's ensuing silence sang of anxiety; Benny imagined that he could sense it – sense waves of the stuff – as she made it to the top of the stairs. Benny pointed the beam into the first bedroom and said, 'We're in here.'

Although Shyleen did not sniff the air as she entered the

room – she was aware of her nostrils flaring. Twitching. She was
trying to smell a sign (any vague sign would suffice) of Chris's
crossing. An olfactory echo of some kind – an electric air, perhaps; a lakeside storm sensation – a salty ozone cologne. But no,
the room stank exactly the same as the rest of the house stank, of
water damage and no through air…

Until the torchlight was extinguished.

'Hey!'

As soon as the light went out, the smell changed dramatically, and this change was accompanied by a hissing sound.

In the filthy darkness, Shyleen tensed.

Hiss.

'What's happening?' Shyleen demanded.

The smell had moved closer to her senses – claustrophobi-
cally close, in fact. The stink of burnt sugar and of muck-spread-
ing on countryside pastures… It assaulted her nostrils while the
hissing sound continued. The hissing sound –

Hisssss…

…like an aerosol can… spraying –

Spraying me.

- spraying its poison into the localised atmosphere.

In order to block her nose as best she could, Shyleen raised
her hands to her face. Both her nose and her eyes had started to
leak; both her mucous and her tears seemed as hot as bathwater
– hot and abrasive… Wanting instinctively nothing more than
to scream or to voice a protest (she wasn't sure which), Shyleen
opened her mouth; not only the stench but a foul taste flooded in,
and Shyleen choked. She coughed.

Surely she had swallowed perfumed fire. No words could
she squeeze out; a coughing fit had overtaken her, but Shyleen
knew that she had to get out of the room. She had to get out of
the house… but one step at a time. Bent at the waist and cough-

ing madly, she walked in the direction that she believed the door to be in - the direction directly opposite the night-blackened window.

Whatever Benny had squirted at Shyleen was affecting her vision – her sense of balance also. Her throat was as raw as gravel; her eyes burned. She couldn't speak. However, what was worst of all was the way that the darkness had started to launch itself directly at her face. She ducked deeper.

...spraying me...

'You are feeling very sleepy,' Benny intoned in a mock-illusionist's stage voice, lightly accented.

The darkness was sapping Shyleen's strength; her consciousness had all but retreated. To the throb in her temples – insistent as a parade's bass drum – she fell down on the stinking single bed that the room contained.

Her mouth was dry.

...spraying me... she thought once more before her consciousness flew away on wings fetid and dark.

10.

Gripping his canister like a truncheon (at shoulder height), Benny waited until Shyleen's breathing had levelled out; until she had exhaled away her panic. Then he flicked on the torch and shone the jaundiced beam at his victim. The approach of her unconsciousness had paralysed her facial features into a mask of horror that could not have been bettered on the face of a French mime. Her mouth was open - invitingly so, in Benny's opinion.

'How long do I have, I wonder?' he whispered to himself.

Shortly after meeting Shyleen for the first time, Benny had pictured her lowering the fly of his trousers with her pursed lips. After all, it had been a long time since he'd stripped and fucked an Asian girl. (And never before had he shared his erection with an Asian *boy*. He had high hopes for Yasser.)

'Why not, as the actress said to the bishop.'

Benny squeezed his trouser pocket − to check on the progress of his tumescence… Nothing doing; soft as a Labrador's turd. But there was time. There was time. If either of the other two outside were to enter the house, Benny would hear the intrusion, even in the throes of passion. He could disengage quickly, and −

'Fuck it,' Benny whispered. Laboriously kneeling down by the side of the bed, he sat about removing Shyleen's trousers.

He'd always been speedy in the sack.

Old age or no old age.

11.

The first thing he thought was that he'd been mugged again.

Thirteen years earlier, he'd been mugged outside London Bridge station, near a throbbing flock of black cabs. A prick with a flick had demanded money. Chris had said no. And the wanker had not understood the mass of the situation. Not willing to practise what he preached, he had held the knife but hadn't used it: he'd lost his bottle. He had fought Chris with fists alone.

And lost.

Chris had pushed the wanker down a flight of stairs and had left him for dead. The wanker had hit his head on a wall. His head had resembled a Bolognese. And Chris had left him.

He'd felt good.

But he didn't feel good right now. Chris imagined that he was the one who had been abandoned at the foot of the stairs. For a few seconds.

Pain information sank codes into Chris's brain. His head pulsed: a headache from the end of the world; an Armageddon migraine… Chris tested the rear of his scalp with numb fingers. He felt wetness, an adhesive quality.

'You piece of shit,' he murmured while attempting to stand.

His fingertips his only guide, he left the bedroom.

He heard commotion. The sounds were distant and extra-terrestrial.

'You prick,' he muttered; and believing that the angel's wing might have saved him from a certain death, and that his luck had held for one more day, he crossed the landing…

12.

'I really don't like this,' said Yasser.

'Nor me.'

Yasser waited. In the field behind the house, a couple of owls performed a brief duet.

'What's going on?' he asked finally.

'You know what's going on. He told us to wait,' said Maggie.

'I'm not talking about Benny. I'm talking about your match-es and petrol.'

'Oh that.'

'Yes, *oh that*… What were you thinking?'

'I'm paving me way.'

'To what?'

'To me future.'

'Oh. And that's cool, I suppose.'

'Quite hot, I'd imagine.'

'…Is that supposed to be a joke?'

Now it was Maggie who waited. The owls sang again and Maggie said, 'That's *two* owls, by the way. One does the *turwit* and the other one does the *turwoo*. Did you know that?'

'I did as a matter of fact.'

'But don't you wonder why the second owl doesn't start the conversation some time? Might be nice to hear *turwoo turwit*.'

'We don't get too many owls in Bury Park,' Yasser answered, and then he realised what Maggie could be saying. 'We're the owls, you mean? You want to speak first?'

'Heaven forfend! Just an observation… Do you think many people were hurt in the fire?'

'That's between you and your conscience, I'd say. You'll find out soon enough when you're in court. On charges of arson and manslaughter. If you're lucky.'

'Oh I won't be going to court, Yasser. I'll die first. By me own hand, as they say. I can't say I haven't thought about it for long enough.'

Again, the owls made whoopee. A bat flapped over the garden.

Yasser said, 'I started to think you wanted me to do it for you.'

'Take my life?' Maggie smiled. 'You could if you wanted to; I wouldn't fight much. Not if I could help it, anyway. But I don't know what my instinct for self-preservation would throw up in your way. We'd be on the voyage together, as virgins.'

Yasser shook his head. 'It's not a voyage I'm going to take, Maggie.'

'But how do you know? Imagine your afterlife! A thousand vestal virgins for killing scum!' Maggie laughed. 'I'm your pass-port to Paradise and you don't even know it.'

'You're a fruit loop, is what you are,' Yasser mumbled, walking away in the direction of the house once more. 'Where *are* they? I'm going in,' he called over his shoulder (a light twinkled on in an upstairs window of the house next door). 'Are you com-ing with me?'

13.

Benny had placed the torch on a shelf near the door; the light it provided was fairly strong but not focussed on what was happening in the room. This defect in illumination combined with the torrents of pain in Chris's skull, and it took Chris a few beats to work out what was going on.

'Get off her!' he shouted.

Benny turned by rotating his shoulder as best he could. He had positioned Shyleen so that she was only just on the bed's edge, on her back, her ankles on Benny's shoulders. Benny himself was kneeling on the floor, pushing his groin against hers in hurried spasms.

Chris crossed the room in four strides – faster than Benny could disconnect and stand up. Chris fell on Benny's body, the two of them landing on the squelchy mattress. Rage burned in Chris's brain – it was hotter than the agony – and punch after punch he landed on Benny's face. Throughout the attack he swore fluently amid tangled, complicated breaths.

'You tried to kill me,' Chris eventually managed to say. By this point he had straddled Benny's torso; apart from the laboured heaving of chests, all action had ceased.

'I thought I had, mate.' Benny gasped breath. 'You must be tougher than you look. I whacked you a coupla good 'uns. You're no use to me, I'm afraid.'

'You took my money fast enough,' Chris argued, immediately regretting the inappropriateness of the remark.

'Overheads,' Benny said simply.

'And what about her? Have you killed her too?' Chris's voice rose in amazed disgust. 'Is she no use to you either. You were *fucking* her, man!'

Benny sniggered. 'Tell me you've never been tempted to crack open a cold one.'

Chris punched him in the face. The nose broke.

'*Jesus!* No! No I didn't all right! She's breathing and she'll just have a bad hangover... I need her. For my collection. First Indian woman, see.'

'My God...' muttered Chris, feeling nauseous, afraid, tired (his biceps ached) – even mildly affronted at not being required by this murdering maniac. 'What do you mean, *collection?* Are you collecting *people?*'

'No, I'm collecting stamps.'

'I'm warning you, mate.'

'*Benny?*'

This was Yasser's voice, from below.

'Up here!' Chris shouted. 'Quickly!'

Benny did not wriggle beneath Chris's weight. Motionlessly they awaited Yasser's arrival, joined together in something like prayer.

Entering the bedroom, Yasser assessed the situation, or as much of it as could be assessed, and demanded to know what was going on.

'Your monkey attacked me,' said Benny. 'When I told him he couldn't have his money back.'

'You liar!' Chris protested. 'Look at the state of me! He hit me with a bat or something!'

'Self-defence,' Benny explained.

'Get off him, Chris,' said Yasser. 'And what's up with Shyleen?'

'He was raping her!'

'Bollocks!'

'Your fly's still undone! Her knickers are on the floor some-where, Yasser – with her trousers.'

Yasser reached for the torch on the shelf; he swung the light across the bed for a better look at everything, including his cousin's vagina. Something bubbled in Yasser's emotions: it might have been jealousy. The reality of Chris having had sex with Shyleen in his house had been bad enough; but to learn that one or both of these wankers had been sliding it to her while she was unconscious… it was too much. It was simply too much. Rage took hold of his reins.

'I told you to get off him, Chris. I meant it,' Yasser said in a determined voice.

Chris complied. His objections, however, were far from over.

'He said he was *collecting* people.'

But Yasser ignored him. 'We'll soon find out who was raping my cousin when she wasn't even awake, you filthy bastards.'

'Now wait a minute,' Chris said. 'I never raped *no one*.'

Sitting up comfortably, Benny took no noticed of the torch's glare; indeed, as he fastened his trouser zip with little self-consciousness at all, he appeared to be on the verge of grinning inanely, amused by the squalor of it all.

'I must admit, son, I *have* been a silly,' he said. 'I've completely forgotten to bring my forensic spunk-testing kit with me tonight. You wouldn't have one on your person, would you, by any chance?'

'The police will have one,' Yasser answered calmly. 'What's wrong with her?'

'Snake poison. Extracted and distilled by my own two hands.' Benny showed Yasser the palms of his hands.

Chris stood up.

'Stay where you are, Chris,' Yasser told him.

'You don't think *I* did this, do you?' Chris asked. 'Shine your light on my face; I can taste my own blood! He fucking belted me one!'

'I can see your blood, mate,' Yasser replied. Then to Benny: 'What does the poison do?'

'What does it look like? It makes the victim dance a jig! It puts the victim into a coma; she's aware of everything, believe it or not, she just can't move. She'll be fine.'

'But why?' Yasser wanted to know. 'Why all the bullshit about another dimension?' Immediately he answered his own question. 'To get us up here one by one?'

Benny nodded his head, and Chris said, 'I told you. He's *collecting* people – he said it as loud as anything!'

'For what reason, though?' Yasser went on.

Chris wasn't finished. 'Only I'm not good enough for him, apparently. Me he just wanted out of the way. So he whacked me blind.'

'Not blind enough,' Benny interjected. 'And *definitely* not mute enough.'

'You need a hospital,' Yasser thought aloud. He took out his mobile and thumbed the buttons to get rid of his text display and to set up a new call.

'Do you know,' said Benny. 'There's a black snake that can pretend to be a rattlesnake to scare off predators? He taps his tail on dried leaves to make the noise.'

'Shut up, Benny.' Yasser's thumb hovered over the third of the three nines that would connect him to the emergency services. It was not only the choice of which service he would name when he was invited to do so – police or ambulance – that made him hesitate. It was also the realisation that he was trespassing; the realisation that there were no innocent parties anymore.

Benny did not shut up. 'Other snakes work together – different *species* of snakes, I mean. One of em does a dance to hypnotise the prey.' Benny used his right arm to show what he meant. 'Then the other cunt nips in and bites the victim on the scrotum. Ingenious, when you think about it.'

'I said: shut *up*, Benny!'

'Bob's your uncle and Fanny's your aunt. Both snakes eat

the prey.'

In the hard wind of Benny's persistent enthusiasm, Yasser could do no better than to shake his head in exasperation. 'Why are you *telling* me this? Why *now?*'

'It's called ironic poignancy, son.' Benny smirked directly into the torchlight. 'If *I'm* the *first* snake, Yasser… who's the second?'

Yasser span on his heels, as hard as he could: it was too late. He had not heard Maggie follow him through the house and up the stairs. Indeed, he had been distracted; he'd been hypnotised.

'Sorry, Yasser,' she whispered.

'Give it him, girl!' said Benny; and what Maggie sprayed into Yasser's face felt dry and cold, with an animal house odour and a burning sensation when it hit the back of his throat.

He choked.

Yasser dropped to his knees, clawing at his neck with short-nailed fingers. He couldn't breathe. His eyes were hot and streaming… he was aware of commotion behind him… he didn't know where he was… his temples throbbed… sickness weakened him… *choking…*

'Don't fight it, Yasser,' a woman's voice said. Maggie's voice. *He was choking, choking…*

…too much darkness… weird light… no air… no… things no Nothing.

FAITHFUL FOLLOWING

1.

    'Okay, got it,' the first man said into his phone, 'reverse and then… yeah, got it… be there in… *yeah*, Benny, I got it. We'll be there in about five minutes. Cool, mate.' He clipped his mobile phone shut. 'Did you get that?' he asked the second man, who was driving the van with one hand splayed limply on the wheel.

    'Something about reverse.'

    'He wants us to reverse up the drive and back into the garage. Then we go in the house round the back and load up. Five bags. Five hundred quid each for fifteen minutes' work, not including the delivery of three and the disposal of two. A grand for ninety minutes? You having a laugh? Fair exchange is no robbery, mate!'

    'I know. But Dad –'

    'Den. Call me Den.'

    'But Den,' the younger man continued, 'why won't he tell us what's *in* the bags?'

    'I didn't ask. None of my business. Bloke's paying us good money not to know, that's all.' Den paused, then went on with a sighed confidence. 'But he's a scientist, right? I expect they're bodies.'

    'Yeah. I think they are too,' the son replied. 'That's what creeps me out.'

    'Why?' Den laughed. 'We can't have new medicines without

testing em first, can we?'

'No.'

'No, of course not. So what? So he's got five bags of dead rabbits or summing. Big deal! All *we* need to know is where we're taking the bags for his keepsies, and where he wants us to take the other two for cremation. Right?'

'Right. Yeah okay.'

'Good boy.' Den laughed again. 'Mean, it's not as if they're gonna be *human*.'

'Nah. Nah they won't be human.'

'Exactly.'

'Exactly!' the son agreed.

'Good boy. Now turn off your lights; this is the road,' Den instructed, in the back of his mind wondering if he'd managed to convince his son against what was obvious or not.

2.

Conducting his endless internal interview with Virginia, Branston leaned into his steering wheel, his arms limp in a vague cross. He watched the house – Number 11. He was part detective, part peeping tom; and when the van laboured into sight, Branston could not have been more content.

He watched it swing wide in the empty road, then negotiate a reverse up the short driveway and into the garage. His pulse quickened. His imagination had been playing with possibilities about the Edlesborough house since he'd arrived in this road for the first time tonight in Yasser's wake. Now the suspense was something harder, like a cramp.

Hours earlier, Branston had followed Yasser to the house up the road, Number 77; he had seen the Asian girl slip around the side, while Yasser rang the front doorbell. While Yasser and the house owner had talked on the step, what had the Asian girl been doing at the back of the building? A burglary? (Branston waited for the reveal.) In a state of serenity Branston had watched Yasser walk away and get back into his car. A long wait had followed. Even pumped up by the mission – by the story! – Branston had grown bored. Then Yasser had started his engine and had driven off.

This had been the most difficult decision that Branston had needed to make. He'd been torn between waiting outside the house to try to discover what had happened to the Asian girl and starting his own engine to pursue his student. Although the house clearly meant something significant, and although the home owner and Yasser were not friends (otherwise why the doorstep conversation at this hour?), there was something appealing about keeping Yasser in his line of sight, for as long as possible, for the sake of dramatic continuity, if for no other reason.

But what if Yasser is just going home? Branston had asked himself… in the voice of his interviewer, Virginia.

Then I'll come back here.

But won't it be too late by then? Virginia had continued, her voice slightly spiky with agitation.

'For what?' Branston had answered in a whisper.

Indeed, for what? All of this time later, and Branston was no clearer about the night's purposes. He had followed Yasser to the Travellers' camp; he had waited outside, not wishing to push his luck. While parked outside, he had even become jittery because of his proximity to the camp's entrance, so he'd driving back the way he'd arrived, fairly convinced that Yasser would drive back to the house in Edlesborough sooner or later.

Yasser had done so, albeit after a length of visit that had shown Branston the opening acts of a new work entitled *Panic at Gypsy Park*. Having waited so long, he had thought that he'd made a mistake. Yasser must have taken the other way when he'd left the camp. But then Yasser had come along, whizzing past Branston (who ducked low in the seat), accompanied by the woman in the film that Yasser had shot; the woman who had snatched the child.

On Yasser's tail once again, half believing that he saw the glow of fire in his rearview mirror, Branston had been led back to Edlesborough, where some sort of party must be gathering at the original house. Or maybe not. When they'd all repaired to the damaged house down the road, Branston had got out of the car and followed on foot, his training shoes making no sound. Not that it would have mattered if he'd clicked along in high heels, he had reckoned - these people were on a mission tonight.

Now that the van had reversed into the garage of the damaged house, Branston believed that they would all move into the next chapter... Having jogged up and down the road a couple of times, Branston had moved his car nearer to Number 11, where he waited now. Not so close, he hoped, that he was easily in sight (although he had to concede that it wouldn't be difficult to be spotted), but close enough to keep a good eye on the place.

However, there was not much to see. From within the garage, the guy who had been in the van's passenger seat was pulling down the door. None of the original four had emerged either. What could they be doing in there? Branston wondered. And what significance did the van play?

Virginia asked Branston a question. *Did you ever consider the possibility that the van drivers live here?*

Branston informed his interviewer that this was a good question, but added: *No. No, I don't think so, and I'll tell you why. The garage door was unlocked, Virginia.* The passenger got out and opened it – without a key. And I don't think men who don't come home from work until this late are in the habit of leaving their garages unlocked in Edlesborough, any more so than they are anywhere else these days.

Someone had unlocked the garage door before the van had arrived, either before the four visitors had arrived (which suggested at least a fifth person present, unless it had been the guy who lived at 77); or perhaps it was one of the four who had slipped into the garage via an entrance adjacent to the back garden.

Why did it matter anyway? Vowing to edit his answers more scrupulously while on surveillance in the future, Branston was contemplating the next move – when the garage door opened again.

The van's main beams flared. Branston heard the engine roar, but he waited before starting his own vehicle. *Be patient. See what the others do...* This advice to self despite the seemingly obvious: the van drivers had come to collect something or to drop something off – something that had required a bit of privacy.

As the van eased out of the garage, a man that Branston had never seen before walked down the path between the house and the garage, the woman from the Travellers' camp a few steps behind him. The man – oldish, ruffled – gave the van a wave in the driveway, then he closed the garage door again. Wordlessly as far as Branston could tell, the two of them walked together on the pavement, not in the direction of Number 77: in the direction of the end of the road, where the park began.

Perhaps they're parked in the park car park, Virginia...

Shouldn't you find out? Start the engine. Follow them!

But where was Yasser? He had not exited the house, which meant that he was still in the property somewhere (minus Maggie, who seemed to have just deserted him), or he had left in the back of the van, with the delivery men.

Did he mean to leave in the back of the van? Was he conscious?

Storyline.

Boy goes to gypsy camp to take back child stolen by lady gypsy. Lady gypsy has had her own child stolen earlier. Boy tries to find lady gypsy's child. Goes to home of old boy with criminal clout. Old boy whacks the younger boy. Dead. Van drivers collect the body…

With no way of knowing how far away from, or close to, the facts this outline was, Branston reminded himself that an Asian woman had gone in there too – as had the man from Number 77. Where were *they* now?

In the back of the van as well, Branston supposed. Why would the three of them hang around in an abandoned house?

Oh I don't know. Ghost-spotting? A sexual threeway? (Branston blinked several times.) *Perhaps they intended a fivesome…*

Yeah right. So who are the guys in the van?

He had three alternatives, and two of them were shrinking from sight.

Follow the van.

Follow the old guy and the baby-thief woman.

Stay put and wait.

Then a fourth choice became clear, quite unexpectedly, as the man from Number 77 stumbled out onto the front lawn, swaying like a sailor, his face filthy with something that Branston did not want to be blood.

As fast as he could, Branston got out of his car and crossed the deserted road. He wouldn't be able to catch the van anyway; perhaps the other two (who knew where they intended to walk?), but not the van: and now it scarcely mattered. The man from 77 needed help – Branston's help – and could hardly stand up straight. He'd been attacked, it seemed.

'What happened?'

Chris looked at Branston – each a stranger to one another

– and in the streetlamp's illumination his eyes were milky and liquid.

'Cut myself shaving – what does it look like? Which way did they go?' Chris asked.

'The old guy or the van?'

'The van. *Which way?*'

Branston pointed in the direction of Chris's house and Chris shuffled off.

'Where's Yasser?' Branston asked.

'He's in the van,' Chris slurred over his shoulder. 'He does *experiments* on them… and my Bernadette's already there.'

'*Where?*'

'Somewhere in Ashridge… Gotta get to my car…' He sounded drunk.

Are you part of this story or not? demanded Branston to himself. The answer took less than a second to compute.

'Get in my car,' he told Chris. 'I'm driving – you're talking. I need explanations… The van can't've got far. We'll catch em.'

3.

Chris attempted to explain to Branston what had happened in the house…

When Yasser collapsed in the darkened bedroom, Chris felt edgy. It was pretty obvious that he was now on his own; it was just him and Maggie and Benny in the room, and Maggie had just nailed her colours to the mast. She and Benny were together. Quite how or quite why was a matter that Chris felt he needn't dwell on. If the crack on the head that he'd received from Benny had not been sufficient to convince him of the danger he was in, he had now witnessed Maggie's deconstruction of Yasser. The stench of the evidence lingered – in the stagnant, compromised oxygen – and Chris pressed a hash-stinking palm to his nostrils.

To run or not to run?

Chris would have to push past Maggie (and step over Yasser) in order to get out of the door; but once clear of the room, of the landing, surely he could make it through the pitch-dark house safely enough. The morning would smell delicious… but then what? It was utterly inconceivable – it was totally *unacceptable* – that he would phone the law. A matter of general principle. But what else was left?

'Do you wanna be on your way?' Benny asked – Chris wasn't sure if the question was for him. Benny sniggered. 'Or do you want your money back?'

So the question *was* for him.

'Yes I do,' Chris answered.

As though nothing more serious than a difference of opinions had occurred in the last few minutes, the three of them walked back down and through the house. Such was the drumming in his skull by this point that Chris did not pay much attention to the others' proximity. If they wanted to attack him again – to boot him down the stairs, to snap his neck – then there was nothing he could do to stop them. His injury had robbed him of his survival instinct. Parenthetically he wondered if he had also lost a life-threatening quantity of blood. He didn't dare check if his wound was still bleeding.

The cold air outside made him dizzy. A few minutes earlier he had asked himself if he was ready to run – to barge out of the house if necessary – but now it was an effort simply to stand up. The black-and-cream lawn, dyed a thousand variations of greyscale by the moon and stars, looked awfully inviting as a place to lay his head…

Chris imagined Bernadette, and how she'd nurse him on those rare occasions when he was ill. She would hold his head;

remind him to drink his Lemsip... Where *was* she? Where was she when she should be nursing him right now?

'Is Bernadette with you?' he asked Benny. 'Wherever you're keeping them all... is she with you?'

'She's the nurse, right?'

'You know she is.'

'Yeah I've got her. She's safe...' Benny sniffed the air and reminded himself of something. 'Listen, mate, I've gotta make a phone call, all right? Chat to Maggie or be on your toes – as you like it. But if you wanna stick around you can see a bit of the process: the collection. I just need to give em a bell for the directions. They'll be here soon.'

Forcing himself to focus, Chris was made aware of all the gaps that he had in his comprehension; not all of these gaps could be explained by the attack either. It was like trying to catch up with a film's plot, thirty minutes in.

'So what do *you* have to say for yourself?' Chris asked Maggie while Benny strolled away (presumably for privacy). Chris took a seat on one of the benches.

Maggie shrugged.

'You don't know, eh? What's to stop me calling the police?'

Maggie shrugged again. 'You don't mean anything to him, in case you haven't realised. You can do what you like.'

Wishing that he didn't have to hear that all the time, Chris rebounded. 'Well, maybe the fucking *law* means something to him. Have you thought of that?'

There was that shrug once more! (Chris would have taken pleasure from slapping her one!) 'You don't understand,' Maggie told him, sitting down beside him. 'He drops hints all the time. I have to expect he *wants* to get caught... but no one challenges anything he does. No one *sees*... For Christ's sake, we're sitting in someone's back garden – why are none of the *neighbours* calling the police? Because they're just like you and me – or like we were until recently. They don't want to watch the show. To watch is... to watch is to get involved.'

Chris waited. While he couldn't query the commonsense nature of what Maggie had told him, the big picture remained cloudy and stormy. *The only way to converse with madness,* Bernadette had once told him, *is to learn its language.*

As her face filled his mind once again (smiling this time), Chris knew that he had to find her, and in order to find her he had to learn the language of madness. After all, she was smiling now; she was aware that he knew that she hadn't left him deliberately. She hadn't run off with another man. She hadn't blown a top-secret Lottery win on a ticket to Barbados. She'd been taken by Benny.

How many others were with her?

'Where does he keep them?' Chris asked.

'A big house near Ashridge Forest.'

Twenty minutes away, Chris calculated. 'Couple of minutes to get back to my car,' he said aloud.

'What?' Maggie asked. 'Are you *going* there?'

Not exactly answering the question, Chris went on: 'There's lots of big houses near Ashridge. Do you have an address?'

Maggie shook her head. 'You can't make it in your condition! You're two minutes from a bloody coma!'

'My Bernadette is there. Please, Maggie... At least *explain* it to me.'

Maggie glanced towards the end of the garden. 'He's coming back,' she said quietly.

'Are you a prisoner too?' Chris pressed.

'Do I *look* like a prisoner?' Maggie smiled. 'The man's me *salvation*. Got shot of some rats in me life... now I'm free.'

'Some rats?'

Benny was five metres from them, and Maggie said, 'He did for me da, the rapist bastard. And Tommy's with your girl Bernadette in Benny's dreamworld... I hope she doesn't get friendly with *that* wanker.'

Maggie stood up, sending a riffle of petrol perfume through the air. 'All done?' she asked Benny.

'Done and done,' the man answered. 'Some new boys – father and son. They'll be here in five... What've you two lovebirds been discussing?'

'Whether he dies here or at home.'

Benny sniffed. 'Fair enough. What did you decide, son?'

Surely there would be a point at which Chris ceased to feel sick and would begin to feel anger; at which the jungle drums in his head would beat an alternative rhythm. Small waves of darkness splashed at the edges of his vision.

Chris lifted a finger and pointed at Benny's chest. 'If I die here, you'll be implicated. It's your house, you said.'

'Indeed it is, mate, but you're not dealing from a full deck. I've got some boys on their way and they're picking up the spoils to deposit elsewhere. They'll be making two deliveries. One to dispose of the dead ones – her old man and you, if you hurry up – and one to my labs, where I'll work on them in due course. So it's up to you, mate – only shit or get off the pot, okay?'

Benny started to walk away, towards the path that would lead around the side of the house. A second later, Maggie moved off after him... and Chris was wrenched between feeling abandoned again – emotionally hurt, indeed – and feeling that he'd crawled out of the worst nightmare known in the history of the superego.

His thoughts were sloppy and ill-formed, he knew they were; but he also knew that when his attackers were gone, they were gone forever, more than likely. And with them, his only hope of getting back to Bernadette.

'Wait!'

They had only walked a few metres, and there was no night noise to spoil his word, but Benny carried on as if he'd heard nothing. On the other hand, Maggie sopped in her tracks; she turned.

'Take me with you,' Chris pleaded. 'I'll be part of it – whatever it is. But don't leave me to freeze.'

Now Benny stopped as well. He was too far away for Chris to read his features, but the angry tone of his voice was unambiguous.

'What part of this don't you understand?' he asked sarcastically.

'All of it!'

'Then listen up, for the last time. *You are absolutely no use to me, twat.* You are weak; you are a piss-ant penny-max stakes fucking gambler. Is *that* clear enough? You have no imagination and you mean nothing to evolution. So die here or crawl home like a damaged cat. *Nobody will care.*'

With which Benny resumed his exit stage left… and Maggie was certain to tail him, Chris knew. However, when he looked at her he saw something that he had not expected. With Maggie being that little bit closer to where Chris was sitting, the fact that she was mouthing words was hard to deny. Chris squinted. And Maggie did it one more time: her silent adieu. And then she was off on her heels, leaving Chris atremble.

Follow us, she had mouthed.

4.

Branston struggled to think of the place that this bashed-up dude would fit in.

The guy was bleeding to death, Branston was certain of it.

Blood was pouring, Virginia.

No.

Not the interview with Virginia, this was the real stamp. This was *it.*

The man was dying.

Ignoring the lolling hulk of Chris's body, Branston drove as fast as he dared. To spin too quickly, left or right, he imagined, would result in Chris being catapulted out of the passenger side window, in a waterfall of smithereened glass. And killed.

Thud.

Sound of the wanker, bouncing on the tarmac.

Thud.

No, not really, it was the sound of Chris as he rammed his temple against the side window, once again.

If the tumble doesn't kill him, I will.

Branston paused to wonder (waiting at a roundabout) if he himself would be the reason for Chris feeling rough with bruises in the morning. It amused him (briefly) that he might be held responsible. If Chris survived this evening, he would be well within his rights to complain about the quality of the chauffeuring service he'd received.

So let him complain, thought Branston.

Never were the Chiltern Hills more luscious than at night. The hills were tipped with dunkings of magnesium light (or was it manganese?). Entrance to the forest wrapped sleeves of darkness around Branston's nippy car. A bare ten metres on, and these sleeves were tied securely. The vehicle felt airlocked. It was lifeless and drained – drained of energy and force: the inside of the car was no different from pernicious anaemia... or so Branston though as he formulated his account of the journey. By this point he was all but damn it alone in the vehicle. Chris's consciousness had slipped away, light as a breeze. Loneliness and anger rattled together in Branston's skull. As a result of these emotions, he summoned up Virginia, in the way that an only child might summon up an imaginary friend.

If he dies, said Virginia – *what then? What's the plan?*

In the interview, Branston smiled in the style more often described as *indulgently.*

If he dies, Virginia, then I've done nothing wrong. Not a thing. I was a Good Samaritan, in the wrong place at the wrong...

Again, no; this wasn't good enough – this was not a film magazine interview.

So what *was* it? A police interrogation?

Seriously, Tim – what is *it?* asked Virginia, dipping her head low to consult the pad of notes that she'd made in preparation.

Up ahead, the vehicle that he was following made a perfectly well-indicated left-hand turn... One thing that Branston had noticed: the driver in the lead was no roadhog – no bitumen prick – and furthermore, he seemed not to give a damn who happened to be following him.

Almost like he was courting the dance...

Well exactly, Virginia... like he wants me there... wherever 'there' might end up being.

The road beneath the car's wheels was stiff and ragged with mud dried into lunar puddles and ravines; the vehicle shook like a cocktail-maker, the red tail-lights ahead describing the ECG reading on a patient's electronic equipment... The road angled left. It decreased in professionalism and became a path. In Branston's vision, the vehicle in the lead bounced manically, the tail-lights sprinkling daubs of illumination.

The house reared up from behind a buttress of hedges. They had arrived, it seemed, at their destination; and although no lights were on within (or none that Branston could detect), this didn't mean that no one was home. Indeed, already parked on the driveway was the white van that Branston had seen reverse into the house's garage, back in Edlesborough. The workmen – the delivery men? the collection men? – had made good time.

Branston tensed at the wheel... and followed the older man and the Traveller girl onto the property. Now was no time to act coy, he reasoned; surely to God they would have discussed the fact that they were being tailed, at *some* point during the drive over. There was no sense in pretending to be invisible now. Apart from anything else, Branston had a series of questions on the subject of Yasser to pose; and he also had a man bleeding to death on his passenger seat... and he wanted to know why.

Wondering where the nearest hospital was for when the time came to drop off his passenger, Branston exited his car. The driveway was awash with a fawn-coloured light (the old man's car had turned on the security beam), which meant that Branston could see fairly clearly – with far greater clarity than he'd been able to in Edlesborough, at any rate. The man's face, in the light, was deepened with shadow; very briefly a comparison with a Halloween pumpkin entered Branston's mind. Then the image fused and shorted out.

'Can I help you, friend?' the old man asked from over the roof of his car. Neither he nor the Traveller woman had moved more than a step from the doors that they'd climbed out of.

Almost as if they're waiting, said Virginia.

They've got nothing to be wary of, Branston told himself (ignoring his interviewer for a second). You've got it all wrong, Tim! They're innocent! And you're on private property in the middle of the night.

Maybe. Or like I say... they're waiting for you, Branston. At the very least they're waiting for you to make the first move.

Branston wondered if he was in a film, right now; wondered if this guy took his security seriously.

'You left a man for dead, back in Edlesborough,' Branston answered. He had not moved from his own driver's door either. There was righteous and there was foolish.

'Is that a fact?' The old man appeared neither perturbed nor put out by the allegation. For all his breezy manner it might have been mid-morning; he might have been asked the time.

'Yeah, that's a fact. He's bleeding in my car.'

'I'd say that makes him *your* problem – and not mine – wouldn't you? Come on, Maggie.'

Benny moved towards the house, prompting Branston to think quickly. A glimpse of Maggie's expression – as flat as pummelled dough – was all it took to recognise the weaker link in Benny's chain. Had something disturbed her? Maybe something the old man had said on the ride over?

Something to do with Yasser?

'Stolen any more infants recently?' Branston called to Maggie.

The woman said nothing in return, but Benny did. Turning quickly to face them, he said, 'Have you *what?*'

'It's nothing, Benny,' Maggie protested.

'Stolen an *infant?*'

It took Branston a beat to understand that beneath Benny's anger was something else: something disbelieving.

Maggie tried to make Benny approve. 'I did it for you. I was going to… donate him to you.'

A *donation?* What horror show had Branston stumbled into?

'…for your project.'

Benny had returned to his side of the car; he and Maggie were conversing across the roof – they might have been in a supermarket car park, discussing price rises or fish fingers.

The word *project* sounded eerie to Branston's ears. Indignation was the fuel in his engine. 'That's not what you told Yasser,' he said to Maggie.

She spat at him: 'Keep your nose out of it… Who *are* you anyway?'

'I'm Yasser's teacher,' Branston answered. 'The one who got a copy of your sex tape.'

Benny was fighting to keep up. '*What* sex tape, Maggie? What the hell?' Then he reorganised his priorities. 'Where's the child? What happened to the *child?*'

'Yasser took him back,' Branston answered, '…back to his parents. She told him…' He indicated Maggie. '…that her dad and a bloke called Tommy made her do it. That's something… that's one of the things I didn't get. Why? But it was for *you*, wasn't it, Benny? She stole the child for *you*… but what happened?'

Maggie had dipped her head. Her accusers had her in a pincer movement; there was no getting out of her lies.

'Hey Maggie, I'm talking to you,' said Branston. 'Benny's got a point. Why *didn't* you hand the child over to him straight away? Why *didn't* he know about the child's existence in the first place?'

'Good question,' Benny piped in.

'Did you fall in love with the child, Maggie? Did you start to doubt what you were doing for this man?'

Maggie looked up and fixed Branston with a powerful stare. 'Why don't you mind your own business? We're going inside, aren't we, Benny.'

'Not yet we're not,' Benny replied. 'The man's questions seem sensible, I reckon. I'm not happy, Mags.'

'Or did you *want* to get caught?'

Maggie frowned. 'Now what eejit *wants* to get caught?' she demanded.

Branston shrugged. 'One with nowhere else to go? One at the end of the road? One prepared to steal a child for the love of a substitute father?'

'This is bollocks, Benny. And I'm cold. Let's go in.'

'Yeah all right,' Benny replied, but his words were slow and indecisive. You could not have accused him of not taking Branston seriously.

'It was you, wasn't it, Maggie?' Branston took his first step away from the car – he almost remembered what it had been like to toddle. 'It wasn't your dad, it wasn't Tommy: it was *you* who made the sex tape. And you who hand delivered it to my door. Wasn't it.'

Now, Maggie looked petulant. Did she also appear embarrassed? Branston wondered. She dipped her head; she had stopped in her tracks.

'Maggie?' Benny's voice was soft. 'Answer the teacher or you're sleeping out here in the cold, darling. Nothing else to be done about *that.*'

'Okay, I filmed it,' Maggie answered. 'It's not a crime, believe it or not. I borrowed Tommy's truck one afternoon when he was sleeping off a late card game. I followed you home. Yasser had told me what you drive.'

Branston examined the evidence, searching for a weakness. *But why bother?* he wondered. There was nothing in it for Maggie. A long shot attempt at getting caught being a manipulative bitch? Unless that's what you're into- getting caught. Maybe. Some people are. Some people like the moment of revelation.

Benny and Maggie walked towards the house's front door.

'Aren't you going to invite me in?' Branston asked.

Once again Benny turned. 'What subject do you teach?' he asked.

'Film.'

'So you've got cameras at your disposal, have you? All the gubbins.'

'…Yes.'

'You ever made a documentary?' Benny continued.

Branston thought about his thwarted ambitions to be a movie director. 'Nothing but,' he answered wistfully.

'Do you want to film us then? Be of use, and all that. How long'll it take you to fetch a camera? A good one, mind. I want it to look pro.'

Branston remained baffled but he responded anyway. 'About thirty seconds. It's on the back seat.' Very calmly he went through his teaching commitments. He did not have a class to teach tomorrow. He had planned to work out and then mark some student assignments that he had printed off earlier on today.

'Juicy. Then come in, my boy. Another witness won't go amiss. Show them intra-rationalists where the new money's growing.'

Benny smiled.

'What's your name again, son?'

'Tim. Tim Branston.'

'I'm Benny. Let's go in. The poor girl's frozen half to death, ain'tcha, Maggie?'

Maggie nodded her head.

THE CANINES OF STRANGERS

1.

Jess was fifteen, and although she had known mobile phones all her life, she was nevertheless aware of the existence of phone boxes. She had never used one – she had never needed to use one – but she knew what they did; she understood their function. She was looking forward to using one.

The problem was finding one.

Through a mildly foggy darkness she had already walked (at a brisk pace) for what seemed like half an hour. But it couldn't have been as long as that, could it? Jess wasn't certain. After so long with so little exercise, the escape had dunked rivets of cramp deep into her thigh muscles; but this didn't mean that she'd walked for long – or walked far, for that matter. Try as she would, Jess could not make her legs move faster or stretch further with each stride, and the suspicion that a hand would land on her shoulder any second was like an emotion, as strong as grief.

So keep walking, she demanded of herself.

Where Jess and Nero had been imprisoned was in a village. However, it was not a village in which the next house stood half a mile away: in fact, by the standards of some of the villages that Jess had visited, this one was positively stodgy with occupation. How come no one had heard their shouts and screams? With every footfall Jess thought back on her time in the house; the images were gooey with mist and dream-grease, the memories both real and unreal. Anger prickled in her breasts; nausea swept through her upper body. *No one had heard them!*

Jess realised that she was emerging from a pocket of shock. Questions sparked at her synapses –

Where am I?

What's the name of this place?

How will I show the police where we were?

– and she understood, with a sickening surety, that in her desperation to be away from the house, not only had she failed to register the property's name or number, she had not so much as looked over her shoulder to commit its façade to memory.

I'll never recognise it again, she thought. Nero and those other people are fucked...

She stopped walking. More of the mist in her head had cleared; whether or not this would enable her to think better was open to question, but at least she'd found a place – psychologically and geographically – where she *wanted* to think better, rather than passively receive a flood of words and pictures, a torrent of pains. It was a start.

So far on her escape route, Jess had seen nothing but houses, most of them gated properties; a restaurant named Habibi was the first non-residential establishment. Surely it would have a phone that she could use. Surely...

The windows were dark. Standing on tiptoes and peering in with her hands around her eyes to form a mask, Jess could make out tables and white tablecloths, wine glasses inverted on table surfaces. But no people. Where *was* everyone? It was dark! Why weren't people settling down to eat at their lovely local Indian?

Jess stayed where she was, in exactly the same position, for the better part of a minute. Perhaps by will alone she would be able to summon up a room full of contented diners, all of them willing to assist her.

However, no one materialised during this period of desperate vigilance. And a voice at Jess's back made her jump.

She was forcing herself to recall if any of the houses she'd passed up to now had had lights on within, when she heard someone say:

'Place is closed.'

Jess twisted so fast that those pains in her thighs reignited. The nearest streetlamp being some ten or so metres away, it was far from simple to make out her interlocutor in the negligible light… but it was easy enough to see that he was neither Massimo nor Charlie. Considerably older than either of her captors, the man who had spoken wore country tweeds and a flat cap; in one hand he held his walking stick's knob, in the other the end of a leash, attached to the collar of a tiny black terrier puppy that was sniffing dead leaves in the restaurant's empty car park.

'Closed by a two-month,' the old man explained. 'People stopped going after the alth scur.'

The what?

Oh, *health*. Health *scare*.

'Rancid kitchen, story run. Positively raaaancid. More rats'n *noives.*'

More *what?* Jess's brain asked.

More rats than knives?

Maybe.

'You larst, girl?' the man continued.

Last? As opposed to first?

'Yes, I'm lost,' Jess answered, the speed of her translations improving – it was only a matter of thinking back, back before any of this had begun. Indeed, one of her own neighbours had spoken with much the same country burr.

'So terribly lost,' Jess finished; then something soft broke inside her face, and tears that had wanted out for some time fulfilled their salty dreams and came running.

2.

Mindful perhaps of all that he'd learned from the news since the 1990s about the repercussions of being perceived to be a child molester (the lynch mobs, the tabloid headlines) – even if one's intentions were utterly chaste and honourable – the old man with the cap and the terrier did not invite Jess into his home. Indeed, his request that she wait in his front garden arrived curt and gruff. But Jess didn't mind: curt and gruff was fine by her, as long as it was curt and gruff *and safe*. Feeling chilly, she sat on a stone bench, near a stone birdbath and a stone cross in a flower bed bearing the single engraved word WILMA.

A minute or so after he'd stepped into the house, he re-emerged carrying a blanket in the hand not carrying the walking stick. Wrapping the blanket around her shoulders, Jess was not in the least concerned that it smelled of pipe smoke and something medicinally minty. Quite the reverse: outside in the chill, enveloped in a whiffy blanket, felt to Jess like the best place in the world. Her rescuer produced a bar of chocolate from an inside pocket of his tweed jacket.

'Always carry one. Blood sugar's not what it were. Just in case… Now what's your name again? Jennifer?'

'Jessica.'

'Well mine's Peter.'

'Thank you. You told me.' Jess tore at the chocolate bar foil.

'Did Oi? Did Oi carl a police?'

'I don't know, sir. You went in – you weren't gone long.'

'Carlem now then, y'say?'

'Please.'

'Carlem now then,' Peter confirmed to himself. Not without

a good deal of effort, the old man shuffled around, turned his back on Jess, and stepped back into one of the village's more modest properties, a slightly run-down cottage leaking warmth from its open front door.

Peter had been absent again less than two minutes when the mauve People Carrier crunched off the road and on to the gravel driveway.

Jess's body tensed. Had they found her missing so soon? Had they come to fetch her back to the prison house?

No. Or apparently not, anyway. Curling out of the front seat was a woman in her mid-forties, her long greying hair pulled back into a ponytail.

'You found him?' the woman said. 'Thank you so much.'

Even as she delivered her gratitude, however, her face displayed an unmistakeable sign of confusion – made worse when Jess replied, 'He found me.'

'Beg pardon?' The woman approached the stone bench, the stone cross – approached Jess. She wore muddy Wellington boots and second-hand jodhpurs.

'He found me. He's calling the police for me,' Jess said, her voice croaking.

'What's going on here?'

The question set Jess's tears in motion once more, and the new arrival was temporarily lost for words.

'Dad?' she then called into the house.

Peter appeared at the door. 'Hello, Sandra,' he said.

'Were you lost again, Dad?'

'No Oi weren't! Oi were alpen this young'un. She were eld carptive agin her will!'

'Oh Dad…'

'He's telling the truth,' Jess interrupted. 'He got us back here safe and sound – or his dog did, maybe.'

Sandra frowned in the porch light. 'What does he mean you were held captive?' she asked, enunciating each word with care.

And Jess started to cry afresh.

Descent

1.

It took them three days to descend the mountain. Although the journey was far from straightforward, the optimistic air that Atchoo created as they trudged – the songs he sang, the conversations he conducted with himself as he led the expedition – was often sufficient to convince the others that they were making good time and reasonable progress. No one questioned his navigation; whether his skill for orienteering was the result of blind luck, or a lifelong exposure to the stories told in the village, or perhaps even something more spiritual or instinctive, he preceded them down slopes that were blessed with neither paths nor landmarks, chanting and laughing, and only raising his voice from time to time when he noticed someone behind him not sticking to the strict single file on which he had insisted at the outset. When a wind dislodged an acre of snow up into the chilled air, Atchoo paid it very little mind; a homing strategy pushed him onwards... even if it happened to be home that he was leaving behind.

The expedition was seven travellers strong. Atchoo had assumed a senior role in the proceedings before they'd left the village that had served as a base camp, single-handedly rounding up three men who spoke little but who seemed willing enough to top and tail the march and shoulder bags of supplies. Each of these men carried a rifle. And as the journey took them down the side of the mountain – a descent on occasion so looped and slalomed that it was hard to imagine much change in elevation had been made in the previous hour, the only sign that progress had been made, in fact, being a half-degree rise in the temperature, and an improvement in the ease of respiration that could not have been faked by even the most resilient sense of self-delusion – the seven pilgrims plodded on through the waves of snow, silently praying for a plateau that might indicate the beginning of foothills.

For long stretches of the march, Massimo and Bernadette kept close together. They talked. The scooped up snow with mittened hands, and drank it at approximately the same time. (A nurse should know when the body needed water, Massimo figured.) When it was time to fill their bellies, the guides from the village boiled water from snow, using a tiny gas stove and a large copper kettle that one of them kept in the bag on his back. They added fistfuls of desiccated ingredients and made a lumpy, sweet porridge that lacked in rich flavour what it gave out in energy. The mealtimes were solemn affairs, and not even Massimo and Bernadette said much to each other after the second of these, concentrating instead on banishing their hunger pangs and wondering why Connors insisted on walking so close behind Atchoo.

2.

At the close of the first day, although light remained in a curiously bronze sky, the guides assembled the tents in which they would spend the night. As ever, they worked to the accompaniment of very little conversation; for the first time in a while, Massimo blessed this silence and sat down on a rug with his legs out.

Bernadette approached and asked, 'Room for a little one?'

'Sure.' Massimo shuffled over a little to allow her some space.

'Not too far. Share warmth,' Bernadette explained, sitting

down with a pained sigh.

'How are you feeling?'

'Well, I know I've done some exercise, I'll tell you that much,' she answered. 'Christ. Had no idea I was so unfit. We're gonna ache like hell tomorrow.'

Massimo nodded. 'And then we do it all again… Bliss,' he added, his voice wet with a new coat of irony.

'I almost did the London Marathon once, a couple of years ago. Four years? I had it all set up. I was gonna do it for breast cancer research. I thought I'd make a few hundred quid if my colleagues sponsored me. Do you what happened?'

'You didn't do it.'

'I didn't do it. I *couldn't* do it − I couldn't even face the bloody tracksuit! Which I'd bought already, *and* some new train-ers. Couldn't so much as *think* about it.' She paused; she laughed. 'Ended up feeling so guilty I got a loan from the bank and gave it to the cancer charity anyway. Cost me five hundred quid, that particular example of cowardice. Six if you count the clothes and the power-shakes.' She laughed again.

'Well you're making up for it now,' Massimo told her. 'There's nothing cowardly about *this* feat of madness.'

'No… but there's nothing especially dangerous about it ei-ther,' said Bernadette.

'Not yet. But they've got a gun apiece; that's gotta suggest something.'

'True. But why do we need *three* of them?' Bernadette con-tinued. 'Atchoo says nothing much lives up here. There's no veg-etation.'

'Nothing *much* is not the same as nothing at all. I was there, remember? He said snow leopards, birds…'

'And how many of these predators have you seen?'

'…None. Your point being?'

Massimo had spread his rug some distance – close to ten metres – away from where the guides were erecting the tents and Atchoo was constructing the framework for the forthcoming fire. Connors had taken himself off in another direction, again to a distance of approximately ten metres. He had not spread a rug of his own. He lay on a snow bank, staring up at the ship of bronze sky and its cargo of rum barrel clouds.

Bernadette disregarded Massimo's question. Nodding in Connors's general direction, she asked, 'Do you feel you know him well?'

'Connors? Less and less.' Massimo admitted that the change in the man – from the cocksure resident of this new dimension, his feet firmly under the celestial table, to the grumbling, moody prick into which he'd changed since the meeting with Atchoo – had left the atmosphere unsettled. 'And all because of a boy!'

'A boy he thinks he met,' said Bernadette. 'A boy he thinks he saw killed, let's not forget.'

Massimo turned. 'What are you saying? He *imagined* the other boy?'

'It's possible, isn't it?'

'It's *possible*… but what about your dog?'

'What about her?'

Remembering to choose a feminine pronoun out of respect for the dead animal, Massimo answered, 'She was with him.'

Bernadette shrugged. 'So he says. How do we know?'

Massimo waited. For an instant he did not know why he felt such an urge to defend Connors; then he remembered why. It was because he'd employed Connors in the first place that they were all here on this fucking Alp. 'He seemed strong.'

'Exactly. Now he doesn't know how to chew his own food… I exaggerate. But you see what I mean.'

'I'm not sure I do.'

Bernadette leaned over and grabbed a fistful of snow; she stuffed it into her face and mouth with all of the precision that her mittens allowed. 'Hark at *me* telling people how to eat,' she remarked, tittering. 'But who would've thought snow would be yummy?'

Massimo watched the guides for a few seconds. They had finished pounding the frames into the snowy ground; now there were unravelling the skins and hides that would act as carapaces. 'That's two things you've broken off telling me,' he said.

'True. The second one first, then. Bereavement. Believe me… I've seen it do peculiar things to an otherwise rational mind. When my Aunt Imelda lost her husband – my Uncle Piers – she slept with his trilby on the other pillow for over five years. She said it made him visit her in her dreams, like he was right beside her. And she wasn't kidding either; she meant it point blank. Imelda believed in an afterlife, and a place where the two existences could overlap – like mixing paints, she would say. And let's not forget, Connors saw Dorman get his head chopped off by flying glass. You'd expect him to be seeing a bereavement counsellor for two sessions a week for three years. Instead he gets lumbered with *this*.'

Bernadette indicated their surroundings with the sweep of her right hand.

'Maybe he's grieving for Dorman, or for someone else who died on the other side. Who knows? I mean… does he have parents, a partner…?'

Massimo shrugged. 'I couldn't tell you,' he admitted. 'I don't know anything about the private lives of those I employ. I never ask. It's none of my business. And I appreciate it if they never ask me either.'

Bernadette smiled. 'That sounded forceful.'

'I'm *feeling* forceful. Maybe I need some more mush in me

belly.'

'I'm hungry too…' Bernadette paused. 'Would you say that our current situation represents a reason to relax the rules a bit?'

'The rules about what?'

'About colleagues asking you personal questions,' said Bernadette.

'Yeah. Yeah I would say this qualifies.' Massimo looked at her. 'What's on your mind?'

Bernadette waited a few seconds before replying. Then she said, 'Do you feel lonely?'

Exhaling loudly, Massimo answered her as simply and honestly as he could.

'I have never, in all my life, felt lonelier,' he said.

'Me too. Are hugs allowed?'

'Hugs are allowed.'

And awkwardly at first they embraced.

3.

Despite what Bernadette had not-quite-promised, she made no mention of the second matter that she had stopped short of discussing with Massimo, not until the third day of their trek, when they'd descended to the mountain's foothills, their leg muscles tight and strong, their stomachs clenched.

They had just spent one hell of a night together; all of them had shared and suffered a strenuous strain of the collywobbles that had affected each person with a different severity, but which had meant that no one slept well. Out of nowhere − almost as if it had laboured for its own life on a breeze − a germ had found its way into the system (probably via a meal) and the upshot was a series of panicky sprints away from the party, to where one could expel one's poisons either through the mouth or the anus - the bug proved to be quite unfussy on the manner of egress.

Ill it was, then – ill and weak and suffering a crapulent hangover that had nothing to do with alcohol – that the party faced its third day of the descent. It went unsaid that everyone looked like death warmed up. Atchoo had gone so far as to cease singing the gee-up ditties that had once seemed fun but which had grown repetitive and dull. The comparative silence was a godsend to all.

The altitude being lower, breathing conditions had altered for the better; a temperature rise of a few degrees meant that the snow appeared threadbare in places, and the sweat on their brows did not chill so quickly… And yet. And yet, despite these improvements, Bernadette was more anxious than ever. Having got used to her new existence on the mountainside, she feared what she did not know – what she could not guess – about what lay ahead.

Was now the right time to confess her worries to Massimo? she wondered. Since the embrace they had shared, was it Bernadette's imagination or had the man changed a tad? Become ever so slightly more stubborn, more difficult? Shied away from her, perhaps… just a little? No?

He might be embarrassed. Clinging together as they had, only partly for warmth, his erection against her thigh had been unmistakeable; perhaps he regretted his own body's indiscretion; perhaps it concerned him, the belief that Bernadette would have found the experience offensive – or even uncomfortable. But Bernadette felt none of these things. True enough, just for a second there, she had experienced an embarrassment of her own, stoked by the anxiety that Massimo had misinterpreted her request for a cuddle. (Had he though? Was Bernadette being truthful to herself about her own motives?) However, it had only been a passage of seconds before she had silently thanked Massimo's honesty.

If he wanted her in a way that he had yet to voice, it was surely preferable a state of affairs than his *not* wanting her. After all, she was as far from home as he was… and nurses got lonely as well.

None of this, however, meant that Bernadette was ready to confess her fears. By no means was she certain that she could have found the right words anyway: it sounded absurd. The notion that the guides expected attack up ahead − or worse, that they intended to use the visitors as bait to bag a larger wild beast (a vast lizard, perhaps) was demonstrably preposterous…

Wasn't it?

Wasn't it, Bernie?

No. No it wasn't a dumb fear at all; not in the slightest. The guides carried rifles for a reason, and no wildlife had been spotted on their way down the mountain, not even a falcon, a deer or a wolf. Nothing. It was only now, as they trudged through aromatic orange heather (it smelt of fudge) and red gorse, that they were able to spot trios or quartets of bats circling, their appearance made all the more wonderful by the brightness of the morning.

'How are you feeling?' Massimo called, five or six metres to Bernadette's left.

'Warmer,' she answered.

'That's good.'

'And like I've eaten four plates of mutton *phal*.'

Massimo chuckled. 'That's not so good.'

'No.'

'Sphincter that glows in the dark.'

'Something like that.'

'Red raw, I am.'

'Yeah all right, Mass, I don't need the details.'

'You're a nurse!'

4.

Midway through the fifth day away from the village, the expedition became aware of the sound of voices, up ahead.

'Signs of life!' Connors announced – the first utterance he'd made in twenty-four hours.

The voices were shouts, guttural and low-pitched; it sounded like cheering. A game of sports? An execution?

The guides spoke among themselves as the party trudged on through patches of snow on the hardpacked pink-and-saffron earth. They passed buildings shaped like domes, made of the same earth, which were thought to be homes; and as the voices grew louder, the trekkers' mood lifted.

A crowd had gathered around a rectilinear piece of land about twenty metres by ten. At either end of this pitch stood a basketball stanchion; and two teams of seven players apiece were engaged in what looked like a game of netball. One team was playing naked; the players were covered in fur from head to foot, and alternated between running on two feet and scampering on all fours. Their chests were protuberant but muscular; no penises were in sight, so the team was possibly female. The other team was dressed in saris made of mirrors; their gender was impossible to determine – they wore mirrors on their faces and heads so that only the three eyes in their foreheads could be seen.

It was not a netball that passed from hand to hand, however. It was a human head.

An Absence of Light

1.

Eastlight woke up in a state of high agitation. He did not know where he was; all he was aware of was pain in both his legs, the sense of a retreating hangover… and the dark physical confines of where he'd been placed. When he tried to stretch out his arms, he understood that there was no space for them to stretch *to*. Instead, his fingers touched the walls of his upright coffin – walls cold and damp – and he remembered the attack that Don Bridges had served him, comprehending in an instant that Don must have shoved him into the hole in the kitchen floor. His heart fluttered. He wiped sweat from his unseeing eyes and tried to dry his hand on a trouser leg.

There were no trousers. Don must have stripped him. There were no boxers either; as Eastlight conducted a touch-search of his own body, he concluded a mental tally. He was not wearing socks; he wore nothing on his upper body. Nothing at all.

He'd been left in a hole completely naked. He'd freeze!

Jesus Christ.

His mind mouthed the words slowly, as if to someone who spoke a different language.

I'll starve to death. He's trying to kill me…

With this realisation planted, Eastlight reached up with both arms and pushed at the underside of the trapdoor. The wood was chilly and dry; it was strong. The trapdoor did not move (had Don placed something heavy on top of it?) and only when his chest muscles burned did Eastlight give up, exhausted and panicky, the pains in his legs excited by the exertion.

But I'm standing, he thought. I'm not crippled... He didn't finish my legs.

It was something: a ray of light in Eastlight's darkness. Or if not a ray, at least a bursting match-head.

Trying to remember what he'd seen while Don had assaulted him with the shovel, Eastlight pushed up against the trapdoor again.

He had seen the trapdoor open, leaning back against its hinges. He had wondered what the hell it was. Then Don had swung his weapon once more...

Locked?

Was the trapdoor locked and bolted; maybe padlocked? How could Eastlight assume he'd ever have enough strength to break a metal lock? But if there was something heavy on the latch, and no locks present, then perhaps with determination... perhaps.

Eastlight pushed one more time, using every grain of power at his disposal. He could not see anything in the darkness, but feel? Oh yes: he could feel plenty. Rivulets of perspiration, for example, rolling down his rotund belly; swimming over the slabs of fat. And something more alarming as well: something trickling between his buttocks. It felt like semen.

He stopped pushing. The discomfort in his anus had been overwhelmed by the agony raging through his shins and thighs. With a deft middle finger he explored the area in question. He'd had sex with his attacker −

No, Charlie. Not 'sex with' your attacker.

You've been raped, mate. The evidence is clear. He bummed you one, Charlie.

Now how does that feel? He knocked you unconscious and then he stripped you. Then he took out his withered old root and he –

Eastlight snarled as loud as his lungs would let him. He punched at the trapdoor, an action that served only to bruise and graze his knuckles. Having shouted Don's name four times (and on receiving no answer), he snarled in frustration once more… but the sound decayed into a whimper – something petulant and forlorn – and he understood, when he tried to sit down, how he'd come to be unconscious but upright in the first place: there was simply no room to sit cross-legged, let alone on his arse with his legs stretched out. His body was a big one; it filled and completed the hole that Don had prepared as surely as earth or sand would have done.

He was trapped.

Tears followed. In his blindness, Eastlight moved his hands in front of his eyes, convinced that he could see them.

I'm not blind, I'm not – and as soon as he could he began pleading with Don from the grave.

'I'm sorry, Don; I'm sorry I called you Donald Duck,' he whimpered. And he carried on calling; he remonstrated and he threatened. He pushed at the trapdoor. He cried again – bitterly – and swore vengeance and begged for water. He promised prison for the old man… and then he learned two things simultaneously, there in his private hell.

The first was that Don was not listening. Perhaps he was not even present.

The second was that he had no chance of punching his way free of his box.

He would have to dig.

2.

Eastlight spent a length of time that he couldn't measure trying to fork his increasingly cold fingers into the compacted earth that was the side of the hole directly ahead of him. During this time the only satisfaction he earned was the feeling of crumbs of mud rolling over his knuckles as his efforts made some minimal difference. It was slow going; but what choice did he have? If he could dig horizontally for a while, perhaps he could generate a kind of cave-in, and if he could make the earth fall in, perhaps he could stretch his arm's length out towards the surface.

Suddenly he stopped digging. Like a mudfall itself, a set of realisations tumbled through his mind; he swore loudly – at himself this time – because he had been so slow on the uptake. And although he could blame the concussion he had received for his mental sloth, Eastlight was not sure this was the case. For one thing, it was not his head that hurt: if Don had brained him with the shovel, it was a wound that had healed swiftly... or else he had been here a lot longer than he'd first imagined. So what then? Had it been the pain caused by the strikes to his legs that had made him black out? Embarrassing, if so; but it was not of primary importance (although Eastlight continued to explore his scalp for bumps and abrasions while the mudslide moved into his consciousness).

He could breathe.

It was the first time that he'd considered this fact, and it arrived like a spiritual revelation.

He could *breathe*.

Which meant that air was entering the hole, from somewhere. But where else could it be coming from?

Eastlight stood on tiptoes, the better to get a sniff of what he was more sure than ever was the trapdoor above him. Due to the pains in his legs, however, he could not hold the ballerina's

pose for more than a few seconds, and the results were inconclu-
sive. Had he or hadn't he smelt fresh air from a gap at the trapdoor's edge? The only thing he knew for certain was that looking
straight up in the darkness had provided him with a neck strain
and a faint sense of vertigo.

'Again, then,' he muttered. This time he eschewed the option of tiptoes; he stared up at his unnatural sky and breathed
deep.

Why hadn't he noticed it before? Trickles of pure air were
coming in, to dilute the damp clammy whiff that escaped from
the mud. Which meant what? There must be a gap (or two)
around the trapdoor's edges! My God! thought Eastlight, and he
knew at once the true definition of hope. The *gaps* were where he
had to dig with his fingers, regardless of how uncomfortable the
exercise would be. And there was no time like the present, was
there? Surely the fact that no light could creep through the gaps
suggested that no light was on in the kitchen.

It was time to dig.

So deciding, Eastlight shuffled his bulk slightly in the confines… and his bare left foot touched something solid – something that felt different from earth or mud. It could be metal, it
could be plastic; he wasn't certain.

He froze.

Then the object below his left foot started to ring.

3.

Too stunned to move for a few seconds, Eastlight absorbed
the information as if through the riddling filter of a dream. The
scant illumination peeking up from beneath his swollen knees;
the persistence of the familiar ring tone… *It's my mobile*, the prisoner concluded; and he set to attempting to answer it before it

rang off.

Easier thought than achieved! Eastlight was forced to squat, the hole's back wall rubbing cold slimy mud along his spine... but there was not enough room to manoeuvre, and the agony in his legs was atrocious. He could not get low enough to reach the phone.

It rang off.

Insisting '*No*' in a gasping voice, Eastlight imagined gravity assuming a fifty-fifty share of the responsibility, but gravity was impotent here in the hole. Not even gravity could suck a tennis ball through a car exhaust pipe; the effort would be Eastlight's alone. And he couldn't do it. He couldn't...

Yes he could.

His bottom slid another few centimetres down the muddy shaft – and his legs, now a quarter bent, complained loudly. Darkness churned in front of his eyes; exaggeratedly he blinked and blinked again, in an effort to ward off unconsciousness. If he blacked out in this position, his legs might seize and he might never stand up again.

Is that right? And how exactly do you plan to stand up again anyway, blackout or no blackout?

One problem at a time, Eastlight told himself, now puffing like a hillside locomotive.

Reach!

His bottom slipped down by another couple of centimetres, and Eastlight felt the pain of some skin being scraped off his tailbone.

Reach, you fat cunt!

Eastlight reached – his legs bent double, pain in shimmering waves – and the mobile phone wriggled away from his touch.

'No...' he breathed. 'Come here, darling – come to me...'

And with a final stretch, he was able to fidget the handset

into his left palm. He squeezed it tight; he loved it. Right at this very moment – almost deaf to the din of pain – the supermarket-bought mobile, nothing flash in the outside world, was probably the most precious thing that Eastlight had ever owned.

Then it rang again.

4.

'When are you gonna let me out?' Eastlight asked as calmly as he could.

'I'm not,' Don answered.

'You can't leave me in here, Donald. I'll freeze to death. I'll starve.'

'That you will, Mr Eastlight. I'll be with you every step of the way – if step is the right word.'

'…What do you mean?'

'We'll be in regular telephone contact,' Don told him. 'The first favour technology's ever done me, Mr Eastlight. I'm going to listen to you die. You can call me anytime.'

And he ended the call.

5.

Having listened to the disconnect tone and the silence that followed for nearly a minute, Eastlight spent another minute in a successful effort to stand upright. Then he stirred himself into action. He had his phone: that was more than he'd thought he had a few minutes earlier. It was a start… He called Massimo but got no answer. Then he called Vig. It rang and rang… and then Dorota's voice slurred sleepily into his ear.

'It's Charlie, Dorota,' Eastlight said loudly but not quickly – he did not want to fluff his chance by acting panicked. 'I think

I'm in Don's hut.'

'You think you're *what?*'

'I've been imprisoned. He intends to starve me to death.'

'Charlie. Are you drunk?'

'I think I am; but this is serious, Dorota. I'm naked and I'm in a hole – an actual hole. I think it's the one in his kitchen.'

'You're naked?'

'Yes... I need you to –'

'He says he's naked,' Dorota told Vig. 'In Don's trap.'

Vig said something that Eastlight couldn't hear.

'What was that?' Eastlight asked, a little sharply. What did they need to take him seriously?

'Vig wants to know where Don is,' said Dorota.

'Well, how the fuck should *I* know? I'm in a fucking *hole*. I'm shivering. And so I'm asking you if you'd kindly get out of bed and come and let me out!'

'Okay okay, Charlie, Vig's pulling on his trousers. We'll be there in ten minutes.'

'*Hurry*.'

Eastlight breathed with a sudden and unexpected difficulty. It took him a moment to realise that this was excitement. It made him shake. No longer did it matter that his phone's display showed a measly two bars of existing battery - his rescuers would be here in a trice.

6.

'This is madness,' said Dorota; 'absolute bloody madness.'

Although Vig wanted to tell her to shut up, he kept his lips sealed as they strode across the gravel driveway and onto the path that led into the woods.

'I want him out, Vig. Tonight. I'm serious.'

'Let's see what's going on,' Vig replied, 'before we make any rash decisions.'

'You think he'd *lie?*'

'I don't know, Dorota. All I know is, I wish I'd never won that bloody prize. It's been nothing but a hindrance.'

'Oh yeah. Because you loved teaching brats to speak German, didn't you? It wasn't *you* cursing about all the books you have to mark.'

'There are other jobs in the world, Dorota.' Vig was trying to keep his cool.

They had entered the woods and the temperature had plummeted.

By the time they arrived at Don's cabin, the angry silence that they'd created hung around their throats like a noose. And it throbbed like a headache.

Wasting no time whatsoever, Dorota rapped on the door. She tapped her foot impatiently; a clutch of desiccated leaves crackled under her heel as it was crushed.

She knocked again.

'Open up, Don!' she shouted.

'He's probably asleep,' Vig mentioned.

'Only the guilty could sleep tonight.'

She had a point, Vig acknowledged: if Don was sleeping, after the grilling he'd been given… then why? Then how?

A murmur of movement from within. A shuffle. A voice.

'I'm coming, I'm coming.'

Voice corroded by drink – and possibly slumber. Say they'd raised the old guy from his pit of dreams… Vig felt a buzz of guilt. If only he could hear a baby's cries, something to verify the claims…

Don opened the door. Dressed in a vest and white long-johns, he held a fizzing snout in his right hand, so he mustn't have been asleep, but his eyes were perimetered red – brandy and enforced wakefulness.

'What is it, boss?' he asked, lifting the burn to his chapped lips.

Dorota jumped in.

'We want to see your hole,' she said.

Don smiled around his cigarette and leaked smoke. 'Hadn't you better buy me dinner first,' he said.

'Don't be sly, Don,' Vig told him. 'Is Charlie here?'

'I thought he was with you.'

'Why?' Dorota's tone was harsh.

'Because his car is in the drive. But come in if it helps. I've had enough of this.'

Don stepped away from the door and waved them in.

'Be quick though, if you would. It's cold as a dead tramp's cock.'

Vig and Dorota stepped in; the smell of roasted chicken remained on the air. The bird had been half-devoured; evidently Don had suffered an attack of the munchies. On the coffee table near his comfy chair were the remains of his midnight snack: chicken skin and bread crusts, ashy smidges of a powerful fix of pepper.

'The hole's empty,' Don told them as he closed the door.

In the kitchen the trapdoor was still open. Vig and Dorota stood over the hole.

It was empty.

7.

Breathe, breathe…

Vig was coiled like a bastard cobra. He could not remember being so furious since two boys had a fist-fight during one of his classes. The phone rang.

Pick it up, wanker, he thought.

'Where the hell are you?' Eastlight demanded into his ear.

'No. Where the hell are *you*?'

'I told you: in Donald Duck's kitchen.'

'No you're not, Charlie. We've just been there. And if you're in my house somewhere, I'm not amused.'

'I'm not… in your house,' Eastlight replied.

'Then where are you?'

'I'm in a hole; a pit.'

'Where?' Vig asked.

'I *don't fucking know.* I thought − you *went* there?'

'The hole's empty, Charlie.'

Eastlight swore. 'Where's he put me, Vig? I'm not joking.'

'I have no idea… Are you sure you're…'

'In a hole?' Eastlight bellowed. 'No, I'm in the fucking Maldives!'

'There's no need, Charlie,' Vig answered weakly.

'No need? *No need?*' Eastlight paused. '*Find me, Vig,*' he said with menace.

'Call the police.'

'Yeah right.'

'They can trace the call. Why not?'

'Yeah right. Just find me.'

And he ended the call.

8.

'Do you know what you've done, Mr Eastlight?' said Don. 'You've just bought yourself a whole day of hunger. I was of a mind to feed you tomorrow morning when I fed the birds. Now I'm not so sure.'

'Where am I, Don?'

'You're in the woods. Where do you think? You imagine I'd

be so backward-thinking as to hide you in me own *home?* You're having a laugh, you must be.' Don broke into a chuckle; it sounded but a shade shy of malicious. 'But I don't suppose a day without food will hurt a fat bugger like you.'

'I'm diabetic. I'll have a seizure.'

'Ah! A shame that'll be,' Don answered. 'Spoil a man's fun, would you.'

Eastlight attempted a different tack. 'I only have a little bit of battery left on my phone,' he said. 'What'll you do when I'm incommunicado?'

'I suggest you turn it off, in that case. I'm not going out again. There's a nip in the air.'

9.

Don knew that it was coming to an end; it had to be. He had almost been found out. He had taken a prisoner, and there was only one way that *that* could finish up. And that way was disastrously. So it was coming to an end; it had to be. And not before time.

He rolled and lit a cigarette. What doesn't kill you makes you stronger, he thought; the chuckle he offered to the room was full of bile – it rattled in his ribcage. As a sixty-a-day man for the last sixty years, the prognosis from his doctor had come as no surprise whatever. He smoked his roll-up with guilt-free relish: the damage to his body had already been done.

And his suicide plan was ready. In fact, it had been ready for months. Free the birds – and then take himself deep into the woods, one last time.

Eastlight would never be found.

GUIDED TOUR OF THE ATROCITIES

1.

Even now – now that he was an older man, playing dangerous games of his own devising – Benny thought back on the excitement-influenza of the stands, the memories of chilled fingers and twitching furled twenties. And he wanted that fire in his bones. He wanted that life. Though decades had passed since he'd last stood among the roaring crowds, wishing home a filly in the two-fifteen at Towcester, it was like an old coat in his closet. Rare was the day that he didn't miss the thunder of voices and hooves, or the hare out of the trap, the confetti of torn-up ticket stubs. Rare was the day that he wouldn't go back there: back into the past, where a Saturday was more than the simple enjoyment of a flutter, it was also the company of gamblers that had made it all worthwhile. The shuttle between elation and despair; the sickening lurch in the stomach – that final wasted fifty of the day, the last knockings – when the awareness of cornflakes till payday bit hard. Ah yes! how he missed it like a favourite holiday, a childhood pet…

And if gambling was an old coat in his closet, it was good to put it on once in a while.

Now relax…

Having returned home at past three in the morning, Benny was tired and wired at the same time; he was ordering himself to *relax*… Relax, you'll give yourself a heart attack, Benny. Have a drink. Have a snooze… And he stood in his library, a vodka in his fist, waiting for his books to calm him down, as they sometimes would. But no, it wasn't going to happen, he knew. This evening and this morning – oh, what a buzz! – had been a little like the old days; the rambling, gambling old days, in the sense that he'd placed a couple of small bets and he'd won big.

Yes. Recently, Benny had won big, thanks to Maggie.

2.

She hadn't minded any of the deception up to now, nor the thinly-veiled disguises, the apparitions, the sleights-of-hand, some of it had even been fun. Most of it, in fact. In Maggie's opinion, Yasser had become a lovely puppet, obedient, erotic and lithe; so no, it would not be fair to say that she lost sleep contemplating how she'd used him. Maggie hadn't minded any of that at all…

However. She really *had* minded blasting Yasser in the face with reptile venom anaesthetic. She had not enjoyed that bit one iota. Not even letting him have his way earlier in the evening – allowing him briefly to become the monster that she believed existed 'neath his skin – had worked as a way of forewarning herself about the guilt that was sure to follow. She'd convinced herself, partly (how? she now wondered) that if Yasser was given the opportunity to slap her around a little, and of course to get his penis wet, then he wouldn't mind it quite so much when he had to face the next act of Maggie's betrayal.

She'd remained fully dressed, and now she stood up and adjusted her clothing. 'I'd like to ask you a favour,' she said.

'Me too. Turn the light off on your way out.'

'I will. Don't hurt him. That's the favour I'm asking.' Maggie wondered if she would also ask another. She contemplated enquiring if he'd mind if she used his *en suite*. There was bound to be some mouthwash or some toothpaste in there... but she'd never entered his *en suite* before. She should ask his permission first.

'...Who?'

'Yasser. You know who.'

Lying naked on top of his duvet, Benny frowned. 'Have I ever hurt anyone?' he asked – somewhat disingenuously, in Maggie's opinion. An affectionate smile brightened his features. Nostalgia? Reminiscence? Unselfconsciously, no longer looking in Maggie's direction, he began to brush his scrotum with his fingertips.

'You hurt *me*.'

Maggie was now by the door. Before she knew what she had done, she had smacked her lips together, the better to generate some saliva with which to refresh her tastebuds in the absence of anything minty. Her breath was crowded with the remains of stale drink; with the taste of burning petrol, the flavour of stagnant moisture from the Edlesborough house's waterlogged air... and now with Benny's own most recent contribution to her mouth. No. There was no doubt about it. Her breath was rank, and it was heartbreakingly so. Maggie had long since got used to the taste of Benny's semen. But she'd been shocked by his penis tasting of another woman's secretions.

'You're special,' Benny answered. 'Of course I won't hurt him, girl. Not interested in that game no more.'

Maggie waited for the unspoken clause, to be added to this blatant lie, but it didn't arrive. If she couldn't find mouthwash or toothpaste, a coffee would make do.

'Thanks,' she admitted finally. Apparently, Benny had nothing more to say. His eyelids had descended.

'The light. On your way out,' he muttered, his hand resting on his quickly drying penis.

3.

While Benny slid the greased chute down into an all-but untroubled sleep, Maggie took her time choosing the right room in which she'd spend the remainder of her darkness (she had never been one for resting in the daylight). In the end she settled for a bedroom on the third floor. It was tastefully decorated, old-fashioned and charming. None of this, however, Maggie noted. For one thing, she had slept in the room before – during one of those nights when she was certain that Yasser would not come knocking – and for a second thing, she was weary to her bones.

Fully clothed, Maggie collapsed onto the delicious double bed. She did not turn out the bedside lamp; the illumination was murky and spot-on. Surely sleep would follow like a dream.

It might have… if she hadn't thought of Yasser, again.

She sat up. She felt dirty. Spastically her fingers twitched, striking non-existent matches until she told them to stop. What to do? The running of a hot bath might wake Benny, so that was out. And besides, there was only one real choice.

Experiencing a resurgence of her desire to see Yasser (to see, to explain and even to confess), Maggie slipped from the bedroom and crept down stairways in the quiet dark. The house was familiar. She knew the groans of its old bones and the creaking secrets of its pressure points, which she largely remembered to avoid, stepping with a dancer's finesse until she'd reached the ground floor.

Just as Maggie was wondering what she'd say if she encountered any of the help on her travels, she was given the opportunity to find out. Up ahead, six or seven doors down on the right, a figure climbed into the corridor's murk and closed a door firmly behind her. It was Eva. Maggie had known her for some months, or at least been aware of her. (Eva was not the type of girl, Maggie thought, that one ever *knew*.) 'Hi, Eva!'

The other woman did not return the greeting. 'You're up early,' she said instead.

'I haven't been to bed. I can't sleep.'

'I have some horse anaesthetic in my quarters…' Eva offered, stepping in Maggie's direction.

'I'll pass. Thanks… I was hoping to see Yasser. Will that be okay?'

Eva shrugged. 'It's not *my* house. You can see who you want, as long as Benny doesn't mind.'

'He won't mind.' Maggie pointed at Eva's right hip. 'Can I borrow that?'

Eva's smile was enigmatic. 'Ever fired a pistol before?' she wanted to know.

'A shotgun. Never a pistol.'

'They're chalk and cheese… but seeing as you and Benny are as thick as thieves, how about this? You tell me why you want it and I'll say no but accompany you, if it's protection you're after.'

'What else would it be?' Maggie replied, her voice harsh.

Eva shrugged again. 'You sound fond of this Yasser.'

'So?'

'So maybe you'd like to put him out of his misery.' Eva turned on her heels and walked back the way she'd come.

Maggie followed. Through her mind galloped murderous images; in one she shot Yasser in his pretty little mouth; in another she disposed of Shyleen so that Yasser would have no choices to make in the future. Maggie it would be, all the way.

Beyond the door was the flight of stairs down to the basement. At the bottom of the stairs, another door. Eva placed her left thumb against the panel that was set at her shoulder height, and the electronic eye decoded the whorls in her print. The door buzzed; a lock clunked.

Eva walked into the vivaria.

4.

As usual, it was the smell that first alarmed Maggie – far more so than the thought of what she knew that the interlocking rooms contained – and her nostrils flared and worried as she followed behind Eva.

The basement stank of sleep. Stank of patients and patience and sickness. Part hospital ward, part reptile house at the zoo, the air seemed mouldy and in need of a set of open windows.

From floor to low ceiling, every piece of wall space was occupied by metal shelving units; on every shelf was a glass tank containing reptiles and the incandescent bulbs that kept the creatures and their habitats at the appropriate sauna temperatures. The bulbs burned brightly; they emitted enough light for Eva not to need to flick on the wall switches.

Machinery hummed; and although it was not cold in the basement, Maggie shivered. The sound of her footfalls, and those of her guide, relayed back and forth between the stone floor and the glass fronts of tanks. As if aware of the presence of humans, the occupant of one especially large tank – a yellow adder – uncurled itself swiftly and butted the front of its prison.

Despite everything that Maggie had seen (or done), snakes continued to give her the creeps. She didn't much like lizards either, but it was snakes that got her the worst - their lazy movements, their cruel eyes… But no more than she could block her nostrils from the scent could she hold her eyelids shut against the sight; the best that she could manage was to hold her gaze straight ahead – at Eva's shoulders – as the two of them moved through the chambers, and to hope that nothing had mastered the art of escapology.

The notion of stepping on something by accident was a horror; it made her shiver once more, and her mouth tasted suddenly of sick and soot.

Here beneath the house, there were no more doors between rooms and chambers; if you had passed the security test at the first door (the recognition of your thumbprint), there was nothing denied. Doorways had been stripped of their doors and their metal fittings; the warren that this had left behind, however, did not feel welcoming to Maggie. It felt threatening. And as they moved from one monk's cell to the next, each one stuffed with more tanks of reptiles, not to mention the crickets, bugs and crawlies on which the reptiles would feed, Maggie longed for the occasional closed door, at which she could have tested her courage – with the intake of a vomit-and-smoke-flavoured breath, a measurement of the tingling in her arms. In the absence of any obstruction, her ride through the vivaria was wild; it felt too fast... even though it was precisely what Maggie had wanted (but dared not hope for - a guided tour of the atrocities. Regardless of the fact that she would have ventured down here anyway (her own thumbprint was known by the system, and she would have marshalled the bravery somehow), Maggie far preferred the assistance of her chaperone. (That the chaperone in question was a hard-nosed bitch, with a pistol erect on her waist, didn't hurt!) But what was the other woman's *hurry?* Slow down! You'll give us both heart attacks!

Maybe Eva had been about to complete her shift, Maggie realised; maybe she'd been on her way to the Land of Nod. Maybe. A show of gratitude, in either case, would surely not go amiss: keep her sweet. 'I'd like to say thanks,' Maggie began – but Eva cut her short.

'Do you know the one they call Connors?' she asked over her shoulder. Her foot hit a sensor and a light was triggered into life in the next part of the catacombs. (This would happen from now on – lights popping awake – and in some places the jogged sensors activated a ceiling fan or an extraction pump.)

'Only by name. Benny's mentioned him.'

'He was telling a story earlier on about his missing brother – when they were kids… Moments like that that I realise what a wretched thing it is we do.'

Maggie thought about contradicting the accusation, but she said instead, 'Agreed.' For it *was* wretched. She *knew* that it was wretched. But she also knew that the wretched could be addictive. And furthermore, she knew that she was hopelessly addicted to suffering (that of others and her own), every bit as much as Benny was.

By now the two women were deep underground, and surely beyond the limitations of the house's walls. The maze of interlocking rooms – some large, some no bigger than a broom cupboard – went on and on and on; and not for the first time, Maggie wondered how long this subterranean workspace – part laboratory, part prison, part mental asylum – had taken to build. And who would Benny have paid to construct it all in the first place.

When she saw the first of Benny's human prisoners over Eva's shoulders, Maggie felt clammy all over. And not only because it was so hot this far from the door. Maggie stopped in front of one of the dozens of four-foot high fans that blew the warm air around this part of the dungeon. She hadn't realised how much her back had perspired; the fan glued her top to her skin.

A few steps ahead, Eva also stopped walking. Having turned to evaluate the hold-up, she followed Maggie's line of vision.

The prisoner was in the nude on his metal cot. At some point he had thrashed his blankets to the mud floor, but for now he was still, albeit with an eyes-wide-open look of horror on his features, his mouth similarly agape, revealing a bowl of gold fillings – like someone who had been photographed mid-scream. Indeed, the only thing that contradicted the horror of which the man appeared to dream was the unenlargeable erection he sported.

'Big soldier, ain't he?' Eva asked, chuckling.

Although Maggie had never seen a penis quite like it in terms of scale, her first thought was of Benny. She wondered if he got excited when he saw his prisoners getting hard-ons in their sleep.

'What's his name?'

'Kuba. He's Polish – last seen walking from farm to farm, offering to pick strawberries and potatoes for minimum wage.' Eva sounded confident; she also sounded flirtatious (to Maggie), as if she was on the brink of divulging a brand new joke. 'Sometimes he talks in the mother tongue.' She shrugged. 'I'm not *encouraged* to talk to our residents, but Benny has never exactly forbidden it either. It's good to be reminded of how much vocabulary you've forgotten in your second language.'

Although Maggie had not come here to listen to anyone's war stories (not even Yasser's), she felt that she might learn something from Eva; but neither the time nor the place seemed appropriate. Something about Maggie's demeanour must have said that she was impatient to proceed. Eva's features tautened, all good nature frittered away. Without checking to see if Maggie was behind her, she walked on.

Lights winked on ahead of them as they approached Yasser.

The Village Idiots

1.

Needless to say, the explorers' arrival had not gone unnoticed. Though the game underway kept hold of the attention of many, there were some who turned to view and size up the new arrivals, their expressions (if they could be read at all) mixing wonderment with candid disgust.

Bernadette (for one) did not enjoy being the object of such open evaluation. Usually it was she who did the evaluating: she assessed a head wound, the result of a sharp instrument trauma; she broke bad news and read faces. It had been a while since the tables had been turned in this way, and she said:

'Guess they don't get many tourists around here.'

The comment had not been meant as a joke – not exactly – but Massimo smiled good-naturedly, and was about to say something like: *I'm not surprised, if that's how they treat them* – when Connors pipped him to the post and spoke first.

'That's Dorman's head,' he said clearly.

The game was brought to a rousing finale a few minutes later, when a shortarse pug on the three-eyed players' side performed a turnaround jump shot of which a basketball professional would be proud. Dorman's battered face did not touch the hoop: the head described a perfect arc, and with a gentle sound it fell through the ragged netting and was caught by one of the opposition's defensive line.

Whoops and applause. A long whistle.

2.

As Bernadette and Massimo embarked on a round of hand-shakes, encouraging smiles and what they hoped were friendly nods (even the occasional curtsey), the better to let the crowd know of their amiable intentions, Connors eschewed all formalities and strode out into the middle of the makeshift basketball court, and sat down. The sit did not appear voluntary: it was more like a slump and a collapse; and as soon as he was established on his backside, he leaned forward slightly and cupped his bearded chin in both hands, his elbows on his knees. No portrait painter could have fashioned a more convincing portrayal of despondency or melancholy.

What to do?

Bernadette and Massimo exchanged glances, their expressions flickering from warmth to worry and back again. Atchoo and the guides were several metres away, presumably telling the story of their travails. For the moment, it was impossible to ask the boy to go over and sit with Connors. Any attempts to offer consolation to Connors were firmly the responsibility of Bernadette and Massimo... and Bernadette was not *absolutely* convinced that Massimo would know what to do either. She was not sure that the two men got along.

No.

Bernadette would do this on her own – she would have to. Many had been the friends and relatives that she'd spoken to and held, following the death of a loved one – an unsuccessful operation, perhaps. Bad news was a language she spoke. Not fluently, granted; but competently.

Making international gestures of abject apology, Bernadette moved through and away from the crowd that was swiftly disbanding. She crossed over to the hunched potato sack that Connors had become. Wordlessly she sat nearby him, maintaining a respectful distance. He noted her presence, then resumed an inspection of his palm.

'First sign of madness, you know,' said Bernadette.

Connors regarded her again.

'Looking for hair,' she explained.

She'd intended it as a joke but it was not taken as one.

'I'm already mad,' Connors told her.

'There is absolutely no way I can tell you to snap out of it.'

'Good.'

'Not after you've seen your friend's head used as a netball,' said Bernadette.

Connors was shaking his head. 'He was no friend,' he answered quietly. 'I hardly knew him more than three hours or so. And it wasn't like I didn't know he was *dead*. I saw it happen.'

'True. But a team sport's a different thing,' Bernadette attempted to rationalise. 'Surely.'

'His *whole* head, you'll notice. I didn't imagine that, did I?'

'You didn't. So you're not mad.'

'I think I am – but not for that. Cuz I saw the cunt's head get cut in half. I fucking *saw* it. The glass chopped it in two in the back garden, right?'

'…Yeah.'

'So how comes his *whole* head's here?' Connors asked. 'That doesn't make a lick of sense, does it? Half of it was left on the grass.'

'I guess so,' said Bernadette.

'I saw it!'

'I don't doubt you.'

Connors paused. 'Really?'

'Yes, really, Chris. The question is, what does it mean?'

'Or what do *we* mean?' Connors replied.

'Sorry? Mean to who?'

'Exactly! Mean to who!' His eyes lit up with a flare of excitement. 'Who's controlling us – right now? Have you thought of that? I think back to when we were in the village…' He might have been talking to himself or to a counsellor; he wasn't talking to Bernadette. 'Very briefly – just for a few days there – I felt like I was on top of the world. Like I got to the end of something… I should've known better.' Now he looked at Bernadette once more: back in the real world. His voice soft he said, 'I'm a puppet. We all are.'

Connors paused.

'But I know one thing,' he added. 'Whoever's in charge here, it's someone with a small imagination for this stuff. He hasn't thought it all through. It's *not consistent.*'

3.

The group's arrival was destined to be a transient pleasure. No more than an hour had passed since the culmination of the basketball game, and already Connors, Massimo and Bernadette were no more appealing than yesterday's news. Did this mean it was over? That their struggle down the mountain had led only to this? This apathy, this lassitude…

'It can't be the end,' Massimo reflected in a murmur, thereby spoiling a long (frightened) silence. But it felt like the end of *something*. There was no more fuel in the tank.

During the preceding forty minutes, a few matters of note had occurred.

First they'd been offered food, at a price. Any sense of goodwill or charity that they might have expected from the villagers as the result of their achievements had evidently been a non-starter from the off. They were not all-conquering heroes; in the eyes of this encampment, much to the singeing of their individual senses of pride, they were jack shit. They were nothing. A source of momentary curiosity, at best. And so they'd politely declined the sale; a little of the supplies remained. Their refusal to buy had been seen as an act of defiance.

It was not a stance shared by Atchoo and the guides. They'd been ushered into what looked for all the world like a mechanic's garage, complete with a rattling pull-down metal front door. From this building the aroma of meat and spices had crept out on the wind and crept up on their senses; it had smelled like an Indian restaurant, and some of the perfume lingered in the air. The sounds of revelry had been a further insult.

When Atchoo had emerged from the garage, he'd boasted a broad, satisfied grin, and a gravy moustache that Bernadette had pointed out for him to wipe away. The smile had intensified. 'I'm saving that bit for later,' the boy had said.

Connors had become angry at the boy's remark – not only because of its glibness, but also because it was something that he himself had used to say to his own mother, when he was a boy. To Connors, the remark was a reminder of home – yet another reminder of home – and of the miles that separated there from here. He had swapped being treated like a king for being treated like a cunt. And he wanted to know why.

'I want to speak to who's running the show,' Connors had instructed the boy.

Connors, Massimo and Bernadette were sitting on a blue rock, near a deep-red pond. On the water's surface swam a coterie of pink creatures that were made not of flesh and feathers but of concentrated overlaps of air. They swam upside-down, their splayed feet above the water (if it *was* water) and pedalling madly, their tubby torsos underneath, breathing like fish. The only time that their spectators saw their bodies was when they inverted in order to snap at some golfball-sized flying insects. Massimo loved them.

'I could watch them all day,' he announced.

'I wonder what time it gets dark,' said Bernadette, idly.

'I'm not going anywhere until I've met the head honcho,' said Connors.

Bernadette was quick off the mark. 'I wasn't suggesting we go anywhere – I was just.'

'At what point did we understand – together – that where Atchoo led us was going to be significant?' Connors wondered aloud.

No one replied. 'We did, though, didn't we? Don't tell me it was only me,' Connors persisted.

Massimo shook his head.

'It wasn't just you,' said Bernadette. 'But I don't remember why we thought *anything*.' She puffed out air. 'Actually I'm doubting my memory in general.'

'Aren't we all?' Massimo muttered. 'Christ I'm hungry.'

'I wonder if you really are,' Connors told him.

'Am what? Hungry?'

Connors shrugged. 'Hungry. *Here.* You choose. We're being played for cunts, Mass. Someone's controlling the whole fucking shebang. You mark mine.'

Circles.

Circles of conversation. The same topic, loop after loop.

'I've got a hunch.' Connors stood up and stretched the muscles in his shoulderblades. 'With enough concentration we could probably change the weather.'

'I doubt that,' said Massimo.

'What do you mean?' asked Bernadette.

'We are sharing something. And we're being controlled.'

'You've already said that a few times,' Massimo reminded him.

'Well exactly. We're not even capable of original thought!' Connors waited; he leaned forward, collecting his thoughts. 'When I first arrived here – on the land, I mean – I was warned about a tribe of cannibals that lived in the hills, right? Well I think – I *think* – these guys here are the sort I was being warned about... Do you feel safe here, Bernadette?'

'Kind of.'

'Me too. I feel *drowsy*. Why do you think that is? I mean, apart from the big walk we did. What if *these* cunts are the types I was supposed to stay away from in the first place? Might be something in the air, relaxing our minds. The truth is, I feel suspicious of feeling so comfortable, if that makes any sense whatsoever. So I'm all for moving on. Shake the cobwebs from between me ears, because I reckon...' Connors sat up sharply; a joint snapped. 'I reckon I can get us back home if we get back to the harbour town where I first came on land. We get a ship – *somehow* we get a ship.'

'Wait a minute,' said Massimo. 'You mean you *really* think they're cannibals here?'

Connors shrugged. 'All I know is, from the moment I saw Atchoo he reminded me of Elvis – the boy not the singer – and the moment I got to this village, or nearly, I started thinking about my approach towards Toenail Island... It felt like *déjà vu.*'

'But why would they offer to sell us food if they intended to eat us? Wouldn't they say: take off your clothes and hop into the pot?'

'I don't *know*. I'm not claiming to be a bloody expert on the subject. I could be wrong – completely – but if you've got a better plan I suggest you voice it pretty sharpish.'

On the pond, the creatures made of air rubbed their webbed feet together to make noises that sounded like quacks.

'Why don't we hear what the head honcho has to say?' Massimo suggested. 'Let's at least have a few more hours' rest, eh? You've asked to see him, after all.'

Connors nodded. 'Okay, but then I'm off. If I'm right – if my gut instinct is right – we can get away before it gets dark.'

'And if you're wrong?' asked Bernadette.

Connors smiled. 'Then we're casserole.'

Massimo sniggered. 'With carrots.'

'And a big bastard *turnip*,' said Bernadette, also bursting into a smile. 'I wonder who's the saltiest out of the three of us...'

They started laughing – nervous laughter at first, which then became richer and more honest. It was a release from the grip of tension. They laughed about being eaten in a stew; about being skewered. And they wondered if the locals enjoyed brains.

Then they saw Atchoo.

The boy was walking towards them, alone. His expression was impossible to read, and he waited until he was a metre away from where they were sitting before he spoke.

'Benny will see you now,' was what he said.

Connors frowned. 'Who's Benny?' he asked the boy.

'You asked to see who was running the show,' the boy explained. 'And he'll see you now.'

Massimo and Connors exchanged glances.

BENEATH A STORM OF VOICES

1.

The storm broke in Yasser's face - an electrical discharge spearing beams of pain directly into his skin, his eyes; a din like competing engines, revving in his ears. All in all, a sickening ordeal. And one which convinced Yasser that at this very moment he was suffering a stroke.

Attempting to stay calm while his body shook, he watched visions unfold in his brain. He saw his home streets; he saw houses, shops, the B&B place up the hill. But nothing was static. The roads writhed and curled, like snakes – mating or fighting. The air was as red as surgery; homes flickered and expired in a kaleidoscope of colour and destruction. His mother and father, swimming for their lives in molten pavement, chased Yasser's computer as it bobbed in swirls and eddies of liquid steel. A bus dissolved in the heat, spreading its solution of wet upholstery and screaming passengers on a hellbound journey through Bury Park.

And then he heard his own voice.

This isn't home, it said.

Another voice – also his own but from a different source from the first – agreed with some passion.

This isn't home, the second voice said. *You're a long way from home.*

In the following few seconds, a host of alternative Yassers, a scrum of serial selves, weighed into the debate, all offering the same advice – that this was not Yasser's home – all thirteen, fourteen, fifteen or sixteen of the loudmouths.

Then whose home was it?

Where am I? Yasser asked the back of his head. He remembered a darkness from which he had failed to escape; the confines of the house... And Maggie, behind him; a betrayal...

Yasser opened his eyes – or his eyes opened, whether he wanted them to or not – and the first thing he noticed was the vision of his home town, compressed and condensed, on mystery wings climbing a sky the colour of aubergine pulp. Luton was flying away from where he lay, from where he'd woken up; such was the despondency that he experienced at this moment that Yasser sat up quickly, to a throb of pain in his temples, and he breathed a denial as his home life thudded into the distance, on wings so colossal that every flap made the ground beneath his legs vibrate.

'No,' he whispered.

Luton was gone. Bedfordshire was gone. Mum and Dad (almost certainly) were gone too... A glance around told Yasser that he was alone; there was nothing to see but the contours of the land, miles and miles of blue earth and red plants. Not even an indication as to the right direction in which to start walking. At the very edges of what he could see, the pale cloudless sky curved down, giving Yasser the impression that he was under a dome of some sort, a bowl or a fishtank.

He stood up. Assessed the damage. No breaks, pains or aches; a little tightening in the chest, a minimal difficulty in breathing, as if he'd been on a gentle run. Nothing serious.

'Hello!' he shouted.

His word did not echo and his word was not answered. Alone. Confusingly alone. Was he the only one who had made it across? What had happened to Shyleen? To Chris? To Maggie?

Maggie had sprayed something in Yasser's face; something that had robbed him of his senses.

Why?

Yasser wanted to believe, despite every scrap of evidence to the contrary, that Maggie had tried to help him. She had sprayed him with loopy juice, true (this couldn't be refuted), but she had done so in order to facilitate his passing to this oddball countryside on the other side. As ever, she'd had her reasons (Yasser wished, now and always, that the woman was better able to *discuss* her reasons with him beforehand), and she'd got what she'd wanted. He'd arrived. And now what?

As he walked, he answered. He held a wet finger up to test the breeze; there was nothing shifting, however, and so the choice could only be arbitrary. Sure that what he'd seen was his hometown being carried skyward on the vast wings of an angel, Yasser remembered Chris's bloodied head. And Benny. Benny, who had done the damage to the same.

Where was Benny now?

To select the direction in which he'd walk, Yasser eeny-meeny-miney-mo'd, hoping all the while that the angel's wings of which Chris had been so proud would bring him better luck than they had to their owner.

As Yasser set out, the temperature was lukewarm and his clothes were comfortable. Although he might have maimed a living creature for the chance of a hot shower, he knew that the transition might have been worse. Indeed, under other circumstances (dramatically other circumstances), the conditions would have been perfect for a leisurely stroll.

2.

Shyleen awoke bruised and angry. She tried to leaf through her nightmares, to get to the end of the chapter faster (she didn't care about the denouement): but the nightmares refused to flutter away. She was made to endure them, paralysed as she was by a nauseous shock.

Something pushed repeatedly against her face. The pressure was not unbearable but it was strange. It was like the first time that she had woken up in her boyfriend's bed (the boyfriend of whom Yasser knew nothing). The boyfriend's cat, accustomed to sleeping on the other pillow, had chosen to sleep on Shyleen's face instead, in an act of territorial defiance. Not a *hostile* act exactly, more an unconfusable statement that there was already a female in the boyfriend's life, and that Shyleen would be well advised to respect the fact.

The difference was that the cat had not stood up and sat down on her head in a repeated fashion. The pounding that Shyleen was currently accepting was metronomically regular, as if...

Shyleen tittered.

...as if obeying the rhythms of penetrative lovemaking; as if some dick were fucking her head, quite literally. As if her head had become her vagina or something.

Shyleen tittered again. It did not occur to her to be frightened of the darkness; if anything, the black wall was a welcoming non-sight. The presence of darkness implied that she need not move: she could lie still and let him finish poking her brains out... So this was what they meant by a head fuck!

Apart from the nameless boyfriend, no other memory insisted on being noticed. Her skull was being pounded; all the neurological stuffing had been knocked out of it. And because of this, Shyleen was free to drift... and to let the currents dictate which way.

Might as well enjoy it, she reasoned. So numb were her fingertips (and so heavy her arms) that when she touched her breasts, it felt like someone else – an invisible demon lover – was in charge of the massage. Said lover stroked her skin, igniting sparks on the surface that buried down into the flesh; her nipples glowed softly, like the eyes of a nocturnal prowler. The demon lover (he, she or it) made her nipples burn hotter and brighter; they now resembled two distant bonfires on two hills, an image as absurd as it was arresting.

Understanding that her mind was playing tricks with her – confusing her signals, shuffling the information – did not panic Shyleen. On the contrary, it felt good to be so lost, so topsy turvy; it felt like abandonment… and she wondered how her pussy would seem, given such emotional weather.

When she touched the outer lips, her vision began to clear; the darkness faded to dove-grey, and as soon as she withdrew her fingers, the darkness clamped back over her head, with a working-bell clang that scared her… Never one to need much of an excuse to masturbate at the best of times, Shyleen took herself in hand now, dipping her first two fingers as deep as she could reach.

It was like winding up a battery-powered torch (she thought of the house, she thought of Benny). The more she exercised her interior, the healthier her eyesight grew. She saw fields of grey (apparently the crop was ash); she saw blackbirds, conversing with uncle eagles, grandfather buzzards… She remembered the weed that she'd smoked with Chris (she remembered Chris), and while wondering if the visions were its result, she also wondered if the man having sex with her was Chris himself. Up till now it hadn't occurred to her to give her paramour a name – or a face, come to think of it.

Why couldn't she see him? All she could see – the ash-fields, the chattering birds – was as clear as a key in a pool of water. The light was good; the temperature warm (no sensory distractions)… Now the birds turned to watch her watching them; and her brain being fogged both by weed and by anaesthetic (not to mention the mind drugs of fear and orgasm), Shyleen imagined an overarching, all-seeing observer, who watched them all, woman and birds.

Watching.

Voice.

I have a voice, Shyleen recalled, somewhat adaze.

Watching. Something was watching.

Shyleen tried to move – and tried to speak. The birds hopped closer to her, a few of them squawking, their tiny feet kicking up puffs of ash.

Go away! Horrible pecky birds!

Suddenly Shyleen imagined herself to be a worm. She was food for these birds, she understood – or rather, for one bird, the early bird who catches the –

NO!

As her mind shrieked the refusal, the body flailed and her fingers slipped free of her cleft.

The vision left her. A familiar face – brown-skinned and topped with a pelt of short black hair – was everything in her sight.

'Are you okay?' the man asked, and Shyleen remembered his name.

'Yasser.' She said it with relief, her voice groggy. 'Am I a worm?'

'No, babe.' Yasser had misheard her –or had wrongly decoded her slur. 'We're nowhere near home. This is Weirdsville, Arizona.'

'Always wanted to visit America,' Shyleen answered… and then her mind closed down once more and the world darkened.

3.

They sat on a rock and compared memories, wondering

aloud what they would do for food. They tried not to panic: they even told each other to try not to panic, which of course made them both nervous. They defecated at the same time, their hands linked together.

Eventually they slept. The air had turned chilly, but if they snuggled up tight it was warm enough. For a brief few minutes, listening to Yasser's heart before her eyes drooped, Shyleen felt comfortable and secure. Somehow they had weathered the storms of temptation and returned to each other; they had found one another, quite literally, in the wilderness. Did it matter if they never went home? she wondered. Maybe not; not once they'd decoded the mysteries of this place.

Perhaps in this place she wasn't ill.

4.

'How did you sleep?' he asked her.

'...Weird dreams... The light's no different,' Shyleen observed, sitting up.

'It didn't change all night – *night's* the right word... Tell me what you were dreaming.'

'You were awake all night?'

'No; I nodded off a few times, no idea how long for...' Yasser held up his left arm; he had removed his jacket at some point to reveal a white t-shirt that looked grubby. 'Notice anything?' he asked.

'Your t-shirt's filthy.'

'About my wrist?'

'Oh. No watch.'

'No watch. It didn't make it through.'

'Mine did.' Shyleen mirrored Yasser's mime, lifting her right arm and stretching until her shoulder clicked.

'Yeah. The time being?'

She looked at her watch. 'Oh.'

'Stopped, right?'

She nodded.

'A time out of time,' Yasser told her; 'and just you and me, babe.'

'How romantic.'

'Yeah: until we need to eat.'

'Speaking of which…'

Yasser nodded. 'Wagons roll? You fit?'

Standing up with her cousin's assistance, Shyleen told him that she felt peculiar. You mean sick? No; not *sick* exactly… as if I'm dreaming and I know it but I can't get out.

'You were muttering some madcap shit when you *were* dreaming, I tell you that.'

'I remember… I was trying to protect you… Yass… do we know someone called Maggie?'

'Not that I know of. Why?'

For a second or two, Shyleen was silent as they walked on. The glimpses of her vision were maddeningly elusive… but the crumbs were present to trail if she wanted to do so.

She remembered the dread that she'd felt – the sensation of being watched; of being controlled, perhaps. By higher powers. By deities. By God.

'Maggie was touching your brain,' said Shyleen. 'In the dream.'

Although she hadn't intended it to be a joke exactly, she was downbeat at the way that Yasser took the information. All of a sudden he was moody and anxious; when Shyleen glanced to her left, she saw his forehead scrunch up like a cornflake.

'What?' she asked him.

'I heard her talking to me,' Yasser answered. 'She was

telling me she's sorry.'
    '…For what?'
    'I don't know.'

AFTERMATH

1.

All through the following day, Don Bridges was conspicuous by his absence. Vig and Dorota had needed scant discussion before arriving at a decision to postpone a planned day out to Cambridge; however, they had both assumed that the other would have cancelled the taxi that was to have chauffeured them there and back (it was Curtis's day off). When the car arrived, as arranged, at nine-thirty in the morning, the driver pressed the intercom buzzer at the front gate, repeatedly, and also made such a racket with his horn that Vig felt obliged to stroll down the long driveway in his dressing gown, the wind pinching at his groin through his boxer shorts, and to pass on the news of the cancellation face to face. Although the driver was not happy, he was partially mollified by the fifty-pound note that Vig waved in his ill-shaven face, and by the promise that they would re-schedule the trip when Dorota felt better. (Vig lied that she had caught a cold.) Then it was time to tell Don that he would have to start looking for alternative employment – or consider a retirement package, which was Vig's idea of a compromise, one that had been criticised by Dorota… But all through the day, Don Bridges would be conspicuous by his absence.

'His hut's empty,' said Dorota.

And Vig replied, 'The birds haven't been fed.'

'Where's he gone?' they both wondered aloud.

So they searched. Dorota drove to the farm shop where Don bought birdseed and provisions like game and carrots; she made enquiries, but Don had not been seen or served. The same story was true when she called in at the post office.

Vig, meanwhile, kept his eyes peeled in the woods. Leaves crackled under his boot heels and every sound was like a different sound, which was typical of a walk among these trees.

Nothing.

Don had run away – or he'd been taken by aliens – and he had left his home, his birds and a cooled chicken carcass; he'd left his bicycle. He had even left behind his pouch of rolling tobacco and a packet of papers – the most sinister piece of evidence of all.

Don was gone.

2.

As dusk approached, Vig took it upon himself (he was the lord of the manor, after all, however unwarranted the status happened to be) to feed Don's birds. How hard could it be? Vig had watched Don go through the motions a hundred times.

Walking along the path to the aviary, however, Vig experienced a sense of mingled loss and dread that he couldn't explain. The sensation changed into a kind of vertigo, even though his feet were squarely on *terra firma* gravel. He had to stop. There was nothing for him to hold on to; the best he could do for a few seconds was stand still, straighten his back and breathe deeply until the nausea subsided.

We have to face this, Dorota had said an hour earlier. *What if he's killed himself? The shame of it all; Charlie Eastlight…*

No, Vig had answered – a refusal that he did not feel in his bones. *He's not the type.*

And what type would that be? Dorota had demanded. *Even when he's not here he's causing trouble!*

A trouble-maker is not the same as a suicide.

No. No of course the two things were not the same; they were not so much as close. Nonetheless, Vig believed that when he reached the cages this time he would find Don's body inside, dead, a new perch for his beloved birds. Either he'd finished a bottle of something with a strip of painkillers, or – who could tell? wonders never ceased! – the stress of it all had summoned up a good old-fashioned heart attack.

The wave of nausea rolled past, and within a few seconds Vig could see straight again. He picked up his pace, ready to meet Don in the aviary.

However, Don was not there.

Nor were the birds.

3.

'He's let them all go,' Vig explained. 'Every single door was open.'

'That wasn't Don. It couldn't have been – that's not...'

'You mean Charlie?'

Dorota nodded. 'Charlie makes more sense. Why would Don...?'

'Because he's saying goodbye,' Vig replied, shrugging.

Dorota was not impressed. 'I wish he'd say it faster,' she said.

4.

Deep in the woods, proximate to the property's eastern boundary – a densely-forested area into which Vig had never had call to venture up to this point – was where Don Bridges was eventually discovered on the second day after his disappearance.

Ironically enough, it was the sound of foxes that gave the game away.

Having spent another rough night, feeling bitty from a lack of quality sleep, Vig had climbed from bed early and had gone downstairs to pull on his wellies. He could not believe that Don had simply gone. There had to be more to the old man's disappearance. Surely Don would not have left without a goodbye – a vituperative goodbye, perhaps, but a goodbye all the same – or a note, a letter... Even a threat of future legal consequences would have sufficed. But no: not Don. He had followed a script of his own composition; remained obstinate to the last.

To the last?

Was Don dead?

The possibility had circled around Vig's mind, on a loop. Say he'd perished in the woods, of natural causes. The very least that Vig could do, as the man's employer, was find him and report the demise, the mishap... whatever it turned out to be.

So it was, with this in mind, that Vig strode out into an early morning, chilly but bright, armed with little more than an indistinct sense of justice needing to be done... and the awful guilt that had long since become commonplace: the guilt that he had taken on this cause – as he would have taken on any other cause if it had presented itself – because he was bored (bored and lonely), a miserable millionaire, oh woe is me! – and he wanted something constructive to do with his time. Money had made him ache; had made him desperate.

Vig chose to stroll further from what could be called (very loosely) the beaten paths. Before long he was deep into the trees, getting scratched by horrible thorny growth that seemed not to want him to progress further. He didn't care. After the first scratch to the back of one hand, what was another scratch to the other, or to the face? It didn't matter and he didn't *care*. If Don was in his beloved trees somewhere, Vig was going to find him. Vig promised himself this… and he made the same promise to Don. So he quested on. And after a while, it had even become fun: it felt like being a child again – an adventurous child.

He'd been exploring for less than an hour, and had started to wish that he'd told Dorota where he was going, when he heard the foxes.

His ungloved fingers, pricked and bleeding, were attempting to pull some sticky adhesive grass from where it clung to his jeaned thighs, when the noise stabbed a space into his consciousness. All at once the thought of Dorota slipped his mind, as did the prediction of how cross she was going to be when he returned as the Human Pin Cushion. Similarly, Vig's thoughts about Don's birds were shattered. (Vig had expected to see the birds among the trees, at least one or two of them; so far he'd seen none.) The distant but gathering doubt that he would be able to find his way home again when this Boy's Own adventure had climaxed – this also was deleted from his mind.

'What the hell's that?' Vig said.

He cancelled any movement. He waited. What had he heard? And where had the sound come from? Vig knew well that acoustics in the trees were treacherous, but it had seemed to come from a matter of metres away.

Again! There it was!

High-pitched; like babies crying… like *babies* crying? And scratching noises, sounded wooden. A creature carving claws into a tree? Then a growl, a series of growls… How many of them were there? Playtime was over; it sounded angry.

Turn back.

The voice in his head was not his own; it was not Dorota's either. Of all people to enter his consciousness at this moment, it was the voice of Phyllie Reydman.

'Why?' he asked his friend in English.

Trust me. Don't go on.

'I have to see,' Vig replied. 'Please understand.' And he wrestled his legs free of the adhesive weed, his fingertips throbbing and raw.

He walked on.

A line of fierce-looking bushes stood directly in front of Vig, too tall to peer over and too dense to stare through any gaps in the branches. Vig turned to his right and strolled the seven or eight metres of required detour – and then he was able to see what was making the squeals and the growls.

Foxes.

A litter of five baby foxes was scratching at a patch of open ground. No adult fox was in sight, but Vig was wounded enough already not to wish further abrasion from an angry or over-protective parent; he approached with caution. More than anything else he wanted to know what was making that noise; surely it wasn't the normal sound of animals pawing at dried earth. It sounded like a fork on a chopping board.

Making clear signs of protest at the indignity of this human invasion, the foxes watched Vig get closer, step by wary step, and they growled. As soon as they'd stopped pawing at the wooden thing on the ground, the noise that had so befuddled Vig ceased too: there was no doubt about the connection between action and audio; but what had the animals discovered that had intrigued and excited them so?

Vig shouted: '*Yaah!*' In the one long second that followed, he hoped that the foxes were not tough enough to face up to a human – especially not foxes this young, and with no mother or father present to offer support.

The tactic was successful. The five foxes scattered off in three different directions, all of them heading for undergrowth and safety.

Vig moved into the space that they'd vacated, raising one bloodied hand to cover his nose partly against the stink that was lifting from the earth. The smell of fox piss, presumable: there was no excreta on the ground for Vig to see... Or maybe not urine either, he realised.

Maybe the smell was coming up from the door in the ground.

5.

It was a trapdoor... and its basic, sturdy design had Don's name written all over it. The trapdoor was similar to the one the man had dug into his own kitchen floor, although there were some minor modifications.

Vig's stomach rolled. The smell from what was hidden beneath his wellies – it surged up in waves. *Down there*... down there in the hole – down there beneath a heavy wooden trapdoor, with its hinges bolted down into concrete slabs embedded in the earth; with its two bolt-locks on the door's opposite side, fastened into concrete in a similar way – *down there* in a hole that Vig could not see...

...something was rotting.

Yes; yes, Vig – you are seeing this for what it truly is. A trapdoor. A door leading into a trap... Are you going to open it up?

...rotting...

Or are you going to run away, crying like a girl? Because it's dead. It's got to be dead; it can't harm you if it's dead – and it's *got to be* dead, right? The foxes wanted to eat it, so it must be dead in there, right? Well, *right?*

Vig spoke aloud. 'It's their mother,' he said. Bending at the waist to unfasten the bolt-locks, he added: 'She fell in the hole, the door was knocked down by accident...'

Why are there locks on the door, Vig? asked Phyllie.

'I don't know.'

It's a prison, Vig, and you know it... You do know it, don't you, Vig?

'Yes I know it, Phyllie...' And Vig snapped back the first lock. It moved smoothly – a recent dousing in oil, grease or WD40?

What about in chicken fat? That would do the trick too...

'Yes it would.'

Vig stood up to his full height and drew deeply of as fresh a breath as he could find (which was not very fresh). Then he bent at the waist once more, his imagination splintering. In the blink of his eyes –

He flicked the second bolt-lock.

– he saw Phyllie, standing nearby at the barbecue that he'd held, with one hand over her pregnancy... the pregnancy that he wished he'd co-created;

– he saw Dorota, waking up in their bed and silently cursing his name.

And he opened the trapdoor.

6.

Vig took a step backwards, grabbing hold of his belly as if he was pregnant himself.

'Oh God,' he whispered. Now that it had been released into the open air, the smell was stronger. Vig turned aside and tried to vomit, but all that climbed the ladder of his gullet was an arsenic-flavoured drool.

He had to make sure... Taking two steps towards the trapdoor allowed him to check his first impressions, and they'd been true.

Charlie Eastlight. Trapped in this *oubliette*, naked.

The only matter to decorate his skin was mud-and-blood. It would seem that he'd put up a fight, but it took Vig a few more seconds to deduce what the struggle might have been against.

It was only when an early-morning cloud shifted slightly that Vig was able to make out the shape at Charlie's bare feet.

An adult fox.

Vig wondered, stepping backwards once more, which creature had killed which. And which had eaten more of the other.

7.

Vig found a spot to sit down, his back against the wide stump of a plum tree. He inhaled and exhaled, like someone suffering from an asthma attack. In his mind the pieces refused to settle, let alone fit into the correct spaces; Vig waited for a few flies to light on his hands and then fly away again. He did not have the heart to shake them off.

'Vig!'

A distant shout. His name, from across the sea of trees. Although Vig knew that the caller must be Dorota, the distance had distorted her voice: she might have been phoning from Atlantis.

He shook his head. Time to wake up and smell the embalming fluid. There was work to do. He stood up.

No.

Vig's knees wobbled. He had caught sight of something across from the trapdoor – something in the next phalanx of trees and growth – and his first reaction was not one of shock or horror. It was one of confusion.

'Why didn't I see that before?' he wondered aloud. His voice suggested that he'd just been struck a blow to the brow.

Not ten metres from where Vig now stood, Don Bridges was swinging from a branch. His feet were half a metre off the ground. He must have tied the noose nice and tight around his neck because the knot and the rope had held his weight.

8.

Part of what I told you was true, read the letter that Vig held in his hands. *Part of it was guesswork. But here are the facts, at least as I see them.*

Four sheets of blue paper trembled in Vig's grip, partly because of his shock, partly the wind gambolling in the woods. There had been no *Dear Vig,* no address of any kind, but Vig had started reading anyway, in a spirit of 'finders keepers'.

'*Vig?*'

Shouted... Dorota was still some distance away, though she was at least searching for him among the trees, which was more than Vig had expected of her. He had time to read on, trembling or no trembling.

My little girl died the way I told you she died, and I swear I hear her from time to time, from the Other Place. Is she a ghost? I don't know. All I know is she was killed and my marriage was never the same after that, as you might expect.

My wife would not believe it – or would not believe that it was the end. She used to say Polly was trying to call for her – and up to a point I believed her. I did. But then I stopped believing and I started to accept the truth. Or did I?

You see, Mr Klossen...

So it *was* intended for me to read, Vig comforted himself. He even exhaled with relief – he wasn't spying on a confession meant for someone else's eyes – and as he straightened his back he heard Dorota call his name once again.

...there IS a place for the lost, and it's a place for those who HAVE LOST. As long as you can feel it in your heart that the person isn't gone, she'd just lost, just missing, then you've a chance to visit that person again. That's what I believe now. I didn't at the time – not even when my wife started to disappear for days and weeks at a time. Not even then. Not even when she would come home, disheartened, saying 'I couldn't find her but I know she's

there, Don, I know it' – and I'd ask her, 'Where have you been?' and she's answer, 'Searching.' And I'd say, 'That's not an answer. WHERE?' And she'd tell me, 'I don't know.'

I never would have guessed she was going into the woods near where we lived – about a five-minute walk away, and she always went on foot so her bicycle wouldn't be discovered.

Well, one day I started following her. I think she knew I was there, I think she wanted me to go with her. And before my very eyes, I saw her disappear, I swear I did, Mr Klossen. She didn't return for a fortnight – she had a tan! We had to pretend she'd been on holiday!

One day she didn't come back at all. Eventually I had to admit to people she'd left me and we were seeking a divorce, which was a lot more difficult to file for in those days, believe me! I changed jobs a dozen times, sometimes by my own choice, sometimes I was 'invited to leave' as we said in those days. And as time moved on – years passed – and I knew (or I believed…which is almost the same thing) that my wife was missing… but she was alive. And searching for our daughter. Tirelessly.

I thought I had to help, but I didn't know how. You'll be surprised, I think, at the lengths I went to – things you might not expect of an old man, though of course I wasn't old then. Hypnosis. Regression. Meditation. And then something called intra-rationalism.

Vig turned over the last of the four sheets of paper. He gasped. The other side was blank. Don had either finished writing it and had forgotten to include it, or he had run out of time. Run out of *time?* What had he done: scribbled this confession while swinging from the bloody branch? How could he have done this? How could he have abandoned it, half-cooked?

'Vig, where are you?' Dorota called – nearer than ever now. 'Vig, I'm worried!'

Stuffing Don's letter back into the hip pocket of the man's tweed jacket from which he had taken it in the first place (the pocket at Vig's shoulder height while the man remained dangling), Vig shouted his response to his partner.

'I'm here, Dorota! Stay where you are! Do you have your phone?'

'Yes!'

'Then call the police! I've found Don and Charlie!'

'...Alive?' Dorota called.

'Far from it!' Vig called back; then he went over to where Eastlight had been buried, and he lowered the trapdoor. The baby foxes would have to find some other form of nourishment for the time being.

9.

'What made you go into his pockets?' Vig was asked. 'How did you find him?'

The questions came as thick and fast as springtime hail, and although Vig tried to answer as well as he could, he imagined that he'd never *quite* finished speaking before the next teaser was posed. He was never finished – and the barrage soon became dizzying; his brain choked in fog. At no point was he sure how he was doing, he answered until his jaw was numb; his mind too. So much talk! Vig wondered (and almost wondered aloud) if it would be okay with all concerned if he just slipped off to bed for a year or so.

'Analyse it any way you want,' Dorota suggested in the lunchtime lull between interrogations, 'I was right about Don all along.'

She scarcely had time to bite the end off a banana before Vig did the same with her head.

'Is that meant to make me feel *better?*' he shouted. 'Does it make *you* feel better? I hope it doesn't.'

'Why are you raising your voice?' Dorota went on, her

mouth full of fruit.

'You had him down for a murderer from day one, did you?' Vig was incensed. 'Funny you didn't mention it, Dorota. And all the *more* funny you seem to take some sort of pride in being able to pick out a weirdo. Maybe it's a skill you could market!'

Dorota turned away from Vig and from his bait; she stared out of the kitchen window. 'I was right, that's all I'm saying; and I never trusted Eastlight either. You know I didn't, unless you weren't listening.' She swallowed. 'But do you want to know what else?' she asked.

'I'm not at all certain I do.'

'I'm glad they're both gone.'

'Say that when the police get back, I dare you.'

'I am.' Dorota shrugged. 'Now it finally feels like our house. No trespassing real estate guy; no birds; and no bloody Don Bridges.'

'Who helped keep the grounds tidy and neat,' Vig reminded her.

'So what? We can't hire another gardener? Don't be stupid.'

'Don't call me stupid,' Vig replied.

'I'm *pleased* they're gone, Vig. What's the word we heard the other night? I'm *chuffed.*'

'So you say…' Vig opened the door to the patio and stepping into the wellies that he had left on the step. 'Where are you going *now?*' Dorota wanted to know.

'To the bird cages. In case he left something for me there. And Dorota?'

'Yes?'

'It's not *our* house. It's *my* house. Paid for with my money… You'd be well advised to remember that.'

BENNY HILL

1.

So it seemed that there was at least one more incline to ascend before things could progress, but by their recent standards the slope ahead of them was little more than a speed-bump on a village road. Though their legs ached from the trek down the mountain, Connors, Massimo and Bernadette had no difficulty with the climb.

What Massimo had a problem with was the signpost that announced the name of this particular slant. On the wooden board at the top of the six-foot pole, two words had been written in white paint:

BENNY HILL

'Oh he's taking the *piss*,' Massimo said.

'What do you mean?' asked Connors and Bernadette as a duet.

'Benny Hill? I ask you...'

'It's Benny – the guy with the reptiles,' Bernadette tried to explain.

'Yes I know,' said Massimo, 'and this is his hill. But what else does Benny Hill suggest to you?'

The look that Connors and Bernadette shared implied that the words 'Benny Hill' suggested nothing to them. Massimo was incredulous.

'The *comedian*,' he almost shouted.

'What comedian?' Connors asked. 'Benny Hill?'

'No, Richard Pryor. Of course Benny Hill! Who else are we talking about?'

'I've never heard of him; sorry. What about him?'

'It's Benny's joke. On us. Benny Hill used to do a routine… you're not *that* fucking young, either of you! You must remember him!'

Atchoo tried to hurry the three of them along: by this point they had stopped in the middle of the dirt track that led up to what looked like one solitary dwelling.

'Shut it, son,' said Massimo, and he wagged a finger in the boy's face. 'You made *us* wait long enough – now it's your turn.'

'It's *his* turn,' Atchoo countered. 'He said *now*.'

'Well, in that case, you can run along ahead and tell him where he can stick his now, can't you, son? I'm talking to my friends.'

'I know,' said Bernadette, 'who you're talking about – the comedian – but so what? His name was Benny Hill. It's a coincidence.'

'No such thing, Bernie. We make our own coincidences… or some wanker makes em for us. I am telling you this is another little joke on our ventriloquist's part.'

'I still don't get it,' said Connors.

'Benny Hill did this routine where he chased women in bikinis through a park, or some bullshit, or they chased him, and it was all speeded up and the music was really fast, like a… what do you call it? Like Kazoo music.'

'What's a kazoo now?' Connors asked.

Massimo shook his head. 'It don't matter. The point is, it was all about manipulation and control… Why would twenty babes chase a middle-aged chipmunk like Benny Hill through a park, or anywhere else for that matter?'

Connors was attempting to warm to the theme. 'To manipulate him?' he guessed.

'No; because *he's* manipulating *them*. Like Benny's been doing, from the start I wouldn't be surprised. He's made us chase him here, hasn't he? A lot more than through a fucking park an' all!'

Atchoo said, 'Come on, please. Come on now. Benny waiting.'

Connors rounded on the boy. 'Have you been our guardian angel in this story, son? he demanded. 'You were there as Elvis in the beginning and you got me as far as I needed to get to start this nonsense. And then, when we got lost, you got us delivered here – a different appearance, a different name: the same kid. Same guiding angel.'

Atchoo regarded Connors with distrust and distaste. 'Benny waiting,' was all he repeated.

As they started up Benny Hill, they argued about running away – in the opposite direction. In *any* direction. But if Benny was godlike in these parts – if the three of them *had* reached the mind of God, ironically – then was it so difficult to imagine a deity capable of engineering a double bluff? If they tried to escape now (they agreed), it would only be because Benny wanted them to escape.

They were trapped. They would do as they were told. Speak the lines they were given, and dance when the hand on their spines squeezed or stroked. Puppets. Being returned to their box.

The house's front door opened.

2.

The ground floor consisted of one large room; there were no divisions. At the far end – no more than seven metres away –

was a green two-seater settee that had seen better days, and three wooden chairs facing. On the settee sat a man whose appearance deflated Massimo's mood of self-righteousness at a stroke. What surged through Massimo was anger, pure and simple; Connors and Bernadette stuck with confusion.

'Who the fuck are you?' Massimo demanded. 'Where's Benny?'

'Welcome to my home!'

The man grinned, slowly opening his arms like fat wings. His khaki-coloured t-shirt was a size too small on his squat and muscular upper body. Fading green-and-blue tattoos poked out beneath the tourniquet sleeves. He was also wearing brown floppy tracksuit bottoms and a pair of scuffed workboots with metal toecaps. His face was weatherworn and tanned. Most certainly this was not Benny.

'I asked you a question,' said Massimo.

The man on the settee made the V for Victory sign with his chubby sunbronzed fingers.

'You asked me *two* questions,' he answered. 'The first one's easy. My name's Tommy. But they call me the Brazilian. Do you wanna know why?'

'I don't care why. Where's Benny?'

Tommy was not about to let an interruption spoil his punchline. The grin that polluted his features was stoic. 'It's because of me tendency to tear strips off a poor cunt.'

He waited a beat for a reaction – and he got one.

'You are aware there's a lady present, I take it.'

'Don't defend me, Mass...'

'Sorry, Miss,' said Tommy, who actually managed to appear sorry too. 'But who *are* you exactly? I was expecting a sturdy Wop.' He indicated in Massimo's direction. 'That'll be you, mate. And I was expecting a twenty year-old weasel dick wanker. And that'll be you.' Tommy nodded at Connors. 'But nobody told me nothing about you, m'darlin. What's your name?'

'Angela.'

'An angelic name, to be sure. And what brings you to me neck of the wood, darlin?'

'Don't call me darling. Or anything else. My name's Bernadette. The Angela was to test your reaction to a lie.'

Tommy smiled. 'Did I pass?'

'Funnily enough, you did. I can tell a liar when I see one, I think,' said Bernadette. Momentarily her mind counted the scraped faces in Casualty, the broken noses, the red eyes... and the promises – oh, the promises. *I've only had a couple of pints... He hit me first, it was self-defence.*

'Which brings me to your second question,' said Tommy, 'concerning the whereabouts of a character named *Benny*. Who is he?'

'The man who gave this hill its name,' Connors answered.

'Benny Hill?' Tommy appeared surprised. 'Well I didn't know that. I thought it was a corruption of *bene* – from the Latin, I believe. But I could be mistaken on that score. Books and me have never been on what you'd call good speaking terms. *Bene* meaning good.'

'I'll give *you* a corruption in a minute,' Massimo told him. 'What the fuck's going on?'

Tommy laughed. 'What was that you said about a lady being present?'

'I've heard worse,' said Bernadette.

'I dare say. Why don't you take a seat? Take the weight off your paragraphs.'

Glad of the invitation, Connors and Bernadette claimed a chair each immediately. Massimo, more wary, hovered, his fingers twitching. After a few seconds, however, he changed his mind and sat down. Although it felt like a relief to do so, his wariness and his dislike of Tommy persisted.

'Now isn't this cosy,' Tommy ventured.

By no means was this the first time that Bernadette had witnessed the strut and flared plumage of an alpha male contest. A woman's word, perhaps, was what was needed.

'Please could you explain what's going on,' she said.

'I could. But first tell me how you got here.'

'There's no time,' Massimo protested.

'Why? You got a dentist's appointment or something.'

'No. Obviously not.'

'Well then...'

'Well then...'

Eventually and at length, they talked.

3.

'So who have you lost?' Tommy asked. 'In order to be here, like.'

While Connors and Massimo exchanged rapid glances, Bernadette took the question seriously enough not to ask for further explanation. Once more (she believed) her willingness to adapt was part of her nursing training; Tommy's query was no different, really, to when she asked a man with facial contusions: *So how many drinks have you had tonight?*

And there was something else, she realised... and the realisation shocked her. Since meeting Tommy she'd recovered a portion of her inquisitiveness – her will to strive on. The sense was upon her once again that by moving towards a goal – by cooperating, really – the path back home would be cleared. She was growing undepressed; she was floating away, slowly but unarguably, from the lassitude that had ensnared all three of them.

'I'm an orphan,' she admitted. As she kept her gaze level at Tommy's face, her eyes meeting his, she was aware of the attention of Connors and Massimo, one on either side of her. 'My dad raised me – and my younger sister – virtually solo. Mum died when I was nine; Rachel was seven. She killed herself. She was a manic depressive and she took herself off to Land's End and jumped off a cliff. I was *nine*. And it was a week before Dad could tell us what had happened… Dad was four years ago. Cancer.'

Tommy nodded his head; his facial contortions suggested to all present that he had no idea what to do with this information.

'Was your mum's… decision what made you want to be a nurse?' he asked at length.

Folding her arms, Bernadette replied, 'How do you know I'm a nurse?'

'About a year ago. A neighbour of mine, Max O'Hara – he decides he'll go in for a bit of street racing with some eejits from Lewsey Farm. And you can't say I didn't warn the cunt. It was me brought him into A&E. You were on duty. You were very good – a lot kinder than I was feeling.'

Bernadette smiled at the compliment. 'He broke his left arm,' she remembered.

'That's the wanker.'

Bernadette laughed briefly. Of all the places to meet someone you've met in the line of your work! Here! 'And how is he these days?' she asked.

'Well he's given up street racing.'

'That's good.'

'Look.' It was Massimo. 'I'm sorry to break up your let's-remember party, but we're here to learn something new, aren't we?'

Tommy's face betrayed no sign of amusement at the interruption. 'Well, *aren't* you?' he demanded.

'Learning something new? No I'm not.'

'Then you're not listening properly,' Tommy told him. At this point he turned back to Bernadette, and added: 'I admire your honesty, I really do. But that's not what I meant when I said lost. The death of a parent is terrible; the loss of two is more than double that pain… but you know where they are. They're not *lost*. Right?'

'Well…'

'You either had them buried or cremated. You know where to visit when you want a word,' Tommy continued.

Bernadette shrugged. 'I suppose so, yes.'

'Then they're not lost,' said Tommy. 'They're absent but they're not lost.'

Massimo was seething. Everything he said was being treated with derision by this stroker, and it had been a long time since he'd felt power drained from his soul so effectively – so comprehensively. Had Massimo been able to read the thoughts inside Bernadette's head (after that time on the road together he could guess them, but he couldn't *read* them), he would have seen her opinions on the disgraceful posturing of the alpha male set-up, and no doubt with a wince of inner embarrassment, he would have agreed with her view. He'd been downgraded. The fact that he did not like the situation was only part of the picture. He couldn't *believe* it, that was the worst part. To have fallen from a state of princely grace – his two willing slaves, Nero and Jess, kept in ignorance and a position of supplication – to *this*. To a belly yawning for food; to penury, exhaustion and a fear that he'd never once more see home. It was shameful; it was humiliating. He had half a mind, right here and now, to confess his crimes to the other three people in the room (and who knew how many others who might be eavesdropping). Just to claw back some respect. Even if the respect manifested itself in the guise of disgust (and who could blame anyone for experiencing disgust at the telling of Massimo's tale?), at least it would mean that he would be noticed again.

As Bernadette said, 'Then I don't think I understand the question…' Massimo felt his buttocks clench, as if he was about to stand up. But stand up and do what? It didn't matter that his instinct was to cross the distance between the three wooden chairs and Tommy's couch in two strides, and then swing for the bastard. What was the best that he could achieve? A couple of blows to the side of the man's face? Pathetic. Connors and Bernadette would be on them like a fall of rain, pulling them apart… No. Better to wait, thought Massimo; hear the man out, with his drivel and his prevarication, and then – when the opportunity arose – to take Tommy somewhere and incapacitate the bigheaded dick-splash. And then bugger him. Hard.

'The *uncertainty* is what makes loss loss,' Tommy was saying. 'And this whole place – everywhere you've walked, every sight you've seen – has been built on the grief of someone's losses. A *world* of grief!' Tommy grinned. 'A whole world, lady and gentlemen!'

Oh, quite the showman, Massimo thought bitterly. *You wait. You'll change your tune.*

'And you don't arrive here without grief,' said Tommy, 'you mark my words.'

Breathing loudly through her nose, Bernadette said, 'Well, I think my dog might count.'

'Your dog?'

'You didn't say the loss had to be human.'

'No I didn't… So what happened to your dog?' Tommy asked.

'That's a good question. No one is exactly sure, but there was a kind of explosion in a house near where I live, just down the street. And my dog was washed away when the sea exploded out, along with Connors…' Bernadette indicated Connors, who had not uttered a word for a while and who was gazing down at the filthy furs that covered his feet – as if he expected said furs to show signs of life of the creature they had once belonged to. He did not acknowledge the name-check.

Tommy frowned. 'Wait a second… You're not talking about a house in Edlesborough, are you? Edlesborough, Bedfordshire.'

'Yes. That's where I live,' Bernadette answered, immediately smiling either in reflex or in reflection of Tommy's own spirited beam.

Shaking his head, Tommy offered his opinion of the situation that they'd reached. 'Fuck *me* it's a small world,' he said. 'That's just down the road where *I* live! It's where I left me da a few hours previous!'

Connors looked up from the perusal of his feet. His voice a little clogged with emotion, he said, 'My brother. For me it was my brother…' And he waited until he was certain that he had not been understood. 'The one I lost,' he clarified. 'The one I don't know where he went. It was my brother. We think he drowned. He was never found.'

STAND-OFFS

1.

Alarmed clear of a shallow doze by the sound of a vehicle, Nero jumped up and tensed his muscles. He knew Charlie's car engine… and this wasn't it.

The male voice that reached his ears was calm, magnified loud.

'*This is the police! We have the place surrounded! Come out with your hands up!*'

'Where the fuck's Charlie?' Nero muttered.

Glass was being broken downstairs, and Nero ran the sweating fingers of his left hand through the hair on his head that had grown longer during his time in the house than he had worn it in years. 'Oh my days,' he muttered. Although he knew the timing to be absurd, he wanted, suddenly and desperately, a head-shave: if he must face the public, in whatever form the interaction would take, he would like it to be while he looked his best… which was only right and proper, wasn't it? Of course it was! The problem, however, that presented itself was this: by no exaggeration could Nero be said at this moment to be looking his best. The contest needed no judge to settle the matter: from his naked chest down to his naked toes, he looked a mess. A sweating, emaciated bundle of sticks and skin.

It was no way to meet the enemy, Nero believed; but what could he do about it? They were entering the building – he could hear them – and the best he might have was a minute or two.

Where the hell was Charlie?

Where was Massimo?

Where were Nero's protectors, now that the time had come to really need them? Nero's brain fizzed with activity; he felt his heart changing gear and moving faster, ever faster. In his right hand he squeezed the stun-gun's grip.

A mantra had started at the back of Nero's head – *they'll be here, they'll be here* – and was marching forward, increasing in decibels. The *they* were Charlie and Massimo. Even now, in the midst of a panicky despair, Nero believed that the cavalry would arrive on time. 'They'll be here!' he shouted – and the sound of movement inside the walk-in wardrobe reminded him that he had a hostage or two if required.

Get the woman out of there, he thought. She was the weakest; she could be Nero's passport out of the house.

But then what?

Nero thought of Jess, and twitted himself for not having left when she'd made the break. Together they might have been miles away by now.

I didn't want to go, Nero reminded himself. *And I don't want to go now either,* he continued.

Hearing footfalls on the stairs, Nero took up a position in the centre of the room.

Voices from beyond the door; mutterings; the swish of fabric. 'Clear!' he heard a male voice announce. They were checking the rooms one by one.

As nervous as he felt at this moment, Nero raised the stun-gun to his own right temple. They would find him ready: nervous but ready. No need did he have for a hostage – nor even a witness to tell his tale as a caution to others in future days. He would be his own passport out of the house: that or sting himself in the process, like a scorpion with a drop of liquor on its tail. They would either make room for him to exit – or they wouldn't. But if they did not, he would never need to know about their decision.

Took less than a second to pull a trigger.

2.

Entering Interview Room 3, Sergeant Maureen Tennan thought back to her Post-Hostage Training with excitement and ominosity. There was no doubt in her mind that she must be the worst person on the Force to deal with the girl inside the room; but the girl had specified a female officer, and Tennan was the only one on duty with the right training behind her. It didn't matter that it was good practice to wait for the subject-experts to arrive from North London: the girl wanted to talk *now*, and Tennan's colleague had said that the girl appeared stoic and clear-headed.

'Hello, Jess,' said Tennan, closing the door. 'How are you feeling?'

'I remembered something,' Jess replied. 'Sorry. Hello. I forgot who I've spoken to so far.'

'My name is Maureen. I'd like to record our conversation if that's all right with you.'

'I don't care. I mean… I don't mind. I was wondering how I'd know the house again: I didn't look at it. And then I remembered.' Jess was squeezing an empty plastic cup in both hands; the recollection caused her to press harder, and it broke with a flamey crackle. 'Just outside the main gate – I had to climb the gate to get out – there's a signpost on the verge…' She sucked in a breath.

'A house name?'

'No. A FOR SALE sign. The house is for sale.' Jess closed

her eyes and cleared the memory of debris, as carefully as an archaeologist brushing sand off an artefact. Her subliminal vision, as it turned out, was 20/20. 'Edmonton and Squires. Estate Agents. Based in Bletchley,' Jess said.

3.

'Clear!'

The bathroom was as empty as the first two bedrooms had been, and now the three officers on the landing – two male and one female, all dressed in combats and carrying guns – addressed the fourth door of five on this storey.

Sergeant Roy Card, seven years on the Force dealing with hostage situations, and with the nightmares to prove it, laid his grip on the handle... and opened the door and stepped in.

In the middle of the room, a black boy stood with a gun against his temple, an expression of imbecilic tranquillity blanking out most of his features. The boy stood stark bollock naked, and exuded a scent of carrion. At the very least this room would need the windows opened for a couple of days, just to dissipate the odour, which also contained something electrical, something stormy – ozone-like, polluted.

'Put the weapon down, son,' Card instructed, taking a further step deeper into the room to allow his colleagues an unhindered entrance. 'We're armed police officers and we're going to get you out of here.'

'I'm going on my own,' Nero replied. 'Try and stop me and I'm zapping my brains out.'

'There's no need, son,' Card told him.

Three guns were now trained on Nero.

'Your girlfriend's made it out safely. We know you two are the victims here. And we'll find your captors, all right? We'll search until we do. They won't get far.'

Nero smiled. 'I'm no one's victim, Mr Policeman. The three in the wardrobe are *mine*. I was left in charge.'

As if on cue, from within the walk-in wardrobe came two male voices and the thunder of hands battering the door.

Having swapped a glance with his female colleague, who had taken up a position to his left, Card said again, 'Put the weapon down, son.'

'I ain't your son, Mr Policeman. Now back the fuck off, man.'

'Your name's Neil,' the female officer informed him.

'Once upon a time, maybe.'

'So what is it now?' she asked.

'You first,' Nero instructed.

'My name's Susan.'

'Pleased to meet you, Susan,' said Nero, the politeness bizarre in the circumstances; the officers' guns remained trained on Nero's bare torso.

Susan continued: 'We're here to get you out of here…' She remembered what she'd learned from the briefing back at The Nick. '…Nero.'

'I ain't Nero no more either. My name's Charlie – King Charlie! And I *rule* this roost, sweet. The prisoners are mine until Charlie comes home.'

'And then what?' Card asked.

Taking a step towards the trio of nozzles pointed in his direction, Nero answered, 'Then he gets his name back. And his prisoners.'

Another step, slow…

'Now leave my room,' Nero ordered.

'You need food and water,' Susan told him. 'You've had a terrible ordeal.'

'Not as bad as the one *they're* getting.' And Nero indicated the walk-in wardrobe with the hand carrying the stun-gun. The gun was only apart from his temple for a second but it was long enough.

Card fired.

The rubber bullet hit Nero in the centre of his chest, the marksman having aimed to miss the area above the mark's heart. In the echo-chamber acoustics of the unfurnished room, the report was an amplified version of a cork slipping free of a champagne bottle. The shot lifted Nero – or King Charlie, or Neil – off his feet.

Nero fell back into empty space; he was not close enough to the wall or the wardrobe door to make contact with anything. He landed on his back, the stun-gun having left his grip during his temporary flight.

As one the officers moved forward. Susan and Card covered the body; the third man in the room kicked Nero's dropped weapon towards the skirting board, beyond anyone's reach.

Not only had Card's shot robbed Nero of a bargaining position, it had also stolen several other of his liberties: namely, a semblance of control over his own breathing; the façade of bravado that he'd worn; and autocracy over his own bladder.

As he squealed and tried to catch his breath, the two actions serving to hamper the progress of the other, he also swore in disbelief… and wet himself. The way he'd landed meant that urine slopped up the brushy beach of his groin.

'You fucking *shot* me!' he gasped.

And he started to weep.

4.

Roger Billie was finishing up a case study, touch-typing it onto the template on the screen (and dreaming of a bigger office) when the telephone rang.

'It's me,' said Phyllie. 'The police are here. They want to talk about Don Bridges and Charlie Eastlight. And something else.'

'That's acceptable, I can pop by in my lunch hour if that's okay.'

'…Who's in the office with you?' Pyllie asked.

'That's right,' Roger answered, pretending to any eaves-droppers that he'd been asked a completely different question.

'Well okay. Just get here, could you? You know more than I do, I think, and I've got morning sickness like you wouldn't believe.'

5.

Sometimes, in the middle of the morning, if it was a day that she did not go to work, and if she was lonely or bored (or in not so distant times in the past, brain dead on cannabis), Phyl-lie would go into the spare bedroom and pretend that she had checked into a hotel room. For the purposes of her masturbatory fantasies, she was usually on a business trip abroad, alone in an Eastern European city, perhaps, or frustrated by the heat of an Argentinian evening.

In her waking dream this mid-morning, Phyllie had un-dressed out of a sandalwood-coloured suit. She showered, she ate the complimentary chocolates (with a cup of *ersatz* coffee), then she phoned in her kisses to the kids. Trying desperately to get a fix on her geographical location, she considered room service and trotted through a selection of the world's trouble spots, in her mind. Islamabad, Afghanistan… Whoever came to rescue her would be obliged to hurdle road blocks, and tapdance and zigzag past armed militia in mustard uniforms, as dextrous as Astaire.

But the picture wouldn't settle: it flickered, crackled and

paused. The real room seeped into her fantasy hotel room; Phyllie sneezed and it melted away. 'Damn it.' She was not even close to her G-spot jackpot; feeling foolish while kneading through her own secretions, Phyllie stopped and wondered what she thought she was doing. (Shame and a sense of lunacy competed for the lion's share of her emotions.) Truly, it was no way to behave, was it, flicking the bean as an avoidance tactic: she had tasks to execute, chores to perform – and now the front door bell was chiming. 'Damn it,' she repeated, pulling her dressing gown on over her sweaty nipples. Her vagina was sore.

'I'm coming!' she shouted to whoever was outside. As she trod the stairboards, a smile inched on to her face.

Her rescuer was dressed in a police uniform. 'I'm Constable Peter Vash,' the young man announced. 'May I come in, Madam?'

Phyllie regretted the lie about the morning sickness to Roger, but she'd had to say something that the officer would overhear that explained the fact that she wasn't dressed at this hour of the day. Morning sickness would do (she could not really say that she'd been masturbating); and at least there was a grain of truth in the explanation: she had certainly felt ropey first thing, which was why she had called in sick in the first place.

'This might seem odd,' Phyllie said to the officer who had been dispatched to her home, 'but do you actually need me here? For when Roger arrives, I mean. Do you need me?'

'Do you need to go out?'

'I'd like to. If that's okay with you, I mean – if you can wait for him… You see, Hartvig's a friend of mine from way back. I'd like to drive over and see how he's doing with all this.'

Although Vash appeared disappointed, he nodded sagely; he even stroked his bearded chin.

'I'll have a sandwich in my car while I wait,' he said, his tone irritatingly long-suffering.

6.

The gates that barred – or should have barred – the end of the driveway were wide open, and Phyllie drove up to the house unimpeded, drawing up alongside two police cars that were already parked there but which were empty of officers.

The estate felt hushed; it lacked the bustle and commotion that Phyllie had imagined would mark a crime scene. As she locked her car door (manually for a change), she wondered where the helicopters were, where the frothing news crews were. It was all as subdued as a parrot with a cloth over its cage... an enforced sleep.

Phyllie did not walk towards the house. Given the fact that no one had come out to greet her – either in a uniform or not – she assumed that no one was in the building at the moment. So be it: if this matter was *al fresco*, then Phyllie could use the exercise. Only last week, her doctor had told her that she was pregnant, not ill, and that a baby inside her was no good reason not to go for a stroll in the fresh air.

And the air did not come fresher than it blew this afternoon! Normal-smelling, good, strong gusts, without the vaguest whiff of blood cavorting among them... Into these guests Phyllie strode, with a heart packed with grief – grief for Vig, not Dorota (not really), whom she neither knew well nor not at all, and whom she neither liked well nor detested. It was Vig – and only Vig – on Phyllie's cluttered mind this early afternoon, and despite the size of the grounds, she knew – somehow *knew* – that she'd find him at the bird cages.

She headed in their direction.

7.

It was not a perfect union of coincidences or instincts, for

Vig had clearly been at the cages for a while. (Phyllie had imagined that they'd rock up simultaneously, albeit from opposite, or at least different, directions.) But it was close enough.

'You look soaked to the skin,' Phyllie told him. 'Has it been raining?'

'No. I've been exercising. Digging.'

'For treasure? X marks the spot?'

'Something like that.' Vig held up a supermarket carrier bag. 'It's Don's phone. His last testament if not his last will.'

'I don't get it,' Phyllie admitted.

'He left me a note,' Vig explained from within the first cage on the left. Holding open the door, he added, 'Care to join me?'

Phyllie stepped into the cage.

'I knew there had to be more than he said in the letter. The old bugger hid it for me to find.'

Phyllie noted the dirt embedded in Vig's fingernails, the excrement and slime coating his hands. 'So he buried his phone.'

'For me. That's right, I'm sure of it.'

'Do the *police* know you're in here?'

'Do the police know *we're* in here, you mean. No they don't. Not unless they're watching with binoculars, which I wouldn't put past them, I suppose.' Vig smiled. 'He must've known I'd be quick – he'd left it on. The phone. With the display reading PLAY MESSAGE question mark. So I played the message.'

'And what did it say?'

Vig's smile widened. 'Wanna hear?'

'Well of course I do,' Phyllie answered. 'Don't tease me, Vig.'

'You'll be shocked. It's a ghost's voice.'

Phyllie shrugged. 'I'll take my chances,' she told him.

8.

'Introduce yourself clearly,' Don said into the ear of Phyllie Reydman. There followed a squawk of noise pollution – wind buffeting the mouthpiece, perhaps – and then another voice spoke, not quite as clearly as Don had, but audibly enough.

'My name is Charles Eastlight,' the second voice said. *'And I am a prisoner of Don Bridges.'*

'He hasn't given him the phone,' said Vig. 'He's holding it for him – at the top of the hole, I reckon.'

'Ssshhh.'

'I am guilty of the crimes of kidnapping and torture,' Eastlight confessed slowly. *'My partner's name is Massimo Sento… but he is innocent of most of our crimes… It was me… It was me. It was my idea. To take the kids.'*

Don interrupted. *'What are their names? For the record, like.'*

'The boy is called Nero – his real name is Neil. The girl is called Jessica – Jess.'

'Good,' said Don.

'Good God,' said Phyllie. 'It's the missing girl from my school. It's got to be.'

'That's what I thought too,' Vig told her.

Eastlight gave the address in Eggington: the address of the torture house, where he had planned to kill Nero and Jess on the night of his anniversary.

Then he gave the date.

'That's tomorrow,' said Phyllie under her breath.

'Exactly. Don's saved that girl's life.'

'In a roundabout way… Vig. You've got to give this to the police right now.'

'You haven't got to the best bit.'

'I recognised him at your barbecue, sir,' Don said into the mouthpiece, as clear as a whistle once more. *'The way one species knows*

another by smell alone. I knew him for what he was, or would be, and the pervert knew me as well, a leopard being unable to change its spots and all that, sir. And I think that's why we disliked each other from the word go. We were fighting over the same prey, so to speak.'

Don left a long pause.

'What does that mean?' Phyllie asked. 'Christ, I can hardly breathe.'

'How far have you got?'

'The bit about… fighting over the same prey.'

As if he'd heard her through the divisions between life and death, Don elucidated his point.

'You see, I was once like Mr Eastlight, and I've lived with it ever since. Until now, of course. I was a brute, sir. A savage. To me wife, to me daughter, God rest their harrowed souls. To stable girls and the youngsters wanting riding lessons. To the horses themselves – and what's a horse ever done, except bring me luck and an income? A disgrace of a human being, through and through, I admit it for all to see.'

Another pause. Wind crowding around the mouthpiece of Don's phone while he gathered his thoughts (or had a weep? Who could tell?).

'Everything I told you about me daughter was true, sir, with one rather large condition. The horse kicked her all right, and God help me when I say it might've been better if she'd died straight away, for she suffered her short life through. Damage to the brain, sir, you see. Affected her development – and ours, sir. And ours.'

Don sighed; his words had started to sound chopped up, as if he was walking away from Eastlight. He didn't want Eastlight to hear this?

'We took it all out on that poor girl, emotionally speaking, the both of us did, when we weren't doing the same to one another. It was a house of domestic abuse, sir – I'll call it no other – and occasionally I was the victim meself. Me shattered knees, for example: nothing to do with the horses. That

was me wife, God save her, when she ran me over in the car. Then reversed. To make it final – or so she thought.'

Don laughed; coughed. The flick-and-catch of a cigarette lighter; an exhausted exhalation. Another cough.

'Swear these things'll be the death of me,' he said, still laughing. Then he coughed again – and seemed to sober up.

'What I wrote in the letter – about me wife's disappearances? – all true. All true, sir. And I tried everything to find me wife and me daughter – or the daughter as she should've been if the horse hadn't kicked her. My lost. My missing…

'Only one man seemed to make sense to me. His name was Benny, and he represented something with the name of intra-rationalism, *which basically means the spaces between alternative planes of being. Or so he sold it to me, any rate.*

Don gave out Benny's address in Ashridge, and said, *'Ask him to see his vivaria.'*

'See his what?' Phyllie whispered.

'Which brings me to my final confession, I suppose: on the subject of children who go missing…'

'Oh God.'

'I can tell you where three of them ended up over the years, and if there's a Hell of burning excrement for me to dwell in for the rest of me days, I know it's for those children I'll dwell there.

'They're in the woods, sir. I've sent you a map of approximately where, sir, to the best of me recollection – I've sent it second class post. I can only plead grief or insanity – which are much the same thing – for those three children… I bought em off Benny himself. He keeps a zoo of human beings in his vivaria. Kept alive but in deep comas. Comas. And a lot of em connected together, for reasons of his own.

'See… I thought the children, if I kept em in the hole in me kitchen – I thought they'd lure me own child and me wife back to me, from the other side – the other place. He convinced me it would work. He promised me it

would. But it didn't. So the freshest one you'll find is in the septic tank — she was recent. The others I wouldn't like to say what condition they'll be in, sir. Sorry about that.'

'Is he crying?' Phyllie asked.

'Or laughing. I couldn't tell,' Vig replied.

Phyllie nodded. 'You'll have entered the address for this Benny guy in your phone, right?'

'Right as rain.'

The two of them stopped talking when a voice said, 'I wouldn't want to *disturb* you in there... but would either of you like to tell me what the hell's going on?'

It was Dorota.

The Intra-Rationalist

1.

For the first ten minutes of the journey, Vig could not think about Don: his imagination was crowded with Dorota. He and Phyllie had left her behind, and when he returned to the house there'd be hell to pay, no doubt; but then again, perhaps she would run away from him – she had certainly been angry enough to do so. She had frothed with rage while he'd used his phone to find the postcode for Benny's property. And she had fizzed with temper while he'd walked away from the empty cages (with Phyllie a stride behind) on his way to the car on the driveway.

Phyllie had tapped the postcode into the journey-planner that Vig kept beneath the driver's seat. Fixing the device to the windscreen for him to see the roadmap, Phyllie had said, 'I'm sorry if I've created a ruckus for when you get back.'

'At the end of the road, in two hundred yards, turn left,' said the journey-planner.

Vig said nothing.

'Should we have told the police where we're going?' Phyllie asked, trying a different tack.

Vig said nothing. Silently he obeyed the direction that the device had given.

'Vig?'

And then he spoke, his words more robotic than the planner's. 'I think it's over between me and Dorota,' he said. 'I think it's been over for longer than I was willing to admit.'

'Well, I'm sorry to hear that,' Phyllie replied.

'I left instructions for her to call the police if she doesn't hear from me within an hour. But it's probably not the best time to be throwing out my orders, in retrospect.'

Phyllie waited before asking, '…What do you intend to do when we get there, by the way?'

'Talk to this guy Benny.'

'If he's there. If he still *lives* there.'

Vig shrugged. 'If he's there,' he agreed.

'And say what?' Phyllie asked.

'At the roundabout, take the third exit,' said the journey-planner.

'I don't know. But Don was not exactly ambiguous about Benny's involvement, was he?'

'…No. But he wasn't exactly sane either.'

'Oh I don't know. Maybe killing himself was the sanest thing he ever did in his life.'

2.

The navigation device took them right to the door. Vig would not have known how precisely to articulate his feelings at this moment (not even in German), but there was something unsettling about the house's absence of protection. No gates or fences secured the perimeter; no long gravel driveway snaked and teased its way from the road to the front door. In fact, to Vig, it resembled nothing more or less than a countryside B&B. It was wide open. Utterly unthreatening… And this had to be a mistake, didn't it?

'No time like the present,' Phyllie suggested.

'Just give me a minute.'

His thoughts of Dorota had been quiet for the last fifteen minutes, but now Vig pictured her standing by the front door, puzzled and furious; she would be waiting for him, her fists clenched. Perhaps she had already packed a suitcase – a suitcase for *him*. He saw the fences around his own property – the security seemed ludicrous now – and he knew that once he walked away, he walked away for good.

'What if Don was having us on?' he whispered. 'It doesn't look…'

'It doesn't look odd enough,' Phyllie interrupted. 'I agree. What better place to hide something? A place so ordinary…'

Vig killed the engine.

'So what impression do *I* give, I wonder. With my gates, I mean.'

'You give the impression of uneasy money,' Phyllie answered. 'You'll be burgled before *this* wanker is… Are you ready?'

They were met at the door by a short young woman who smiled at them pleasantly. 'Can I help you?' she asked.

Vig recognised an Eastern European facial structure when he saw one. The lady at the door even resembled Dorota, and Vig was a breath away from addressing her in Polish when she spoke again.

'Is Benny expecting you?'

'No. No I don't think so,' Vig replied… and he immediately wondered if this was true.

For a second the woman's eyes lost their distant ethereal quality; they focused, something sharpened to a point… and Vig was convinced that the interview was at an end, almost before it had begun. Partly because of embarrassment, he avoided the woman's expression and averted his eyes in a downward glance. By doing this he was able to see what the woman had made no attempt to hide.

On her right hip she wore a holster. Poking from the top of the holster was a gun butt.

'You can come in,' she said, standing aside – but the decision that she'd made had armed her with a smile that Vig didn't like, and he was certain that he wouldn't like the hospitality on offer.

Telling himself not to be a baby, Vig stepped into the house. The woman had been out the back somewhere when they'd called. Target practice or something. Country ways... Didn't Vig himself enjoy a shoot? Sure! Sure he did! The difference was, he was not in the habit of answering the front door carrying a shotgun.

'He'll be in the vivaria,' the woman called over her shoulder. Indicatating to her right as she walked, she added, 'Perhaps you'd like to wait in the library. I'm Eva, by the way.'

When they were certain that Eva was out of earshot, Phyllie and Vig spoke industriously at low volume.

'She had a gun!' said Phyllie.

'Didn't even ask our names,' said Vig. 'He's not frightened of anyone or he's stupid.'

'I should've waited in the car.'

'Why?'

'Because *she has a gun.*'

'So? His daughter, do you think?'

'Maybe.'

'What the hell is this vivaria that everyone keeps mentioning?'

Phyllie's faced pinched as she attempted the recollection. 'Something to do with animals, I think.'

'I've got a sense of déjà vu,' Vig admitted. 'I remember talking to Charlie in *my* library when Dorota and I had just moved in. Now we're in Benny's – it's like one of those Russian dolls. And now he keeps animals, you tell me. Like Don did. It's too weird.'

'You should talk to Roger about patterns of behaviour. I'm sure he'll appreciate the chance to sing his old hymns.'

'Yeah, I'll do that if we don't get shot. And fed to the creatures… Does he know where you are, by the way?'

'No.'

'Why not text him,' Vig advised. 'Be on the safe side.'

They were wordless for a few moments. They listened for clues – for anything inside the house, a moan, a cry – and then Phyllie said, after removing her phone from her handbag, 'It's snakes. Vivaria is the plural of vivarium. It's where people keep snakes.'

3.

'What magazine are you from?' Benny asked, smiling. 'Excuse the wet hair – I'm off out tonight. Shower.'

'It's fine. We're not from a magazine,' said Phyllie.

'Ah. You're not here about the reptiles, then.'

'No.'

'I have to say I was wondering why no camera. So what then?'

'Don Bridges,' Vig answered.

'Who?'

'Don Bridges.'

'Yeah I heard you. And I asked you: *who?*'

'He used to work for me. Groundskeeper. He had a few choice words for you, Benny. It *is* Benny, isn't it?'

'It is.' Benny sat down on one of the plump chairs, indicating for his guests to do likewise. 'Please.' Memories creased his face. 'This Don Bridges. He used to be a jockey, did he?'

'That's the one,' said Phyllie.

Benny nodded. 'Yeah. He worked for me for a while. Yonks ago. What about him?'

'He killed himself,' Vig replied.

'Sorry to hear that. Did he leave me something in his will?'

'I don't know.'

'See, I'm trying to grasp why you're *here*,' said Benny.

'He alluded to your experiments. With people.'

'Did he now. Well the cunt was finally good for something. Who'da thought it?' Benny smirked. 'I'd given up on the prick.'

'Would you mind telling us about the experiments?' Phyllie asked.

'Not at all.'

He doesn't know our names, Vig realised, and yet he'll tell us all about his experiments. What the dickens?

'*Eva!*' Benny shouted. 'Something for my guests, if you'd be so kind.'

'I *am* a bit parched,' said Phyllie, 'as it happens. Thank you.'

'*Eva!*'

'I *heard* you, Benny. Give me a second,' said Eva, appearing at the room's threshold.

'You can't get the staff,' Benny joked, loud enough for Eva to hear as she walked away. 'She's a good girl, is Eva. From Czechoslovakia. Or the Czech Republic, I should say. Czechoslovakia in old money. Only came here to be a nanny when she was eighteen. Now she's twenty-seven and looking after a load of fucking zombies. But at least the pay's better.'

Vig did not know what to say; he was relieved to hear Phyllie say, 'I'm not sure I understand you, Benny. What do you mean by zombies?'

Why doesn't he care about our names? Vig wondered. Either Benny wanted them to speak of this encounter… or they were not expected to leave. Which was it?

'I'll show you in a minute. Always happy to show off me wares. Things've evolved a fair bit since Don was around.'

Benny paused.

'How much do you know?' he asked.

'Only what he left in his suicide note,' said Phyllie.

'Which was what?'

'It was about you,' said Vig. 'About your experiments.'

'Oh that. Well, allow me to expand on what you don't know.

'You might call evolution my *grand plan* – I've renounced a good number of em as I've gone along, I don't mind telling you.'

Eva entered the room, carrying a tray on which cups and a teapot had been set. Her face said nothing. The look of ethereal distance had left her.

Waiting for Eva to pour and to do the honours, Benny said, 'What I'm about to tell you, I've told a hundred times before, to a hundred different people like you – seeking answers. Some of em listen and some of em don't. And I insist on being heard, so are you listening? Listen to this. It's been my reason for living for a little while – a couple of years. Evolution, mate. *Evolution.*' He settled back into his chair and added quietly, 'Evolution.'

His repetition of the word like a mantra had not cleared anything up, however.

'…Meaning what?' said Phyllie.

Benny's lower eyebags were cushions of bad stitches, especially when he smiled, which he did now. The facial tan adopted a depth of varnish.

'I am overwhelmingly interested in the capabilities and capacities of the human body and spirit. And the corruption of the same… Do you follow me?'

'Not yet,' Vig admitted. He did so with an inner alarm bell chiming. For the first time he got the impression that Benny, despite his years, was not a man not used to getting his own way. Nor was he a pacifist: not by a long chalk. He had something about him of an old East End villain, maybe suntanned (and pickled) on the patio of a second home in Marbella; he was dangerous. He'd invite you into his home but he'd work on you later.

'Scientists disagree on the numbers,' Benny continued, 'but let's assume the figure is ten per cent. The human brain uses ten per cent of its total functionality. First I'd ask: How do you know? Secondly, why do we assume there's more to make use of? If we don't know what ninety per cent does then maybe it does the square root of bugger all.'

'So you're…' Phyllie sipped her tea. '…you're conducting experiments on people's brains?'

Benny sniffed. 'Among other things. One of me projects being what some would call our spiritual selves – the unopposable force of will, if you like. Or even if you don't like.' And he laughed at his own 'joke'.

'I'll write a book about it, I reckon. Well, *I* won't write a book about it… I'll dictate a book about it. I've submitted a few papers to peer reviewed journals, but I'm no academic. They've come back – nonsense about clarity of me argument. *Ethics* if you please. What's so fucking *ethical* about living in ignorance, I ask you? Nothing: that's what. It's wilful naïveté – a disgraceful, diabolical human trait.'

Continuing to flounder somewhat, Vig took a swallow of his tea and selected from a list of possible questions.

'Do you mean – sorry if I'm being slow here – do you mean you perform surgery here? On people's brains?' He endeavoured to edit the horror from his voice.

Either the subject itself or Vig's efforts at self-censorship amused Benny. His eyes twinkled. 'Well I've done a bit of incision and excision in me time, but I don't know you'd call it surgery. It was mainly gangs in them days. Non-payment for this or that. Occasionally you'd be obliged to inform some insect that he wouldn't be needing his reading glasses anymore.'

'Christ. You put out his eyes?' asked Phyllie.

'No no no; nothing so serous, darling. I just cut an ear off. Only once or twice, like. Twelve times to be precise.'

'That's sick. I hope that's an old gangster joke,' she told him.

'Regrettably not; but those were harder days… and bear in mind we're talking about scum. Total pus. *Who won't learn a lesson any other fucking way*. And it's like in any other walk of life. It's reputation. You can't have it get round you've been *ignored*… Anyway. That's a younger man's game. Gave it all up a long time ago.'

'Because of your conscience?' Vig asked, hoping desperately for a Paul-on-the-road-to-Damascus-type conversion to a more equable industry, however unlikely this appeared to be in the offing.

He also asked himself a question; a question that he hoped Phyllie was asking of herself as well. *Why is his telling us this?* It was not as though Benny seemed contrite, and there was no feel of the deathbed confession about his words.

'Conscience? Not in *this* lifetime. No, mate. What goes on in a man's conscience is between that man and his conscience. An overrated stimulus anyway, if you want my opinion. Those tinker toy psychology programmes they force you onto in prison… either of you been inside?'

Vig and Phyllie shook their heads.

'Good job. Stay out as long as you can: that's my motto. And do you know how I achieve this? By control and manipulation. Control plus manipulation equals distance. There are people with a dotted-line connection to me, in terms of management structure, who *don't even know my name*. And that's just the way I like it… But what was I saying?'

'Oh yeah, conscience. When you're inside, in a rec room with fifteen other overweight fuckwits whose *names* you don't want to learn, let alone what crimes they committed, and you've got some underpaid do-gooder asking you *to think about your crime* and *think about your victim* – how do you think your victim *feels?* – and half the time what you're *really* thinking is *get me out of here* and *the wanker feels nothing* – he's dead – that's when you learn what a useless thing a conscience actually is. It's unnecessary. Actually, it's a hindrance - stops a man doing his work, I reckon. Easily removed. Like the appendix. What good's a conscience if it can be bought and sold? Anything – this is a theory I've developed, see what you think – anything that can be bought and sold is essentially worthless. Worthless in the literal sense of without value.

'No. My retirement from violence was essentially a financial decision. You'd be surprised at how little you actually *earn* in organised bodywork. All the money stays at the top. So you're scarring a man's torso for what? For thirty *quid?* Stroll on! I made myself a wealthy man by selling what didn't belong to me. And I'm good.'

'…You're a fence,' said Phyllie.

Benny wrinkled his nose. 'Never cared for that term,' he replied. 'I prefer a transferral executive. But yeah, essentially, you've got the right idea. I only dip me toes into actual violence rarely… and it's rarely about money. I need people for my intra-rationalist work. Sometimes they don't wanna volunteer.' He smiled fondly at a memory. 'Oh, and the grass who put me in the nick that time, of course. I had to tell *that* prick his fortune… Do you know what we did? The prick was into amateur dramatics, right – on the side? Straight up. Loved a bit of Gilbert and Sullivan and that game. And when it comes to revenge, your best bet's to hurt what's gonna hurt worst. Now with me fresh out of prison, he's gonna be thinking: *That Benny won't risk anything straight away. People'll be watching him.* So that's when you strike. You double bluff em. The *last* person he'll expect is me *in person*. Wouldn't even cross his mind I'd take the chance.

'So my choice was this. The prick likes singing and dancing in Gilbert and Sullivan. Fair enough, each to his own. So what would hurt worst? Never singing again or never dancing again? I couldn't decide. So I made him gargle with a corrosive compound. And then I set fire to his feet.'

The comment caused much concerted tea-drinking… until Phyllie asked, 'And will *that* particular story appear in your book as well?'

'Phyllie…' Vig warned.

'He's talking crap, Vig. Living out a wish fulfilment fantasy in his dotage. No offence, Benny.'

But Benny was still in a state of amusement; umbrage was the furthest emotion from his mind, it seemed. He waved the very notion from the air.

'Come on, Vig – we're leaving.'

'I seriously doubt that, my dear,' Benny replied. 'It's one of me favourites – a concoction I'm especially proud of. Made with me own ingenuity and instinct.'

'What are you talking about?' Vig wanted to know.

'The poison you've been drinking in your tea. It works from the feet up. You don't feel a thing until you try to walk.'

Phyllie snorted. 'Well let's put that theory to the test, shall we?' And she stood up.

Her legs were not strong enough to support her. Her knees buckled and she fell back onto her chair.

'Now the first thing to mention,' Benny continued, 'is the worse you'll encounter is a bad headache. The poison works on your muscles – the brain's last on his journey.'

Vig made a move – an atavistic response to the threat. He did not raise himself to his full height, however: the sense of weakness in his feet and shins was emphatic. Suddenly he felt too weak even to curse.

'What I'm interested in – obsessed you might say – is the evolution of the group mind. Down below our feet I keep thirty-odd waifs and strays in a state of suspended animation. Injections. Administered by the lovely Eva and some other members of my team. And what I've *found* – to my surprise – is for want of a better expression, their dreamworlds have started to overlap.'

Phyllie had not caught Vig's temporary speechlessness. 'You're a madman,' she breathed; for all her cool, irate demeanour, however, she felt hot. Sweat prickled on her brow and in her oxters.

'They're not really unconscious, you see. It's like they're talking in their sleep. The funny thing being, some of em talk *to each other*. They talk about this place they've gone to. Jung might have had something of the kind in mind when he wrote about the collective unconscious. I wouldn't know, never read the cunt. Just like the term – collective unconscious. Certain ring to it.'

There must be something we can do, Vig thought. But how would he get over to the other side of the room, without the use of his legs? Even if he crawled... what then?

'What will it cost us for the antidote?' he asked.

'The antidote? You'll have to work for it, mate. How do you normally earn anything?'

'This doesn't make any sense,' said Phyllie. 'You didn't know we'd be coming here...'

Once more, Benny waved the suggestion away like a wasp.

'Oh there're visitors all the time,' he said. 'I welcome them all. Some are suitable; some aren't. Most of my subjects I collect from various properties in the general area.'

'So what do you want from us?' Vig asked.

'*Vig!* I'm not going to be his puppet! I'm not a plaything! I'm pregnant for Christ's sake!'

Benny's face brightened further. 'Are you? That'll be a new

one – never had a *foetus* to work with. I've had a *dog.* Always felt bad about that dog. See: I arranged an explosion and a flood in a house I rent out in Edlesborough. I made sure the tenants wouldn't be home – they were at a funeral – and I arranged for a couple of expendable guys to get into the blast. I wanted to see how water might influence what they thought about when they were back here. Some *extremely* interesting observations.'

'Oh *sod* your fucking observations!' Phyllie shouted. 'Didn't you hear me? I won't do it, whatever you want me to do. I'll drag myself out by my fingernails if I have to.'

'Be my guest. I only need your husband,' said Benny, 'though I'd prefer you both, I must admit. I wanna see if some-one who *knows what's going on* influences the balance of the world they've created for themselves.'

'But we *don't* know what's gong on,' Vig argued. 'The bit about the dog…?'

'Ah. An unfortunate soldier of circumstances, that dog. I don't like unnecessary harm to any creature, which you might find ironic.'

Vig was sweating as well now. But he wanted to know more; indeed, he imagined that his only chance lay in learning.

'When the water smashed the house up, there was a neigh-bour's dog there. The poor thing drowned. I tried me best. The funny thing was, one of the burglars – the one that didn't die, obviously – thought the dog had gone across the threshold with him. It made for some interesting pillow talk, I can tell you.'

'Vig, I'm frightened,' Phyllie said. 'If this harms the baby…' With which she tried again to stand up. The effort was no more competent than the first attempt. Before she could scream or shout, she burst into a torrent of impotent tears.

Perhaps it was this squall that reminded Vig of when he'd used to teach German: it had the temperature and ferocity of an adolescent tantrum over the incorrect usage of the accusative case. Though Vig said nothing to soothe Phyllie's panic, he was pleased to note that the crying had given him an idea. And he owed it all to his experiences with stroppy teens.

'What's in it for me?' he asked. A bead of sweat trickled into his left eye and he squinted; Benny must have misconstrued something menacing from this because his own expression hardened.

'Are you *bargaining* with me?' Benny demanded.

'Are you bargaining with him?' Phyllie also wanted to know.

'I am. What do *I* get out of this? You want us to visit this place they've created – but I already know it won't be real... even if I find it. So I don't even have the prospect of an adventure; so I'll ask again. What's in it for me?'

Benny paused. Then he said, 'I've got money – you can see that. Name a price. Name a *fee*.'

'I'm a Lottery winner, mate. I've *got* money. I own the place where Don Bridges worked.'

'Then what? What do you want?'

'I'm a teacher, Benny. I'm an educator.'

'You wanna teach people when you get there? Be my guest. Fill your boots. You'll be a prophet there, son!'

'No,' said Vig. 'I want to teach people *about* what you've discovered – or created, depending on how you view it.'

His frown melting, Benny said, 'That's exactly what *I* want. At my time of life. I want the scientific community to sit up and take notice. To give me credit.'

'For which I'll want fifty per cent of all future sales.'

'...What *sales?*' Benny demanded.

'Whether we market it as... I don't know... a holiday opportunity... or training conditions for the military, for example,' said Vig.

'Now wait a minute…'

'You're talking about psychic phenomena and yet…' Vig's mouth was as arid as a camel's hoof. '…and yet you've got all your subjects *in one place*. What'll happen when you've got centres in Vladivostock and Cairo, all talking together across the seas. You're *thinking too small*, Benny.'

'I am not!'

'And that's why the scientific community takes you as seriously as Norman Wisdom.'

Benny protested. 'I'm a one-man band, son.'

'Not now you're not.'

Phyllie retched and some of the spiked tea dribbled down her chin. Her face had lost colour; her skin was the shade of a Greek column. When she tried to say Vig's name once again she lost consciousness. Her passing-out sigh fluttered like a swift.

'We're business partners, Benny. Fifty-fifty.'

'Or what?' Benny argued, the old resilience leaping back into life, almost as if it had supped nourishment from Phyllie's departure. 'In case you haven't noticed, I happen to be holding all the tools. You've nothing to work with, son.'

Vig managed one final conscious smile. 'I'll tear the fucking thing to pieces from inside,' he said. And then he closed his eyes. The smile did not evaporate from his lips.

CHILDREN OF THE OVERLAP

1.

'Mummy? Mummy, wake up!'

Phyllie gasped; snored; tried to settle.

'*Mummy!*'

And she opened her eyes… to see the little girl kneeling to the left of her head. The girl was four or five; her expression was pained and worried.

'We have to wake up,' the girl explained.

I'm not your Mummy, Phyllie wanted to say, but she sat up anyway. The indistinct scenery around her read her mind; it tried to copy her thoughts. However, the blue sky was pale and indecisive; so Phyllie thought harder – projected harder – knowing that this was all in her skull.

The little girl stood up and took a few steps away from her mother. She kept looking left and right; she was nervous. Someone was pursuing them, perhaps.

Examining her own clothing and finding it to be intact (and as she remembered it), Phyllie climbed to her feet.

They were inside a building that did not have a roof. Water had damaged everything… there would be no more lessons taught here. She was back at school. She was in her former classroom, back when she was twelve, despite the physical evidence of Phyllie's fully-matured womanhood.

She felt her stomach, punched by panic. No baby breathed

inside her skin. Then she relaxed. Of course not: her baby was now four years old, and was urging her to go somewhere else. Her baby was guiding her. Her baby –

'Claire?'

The girl's head stopped in one place for a few seconds; her eyes were Phyllie's own, the mother realised – years before the embarrassments at school that would eventually lead to a diagnosis of myopia, to spectacles, and later to contact lenses.

Phyllie and Roger had settled on Claire if it was a girl; Vincent if it was a boy. The second option had been rendered redundant.

'Where are we going, sweetheart?'

'Mummy, *please…*' The girl was at the classroom door, which was warped on its hinges (it looked like a cow's tongue).

Firmer now: 'Where, darling?'

'To the *Overlap*,' the child whined, as if this was the most obvious thing in the world. And perhaps it was… in *this* world at least.

Wondering where Vig had been taken, Phyllie followed Claire out into the corridor… How long had the school been abandoned? she wondered. Beneath the pale blue sky, the damage to the building was well enough lit. The corridor was slippery in a porridge of dirty and filthy paperwork; textbooks spreadeagled, ruined and trampled, posters and staff announcements, pleas for club enrolments, Sports Day achievements… Phyllie saw a picture of Ben Nevis that she'd painted in Art at the age of eleven, it lay in some crumbled plaster and the remains of a bird's nest. She remembered the gold star that she'd earned with that painting, how her teacher, Mr Madden, had urged on a talent that Phyllie had not only jettisoned but until now had forgotten ever existed.

Phyllie took charge and gripped Claire's hand. Together

they negotiated the corridors, Phyllie quickly learning to reduce the length of her stride in order to accommodate her child's less certain movements. As they approached, step by step, the building's rear entrance (leading on to the playground, as Phyllie well recalled), Phyllie saw artefacts from her childhood and from later on. This abandoned school was where her memories had been deposited, it seemed. A photo of her first boyfriend, Dean, hung by one corner from a waterlogged notice board, the image's smile reminding Phyllie of why she'd slept with him at the age of fourteen. As the memory returned that Dean had died in a car crash at the age of twenty-two, the image in the photo grew a blonde beard in seconds, grew gentle laugh-lines around the eyes, stopped smiling and lowered its eyelids. He was gone. She had mourned him. Along with other former school friends she had taken a train south from her university town to attend his funeral.

In this new existence, Phyllie wondered, was Dean still alive?

She tried to recall what Benny had told her and Vig. Only while so attempting did she acknowledge the fuzziness in her skull. The long-left-behind was as clear as day; the more-recent needed extra time to sleep... or so it seemed.

It occurred to Phyllie that Vig might be somewhere in the building, perhaps hurt; that by exiting, she and Claire would not be permitted to re-enter. Although the little girl was adamant that they must be on their way to the Overlap (whatever *that* might be), it bit Phyllie's heart to imagine she might be leaving Vig here, and in pain. Perhaps if she could understand the child's urgency she would be better positioned to make a reasoned decision.

They stepped out onto a path that led to a playground. Taking in the unexpectedly diminished dimensions, Phyllie stopped in her tracks. The girl walked on, like a dog at the end of its leash, she felt a restraining tug (they were still joined hand to hand), and she turned to her mother with a quizzical expression on her face.

Phyllie didn't notice it. True as it might be that there was nothing to see in the playground, the littleness of where they'd played – where they'd shouted, where they'd sulked – had grasped hold of her breath. In a trance she saw a parade of boys from the lower years, walking in file around the perimeter, ghostly, dead soldiers now, perhaps, chanting *Who wants to play… war-ore!* Always the word *war* in two syllables: the rhythm of their mantra. Playtime after playtime, the line of willing conscripts growing, but never enough time to actually *play*. The collection was everything… Skipping ropes flicked the summer-hot asphalt. Johnny Hodgins fell from the climbing frame one lunchtime – not even from its summit – and broke his left arm. Phyllie had witnessed the accident; terrified and heavy-bladdered, she'd been summoned to Mrs Barter's office to provide an eye-witness account, and now Phyllie saw Johnny fall again and again, in a loop, from the frame that she had always been too scared to scale herself.

'Mummy?'

'Just a second, Claire.'

More and more children filled the playground as Phyllie kept watch; children whose names were now buried under strata of other memories, but whose faces were familiar. The Gillis Twins, who had frightened everyone; that poor girl Jeanette, an old face on a young girl, born with a hole in her heart, not long to live while Phyllie had known her.

'Mummy, we have to…'

'Claire, *be quiet*,' Phyllie snapped, squeezing her daughter's hand too hard (a bone clicked, hers or Claire's?). When the child started crying, Phyllie stared still at the playground for a second, seeing girls bobbing on a hopscotch grid, little boys with twigs for rifles, shooting bullets of air.

Phyllie decided that this was a place of fears; this was where she had once been frightened. And remembering (a little) what

Benny had taught, she knew that it could not harm her now. If it had lacked the power and the will to harm her *then*, it most certainly had no evil charms to freeze her blood if she was an adult.

But *Claire* could be damaged, she understood.

The notion made her drop down into a crouch. 'I'm sorry, darling,' she said, 'I'm sorry. I'll kiss it better…' It was what her own mother would have done to her in a similar situation.

The ghosts in the playground stopped playing; whispers passed on a breeze; and such was the suddenness of the games' cessation that the absence of energy caused a pulling sensation on Phyllie's skin. Tension rippled in the air, the atmosphere was off balance, shaky.

If nothing moved in the playground, why had butterflies appeared in Phyllie's stomach? Partly she was nervous on Claire's behalf, for the girl had tensed from temple to toe, the squeezed hand forgotten. The girl was watching for someone… or something.

'Claire. What's the Overlap?' Phyllie wanted to know.

The girl did not respond. Any signs of positivity had been snatched from her; she jumped when a screeching sound reached their ears – something metallic.

Calm. For the sake of the girl, calm.

'Claire-darling… Claire, look at me.' Phyllie smiled. The girl looked at her. 'Thank you. Do you know what's happening?'

Was the question more useful or less so, worded in such a vague fashion?

The little girl nodded her head.

The metallic screech again, laden and more insistent. Although Claire said nothing, she raised her right arm and pointed a finger… at the climbing frame from which Johnny Hodgins had once fallen and broken his arm.

It was domelike in shape, constructed of curved metal bars:

radically upscaled, it was something like a large vessel to strain vegetables, set on its base. The objective for the braver kids was to climb to the top of this spindly crown – and then to climb down again, mission accomplished. And Phyllie had always felt anxious beside it, back then. The climbing frame (years before the term Jungle Gym existed in the UK) had often put her in mind of a giant spider. No - a giant cranefly – a daddy-long-legs. When the wind had puffed up and lashed one of those rare winter rainstorms across the yard, the child that Phyllie had once been had fancied that she'd seen the metal monstrosity twitch.

A trick of the light, at the time; a weirdness reasoned away from childish shadows by retrospective logic, by adult luminescence. No?

No.

Apparently no, at any rate: the construction was moving right now, or attempting to. A pet tethered, it was tugging at the bars buried in the asphalt. It wanted to escape.

No.

Again, no.

Not a pet tethered - a daddy-long-legs trapped under an inverted pint glass. One or more limbs tightly secured.

Pulling.

2.

Unlike Phyllie, Vig did not wake up in a new place, pining for a return to the old. Indeed, it took a morning of his going through his ordinary business, while plagued by flashes that he couldn't decipher – images, sounds and smells that seemed no more than dreamlike – before Vig even remembered that there *was* an old from which he'd been snatched, and by then he was German again.

You know you've mastered a language, someone had once told him (a philosopher? a professor?) *when you start to dream in that language.* Which was all well and good… but where did it leave Hartvig Klossen, whose lessons in English were only a term old? Hartvig, who was now in a forest.

There were children all around him, boys and girls, all determined to find something among the trees. What was the treasure? For a moment he could not remember; snatches of the English language would sneak into his skull, transmitted from he didn't know where. His cranium had become an aerial.

Was he ill?

A boy ran past him, beaming, and calling, '*Ich habe den* _____ *gefunden!*' Face all smiles, triumphant; a winner. But Hartvig had not caught the missing word. 'I have the [SOMETHING] found,' his brain translated into English… but why was he translating *anything* into English. *I have found the [SOMETHING].* What were he and his friends searching for? No. Not friends. Classmates; schoolkids. What were he and his classmates searching for in the forest? On this field trip. This Geography field trip.

You're searching for me, Vig remembered, his adult conscious-ness casting a tarp of awareness over the scene. The boy who had just run past, he had run to collect help. It hadn't been smiles on his face: that was horror. *He was the one who found me.* He had not seen Vig on the forest path; he had seen a little boy, little Hartvig, and unconsciously he had assumed the worst scenario, for the missing word was *Körper.*

Ich habe den *Körper gefunden.*

I have found the body.

Not: *I have found the missing boy.* Not: *I have found him.*

'I have found the body.'

Comprehending which, Vig sensed his adult world take on solidity and greater amassed form. He thought of Benny. And not only that, he was *grateful* to think of Benny, for if the scene with Benny had occurred, the little boy Hartvig could not have perished in the forest on that field trip. He had slipped down a long and treacherous slope, true enough, but he hadn't died; he had knocked himself unconscious and lost two pints of blood. But that kid from one of the other schools had found him…

'Carlos.'

Although Vig said the word with no great volume, more with the snap of something dug up from a deep mental place, the boy who had passed him stopped running away. As he skidded to a halt he kicked up twigs and dirt on the path.

The young Carlos and the adult Vig, they walked towards one another, both more than a little cautious. At a distance apart deemed respectable by both parties they stopped.

'I don't know if you can hear me,' Vig began.

'*Bitte?*'

Vig repeated what he'd said, this time in German. The boy replied that he could hear him fine. Was Vig one of the search party? he asked.

'I don't know if you can hear me as an adult,' Vig went on.

The boy cocked his head to one side, confused.

'But I never said thank you. For finding me… For saving me. I might have bled to death but you found me and they lifted me to the mountain clinic. I didn't say thank you. From the bottom of my heart… Carlos. Thank you.'

3.

Five metres high, a skeletal dome-shaped nightmare, the cranefly yanked the first of its eight legs from the playground's asphalt, the bolt-and-screw combination that had held it spring-ing free with a noise like a bullpeen hammer on an anvil.

Little more than ten metres from this act of emancipation, Phyllie crouched on the pathway, attempting a motherly grip. Phyllie's lower jaw dangled somewhat, the lips were parted. The child had turned her face towards her mother's neck (Phyllie could feel the girl's snot on her skin)...

And the cranefly released a second leg. Once again, a bolt and a screw were catapulted out, this time as high as a clay pigeon.

Phyllie expected a gun shot to knock the screw into smithereens – a constellation of carbon – but nothing followed for a few more seconds.

Then the metal screech again, and another leg extracted itself from the ground in which it had been implanted... and Phyllie was not sure that she could bear to see the daddy-long-legs walking free.

Phyllie lifted Claire to chest height... not that the movement was a cinch. On the contrary, it was an agony - the lower spine, the kneecaps (her muscles were not used to this particular exercise).

Meanwhile, the cranefly had released the fourth of its eight legs.

Ping.

Clang.

The options were to sneak back into the building or to run forwards, into the playground. Phyllie chose the latter with little hesitation. The school had adopted, in her mind, a creepy quality, although she mightn't have been able to articulate exactly why, or why not, she did not intend to return to her past. Not unless there was no alternative.

Absolutely none.

Enduring the girl's sudden squeals in her ear, Phyllie carried them both towards the playing fields beyond the playground.

She stepped close to the cranefly as it worried free its fifth leg. She paid it no attention. The only goal was to run beyond the school's boundaries. Or rather... the only goal was to stop Claire's tears, and this might be achieved – it might not – by stepping over the school's boundaries.

No one was taking *her* daughter.

4.

Vig followed paths into areas that reminded him of the woods on the grounds of his home – the woods in which he'd found Don Bridges dangling. The trees looked identical... But they would, wouldn't they? Trees are trees. In Europe at least... No? Yes? No? Maybe this was the point, he considered; these trees were of his own creation. By tramping along these beaten tracks he was doing nothing more than walking into his own memories. Not only the memories of when he'd slipped down the slope on the school trip; there was also the discovery of Don's suicide to process, with this stroll through the trees acting as therapy. Not the talking cure, the walking cure.

This meant that he had to find Don again, in order to confront what had already gone stale in his soul – and would one day begin to rot. However... if Vig could find Don (and assuming that all logical bets, all wagers of logic, were squarely off), then what was to stop him locating the old guy *before* he killed himself? Before he'd even set the birds free...

Or why stop there?

What if Vig could find Don while *Eastlight* was still alive? If he could stop Don Bridges starving Eastlight to death, then Don might not kill himself either. Everything would be different. Vig would not have driven to Benny's, for one thing.

Benny.

How could Vig have forgotten that wanker in all of this? And whereabouts in this forest did the wanker reside? He had to be *somewhere*... Didn't he? Benny had said that each traveller made for himself or herself something new, something original... something different from other people's retreats. But surely it could not be only Vig and Phyllie who knew of Benny's existence in the real world, and therefore they must also have created a version of the wanker herein in this world.

To Vig this reasoning made about as much sense as any-thing else did, so why not? Why not seek him out?

'These are the woods on my grounds,' Vig said aloud. 'We are not in Germany, we are in Buckinghamshire.' He tipped his head back and shouted: *'Does everyone hear me?'*

The forest creaked with wildlife and with a crackle that sounded like fire, albeit a baby blaze.

'No!' Vig shouted. 'You will *not* burn down my woods! Do you understand me? You will *not! I* own these trees and if they're to be burnt, it's me who'll strike the fucking match!'

Silence. No response.

'Don't make me angry!' Vig bellowed into the trees. 'Either I employ you or you're on private property, and I will prosecute.'

Silence. No response.

How did I find Don? I scrambled away from the beaten track... I followed the sounds of the foxes...

Not this time, Vig decided. I own what I see – and I'll own Benny too before I'm done.

'Come here *now*, Don!' Vig shouted. 'As your employer, *I order* you to appear now.'

Suddenly Vig noted birds on the branches of the trees – birds that had no place in an English woodland setting.

Don's birds?

And summoned by Vig's order, Don himself appeared on

the path in front of Vig, looking sheepish and afraid. Chin dug into the top of his chest, flat-capped and wearing his poacher's waterproof coat and his mud-streaked wellington boots, Don entered with neither fanfare nor avian applause from the creatures that he'd looked after so diligently.

He wore his noose like a necklace. The rope from which he'd hung dragged behind him – a tail of shame.

'Good day to you, sir,' said Don.

'You owe me an explanation.'

And Don looked up, something steely in his eyes. He took his time rolling a cigarette, using a pouch of tobacco that he plucked from his coat pocket.

'No, sir. I believe I was clear as day, sir. If I might be so bold ... *You* owe *me* an explanation.'

5.

Claire wrapped her arms around her mother's neck and shoulders. The faster Phyllie walked (and she was definitely lengthening her stride), the tighter the little girl clasped. It got to the point, about a quarter of the voyage across the cricket field, when Phyllie worried about passing out due to a lack of oxygen.

'Honey…'

She had not settled on a term of endearment for Claire.

'Honey, let Mummy's neck go a bit…'

She stopped striding, her breathing lumpy and harsh in her throat. Claire loosened her hold and they turned to see what was behind them.

The climbing frame was following, but not at any great pace. Its every step sending shocks through the earth, it lumbered awkwardly, no doubt keeping mother and daughter in its sights (if it *had* sight); but beyond the macabre nature of its pursuit, there seemed little danger. If it really was after the humans, it was taking its sweet time about it.

Phyllie held the child out away from her body and said, 'Sweety? Sweety, listen.' The child thrashed. 'Claire, listen, please, to Mummy.' She waited until she had the girl's attention. 'What happens at the Overlap? It's very important you tell Mummy.'

Claire had swapped looking terrified for looking confused, and Phyllie was not sure which she preferred. While she waited for her daughter to respond (the ground shook - another heavy step), she tried to remember what Benny had told her and Vig. Something about everyone living in a place of their own creation. They constructed their own islands, their own worlds... but they talked in their sleep, some of them, in the place where they were held captive. They influenced one another; they formed groups, they melded...

They overlapped.

Could that be it? Claire's silence had suggested something close to unthinkable, but perhaps her vocabulary was simply not the concept's equal. And if so, whose fault was that? It was she, Phyllie, who had given the child such characteristics as she owned; it was hardly fair to blame her for freezing now. She needed help, not harsh judgement.

'Is it where all the people meet?' Phyllie asked. 'All the people from all the different places?'

'Not all.'

'But some.'

Claire nodded. 'Mummy, I'm scared,' she said – but her voice had changed: it had deepened. It was Phyllie's own voice. She was talking to herself and probably would be from this moment on.

It came as no surprise when Claire began to lose colour and fade, there in her arms. However, she needed the girl for a few more minutes. All the fantasies that she'd used over the years of someone rescuing her from danger, they had all been a crock. The only person who would get her out of this jam was herself.

'Is that where Vig is?' Phyllie asked Claire, 'at the Overlap?'

But the child declined to answer. Her colours seeped into the air and rose like will o' the wisps, a multitude of them; the lines that defined the girl's face blurred and smudged, lost distinction.

'Where is it? Where's the Overlap?' Phyllie demanded, furious at the girl's silence. She shook Claire hard. *'Tell me where.'*

'It's near the sea,' the girl answered in Phyllie's voice... and now, as well as the colours fading, the skin was ageing, tightening...

'Which way?' She rattled the wraith once again. *'Which way, you little bitch?'*

Claire threw her right arm out in the direction in which they'd been heading: towards the boundary of the cricket pitch. Where the ditch waited, Phyllie knew from memory- the ditch where some of the girls had hidden during after-school games, in their P.E. kits, skiving sports and smoking cigarettes stolen from their parents. A gang to which Phyllie had briefly belonged. The Bitch Ditch.

And then Claire vanished. She was gone. Her work was complete.

Breathing deeply and trying not to over-examine what the girl's early demise might imply, philosophically speaking, Phyllie faced the lumbering climbing frame as it moved towards her.

'And *you*,' she said loud and clear to the monstrosity; *'you* can fuck right off as well!'

At which it stopped walking. Shamed and humbled, it gave the impression of a naughty dog, bested by an owner.

Phyllie showed it her back and strode on, as fast as she could.

6.

Vig regarded Don with astonishment.

'*What* did you just say to me?'

'I think you heard me, sir.'

'I meant an explanation about Charlie Eastlight, about your suicide.'

Don nodded. 'I was aware of that, sir. I apologise if my letter was not the full ticket. But sir, you have to understand, I'm already off your payroll… I'm a bit on the dead side, you see, sir.'

He had a point. Not that Vig was delirious to concede.

'Where's Benny?'

'I wouldn't know, sir. It's a lot of trees.'

'Don't patronise me, Don.' Vig lifted his voice. 'I repeat,' he shouted, 'this is *my* construction… on *my* owned land… not Benny's… and I want to see the following people.'

On branches above him, Don's owls, kites and falcons fussed and flapped. A fox had appeared at the door to the chicken-house.

'Charlie Eastlight! Where *are* you?'

'I'm here… Viggy-Loo, Viggy-Lay!'

The voice came from behind Vig, who swivelled expecting to see Eastlight plump and suave in an expensive suit. There was no suit. There was virtually no skin either: evidently the fox that had gnawed at Eastlight's skin when Vig had found the man had not finished its meal in this afterlife. Eastlight's body was all-but a skeletal frame. The fox (or a collection of foxes) had eaten most of the skin from Eastlight's bones. Most of the internal organs too. What remained was not worthy of the word *body*.

'Don't tell me,' said Eastlight. 'I've spilt some soup down my tie again. You look like I'm not welcome in your dinner club.'

'You're not. You owe me for my hospitality…' Vig indicated to the oldest man present. 'So does Don.'

Eastlight chuckled. 'Your *hospitality?*'

Vig appeared stoic. 'How much commission did you make on the house you sold me?'

'A good chunk of change – and thank you very much. So?'

'So I didn't give you permission to sleep on my land, Charlie.'

'Viggy-Loo…'

'I didn't, Charlie. How many nights did you stay as Don's guest? I'm not running a *hotel.*'

Eastlight's laugh sounded less certain. 'It wasn't exactly my intention, Viggy-Loo,' he began.

'Nevertheless. You *did* stay. So you owe me. You owe me *for rent.*'

'…You've got to be kidding.' Eastlight's smile was fading. '…You're serious.'

'You owe *me* for rent and you owe the people you hurt.'

'…What's the price?' Eastlight asked.

'You and Don.'

'Yes?' Eastlight and Don asked in unison.

'A team. You're working as a team. We're going to close down Benny's operation, do you hear me? You both left before discharging your debts.'

7.

In control, calm and sane, Vig exited the woods, expecting to see the large house that he knew he would sell when he was given the opportunity (he'd take a loss for a quick sale: he didn't need the money) – the house and maybe Dorota. After all, why shouldn't his partner be in this fantasy, even if she was about to be an ex-partner? (Things were going to change when he got home.) But neither the house nor Dorota was present.

Phyllie was.

She stood on the other side of a chainlink fence that stretched in either direction for as far as the eye could see.

'Fancy meeting you here,' said Vig.

'Small world.'

'Literally… So what happens next?'

'I'm trying to get out of school,' Phyllie replied. 'I've walked all the way round – there's no door and no gate.'

The fence was also (Vig estimated) ten metres or so high.

'And you don't fancy a climb, I suppose,' Vig suggested.

'In these shoes?'

Vig tested the strength of the chainlink with one hand; he squeezed to see if it would break – perhaps it was rustier than it appeared… No, it wasn't.

'What's in there?' he asked.

'I told you. A school. *My* school.'

'I thought you were joking. I met Don and Charlie. I told them they had to work together. I sent them off to do my bidding.'

Phyllie smiled. 'Bet they loved that. Doing what?'

'Spreading the word. That all of this is an experiment; it's not real.' Vig shrugged. 'If we can sow a few doubts, that can hardly be a bad thing.'

'And what if no one believes them?'

Vig shrugged again. 'Negative news spreads as fast as positive. Faster, probably.'

Phyllie leaned against the fence and gripped a couple of links. 'Come on, this is like *A Letter to Brezhnev*. Get me out of here, Vig.' And she sang the first bar of 'Rescue Me'.

'Benny said this was all ours to control, right? So why don't we abuse the responsibility we've been handed?' He cleared his throat. 'Listen to me, fence,' he said in his best English accent (he sounded like the actor Trevor Eve). '*You do not exist. I unmake you. Go…*'

Vig even flexed a karate chop at the fence – hey presto! – for extra panache and *shazam*.

Nothing happened.

Bursting out laughing, Phyllie managed to say, 'Oh your *face*, Vig. *Bless.*'

'Why didn't that work?'

'You look crestfallen…' Phyllie was still chuckling. 'You didn't think I might've tried that then? Thanks for the vote of support.' But she wasn't offended, in fact she found the whole situation very close to hysterically funny. 'You look like you've knocked your tennis ball into the neighbour's garden. And there's a nasty little yapping dog playing with it.'

Somewhat sulkily Vig replied, 'The situations are not a million miles apart, in case you haven't noticed, Phyl.'

'Am I the dog or the tennis ball?' Phyllie started laughing afresh.

'I could always walk away, you know.'

'Oh don't whinge.'

'Seriously. I don't know why that didn't work.'

'You didn't make it,' Phyllie guessed. 'Maybe it's mine to dispose of… only that didn't work either.'

'If I wanted to conjure up a shovel, would I be able to?'

'A shovel? Are you planning to *dig* me out?'

'Or a pair of shears then! What am I, some sort of expert!'

'Well what am *I*, Vig? You're treating me like an old hand.'

'…Sorry.'

'Where are they, by the way? Charlie and Don: where did they go?'

'The road not taken,' Vig answered. 'We hit a crossroads a mile or so back. I told them to go left and I turned right… They're to find me at a place I want them to find me: that's the challenge I set them… I don't know if that's metaphysical or just vague and woolly.'

'It's the Overlap,' said Phyllie. 'My daughter told me about it. Sort of.'

'Your daughter…'

'Yes, I have a daughter. It's complicated. Another time, Vig. I think I need to get out of here.'

'Or I have to get in.'

'To my school?'

'No you're right. Start climbing, Phyl. And that's an order.'

'Ooh. I love it when you talk dirty.'

8.

They walked over hill and dale, where the winds had colours but the animals and plant life did not. Rabbit-shaped absences of colour hopped in front of their footfalls; bird-shaped absences of colour swooped over their aching heads.

But were they getting anywhere? It was hard to tell if they had made any progress, the sky remained cloud-covered for a mile after mile, the cumulonimbus a gorgeous aquamarine hue against the dirty cream sky. Besides which, neither of them wanted to question the assumption of progress being made (by placing one foot in front of the other, surely they were moving towards an end-up point somewhere); for both of them, a walk was anyway a welcome break, a way of spending the poison-induced hangovers that they surely must be nursing, back in the real world. A walk was a way to discuss their home lives.

Vig admitted that he and Dorota were at a standstill, developmentally and emotionally speaking. 'And Don didn't help much, I must say.'

'No. No I don't suppose he did.'

'…How's it going with you?'

Never in living memory had Phyllie stepped so close to blurting out the truth: that she was frightened of her time at home. A host of conflicting fears troubled her, here, sufficiently far away from that existence that she could view it, stripped of any inevitable proximate passion, with objectivity. Contemplating Vig's question, Phyllie sighed and wondered where to begin. Not only was she frightened of Roger's escalations of libido, and the new and *outré* acts that they would share together to quench it, she was frightened that one day (soon) he would stop wanting to achieve these sexual complicities. That one day he would cease fancying her, either for the duration of her pregnancy or longer. That he would move on to person new (not necessarily women either). That the baby inside her had brought their love life to an end, and not with a bang but with a whimper.

'Roger has a theory,' said Phyllie, 'all women eventually marry their fathers.'

'With respect, I think Freud might've come up with something along those lines first.'

'Well he was right, whoever it was. I married my father when I married Roger. They've even got the same name! That should've been a clue, don't you think? I've been punishing myself for something ever since.'

Vig spent a few seconds tiptoeing through his thoughts.

'Was your dad a psychologist too?'

'No. He sold used office furniture and dreamed of winning the Pools... He was in *The Sun* the other year.'

'I didn't realise the Pools were still going.'

'Not for that... I have no idea. He was a regional slimmer of the year for East Sussex. Lost fourteen stone in eight months... He'd ballooned up to twenty-nine stone after Mum died. Lived on four pizzas and a bottle of brandy a day. Eighty-a-day on the snouts.'

'Wow.'

'…I think it'd be fair to say it was more than a cry for help. He wanted it over and done with.'

'So what changed?' asked Vig.

'I will never know – he won't tell me. I've stopped asking, to be honest: it gets embarrassing after a while.'

Vig made the mental adjustments that needed to be made. Up until this point he had assumed Phyllie's father to be deceased. Fortunately he had not asked Phyllie if she missed him terribly.

'Saul Bellow wrote that it's a rare man indeed who isn't affected evermore by the sexual advice of his father… or words to that effect.'

Phyllie sniggered. 'And where does that leave girls?'

'I have no idea… I can't help questioning whether I think it would be better or worse to meet some other people, on the trail as it were – the trail of the lonesome pine.'

'Worse, would be my vote. I'm actually enjoying myself – I'm sure that's not supposed to be how it works.'

Vig smiled as a butterfly-shaped absence of colour floated past. It was almost too cartoonish to be true.

'Only one thing would make it perfect,' Phyllie suggested. 'Do you think we can turn the world's lights off?'

Vig said nothing.

'It's been a while since I had you alone, after all. And technically… it's not cheating if we're actually not here. We're in a room somewhere, not even touching.'

'As far as you know.'

Phyllie laughed. 'As far as *we* know.'

She stopped walking. The wind blew through her hair in streaks of orange and gold. She felt pained – she felt threatened – by the chance of rejection. Uxoriousness was one of Vig's more regrettable traits. She waited.'

'*Al fresco?*'

'As if there's a choice.' Phyllie started to unbutton her blouse.

'No, let me,' said Vig. 'We've waited long enough. I don't want to rush it now.'

'We won't rush... Let's try to make some stars,' said Phyllie.

'You mean real ones? In the sky?'

'We'll decide as we go along.'

GROUP ACTIVITY

1.

Barely sentences into an excavation, a dig for a particular lode of memories, senses and impressions, Connors stopped in the middle of a word (the word was *reservoir*) and let the dash that bisected its syllable stand for the whole, unwilling and impotent to strike deeper, and not possessing the correct tools to do so anyway.

It was Bernadette who provided him with an implement. She did so by completing the thought that Connors couldn't manage.

'Your brother died in the reservoir,' she said softly. 'That's what you're telling us, isn't it.'

Connors nodded his head.

Bernadette, Massimo and Tommy watched him closely, each individually wondering what emotion the man would be led to explore. For the moment, no emotion was obvious: Connors was still alternating his shovel and his pick, dig-dig-digging in the mine.

'We think so,' Connors continued. 'The problem was, he was never found. They never found his body.'

'In a reservoir?' asked Bernadette.

'They searched for a week, I found out later. Me, my mum and my mum's fella – we all watched him fucking about at the rail and fall in. But he didn't even bob up, struggling-like. Spitting and coughing. Nothing. A big splash… and it was like he was never there. Goodnight, Vienna. We never saw the cunt again. He left this world, like… or *that* world I should say. A whole seven days to declare the poor cunt dead.'

'It's like you never knew him at all,' said Tommy (surprising everyone). 'Like you made him up or something.'

'Sort of.'

'…And do you think you're going to find him here?' Tommy went on, his tone interrogatory but not unkind.

Once again, Connors nodded; then he shrugged. 'I have no idea. But here's as good a place as any. Looking on the bright side.'

And he was about to resume the story of his brother's drowning – when there was a knock on the door through which they had entered Tommy's house on Benny Hill.

Tommy stood up and walked over. On opening the door wide, the party was able to see two visitors: one fat and one thin, short and old. Both of them looked too weary to be awake.

'Sorry to bother you,' said the younger of the two – the fat man – 'but we have a message you need to hear… None of this – absolutely none of it – is real. We are all being held in a cellar somewhere.'

'Any questions?' added the small old man.

And Massimo said, '*Charlie?*'

2.

Tommy invited the two men into the house.

The fat man, wearing a frayed and soil-spotted suit that he had stolen from a man they'd found dead in a ditch, walked with a limp so pronounced that it was more a matter of humane courtesy than of English manners that lifted Massimo, Bernadette and Connors to their feet in order that they might offer the visitor a seat.

'Thank you,' said Charlie Eastlight, spoilt for choice and selecting the chair that Connors had vacated.

It was only once he had sat down that the group paid any attention to the bloody state of Eastlight's lower limbs and the shredded strips of his trousers.

'What the hell happened to you?' asked Massimo, giving voice to what everyone was thinking... but his voice was all but breathless. He meant more than his partner's damaged legs.

Eastlight grimaced. 'It was this cunt,' he answered, gesturing towards Don Bridges (who was seating himself in Bernadette's vacated chair with a nod of thanks). 'Fed me to the foxes, didn't he, the wanker.'

'You bloody drama queen! It was only *one* fox,' Don protested for the benefit of the group. 'Christ that feels better to sit down.'

'Oh that's all right then,' Eastlight continued sarcastically. 'It was only *one* fox, everyone, who fed on me. This murderer threw a fox into the trap where he had me!'

A momentary silence ensued. Bernadette felt the sort of sorry embarrassment that she had used to experience when her parents argued upstairs... Tommy, meanwhile, gave no indication that he had a clue what was going on, his expression flitted between confusion and fury.

It was only Massimo who seemed willing to move the two men out of their verbal deadlock. He bent at the waist and kissed Eastlight on the cheek. Only seconds had passed since Connors's story had been interrupted (to his relief but also to his consternation) but it seemed as though Massimo and Eastlight had been afraid of acknowledging one another with an appropriate sign of fondness. The kiss served to remind them of one another, the good and the bad events blurring, transforming…

'So how are things back home?' Massimo asked, unable to keep a grin away from his lips.

'Oh, so-so.' Eastlight looked away, taking in Bernadette with a nod. 'The kids left home.' And he laughed.

And he laughed some more. There was something deranged and uncontrolled – uncontrollable – about this laughter.

Frowning ever so slightly, Massimo explained: 'This is Charlie. My boyfriend. Partner. Whatever you want to call it.'

'You's benders?' asked Tommy, also frowning, but frowning a good deal more urgently than ever so slightly.

Massimo faced him. 'Yes. To make sure we're all clear on this, Charlie and I are homosexuals with violent streaks.' Charlie's appearance had made him bold and loose-lipped. 'We had a couple of teenagers as hostages until recently. We were planning to kill them.'

Bernadette flinched. Massimo shot her a glance that he hoped would express an apology.

'Now now, Mass,' said Eastlight; 'no bean-spilling at the party until we've all been introduced.'

Ignoring this, Massimo turned to the old man.

'You fed him to a fox?' he demanded.

Don nodded. 'I did. After I smacked his legs with a spade. For the trouble he's caused me.'

Massimo shook his head. 'I'm surprised you're still alive. Charlie, why haven't you –'

'I'm not,' Don replied.

'…You're not what?'

'Alive. I strung meself up from a tree in the woods. Suicide: the best way, all things considered. Wouldn't you say, Eastlight?'

Eastlight had stopped laughing. 'Fuck you, Donald Duck.' Noticing Massimo again, he added, 'Yeah. Me as well. Sorry,

Mass. Dead as a doornail. He buried me in a trap in the woods.'

'You don't look very dead,' said Tommy.

As surreptitiously as she could manage, Bernadette inched closer to the door. The mention of a plan to kill teenagers was what had done it, what had broken the emotional glue. No less than she had ever wanted anything in her life, she now wanted out of this building. Away from these murderers, away from Benny Hill...

Home.

Bernadette wanted to go home.

'Are you suggesting, sir,' Don went on, 'that Eastlight could've killed *me*?'

'That's exactly what I'm suggesting. No offence.'

'None taken, sir.'

'You don't know what I'm going to say yet,' said Massimo.

'Oh I think I do, sir. You see an old man with ruined knees...'

'Not as ruined as mine!' Eastlight interjected.

'...and you think he must be weak.' Don grinned. 'Believe me, sir - whatever harm you've done to man, woman, child or beast... I've done worse. That's a promise.'

Tommy moved away from the door. 'But why are the two of you together, that's what I want to know.'

The door had been left ajar, Bernadette noted. A matter of a few steps... and out. How tired were her legs? Could she run? Maybe not; or maybe not far, or maybe not fast... but she couldn't stay in here, no – not with these animals.

But.

Abandoning Benny Hill would mean abandoning any hope of an answer. Any chance of progress.

Should I?

Images of Massimo and Charlie kicked in hard, completely made-up images; horror film, constructions. The torture of teens.

(She couldn't help it.) She helped them roll flesh away from sinew on a victim's thighs... By picturing it – she knew – she was guilty, she was present. No longer a healer, she was its obverse.

'Vig told us to tell you,' Don explained, replying to Tommy's question. 'We're no more content about it than you are... but there you go.'

'Tell us what?' asked Connors.

'Tell you this,' Don answered, cutting in before Eastlight's open mouth. 'The world you see is false, ladies and gentlemen. It's a world of your own creation. And a world for you – a world for you to obliterate.'

Bernadette decided to stay.

SCENES FROM THE VIVARIA

1.

'*They* didn't waste any time,' Maggie said to Benny.

'Dirty bunnies,' the old man agreed.

They were in the vivaria, observing Vig and Phyllie, who were side by side on consecutive bunks, stark naked and already wired up to monitors.

'Big boy,' Benny continued, referring to the dimensions of Vig's unmistakeable erection. 'She'd be a lucky girl if they were doing it for real.'

Maggie watched Phyllie's hands, one of which stroked its owner's left nipple, the other of which had angled between her legs, the fingers typing on and in her flesh. There was no denying that the woman's ministrations were a source of arousal for Maggie as well.

Perhaps Benny recognised this. 'Which one do you want?' he asked.

Confused by the question, Maggie tore her attention away from the floor show in front of her. 'Want?'

'Well, *he's* got a cock like a baby's arm and she – I can smell her from here. Wouldn't be fair to have em all dressed up and no place to go, would it now? So who do you want? To give em a fuck of a lifetime. Fucked by the gods no less, from their point of view… Which one?'

Maggie thought of Yasser, cursing herself for a guilty pang

that arrived unawares. Accommodating a second penis this evening might feel awkward (Benny had been rough with her; she was sore) so she said, 'The girl.'

'Thought you might. Well fire away.'

Benny sat on a wooden chair and watched Maggie undress. He flipped out his half-erection and moved his gaze between Maggie and Phyllie, with the patient reptilian attention of a snake. Indeed, to Maggie's mind, as she unbuckled her belt and pulled down her trousers and panties, Benny actually resembled a snake. Had a forked tongue poked out of his mouth in this moment of his lascivity, she might not been much surprised.

Once she was nude, Maggie fought for space on Phyllie's small bunk (Army issue, these bunks had not been designed for two people). It wasn't comfortable; Maggie wondered if she might be better suited to standing by the side. Then she hit on the idea of reversing her direction, and everything fell simply and naturally into place. With her knees planted either side of Phyllie's head, she lowered her pussy onto the comatose woman's face, immediately gratified by the sensation of a tongue on her swollen lips. Leaning forward down Phyllie's body, she took a look over at Benny (who was masturbating slowly, languidly, his expression unreadable), and she dipped her face into the pool of Phyllie's water, joining in with her tongue with what the woman had begun with her fingertips.

Although she was not in control of the situation – Benny was very much at the top of the pecking order – Maggie felt excited to wield powers over this prisoner. When Phyllie moaned, the vibrations it sent into Maggie's vagina were enough to make her shudder. Also, it was good to espy Benny as he took a few strides along the road to his own self-gratification. In much the same way as she'd enjoyed manipulating Yasser (to begin with; she'd felt guilty later on), she enjoyed knowing that, despite the undeniable chain of command in operation, there remained certain things that she could do to make Benny uncertain of his bearings for a moment or two.

Like now, for example. Unable to resist any longer, Benny stood up and approached the bunks, led by the hard-on that poked out of his slacks. Maggie guessed what he'd want - either Phyllie herself, her ankles resting against his earlobes while he pushed into the wetness that Maggie had helped the woman prepare; or Maggie, in exactly the same position as she had adopted, with her labia straddling the prisoner woman's lips and Benny buried deep in the ditch of her buttocks.

She was wrong. To Maggie's surprise, Benny bent almost double over the adjacent bunk, and received Vig's erection into his mouth. Such was the unexpected nature of this action that Maggie was immediately turned on further. She was hot and flustered – one of several emotional precursors to any orgasm – and the feelings deepened and sharpened as she watched Benny suck and she watched him rub the man's scrotum.

It was Vig who came first. Benny and Maggie kissed, exchanging the man's semen from mouth to mouth, which Maggie then swallowed while orgasming herself, twitching her secretions into Phyllie's mouth. Phyllie was third. Maggie owed it to her to do her best to make it a good one, and the woman's body shuddered and writhed; her toes stretched. Then she relaxed.

Benny instructed Maggie to help him turn Vig onto his front… Maggie was the sole member of Benny's audience when he started to push into Vig, but this was not so by the end, about halfway through, Eva joined them with a camera. She filmed the rape one-handed while she and Maggie held hands, either sisterly, supportively or in the throes of lust.

Maggie was not sure which.

2.

Branston had slept very little on the night he'd entered Benny's house. Apart from the fact that he was adrenaline-loaded and mining a deep lode of something resembling disbelief (and disbelief being a source of energy for a film-maker, in both a good and a bad way), there was also to contend with the issue of a job to be done, a task executed, and a film (of all things!) – an actual film to be made. And for Branston, excitement was a more efficient pick-me-up than caffeine; the combination of excitement and (forthcoming) pride in one's work was a more reliable combo than a dozen *espressos* and a bowl of coke larger than a gorilla's skull.

He had a commission!

Virginia, I was commissioned to shoot human subjects...

An actual commission to make an actual documentary!

The commissioner had even mentioned a fee of ten thousand pounds, payable on completion... Ten grand!

One third of his annual teaching salary for a couple of evenings' work.

It was candy from a baby, Virginia.

Emitting, he hoped, words of insouciant bravery, Branston followed Benny through the house and down a flight of stairs. Benny placed his thumb on the panel and the door buzzed and a lock clunked. He opened the door.

'Welcome to the vivaria!' Benny announced.

For an increasingly seasick half-hour, Branston was led around the chambers and rooms. He filmed. His batteries would not last forever, he knew, but he'd film what he could... and then, maybe later (much later!), some of this concentration camp nightmare would make sense.

As they walked, automatic lights were triggered, and Benny was as efficient a tour guide as ever sang praises on a city tour bus through a mike. He named names; he gave bone-crunching, sickening details; he was proud. More proud of his work than Branston was of his own.

When Branston was shown to his room, he threw up.

3.

Eva had been in Benny's employment for long enough for her to have witnessed or carried out most of the activities that an employee should never have to contemplate. She was good. All the same, Benny did not wish to entrust her with the disposal of that nuisance Chris. It wasn't as if there was a Union that she could complain to, citing unreasonable demands; it was more the case that Benny wanted to do the job himself. For Benny it was a matter of balming a sense of stung pride.

More than a day had passed between then and now – between Benny's nod of praise to the patron saint who protected thieves, the saint who had so contrived fate that Benny had ended up financially secure enough to afford a state-of-the-art chainsaw, and a home sufficiently remote for him to be able to use it at three in the morning without spooking the neighbours – and this four a.m. amble around the estate. Experiencing both hollowness and contentment, Benny strolled in the held-breath hush; the wind sharpened its claws on his nose and cheeks. On nights such as this, when sleep danced distant from his brain's grip, when nothing seemed the right thing to do, Benny was often to be found among his fields, his garden, his arable land, a pensive *flaneur* (as he thought of it), an explorer. One who has what others lack.

Becalmed by the weather, Benny returned to the house to prepare a drink. Perhaps a Margarita. No, too much faff, too much effort. Neat vodka with a twist of lemon and plenty of ice, the very ticket… But what was this? Alas and alack! Opening the fridge's freezer drawer in the library (Benny's favourite place to sip and ponder) revealed an empty hole. Not only was there no Smirnoff inside, the icecube tray was empty as well! A tumbler in his right fist, Benny set out to forage for replenishments.

The kitchen was the most obvious oasis, but events downstairs in the vivaria had been hectic; it wouldn't hurt to see how the new guests had settled in, or what Maggie was up to (as she continued to moon over that window licker Yasser). So Benny plumped for a visit to the vivaria, regardless of the hour.

It was only while descending the stairs to the basement that Benny remembered Chris, and where he'd stored the parts of the man's dead body. Clumsy. *Clumsy work, me.* Benny tutted with self-reproof: he really should have warned Eva of what she would find in the underground chest freezer, should she open its lid. Clumsy! Forgetful! *I've had a lot on me plate. Sorry, darlin',* Benny rehearsed, imagining (with embarrassment) Eva going into the freezer (where some of the poisons and some of the antidotes were kept in careful file)… and the poor girl coming eye to eye with Chris's frozen head! Frit the life out the girl, it would!

When Benny heard an isolated shriek from behind the door, he guessed that Eva had found Chris's corpse. Typical! For the sake of a few more seconds – not even minutes: *seconds* – he could've tipped her the wink and said *Eva, before you lift that lid…* and all would be ticketyboo.

The shriek came again.

Wait a minute – Benny lifted his thumb to the panel – *maybe it's not Eva. One of the guests.*

Another squeal! A different voice…

Benny stepped over the threshold.

…but not a squeal of horror, or even surprise. It was laughter! Two woman (maybe more?) were having a laugh down here!

Maggie?

Surely not *Eva*…

Benny trod quietly through the rooms and chambers until he found –

'Jesus.'

In one of the larger areas, Maggie and Eva kept on with what they were doing, until they noticed Benny. They stopped immediately. Like a schoolgirl caught with contraband, Maggie even attempted to conceal what they had been throwing from one to the other.

Benny was livid. 'So you found him then?' he demanded and accused.

The women hung their heads, all laughter at the childish pleasure of games of catch soon forgotten.

'Talk about *disrespect*,' Benny continued. 'Give it here.' And he held out a palm to Maggie.

She and Eva had been playing Frisbee with Chris's left hand, its fingers extended and frozen rigid. She placed Chris's hand (it was slippery with ice) onto Benny's left palm. Not for long did it remain there, however, such was the force of the right fist that Benny aimed at Maggie's face that his balance was momentarily to cock; and the sound of Chris's dropped hand hitting the floor, and the sound of Maggie's nose breaking, were almost simultaneous.

But the latter was louder.

4.

Camera in hand, Branston was underground, directing the documentary (no mean feat considering the comatose natures of his key players), when he entered the chamber in which Yasser slept on the troubled dozy tides that would sometimes send him so close to the borderline with consciousness that Branston wondered how he failed to cross over and wake.

Maggie was seated on the end of Yasser's narrow cot. Although she looked up at Branston's approach, she did not appear startled or surprised.

'How's it going?' She asked in a friendly manner.

'Fine,' Branston answered, well aware that the response was trite and lacking. 'Weird' would have been more honest. Experiencing the burden of confession on his soul, he added, 'I meant to ask you last night. Would you be prepared to go on the record?'

There was no need for Maggie to seek much clarification. 'In your film? Sure; why not? It's all over for me anyhow.'

'What makes you say that?'

Maggie resumed her perusal of Yasser's inert expression. 'I've sort of burned me bridges,' she explained, 'as well as me home. There's no way to go back – and I doubt I'll be interesting to Benny forever.'

She allowed the meaning of this to filter through the stuffy air.

5.

'What next?' Benny asked, his voice ominously low. 'A game of golf with the cunt's leg? Eh?'

'Sorry, Benny.'

'Sorry, Benny,' Eva echoed. 'We were blowing off steam. I haven't been out of the house in a month. I've been filming, injecting… doing everything you want. I needed a break.'

'Not a prison, is it?' Benny countered, aware of the irony. '*You* can leave when you like. So can you. Gainful employment's what I offer: there's nothing to stop you handing in your notice, ladies. I'll even write you a respectable reference, as far as I'm able. But I will *not have* a man's body ridiculed. Not for someone else's amusement. Too ghoulish. Christ. You're like a coupla *Nazis!*'

As Benny raged on, Maggie tried to imagine what Eva was thinking. Though sure to pay attention to Benny's empassioned soliloquy (fearful of pitfalls, sudden questions or a test at the end), Maggie was also totting up all that she knew about the other woman, which didn't take long. But there was no doubt that Eva's granite reserve had crumbled tonight. There'd been something in the air. And if Maggie's own disloyalty appeared bad enough (through a lens of objective retrospection), it was the change in Eva's persona that had seemed nigh-on remarkable, transforming as it had from diligent worker to reprobate.

Something in the air, she repeated to herself; she mulled as Benny ranted.

'Last night,' the man said, 'I granted the poor sod you were playing with a dying wish. He knew he was gonna die and so did I, of course; but how often do I do that? *Not* often, that's how often – that's how much the cunt earned my respect. For the sake of the love of his woman. And I admire that. He fought hard to the end; fair play to the cunt… So when he asks me: *Can I see her? Can I see me Bernadette?*, what am I gonna tell the cunt? *No? You're a nuisance?* Nah. I've already cut off his hands – he was no threat. He was weak… Dying wish, I thought. He *earned* it.'

'I'll resign if you want me to,' said Eva, the interruption a risk in itself; but she clearly wanted no more punishment or admonition. She'd rather leave, thought Maggie. Perhaps she has somewhere to go. Perhaps she'll take me with her…

Hoping that Eva wouldn't mention the vodka that Maggie had stolen from the fridge-freezer in the library – the vodka they'd drunk together, while attempting to tweezer secrets from one another's unconsciouses – Maggie asked, 'What can I do to make it up to you, Benny?'

Her voice sounded different, now her nose was busted: more nasal, bunged-up, as if she had a cold: not unattractive actually, she considered. She wondered what she looked like... Karl Malden, possibly. Maybe Benny wouldn't want to fuck her anymore, not even as a punishment – not even the rough games – and this worried Maggie in an instant. What else would he keep her here for?

Sounding smug (and now crossing his arms defensively), Benny said, 'What do you suggest?'

Maggie made a decision: to give the hint of solidarity with Eva. The word *we* should do it.

'We noticed something odd tonight, Benny,' said Maggie. 'The atmosphere down here was different. Tim noticed something too. Something is not right with the patients.'

Benny leaned forward slightly, the whites of his eyes bulging like flexed muscles.

'*Branston* saw you fucking around?'

'No. He was here earlier, filming. He didn't see anything.'

Lie. Branston had shot Maggie lifting Chris's head and left foot from the chest freezer, one by one – the head so slippery that she'd had to cradle it to her breast like a Christmas turkey en route to the oven. Branston knew plenty.

'The word that kept cropping up in their sleep,' said Eva, thereby accepting Maggie's show of union – for how long remained to be seen – 'was the Overlap.'

6.

One of the reasons that Branston had entered the profession of education was his love of film (obsession with film?) and his notion that this love could be communicated to a willing listener.

Another reason was that he had never made much money as a private or corporate film maker. He had never contracted that lovely virus called Luck.

These two reasons were all well and good; they were long since on the record with Virginia, his future interviewer –

(No. Biographer, not interviewer. Life had swollen too vast for Branston now to be satisfied with the prospect of future interviews; no less than a life-and-times would suffice.)

– but another reason existed. Another reason existed as to why Branston had gone into Further Education as a practitioner. The reason was bullying.

From the age of ten to the age of thirteen, Branston had had the misfortune of being taught Technology by a bully named McGregor. To this day, whenever the word *bully* was overheard, Branston could not help picturing the corpulent pud-puller; his inexpertly trimmed moustache, his greasy skin, his flatulent fly-attracting aroma.

From now on, the word would summon up a different face. Benny's face.

After Branston's second night in Benny's house, he sought an audience with his new commissioner. It was seven a.m.

'I'll need to go home today, Benny. I've a class to teach this afternoon,' he said.

Fondling a pensive Irish coffee in the library, Benny nodded. 'Course you have, Tim,' he answered, as friendly as you like. 'Come and go as you need to. And tell me is there anything you need from me to make our film? The lighting conditions down there aren't the best, you don't need me to tell you. If you need to hire some Kleig Lamps, that's fine by me. I'll pay. I don't want this to look like the fucking Nativity Play at Sunday School. The whole *point* is to be taken seriously – by the scientific community, among others.'

Before Benny sipped his drink, Branston expected a kind of punchline; a defining clause along the lines of *But if you don't return I'll come and find you.* Nothing. The man sipped (what Branston took to be Americano) coffee and appeared happy with Branston's decision to leave.

Branston drove home and was ill as soon as he spied his toilet. To whom would he report what he'd heard and seen? (Who would believe him?) To whom would he show what he'd filmed up to now?

The Council?

The BBC? Channel 4?

He didn't know. The question itself felt as frightening as diabetes; the mere contemplation of his hours-old memories tripled his heartrate... Branston stripped to the sweetbreads and repeated ten sets of twenty push-ups and five sets of thirty sit-ups. Practised his boxing in the bedroom mirror. Practised his karate chops.

You have to go back there, Virginia told him.

There was more to consider than the guests in their states of suspended animation.

There was Chris.

Chris. The man with whom Branston had conversed for less than twenty minutes; the man who had led Branston to Benny... The man who had nearly died in Branston's car.

Chris was dead. His head in an ice box.

What am I supposed to do about it? Branston inquired of Virginia (or anyone else listening).

Chris's blood would be in Branston's car. The sooner Branston notified the law, the better... No? Wasn't this the way these things were handled? The film would have to wait. Chris was his responsibility now.

While packing a bag (a shirt, some underwear, a wash

bag: an overnight stay), Branston hummed a tune that at first he didn't recognise. Only when he was one leg out the door could he place it.

'In the Air Tonight' by Phil Collins.

And no more than that, Branston promised himself, closing the door and unlocking the car with a sweaty thumb. It took him a few seconds to realise that he was still crying.

SKULL RENDEZVOUS

1.

In time, as they knew they would, they came upon other people on their travels. Nearly everyone they met had something missing, whether it was a limb, an eye, an ear or a voice. In one case, a head! The man wandered along tensely, testing every other step with a foot before committing to the next stride.

What does it mean? was not a question that required an answer: it was obvious. People of varying degrees of importance (to both Vig and Phyllie) had been taken, made missing or killed (the ultimate in absence), and surely these poor unfortunates were adaptations of those real-world events. The once-missing schoolgirl, Jess, for example, was now an old lady with an amputated left leg. There was no one to tell them that this couldn't be true. Why not? Because, as Vig and Phyllie had swiftly discovered, there were no strict rules to follow (not even their own); and anyone they attempted to engage in conversation exhibited a depth of mystification that made the travellers wonder if anyone here spoke English.

'If we can't communicate,' Phyllie wondered aloud, her most recent attempt to engage the attention of a stranger with no nose or lips having failed, 'how the hell are we getting out?' Although she had not given up her hopes for the Overlap, these setbacks had whittled away, one by one, at her natural optimism.

Phyllie felt blue and Vig knew it.

'Two things I've considered,' he replied, with the rare but not unknown recourse to a clipped style of no-nonsense speech that was not quite natural English (or so he believed) and not a translation from the German language either. To Vig, his words sounded like an English man *pretending to be* a German.

What could it mean? he wondered (and wondered in parentheses that he could actually *see*… in the form of silver-coloured bracket-shaped breezes). *What does it mean when I stop sounding like myself?*

'You look like a dog chewing a wasp,' Phyllie told him. 'Don't zone out on me now, Vig. Or leave me in suspense.'

'What?'

'Two things you've considered…'

'Oh right… Phyllie. Suddeny I don't feel well.' Vig saw the crossness on Phyllie's face and decided to move on lickety-split. 'But okay – two things. One: they can't *see* us, or they only see us… spiritually. As visitations.'

'Ghosts?'

'Why not?'

Humming an unconscious *reason* why not – or rather, an affirmation of her scepticism – Phyllie said, 'And two?'

'Two. Two, we're doing things in negative. Like the coloured wind and the no-colour animals… Phyllie. What *colour* am I?'

Phyllie was in the process of berating herself for that previous non-committal hum (the one that implied: *You're talking wank*). Once more she had reminded herself that there existed *no rules*: or, perhaps a shade closer to the truth (she had thought again), there were rules that neither of them could fathom. So what? So maybe they *were* ghosts. Life, only recently, had been much stranger, had it not?

With this in mind, Phyllie took seriously – perfectly seriously – Vig's question.

'Your face is white. Your hair is brown and your eyes are grey with long black lashes that remind me – I've never told you this – of a bear I saw stuffed in a natural history museum in Tring when I was about nine. Your willy is of average length and perfectly pink. It knows its work.'

'Yes yes yes.' Vig was in no mood for flirtation, though he accepted (even appreciated) Phyllie's attempt to lighten their psychic load. '…Phyllie, we're the *wind* to these people. We have too much colour!'

Voices on the breeze, Phyllie conjectured. 'Is that a banshee?'

Vig did not follow the train of thought, but he nodded and shrugged simultaneously. A smile had taken root on his lips.

'Okay we're banshees,' said Phyllie. 'I've been called worse… How do we lose colour – one – and I know I'm sounding like you at this point – and two, how come *we* could see *them?*'

'They're not real either,' Vig answered. 'They're lost – like us. They're somebody's missing, just like we'll be. The difference *is*, those poor sods won't know they're actually being held captive in Benny's dungeon… or whatever we want to call it.'

Phyllie thought before responding. 'If you're right… they're close enough to us to hear us talking in our sleep, but they don't know we're talking to *them*. I can buy that. We're sharing parts of the same fantasy: I can buy that too – even though… the missing limbs, I'm not sure about that anymore.'

'I never was.'

'…the question is, where does it get us? We're still no closer to the Overlap.'

'But I think we are, Phyl.' He stopped walking. He waited for an animal with no colour to pass his way in some fashion – either airborne or on the ground – but nothing did. He went on: 'What if it's not a place? What if we're being too literal? The

Overlap is something that we made up, right? Or *you* did, to be accurate.'

'My daughter did, to be more accurate still.'

'But how would the other people Benny's got know about it, other than through our words?' Vig's voice, as he thought out loud, had moved from a slow, quiet, almost shy mode, to something more direct and with greater volume. 'Benny said his prisoners, some of them, under the influence of… whatever we've got coursing through our veins at the moment – he said they share parts of whatever existence they create, right? And then talk about things – the stuff he records, right?'

'Yes,' said Phyllie, failing to see Vig's point entirely but not wishing to halt his excited flow.

'It's telepathic; it's got to be! It's more than words, Phyl… or less, I should say. Words are too direct. It's *thoughts* we need to create the Overlap. The people who are *representations* of those in the dungeon – and those who are – you know – the ones we make up ourselves. The moral of the story being…'

'Stop chatting and start noodling,' said Phyllie.

'Well exactly.'

2.

Hand in hand, Yasser and Shyleen stood in a crowd of people, at the top of a hill, waiting for a speaker (a prophet, a preacher) to make himself known by standing up on the rock around which the gathering had taken place. Yasser pictured the man in robes; he was lifting his smooth hands for silence…

Though the congregation was no more than forty-or-so strong, the energy was palpable – a lynchmob intensity – and something dramatic or violent was about to happen. It had better, Yasser thought - the faces and muscles around him would not be satisfied with anything less.

Yasser addressed a man to his left – a man stripped to the waist, his modesty shielded only by what looked like a nappy – whose dark skin was prodigiously covered with tattoos of birds, of all sizes and species.

'Yes?' the man answered, doing so without moving his lips. The voice came from a tattoo of a puffin on his chest; he had even flexed his pectoral muscle to make the bird's beak open and close.

'What are we about to see, please?' Yasser's eyes were drawn to the puffin's features.

'I'm not entirely sure,' the seabird confessed. Different muscles were employed to make its wings flap, an impressive trick, Yasser thought. In the same way that he'd keep a close eye on a cardsharp, or someone betting fivers in a game of find-the-lady, Yasser wished to learn how it was done.

'You know how a crowd begets a crowd.' The puffin shrugged. 'But the word on the street is… this'll be bigger than Elvis.'

'Did someone say my name?'

A skeleton scarcely decorated with flesh and sinew, standing in front of the tattooed man, turned around. The build suggested a boy; the flayed quality suggested a corpse – it was a miracle that he could stand up, let alone speak. Let alone smile… which he seemed to be doing now, unless the absence of lips was what gave this impression.

The tattooed man's facial features didn't change, but all over his skin the flocks of birds flapped their wings, chirped and squawked. 'Turn around, son,' said a parrot inked on the black man's left shoulder, 'and don't step on my blue suede shoes.'

Looking down briefly, Yasser saw that the ventriloquist was indeed wearing a pair of blue suede shoes… and not a pair of filthy flip-flops. When he looked up again, the flayed boy was holding out his hand.

'I'm Elvis,' the lad said to Yasser; 'pleased to meet you.'

He and Yasser shook. The grip was clammy and adhesive.

'I'm Yasser… This is Shyleen.'

The boy reached out for Shyleen's hand too, which she took and shook.

'This bully is my loving Teddy Bear,' said Elvis, referring to the tattooed fellow. 'Don't mind his grumpiness. You'd think *he* was the one eaten to death by insects!'

'*What?*' said Shyleen.

'A little less conversation, a little more action, please,' said the parrot.

'Eaten alive?' Shyleen asked.

'Oh yes. I'm as dead as a fried peanut butter sandwich.' The boy giggled. 'I was supposed to chaperone a man called Connors… Do you know him? I keep thinking I'll see him here…'

Yasser shook his head. 'I'm sorry, I don't know him.'

'I think *I* do,' Shyleen interrupted. For a few seconds, she looked around and about, searching for a horizon to peer out at but too short to see past the motley crew of pilgrims on the mount… Taking in the crisp mid-afternoon seaside air, tangy with brine and washed-up kelp, Shyleen formed her thoughts from a jigsaw of disconnected memories, and her nostrils spasmed. 'I heard his name on the wind last night, while you were asleep.'

The air now a marked contrast to how it had been then: chilly, obsidian, and fizzy with drizzle and midges. And a voice – a woman's voice, one that Shyleen had wanted to know, to remember – had trailed from wallet-shaped cloud to wallet-shaped cloud, trailing like a comet's streak, something visible, a string lacing buoys together.

A roll call in the heavens.

'Connors was one of the names,' said Shyleen. 'She was

telling us about the people we'd meet.'

'Who was?'

'I don't know… Someone *spoke* to us last night, Yass. Like we heard before.' Shyleen addressed Elvis – and Teddy Bear's decorated chest. 'Have you any idea what I'm talking about?'

A pause.

Then a parakeet said, 'I think *I* do.'

And Yasser said, 'I think I do too. It's all coming back to me.'

3.

When a man and a woman climbed up on the rock, an air of expectation rippled through the crowd and felt like a change in atmospheric pressure, the approach of a summer storm.

The man spoke first.

'My name is Vig,' he said in a loud voice, 'and just like you, I believe, I live in the Home Counties in England… A quick show of hands, if you'd be so kind. Who here knows what I'm talking about when I say the Home Counties?'

Murmurs; nothing committal. Too early in the performance for audience participation.

'Think hard,' Vig advised. 'Tell me where you were born, where you live. Shout em out!'

'We were born *here*!' a man shouted from somewhere near the front. He sounded angry.

Undeterred, Vig made the invitation once more. 'Who's heard of Leighton Buzzard? Dunstable? Hemel Hempstead, Harpenden, Flitwick…'

'Yo!' another voice called.

'Flitwick?' Vig asked.

'Harpenden! I work in a travel agent's… in Harpenden.'

'Good! Anyone else?'

The first man who had spoken now spoke again. 'What's this nonsense about?' he demanded.

Vig showed the palms of his hands and made a plea for the dissenter's patience.

A woman called out that she was born in Linslade, adding that the town was joined to Leighton Buzzard. Although Vig was not entirely sure where Linslade was located (even with the woman's geographical clue), he was energised by the cooperation.

'Who else?' Vig shouted.

Group psychology – the mystical social adhesive of the mob – was what it took for the spell under which they'd all suffered to decay. As more place names were bellowed out, confidence grew among the ranks. The fact that some of the towns mentioned were not even close to the Home Counties was not important. The important thing was the remembering. The crowd was picking holes in its amnesia.

'We are not really here!' shouted Phyllie, her voice riding a wave of murmurs – agreement and dissent in equal measures.

Running with the baton now, Vig added, 'We're all prisoners – in a man's home! We're in the dungeon he's built, under lock and key! Under sedation! But we can escape! If we all fight together… there's a lot more of us than there is of him!'

The murmurs had become cheers, in parts of the congregation at least.

Turning to his left, Vig watched a young Asian man work his way through the crowd. Politely but insistently, he moved forwards, his expression (to Vig) unreadable – neither hagiographic nor hostile. When he was close enough to call out, he said:

'Can I get up there with you? Few words?'

Vig and Phyllie exchanged looks and the twitchiest of shrugs.

'Be our guest,' Phyllie answered.

4.

    'My name's Yasser,' he called out, 'and I'm from Bury Park in Luton, Bedfordshire... Some of you might know it. It doesn't matter if you do or don't... The important thing is, I'm a visitor here, like all of you are. And the man here is right... Did you say Vig?'

Vig nodded.

    'Vig is right. We're here against our wishes,' Yasser preached. 'Me and Shyleen, my cousin, I mean – but I bet it's all of us. *All of us,* yeah?'

    Cries of *yeah!*

    'And if you're in any doubt,' Yasser went on, 'I've been learning some of your names. You see, wherever we are really – and I believe Vig if he says it's a madman's dungeon – in fact, I can almost remember him... an older man... Benny!... Do any of you remember a man named Benny?'

    The cries of *yeah!* sounded more surprised this time. Benny's name echoed and hovered.

    'There's a woman I know who must be with us – with our physical bodies, I mean. And she talks to me and Shyleen; tells us what's going on in the real world.' Yasser smiled. 'At first I thought she was a kind of goddess... she'd love that!' He laughed. 'But then I realised – or Shyleen did, to be exact – that she was talking to us in our sleep. In our coma! She wants to help us!'

    More murmurs; more cries... Vig's reciprocated glance at Phyllie was an exchange of mostly optimism. It seemd as though the Asian lad's words were working wonders. The hollers of disapproval, now, were no more than a quarter-of-the-throng strong, or so he guessed.

    He was winning.

    Yasser had not quite finished.

    'I came here as the result of some violence in a house in

Edlesborough – one of the ways Benny gets us here. At the same time, roughly, some other people were attacked in the house, in one way or another.' Yasser paused. 'Is there a Connors in the crowd? A Chris Connors?'

'I'm Chris Connors!' a young man shouted from midway into the crowd.

'Do you remember the house?' Yasser asked. 'You were there to steal from it… but you were set up. You and the bloke with you. Benny wanted some new blood for his project.'

It was not Connors who spoke next.

'How do you know all this?' a man called out – a man who was standing near Connors.

Yasser replied, 'The goddess *told* me… Who are you, if you don't mind me asking?'

'My name's Massimo. I'm the one who employed Connors and Dorman to rob the place… It was Benny who set us *all* up!'

Yasser raised his arms in a gesture that said: *There you are then! We're all in agreement!*

And with every second that passed, there were more people joining the crowd – more people to agree with Yasser's sentiments, message and rage. Among their numbers, newly arrived, were Don and Charlie – even Dorman. Not everyone knew one another individually… but the crowd absorbed these new arrivals with the hive mind of species recognition. All were welcome… and all would be there in due course, drawn towards the sermon by instincts impossible to ignore. The dead and the living, together on one final battlefield, their anger fed by the memories and thwarted ambitions of those in Benny's dungeon. Memories creating a false and gruesome nostalgia sometimes, and at other times the purest of factual recollections, which also had to be addressed in blood. Revenge and violence was in the air, like a coalescing storm.

Vig raised his voice and addressed the swelling numbers. 'So we're all in agreement!' he shouted. 'It's time to tear this place to shreds from the inside!'

THE CAN-DO SPIRIT

1.

At Maggie's behest Eva had brought Benny down into the vivaria.

'I thought you should see this,' Maggie told him. 'In the absence of our noted film maker... who is where, by the way?'

Benny walked closer. 'He had a class to teach... How long has this been going on?'

'I only just got here,' Maggie told him.

Holding a digital camera on the unfolding events, Eva answered. 'About fifteen minutes.'

Although the prisoners (or scientific subjects, as Benny preferred to think of them) remained asleep, a discernible shift in posture had overtaken as many of them as Benny could see in and from this chamber. The bodies of some had stiffened, where before they had been relaxed in their comas; others had sat up on their cots. One or two had even opened their eyes.

'What's happening?' Benny asked hopefully. 'Is it Vig and Phyllie?'

'It was,' Eva answered. 'Right now it's Yasser... he talking to them *all*.' Her voice sounded somewhat awed.

So did Benny's. 'It's working... All of them?' he wished to clarify. 'They're all listening?'

'As far as we can tell,' said Maggie. 'They're talking about you.'

'Fame at last... You sure that thing's got batteries, Ev?' And he looked straight into the camera.

'It's fully charged,' he was assured.

'Good.' Benny made certain his shirt collar was straight, muttering something about wanting to wear a tie; then he turned to face Eva's camera and he gave the date.

'It's three-forty-five,' he continued, 'and there've been some interesting developments. Or so it would appear… For the last fifteen minutes, there's been signs of spontaneous psychic activity. The catalysts I used – Vig and Phyllie – have agitated the state of ennui that was the case for the last…' Benny fidgeted. Because he had not prepared for this, he did not have the facts at his tongue-tip. '…the last little while,' he busked. 'Vig and Phyllie were the only subjects who went in with the knowledge – or the *certain* knowledge – of what they'd find. So *scientifically*, I'd argue, they have to be the ones responsible for this intra-rationalism.'

This was when the former soldier, for whom Eva had the hots, began to move. Still naked and somnambulant, he swung his legs free of the bed and tried to stand up.

2.

One by one, the prisoners moved on their cots; suction pads were torn from dried patches of skin on their bodies, and dangled from monitoring devices. With the machines' readings thereby knocked off-kilter, the air was alive with the sound of angry and admonitory beeps. Hydraulic pumps writhed; saline drips spasmed like skeletons dancing, such was the movement in the chambers, the commotion of the prisoners as they tried once again to learn to toddle and stroll.

3.

'Do you think you should get out of the way,' Maggie asked, 'for when they wake up finally?'

Benny asked, 'Why?'

'Because they'll be angry, of course.'

'Good. I deserve their anger – and *science* deserves their anger… I was right all along, girl,' he boasted. 'Now where's that Branston to record it all?'

4.

The answer to Benny's question was: outside.

At just after four p.m., camera in hand, Tim Branston arrived at Benny's front door.

Accompanying him was a man named Lydon, a journalist for the *Beds on Sunday*, and police officers Peter Vash and Maureen Tennan. Other officers were also *en route.*

Branston was wondering if it would be him or the officers who knocked on the door… when the door opened wide. Wearing blank expressions, Maggie and Eva backed out into the afternoon air. The red light on the camera in Eva's hand was still on.

Inside the house, someone screamed the first of many screams.

THE END

David Mathew is the author of two previous novels, *O My Days* (Montag Press) and *Creature Feature* with M.F. Korn (Post Mortem Press) and *Paranoid Landscapes*, a volume of short stories. Born in Bedfordshire, England, David has travelled widely, working in a variety of countries. He has since returned and lives in Bedfordshire once again. As a researcher and technical writer, David publishes academic work and focuses on developments in education, health and psychoanalysis.